Derek,

Enjoy the
adventure!

Seth
Josh

PENANCE

Seth Sjostrom

wolfprint, LLC
Camas,
WA, 98607

Trade Paperback KDP
ISBN-13: 978-1-7349376-0-2

1. Alex Penance (Fictitious character)-Fiction. 2. Terrorism-Crime-Political- Fiction. 3. Penance Series-Fiction I. Title.

First wolfprintMedia Digital edition 2020. wolfprintMedia is a trademark of wolfprintMedia, LLC.

For information regarding bulk purchases, please contact wolfprintMedia, LLC, at wolfprint@hotmail.com.

United States of America

To our law enforcement agents and first responders who come to our aid when we need them, even at risk to themselves.

To God, who through all things is possible.

PENANCE

ONE

Special Agent Alex Penance lifted two fingers in the air, the agent at the door nodded in understanding – breach in one...two! The butt of the ram slammed into the door handle, its concussive force splintering the door inward from its frame in a shower of wood and metal shrapnel. Before the door had cleared its space, Penance and two of his men burst through the entrance of the six-story brownstone.

Penance swung his forty-caliber Beretta in front of him, his eyes following its sightline from room to room. His ears told him what he needed to know as shattering glass exploded somewhere in the back of the historic apartment building. Not taking any chances, Penance and the half dozen agents who trailed him maintained their point to point sweep as they hastened their way towards the back of the apartment.

The hallway emptied into an open room, housing a kitchen, a tiny eating area, and living space. Cool, moist air met the agent's face from the shattered window. Penance paused for a moment as he took in the maps laid across a dining table, boxes of empty ammunition, and chargers for cellphones and blue tooth devices that littered the back room. Pasting his body next to the window frame, the young agent peered down the fire escape and to the quiet street below. The pair of Boston police officers that served as back up were staring up and radioing into their shoulder-mounted microphones what they were seeing.

Moments later, their words were crackling through Penance's earpiece. Two assailants had crashed through the window, took note of the officers on the street, and climbed up the fire escape. Penance motioned for Moyer, the junior member of his team to remain in the apartment to dig through the evidence as he and the rest of his men cautiously made their way out onto the steel grate of the fire escape. Above his position, the federal agent could hear heavy footsteps making their way towards the rooftop. Reluctantly holstering his weapon to free both hands, Penance pulled himself up to the ladder and began his pursuit.

Rung over rung, Penance scrambled up the metal staircase. Squeezing with each handhold as the early morning fog slathered a fine, slick film on the rusty metal. Reaching the top, Penance paused, listening to the sound of footsteps crunching along the tile roof. Drawing his handgun, he popped over the ledge, seeing two figures hover at the far edge of the roof.

The agent leveled his sight at the fleeing men, "Freeze, Federal Agent!"

Climbing onto the roof itself, Penance watched as the men looked over their shoulders at their pursuer, conferred, and leaped off of the roof. Cursing, the agent sped across the rooftop after them. Nearing the edge, he could see one man hanging from a balcony of the next building. A terrible cacophony of bones and flesh in the alley below told him the fate of the second suspect. Watching the first scrambling up onto the balcony, Penance sprinted to the edge, using advantage of momentum and launched himself across the alley. His hands slapped hard against the metal rail, bruising his wrists, but affording him a stable hold. Yanking upward with his arms, he vaulted over the railing and onto the balcony.

Following the path that the suspect had taken, he jumped through an apartment window. Further inside, Penance could hear items crash and footsteps scamper down the hall as a series of locks unlatched at the front door. Darting through the apartment, Penance rushed toward the fleeing man. Weapon drawn, he careened against the door just as the suspect's body was sliding through the opening. Penance's force pinned his foe between the door and its frame. With a free hand, Agent Penance yanked the suspect by the collar, pulling him back into the apartment and down to the floor. With a quick kick, he dislodged the terror suspect's weapon and slammed his knee into the man's back.

"Federal Agent, the less you move, the less you'll hurt," Penance snapped as he drove his weight into the man, knocking the air out of his lungs. The suspect's momentary struggle for air was enough time for the agent to pull a zip-tie from his pocket and snap it around the suspect's wrists. Calling into his radio, the agent summoned the rest of the team to his location.

Pocketing the man's gun, Penance pulled him to his feet and directed him down the apartment hallway. By the time he reached the stairs, four teammates had joined him. "Sir, we have Johnson with the man in the alley, he's dead," agent Ramsey informed the Special Agent in charge.

"I figured," Penance acknowledged. Once in the empty stairwell, he stopped. "Ramsey, take the top of the stairs, Jackson, the landing below. Do not let anyone up or down." The two agents nodded and headed for their posts.

Facing the suspect, Penance leveled his eyes at the suspect's. "You are going to tell me what your plan is. Where is your crew?" he demanded.

The suspect eyes glared through heavy lids and turned away from the agent. Like a snake striking its victim, Penance's hand shot forward, catching the suspect by the throat, "I asked you a question. We know there is a terror plot in this city today. We know your pathetic interests like to take aggression out on innocent people, children…like cowards. Where is your team headed?"

His questions met with a mere indignant grunt. A slight smirk appeared at the corners of the suspect's mouth.

"Jackson," Penance called out, "Move down a few steps…"

The agents in the stairwell exchanged questioning glances, their mouths agape as Penance delivered another lightning-quick blow to the terror suspect, this time to the back of his head, sending him somersaulting down the concrete steps, slamming into the landing below. Calmly descending the staircase, Penance stood over the man, who found himself once more gasping for air.

"You can't hurt me," the man glowered in his guttural accent.

Grasping the man's shoulder, Penance snatched him up to his feet. Before the man could stabilize himself, Penance slammed his head through the window, driving his body over the sill in a shower of glass. "How about you check on your buddy down there!" Alex growled. His captive flailed wildly in the air as the agent held him with one hand clenched around his belt, leaving him to dangle helplessly over the side of the building.

"I'll never talk!" the suspect gasped.

"Ah, yes. Your code. Allah accepts martyrs into his kingdom. But suicide…that would shame your entire family. Sure, maybe Allah would know the difference, but your family…your compatriots…they'll live out their days believing you a coward," Penance snapped, "You have any sons…"

"Yes, they'll not believe you!"

"Sure, they will. See the news crews out there? They'll catch the whole thing…splash it up on YouTube and poof, all your prideful work out the window," Penance cooed.

"It's too late. Your foolish American pastimes, your indulgence makes you easy targets!" the man spat.

"Pastimes…the baseball game! Fenway Park!" Penance declared. Pulling the suspect back through the window, the agent shoved him towards Agent Jackson, "Take him to H.Q. see if you can get anything more from him. Ricks, Seaver, Cruz…with me!" Penance was already sprinting down the steps, calling his deduction in over the radio.

Darting through the burgeoning crowd, Alex made his way to his blacked-out SUV. Three of his team members slid inside as the vehicle roared to life, and Penance pressed hard on the throttle. Weaving through traffic, the meaty V8 growled as it maneuvered the busy Boston streets. As they neared the ballpark, progress slammed to a halt. Bouncing the SUV over the curb, Penance brought it to rest in a nearby alleyway. Checking his weapon, he called to his men, "Be on the lookout for anything out of sorts. These guys want to make a splash in a big way. The Red Sox-Yankees game is perfect for them – dense crowd, chaos…probably a dirty bomb of some sort, it would maximize casualties."

"Who are these guys?"

"We're not sure…al Quaeda, Hezbollah, Yankee fans…we just know they have purchased the right materials for putting together explosives, and intel picked up reports terror plot targeted for today. We tracked them to the apartment here in Boston," Penance shrugged as they pushed their way through the massive crowd formed around Landsdowne street. "Split up. You two take the Jersey Street entrance. We start with Ipswich and work our way through. Two on the outside, two on the inside. Command has notified security."

Making their way through the rowdy pregame fans, the agents surveyed the building and the individuals. "Ricks, how would you plant a device at a game like this?"

"Mass effect? Anywhere within five blocks of the stadium right now would kill or wound thousands, probably affect no more once on the inside and a lot more risk," the agent replied.

"Yeah, I think you're right," Penance replied, swiveling his head around the area. His eyes caught two men with brand new, ill-fitting red Sox caps on. Each wore

equally new backpacks and, after conferring, moved quickly
in opposite directions. "There, those two!"

Ricks nodded, and the agents snaked their way
through the crowd. Penance closed in on his man, reaching
out, he grabbed the man's backpack by the strap. Surprised,
the man spun to face Penance, his face fearful for just a
moment. Without hesitation, Penance tugged on the zipper
and looked in at the contents despite the man's protest.
Pushing items aside, Penance got to the bottom of the bag,
finding nothing but Yankees souvenirs. The man stared
silently at Penance, still in shock over the abrupt disruption.
Cursing, Penance slammed the bag into the man's chest.
"Next time, either have the guts and root for your team or
do the right thing, become a Red Sox fan." The agent
radioed to his partner what he found. Ramsey concluded he
saw more of the same. "Continue your search along the Van
Ness perimeter and let me know if you find anything."

Penance's head swiveled around the overflowing
streets. Imagining a device detonating near everything he
observed. He thought about the effects of a dirty bomb. A
concentric spray pattern would deliver the most devastating
blow. Outside the Brookline entrance, Alex noticed one
group of hotdog vendors offering their Fenway franks
formed their carts in a half-circle. The Brookline and Jersey
convergence entrance was the original main entrance and
garnered the most traffic.

Shuffling ahead, Penance reached the vendors, each appeared to be of middle-eastern descent, from Penance's experience of attending Red Sox games not novel in and of themselves, but today warranted enough suspicion matching the description of the men from the Brownstone. Ignoring the chorus of "Hey wait in line, buddy!" Penance pushed to the first of the carts. In an instant, a vendor stepped in his path, "Stay behind the line, please, sir."

"I'm afraid I need to inspect your cart," Penance declared.

"We have already been inspected today," the man remained solid in front of him.

"Not by me."

"Sorry, sir, we are too busy," the conversation had picked up interest from the other three vendors, each stopping what they were doing to observe the exchange.

"They don't seem too busy now," Penance offered, taking a step forward.

The man blocking his path jabbed something into Penance's side, "This is really not a good time, sir."

Stopping in his tracks, Alex recognized the steel instrument butted against his ribs. He squinted as he studied the vendor's associates. Neither had resumed their work despite the growing throng of impatient customers. Taking in a calming breath, he relaxed for a moment, causing the man to back off slightly with his weapon. As suddenly as he relaxed, Penance tightened his body, springing his muscles into action. His hand darted to his side, catching the man's weapon by the frame and, with a simultaneous twist, freed it from the man's grip.

One of the other vendors moved to raise their weapon before they could point it in Penance's direction, the agent had fired off two shots of his own. Without a wasted movement, a third shot met the final vendor in the chest as he stooped to withdraw a gun from inside the stainless-steel cart.

The first vendor recovered and drove a knee into Penance's side, reaching to wrestle back the gun he lost within the beginning of the assault. Letting out a gasp, Penance reeled back from the blow. Using his assailant's momentum against him, the agent planted his back foot and torqued his body as he grabbed the terrorist's wrists, sending him sprawling to the ground at the base of the stadium.

Ricks, Cruz, and Seaver appeared and began working the two injured suspects. Penance cautiously inspected the carts. Carefully, he gently tugged at the door of the one closest. As he slid it open, he felt resistance. Stopping, he studied the crack between the door and the frame of the cart. Between the two, he saw a magnet that he had slightly begun to move out of his place. A closer inspection, he could see the magnet had a piece of metal attached to it that would rub off if he continued to open it. At the bottom of the metal cabinet was a jar with a series of wires running out of it.

"We got it, tell the Boston P. D. to search all vendors near the park and have the bomb squad check out the carts. If you yank a door open, this magnet releases a metal disc that allows a sodium tablet to drop into a solution, charging an explosive device," Penance shouted.

Morgan nodded and began to call it in. Ricks stepped close to Penance, "They're likely timed. If they've hedged their bets, they probably have stands like this by all the entrances. The bomb squad will never be able to get to all of them. Do we begin to clear the streets, shut down the park?"

"You can try, but with this crowd, any excitement like that would cause pandemonium and lead to collateral injuries," Penance surveyed the area for ways to minimize the damage. "Call for garbage trucks at each of the entrances, have them provided with police escorts! They usually have them on call for gamedays when the games let out."

"They'll never get here in time!" Ricks pleaded.

"Push the carts across the road, into that alley!" Penance called, careening a cart out onto Jersey Street. Ramsey and Morgan followed in hot pursuit. Once in the alley, Penance had the carts massed together, "Come on, help me turns these over!"

Rolling a steel trash container into position, Penance and the other agents strained to get it to tip. The fulcrum slid some of its contents forward, helping to make the container front heavy. With all of their might, they strained until the dumpster slammed over the top of the hotdog carts.

Further distancing the crowd from the explosives, the three emerged from the alley with their weapons drawn. Penance squeezed off several shots, encouraging the crowd to push away from the lane. In the excitement, several fleeing spectators got pushed down in the path of the frenzied crowd. One child got separated from his parents and began to cry in the middle of the street.

"Clear the nearby stores!" Penance ordered as he sprinted to the middle of the street, snatching the boy up in his arms and towards the Jersey Street entrance. "You going to the game today, buddy?"

The boy nodded his head, frightened eyes staring at the agent. "Alright, how about we get you a sneak peek at the field while we try and find your parents?" Hesitantly the boy nodded. Being inside the stadium felt better than being alone on the street. Displaying his badge to the security guard and helped the boy inside the building. Turning back, Penance saw the dumpster raise into the air as a blast deafened him. He watched as straggling fans ran for cover, and his agents dove to the ground outside the blast zone.

Shrapnel rained down in the confines of the alley with a few fragments reaching the street. Similar blasts sounded from around the stadium. Penance prayed the Boston P. D. had been successful in containing those as well.

Wincing, he glanced at his radio. His heart began to beat again as a jubilant "all clear" sounded through his earpiece.

TWO

Alex Penance barely had time to clean up before receiving the text from his boss. The Boston Field Director wanted an immediate, personal debriefing of the incident. As he strode into the office, he saw two men in suits sitting across the desk from his boss. Hastily patting the wrinkles out of his jacket, he tapped on the office door.

"Special Agent Penance, come in," Director Tracy called, motioning Alex to have a seat. "This is Ron Oswald from Homeland Security." A gray-haired man smiled and shook the agent's hand. Nodding to the second gentleman, the director shared, "This is Director Armand of the Bureau's Terror Command Unit in D.C. They asked me to arrange a meeting with you."

"Thank you, Director. Special Agent Penance, that was fine work out there. You had very little time to find the cell, uncover their plot, and diffuse it. I don't need to tell you that the casualties had that cell been successful would have been catastrophic, akin to the World Trade Center," Oswald declared.

"From the reports your team submitted, you acted swiftly, without hesitation, and with clear logic. Impressive for such a junior Special Agent.," Director Armand agreed.

"Oh, what happened on the stairwell? Witness reports have an agent holding one of the suspects out of a window?" Oswald asked.

Penance grimaced with a nod, "Yessir, the suspect in custody tried to escape, he smashed the window with his face, and I was able to catch him with his belt and pull him into safety...after a momentary struggle."

"Ah, I see. Was that before or after you got the clue to case Fenway Park?"

"Right about then. Must have seen his life flash before his eyes and decided to come clean," Penance shrugged.

"Hmm. So, you lucked into it. I was kind of hoping you weren't afraid of necessary interrogation. The role I am suggesting for you might demand such a willingness to extract information," Armand said with an eyebrow raised.

"Could you handle today's type of action on a regular basis, Special Agent Penance? I need a Deputy Director with your type of swift decision-making and decisive action. We've been watching you since the academy. You have top scores on the written tests and bested our top hand to hand instructor – and he swears he was trying to beat you into submission."

"Director Tracy has nothing but glowing remarks about your missions since being promoted to Special Agent. You have all the pre-requisite skills we like to see in our leadership. We would like to offer you the Deputy Director Position in D.C. You would be responsible for Bureau and Homeland Security personnel within this post," Oswald added.

"You would be the youngest deputy director the department has ever had," Director Tracy concluded, "They want you to get your affairs in order and begin next week."

"Would you like a day to consider the position?" Agent Oswald asked, handing Penance an envelope.

Without opening the seal, Penance beamed and shook each man's hand, "I'll report on Monday."

At Penance's acceptance, the visitors rose from their seats. "Very well, Agent Penance, welcome to the big time."

As the men left and Penance sunk in his seat, opening the envelope. Glancing past the folder, he eyed his boss.

"Congratulations, I hope you understand what a big honor has been bestowed on you, though well-deserved. You are one of the best agents I have ever worked with," Director Tracy said.

"Thank you, sir."

"Now, I imagine you have a lot of things to get done regarding your big move. Get out of here. I look forward to hearing about your rise in the Bureau," Director Tracy replied, "We have a final debrief tomorrow morning."

Penance nodded and left his supervisor's office. Trained for complex scenarios, he could maintain composure at all times, but this news caused his head to spin, dizzy with pride and excitement. With the envelope in his hand, he strode out of the office onto the busy streets of Boston. As he walked, he felt as though he floated along the sidewalk.

Enroute to his brownstone apartment, he ducked into his favorite store, which housed a coffee stand. Waiting his turn for the barista, a perfect storm of heightened confidence and luck collided in the form of five-foot-ten, flowing hair and inviting smile. As he stood in line, he heard a slight crack and, in the corner of his eye, spied a figure looming in his direction. Spinning, he reached forward, his arms darting through the air just in time to catch a stunned woman, falling towards the ground. The woman stabilized in his arms. He freed his right hand, which struck into the air, snatching a package that sailed airborne as she flailed.

"Are you alright?" Penance asked.

"Yes," the woman gasped, "My heel broke. Ugh, these were my favorite shoes…"

"Sad to say, I don't think they're going to make it."

Alex smiled politely at the woman and helped support her as she slipped off both shoes to make her stance even.

"And you even saved my package, you are indeed my hero," the woman gushed.

"Doesn't happen to be another pair of shoes in the box, does it?" Penance asked with a mischievous grin.

"Not so lucky," the woman frowned, holding out her hand, she introduced herself, "I'm Tiffany."

"Nice to meet you, Tiffany. I'm Alex," Penance took her hand and then held out the package for her. "Uhm, I think I saw a shoe store around the corner. Would you like me to walk you there? I mean, you can't go barefoot and hobbling all the way there…"

"You are so sweet…I uh…you know, that would be lovely," holding out her arm, she let Penance hold her erect as her legs managed their three-inch differential.

The federal agent rather enjoyed his escort duty. The woman, he guessed to be in her mid-twenties, was striking. Her face was soft and glowed radiantly, framed by long honey-blonde hair allowed to drape neatly over her shoulders. She reminded him of a Barbie doll – in a good kind of way. What struck Penance the most, was beyond the beauty, was time-stopping smile and bright eyes. She was elegant, startlingly beautiful, yet somehow accessible.

Maybe it was the promotion of talking or merely the innocence of a woman he was able to help. He was undeniably attracted to her, accidentally so.

"So, Mr. Hero, what do you do for a living?" Tiffany smiled.

"I...uh, I work for the government."

"Government, huh? You're not a politician, don't seem like a mailman...ohhhh," Tiffany gasped, her eyes wide, "You're a g-man!"

Alex gave her a perplexed look before confiding, "Yep, I'm a fed."

"Field agent?"

"Was until an hour ago, I just got promoted," Penance beamed.

"We have to celebrate!" Tiffany's eyes brightened and then narrowed, "Unless there is a Mrs. G-man..."

Penance paused for a moment, then inexplicably jumped on the wave of his perfect storm, "No, not attached."

"Then let's do it. I can repay you for your chivalry...after I buy a new pair of shoes, that is."

"You don't have to repay me," Penance stated as he opened the door to the shoe store.

Tiffany squared up to her escort, looking him straight in the face as she balanced on her one functional heel, "I want to. It'll be fun, unless you don't want to, of course."

Penance sighed profoundly and looked through her Caribbean blue-water eyes, "Alright, I suppose it beats the lonely celebration I was planning on my own."

"Then it is settled! I have the *best* place to take you!" Tiffany shrieked, retaking his arm as she entered the store.

The late afternoon blurred into evening, the evening into night. Without the burden of a broken shoe, Penance still held Tiffany as he supported her up the steps to her porch. His heart quickened as his mind reeled about how to bid her a goodnight. A part of him did not want the evening to end. Tiffany's smile, her wit, and genuineness he found more intoxicating than the two bottles of wine they toasted his promotion and their chance meeting. The five-ten beauty spun into him as they reached her door. Each seemed to breathe a little more shallow, neither appearing sure about their next move. Penance, true to his soul, snapped into action and moved to plant a gentlemanly kiss on her cheek. Tiffany caught him with a finger on his chin, staring deep into his eyes, she firmly tugged on his chin to turn his lips to meet hers.

Their moment was soft at first; then, an errant breath slid them down a path of deep, passionate kisses. Tiffany pulled Alex as close to her as their molecules would allow. For her, it wasn't close enough. "Come in," she whispered.

Penance stared at her in silence, unsure whether his evening should end there. Perhaps he knew it should. His body frozen in rare indecisiveness, renowned for his snap-thinking agent and laser straight judgment, Penance for just a moment, found himself at a loss.

"Now!" demanded the alluring siren, wrapping her fingers through Penance's collar, pulling him into her apartment. They kissed and teased their way down the hall, their minds and bodies relentlessly tempting the other. "I don't normally invite men into my home. There's just something…."

Penance stopped her with a kiss that met with a growl from Tiffany. Leading the way, she pulled him up the stairs and, in their embrace, crashed through her bedroom door and landed in a heap on her bed. Their passion burned in a blur of impatient imprudence.

Neither could determine how long they lay intertwined. Neither cared. Penance wrapped his arms around her Tiffany and pulled her tight. He reveled in the smell of her neck, the pattern of her heartbeat.

Tiffany broke their silence, "I promise I don't do this. You, you're just so gallant, unbelievably handsome, so powerful. I genuinely enjoyed spending time with you over wine."

"I'm kinda new to impetuous actions myself," Penance admitted.

"I'm glad you did. I like you, Agent Penance."

"You're not so bad yourself, Miss Tiffany."

To the rhythm of their synchronized heartbeats, they drifted off to sleep.

The click was subtle but unmistakable. Penance shot up in bed, listening. The softest footstep confirmed what his ears had already told him, "Are you expecting somebody, Tiffany?"

The whisper was just enough to stir the slumbering beauty, "Wha...someone's..." She too shot up and gasped, "Oh no! I thought he was out of town until Monday!"

"You're married?"

"My boyfriend, kind of. He must have kept the key I let him borrow!" Tiffany stated.

"Uhh, this is not going to improve your relationship. How would you like me to handle this?" Penance asked politely as he quickly piece himself together.

"I don't know....," Tiffany groaned.

"You have a fire escape? I can climb out the back."

Tiffany shook her head and covered herself as footsteps suddenly thudded up the stairs, and the hall light switched on. Alex scrambled to gather shreds of his wits, hastily gathering his things. He was too late before a figure stood in the doorway.

"What the...who the hell...," a man's voice stammered, "Tiffy, what is going on!"

Embarrassment in Penance's head washed with recognition. He had heard that voice before. His thoughts were interrupted by the man striding forward, with a grunt, he swung his arm out and caught Tiffy in the face. Penance snapped, leaping over the bed, swinging the man face-first into the wall with the hand that wasn't shoving his belongings into his pockets.

"I'm sure you're upset, man, but I promise touching her like that is not the way to handle it," the agent growled.

Alex was distracted by a barrage of footsteps coming up the stairs. Two more figures appeared in the doorway. Penance recognized the type – armed security. Pushing the apparent boyfriend toward the door, he readied himself for an altercation. His wait was not long, as one of the burly guards approached, taking a wild swing at Penance's face. Ducking back, the agent grabbed his assailant by the arm and flung him over his shoulder using the big man's momentum against him.

The second guard was already in play, grabbing Penance in a headlock. Jabbing his heel backward, Alex caught the guard's knee with several vicious blows. Releasing his grip for just a moment allowed the FBI Agent to break free. Spinning, Penance deflected a blow from his attacker. Recovered, the first guard jumped Penance from behind, wrapping massive arms around Penance's own, trapping him for guard number two to get in several shots to the agent's midsection. Held secure, he pulled his knees to his chest as another blow sailed his way. Pushing out with his feet, he caught the guard in the chest, sending him sprawling backward toward the hallway.

Twisting, Penance wormed his way out the hold. Slapping away shot after shot, he used the slightest pause from his offender to deliver a kick to his ribs, sending the big man flailing backward, slamming into Tiffany's window, shattering the glass and the pane. The second man rushed in from the hallway only to be seized by Penance and flung in the direction of the guard recovering covered in glass and splintered wood. The two guards collided, sending one back through the window he just pulled himself from, only this time, the force popped him into a free fall towards the sidewalk below.

During the scuffle, Tiffany was yanked from her bed, dragging a sheet behind her to attempt and cover her barely draped body. As Penance began to follow, tripped up from behind, this time, the guard had a revolver pointed at the agent. Penance kicked free just in time to slip into the hallway before a shot rang out. The bullet embedded in the wood frame of the doorway, Penance shot his arm out, catching the guard by the wrist, with a mighty twist, he had the guard on his back and weapon freed. With a foot on the guard's throat, he pointed the recovered .38 at his assailant's head. "Enough! I'm a federal agent. I'm pretty sure your partner outside needs medical attention. Do you understand me?" Penance growled.

The guard nodded. Lifting his foot, he called out, "Tiffany, are you okay?"

"I'm fine!" Tiffany called back weakly. Over the railing, he could see that she wrapped up in a sheet and huddled on her couch. Her boyfriend paced in front of her, cast an angry glare Penance's way.

Grabbing the rest of his things, Penance motioned with the gun, "Move!"

The guard complied and sauntered down the stairs in front of the agent. As they reached the living area, Penance urged the guard to go outside and check on his friend. "Tiffany, call 911 and then go get some clothes on," Penance demanded, turning to Tiffany's boyfriend, he said in an even tone, "Senator Castadine, I thought I recognized your voice."

The senator glared menacingly at Penance. The agent shrugged, "I had no idea she had a boyfriend. You send your goons after her or me, I'll come after you. If you touch her again, I'll be coming after you. Am I clear?"

The senator paused in his pacing to square up with the agent, "I understand."

The door to the apartment opened up, and one guard helped the other hobble inside. Tiffany came down in silk pajamas with her phone in hand. "Don't call 911," the senator snapped.

Tiffany looked nervously at Penance and then at the guard in obvious pain. Shrugging, the agent replied, "They're your problem." Walking to Tiffany, he touched the crook of her arms softly, "Are you going to be okay?"

Tiffany nodded. Penance pulled a business card from his wallet. "My number may change, but they'll know how to get a hold of me. If you need anything…" he looked over at the senator, "Or have any problems, you give me a call."

Again, Tiffany nodded meekly, "I'm sorry…."

Penance smiled lightly, turned, and walked past the guards, cast a final warning glance at the senator, and left the Brownstone.

THREE

"Penance!" Director Tracy roared, "My office – now!"

Grimacing, the agent reluctantly complied.

"Close the door behind you."

Penance shut the door and sat across from his boss.

The director stared directly at his agent, "What in the world did you do?"

"Sir?"

"Just yesterday, you were the golden child. Your career was on the fast track…," the director sighed and looked down at a piece of paper on his desk, "I don't know who you pissed off…you've been reassigned."

"The D.C. job?"

In a mock bellow, Director Tracy guffawed, "Oh no. Deputy Director for the terrorism unit is off the table. You have been forcibly reassigned; instructions are in this file. You leave in two hours. I'm sorry, Penance. You are an incredible agent."

Penance opened the file and began to flip through it, visibly angry, he looked up at his boss, "Sir?"

Director Trace waved his hands wildly, "Oh no, friend. This came from *way* over my head. Right from the office of the Department of Justice, …you are hosed. I can't help you. Care to clue me in on who's cereal bowl you seemed to have wet yourself in?"

"Not really, sir. I have no questions about who. Is there anything that…"

"No. From the top. Someone with power, *real* power has you in their sights," the Director cut him off. Glancing at his watch, he added, "You had better get going. If you are not at your new assignment by the end of the day, you will receive a reprimanded in your file. This could lead to a demotion."

Defeated, Penance nodded. "Thank you, Director Tracy."

"Good luck to you, Penance."

The air inside the prop plane was hot and still. A silent Alex Penance stared blankly out of the tiny window. Despite the oppressive heat and the sweat that was boiling from within, the agent refused to loosen his tie. He maintained his impeccable attire, sitting straight in his seat.

Quietly he fumed about the turn that his life had taken. In fact, for the first time in his life, he wasn't sure what direction it *had* taken. He was entering eighteen straight hours of kicking himself. He was a trained profiler. Then again, it wasn't as if he had missed the signs. He recalled the spare toothbrush on the shelf in the bathroom, the late-night text, and missed phone calls signaled by the blinking led on her cellphone, the diamond jewelry that had adorned her wrist and ears – both subtle but unmistakably out of her price range. No, he *chose* to ignore them. He was riding the high surf, and though unlike him, he allowed himself to let his guard down. Way down.

All he knew, as the landing gear ground into place beneath him, he had no idea where he was. As the cabin door opened, the already hot air intensified with a blast of searing humidity. Slinging his carry-on over his shoulder, he stepped out on to the tarmac. Encased in bands of mirage-like evaporation, he squinted as he pulled his sunglasses out of his pocket.

Pausing outside of the plane, Penance surveyed the airport. It was a single building, no bigger than an average house. Following the path to the terminal, the agent passed through the sole gate and into the airport. Walking through security, he was surprised to see a man approach him.

In a deep drawl, the man smiled, "Special Agent Penance, welcome to Sawyer."

Penance paused and took in the man. He was tall and lanky, his short-sleeved plaid shirt stuck to his chest from sweat, constantly pulling a handkerchief from wrinkled khakis to wipe his brow. "I'm agent Roth. You can call me Timothy."

"I'd ask what you did to get this assignment Agent Roth, but I think I get it," Penance quipped.

"Oh no," Roth shook his head, vehemently, "I *chose* this office. Close to home."

"Huh, how about that," Penance grunted.

"How was your flight, sir?"

"Okay, first, how old are you, Agent Roth?"

"Twenty-six, sir," Roth replied.

"I'm Twenty-eight. You can drop the 'sir.'"

"But you are a pay-rank higher…," Roth stuttered, "And it sounds like almost several, sir."

"Yeah, almost," Penance nodded, "You asked about the flight? A six-seat sauna dropped into the middle of…where the hell are we?"

"Sawyer, sir."

"Sawyer. With Jethro or Billy Bob flying the only plane in here– about as you might expect," Penance replied curtly.

"Oh, that's not Billy Bob, that's Dewayne. He's a good pilot."

"Right," Penance mock agreed. Then as he was led to a last generation sedan almost exclusively sold as police cruisers, he cocked his head curiously, "Your car?"

"Yes sir, runs smooth."

"Why not just cruise around in a black and white?" Penance retorted.

"That wouldn't work very well when I need to go undercover, sir," Agent Roth replied with a quizzical expression across his face.

"No, Roth, no it wouldn't."

Tossing his bags in the back seat, Penance climbed into the passenger seat. He stared out the window, taking in his surroundings. He watched as the rural setting and cotton field surrounding the airport melded into a semi-urban area. Basic office buildings sprinkled in with classic antebellum architecture.

Wheeling into the parking lot of a small, one-story office building, littered with a handful of similar last generation police sedans, "Here we are, sir."

"It's as fabulous as I imagined."

"You'll like it here," Agent Roth foretold.

"Not likely," Penance mumbled.

Pushing into the dark office, the pair of agents the pungent smell of cigar smoke greeted them. A voice bellowed from an office in the back, "That you, Timothy?"

"Yessir, I have Special Agent Penance with me."

"Send him back!" the voice called.

Somewhat reluctantly, Penance followed the voice. Stepping into the Field Director's office, he took in the room. It was sizable, rows of bookcases lined with leather-bound texts and a handful of photographs. The shards of sunlight shooting through the blinds highlighted the light cloud of smoke that hung in the air over a large mahogany desk. Behind the desk was a man smiling through clenched teeth that held a cigar tight between them. A glance revealed a man - balding, evident as he held his brimmed hat in his hand, drenched in sweat – rings soaked into his wrinkled tan jacket. His barreled chest gave way to a barrel gut. He reminded Penance of a jolly southern Santa Clause.

"Come on in," the Field Director rasped, "Welcome to Sawyer. Son, you must have pissed off someone pretty good to have ended up here. Congratulations, kid."

"Common for black-balled agents to end up herein...Purgatory?" Penance grumbled.

"Just the ones afraid to unbutton their suits in ninety-five-degree heat and flex their smart mouths," the director retorted, "Relax. Do good work here, and you'll be taken care of. Who knows, you might actually find that you like it here."

"With respect, sir, I'll do my time and move on," Penance replied.

"No, I suppose you wouldn't look to stay here long. Not with your record – Valedictorian at MIT, first in your class at the academy, accommodations from Field Director Tracy, and a dog's breath away from your own Deputy

Director role. We'll see how much we can control and how deep memories run," Field Director Dixon drawled.

Dixon points to a desk outside of his office, "You can set up shop there."

"Thanks, though I don't plan on staying long," Penance professed.

"Well, until things sort out for you, might as well be comfortable," Field Director Dixon suggested, "We don't get a lot of action around here. Occasionally, we'll get pulled into a case with the boys in New Orleans or Mobile. Here, we just take care of the locals, interstate passersby, drug stuff – that kind of thing."

Studying Penance's buttoned-up appearance, "By the way, we're pretty informal around here. Don't want to scare the taxpayers."

Penance opened his mouth to offer up another remark, but was cut off by the front door opening. A vibrant, attractive woman burst into the office, her sundress flowing in her wake.

"Dixon! We could use your help...oh, who's this?" the woman snapped and then paused to take in well-tailored, well-coiffed Penance.

"Miss Hunt, I'd like to introduce you to the newest member of our little family, Special Agent Alex Penance," Field Director Dixon replied, "Special Agent Penance, meet Assistance District Attorney Annie Hunt."

The two exchanged pleasantries before the attractive ADA snapped back to business, "Denny, we have a bail jumper penned in downtown, I thought your office might want to provide oversight."

"Miss Hunt, you know we're always here to help you. Why don't you take Special Agent Penance with you? Get him an opportunity to get acquainted with our fair city. I'll set out with Timothy momentarily," the field director suggested, speaking of the third agent assigned to their office.

"Well, *Special* Agent?"

"Sure, why not," Penance shrugged.

"Here," Director Dixon tossed a set of keys towards his newest field agent.

"Shall we?" Penance held his arm out for the A.D.A. to take the lead.

Following her out to the parking lot, he pressed the button on the keyfob. A dust-covered burgundy unmarked police cruiser flashed its lights in the corner of the lot. "At least they won't see us coming in that heap," Penance muttered.

"Aw c'mon, it'll be fun," Annie smiled, jumping into the passenger seat.

FOUR

Agent Penance jammed the key into the ignition and urged the Interceptor engine to life. Turning the wheel and pressing the accelerator, the well-used sedan let out a horrendous squeal as the tired fanbelt labored in the engine bay. Penance shot the Assistant District Attorney Annie Hunt a disapproving glance. She met him with a pleasant smile and a finger indicating which way for him to turn on the street.

Willing the car down the road, they passed several historic-looking storefronts before entering the town square. A fountain gurgled in the center as Penance wheeled the car around. Three police cars and an ambulance, along with a crowd of spectators, told Penance they headed for the hardware store, which was the apparent center of attention.

"There are several apartments above the hardware store. We found Willie Benson up there. He took a few shots at the local police officers and then barricaded himself in the store," Hunt filled him in.

Getting out of the car, Penance walked over to a group of officers standing behind a patrol car. "You must be the new fed, welcome to Sawyer," one of the men called out.

"Chief Pruitt, this is Special Agent Penance. I thought maybe you wouldn't turn a little oversight away."

"Aw, heck no. Benson has gone nuts. He's taken two shots at my officers already. I have another pair out back, making sure he don't slip out that way. I'm afraid he's gonna hurt somebody," Chief Pruitt replied.

"What's his rap?" Penance asked.

"Busted for drug running. Got into a scuffle with the first cop who tried to bring him in. Somehow made bail and first chance he had, he was on the run. Gotta tip he'd be coming here to pick up some money owed to him. Soon as he saw us, just started shootin'," Pruitt filled in.

Just then, another shot rang out—this one shattering the passenger seat window of the patrol car. Penance grabbed Annie and made her sit behind the rear wheel of the patrol car. "Not sure what you know about bullets, but a little sheet metal doesn't stop them," he warned. As the federal agent's head swiveled around the tiny strip of merchants, his eyes caught a hefty patrolman huddled in a nervous ball in the shadow of a large blue mailbox.

With his face screwed into a look of bewilderment, Penance looked to the chief, "What's *he* doing over there?"

"Oh, that's Officer Jeffries. He was on his way to try and talk to Benson through the hardware store door when the first shots were fired," Pruitt answered.

"Humph," Penance snorted, watching the officer do his best to keep his bulky frame behind the presumed safety of the mailbox, "Looks like he's about to soil his pants."

"Yeah," the chief nodded, "He hasn't moved an inch for the last twenty minutes."

Biting his lip, Penance scowled as he once more shifted his gaze around the setting, making tactical reference points. Unsnapping his sidearm, he stalked to the edge of the patrol car. Watching the gunman train his attention where the chief was standing, Penance sprinted to the mailbox and rolled to his knees next to the frightened officer. The giant, African-American cop barely fit behind the blue box.

"How's it going?" Penance asked casually.

"I, uh, kinda got penned in," the officer replied.

"Yeah. I see that. I'm gonna guess with your speed you did the right thing by hunkering down," Penance stated and then asked, "What's your name, officer?"

"Bubba."

Penance looked at him with a stunned raised eyebrow, "Of course it is. Okay, Bubba, here's the deal. If Willie up there moves to the far window, he's going to have a clear shot at you. A fair shot at your pals over by the first car too. Here's what we're going to do, I am going to draw his fire by moving to that car parked right out front. He'll probably take a couple of shots. I want him to. *Do not fire at him.* Your job is to get to a safer position. You can fall back or move inside that shop next door. Once you get in, stay away from the windows and get flat. Got it?"

"But what if my movement gets his attention?" Bubba asked, his voice dripping in nervousness.

"Leave that to me. I'll keep Benson interested," Penance promised, "When I roll, you go."

Bubba nodded.

Slipping his Beretta from its holster, the FBI agent took a quick breath and bolted for the car closest to the hardware store. By the time he had taken his second step, shots had come roaring from above him, peppering the sidewalk at his feet with concrete and asphalt shrapnel. Without looking up at the window where Benson was shooting from, Penance raised the Beretta and squeezed off several shots as he ran. Nearing the vehicle, he took one look towards the side of the street where Bubba was lumbering towards the donut shop next to the hardware store.

Penance settled down in the safety of the car; all eyes would be on the portly police officer. Bubba would be a sitting duck. Penance dropped to a knee, ignoring the poorly aimed shots that were delivered in his wake and defiantly took careful aim at Willie Benson. Squeezing the trigger twice, he saw Willie spin away from his position and retreat further into the building. A glance told him that Bubba had just slipped into the donut shop. In a flash, Penance hunkered down next to the wheel of the old Plymouth Duster parked directly outside of the hardware store.

It didn't take long for a resurgent and seemingly angrier Willie Benson to once more begin firing on the police. Several shots slammed into the sheet metal of the car that Penance himself was using for cover. Penned in himself, he assessed his situation. From his vantage, as soon as he popped out from the car, he was dead.

Pulling out his cell phone, he dialed his new boss. "Hey, anyone over there got a lighter of some sort?"

"Why, you think you need a smoke?" the field director asked sarcastically.

"Yeah, because that is what is on top of mind right now," Penance retorted, "Will you just toss me a lighter?"

"What are you gonna do?"

"I'm going to get the bad guy," Penance said, snapping off the phone. As the clatter of a Bic bouncing along the street met Penance's ears, he removed his shoe and pulled off his sock. Spying the lighter several yards away from the Duster, he muttered to himself, "Nice throw."

More bullets pelted the old car as Penance stretched for the lighter, putting his limbs in jeopardy.

A barrage of shots streamed from the row of police officers lined up behind the FBI agent. Chief Pruitt saw Penance needed cover fire. Lunging for the lighter, he snatched it and rolled back to the relative safety of the steel wheel of the car. Sliding under the trunk of the vehicle, Penance spun the gas cap, stuffing his sock in the filler hole. Furiously flicking the lighter, he got the sock to catch. Scrambling away from the rear of the car, he rested at the wheel towards the front – a precarious position that, with a slight shift from window to window from Benson, would negate any cover afforded Penance.

Soon, the Duster burst in flames, black smoke billowing from the rear of the car. Spinning along the vehicle, Penance rose from the cloud of smoke, his hands in the air. He had swung his Beretta, so it dangled from his thumb in clear view.

"Are you crazy?" Bubba hissed from somewhere in the bowels of the donut shop.

Ignoring him, Penance pressed forward. "Benson, come on, man, we've got to talk. You can last for a while in there, but let's face it, you're stuck. Let's find a way out for you!" Penance called, taking several steps past the flaming car, staring up into the window where he had last seen Benson.

"Boy, you gotta death wish or somethin'," Willie Benson called back.

"Nah, just trying to work something out. I'm Special Agent Alex Penance. I have clearance to get you safe passage that no one else here has," Penance lied, "See, here's my gun. No way I can get it into firing position before you drill me full of holes. Move to the lower floor, three steps left of the entrance."

"Why I'd wanna do that?" Benson asked.

"Because if you do that, you are out of the line of fire from the local cops back there," Penance called back.

Nearly a full minute passed before Benson appeared in front of a window before the FBI agent. A quick check told the gunman that the FBI agent wasn't lying to him. "I don't think even you can help me Special-agent-man," Benson looked pensive for a moment. Casting a glance at the policemen scrambling to get clear of the obstructed view and resight on him and the agent, "Nah, I think I'll take as many of you out as I can!"

Benson tightened his grip on the rifle he had aimed at Penance. Before he could pull the trigger, the gun in Penance's hand whirled into place, and two quick rounds fired from the Beretta. The first shot slammed into the gunman's wrist, three inches from his tightening trigger finger. The second round slammed into the Benson's chest, knocking him back.

Without hesitation, Penance charged, vaulting through the open window, pouncing on the man howling in pain. Kicking the rifle away, Penance slammed Benson against a rack of loose nuts and bolts, a cascade of galvanized metal pieces raining over him. "Willie, you should have tried to make a deal," Penance announced.

"Wha...how, I should have shot you, I didn't even get a shot..."

"Yeah, bet you never had that trouble with a whitetail or whatever it is you hunt with that thing. They don't typically shoot back, huh," Penance grinned as the doors to the hardware store burst open.

Half a dozen policemen, the pair of FBI agents, and the Assistant DA streamed in. Silence overwhelmed the store as the crowd of law enforcement personnel took in the scene. A sea of metal fasteners scattered, creating a metal blanket over the tile floor. The smug FBI agent seated on an overturned bucket offered a nod as he casually observed the bleeding Willie Benson. Just outside the shattered store window, the completely engulfed Duster billowed black smoke and crimson flames.

Analyzing Benson's wounds, ADA Annie Hunt nodded in approval, "Nice shooting. Cleanly disabled without causing mortal harm."

Penance shrugged, a mischievous grin crossing his face, "I aimed to kill, just not as good shooting with my left hand."

A huffing, profusely sweating Bubba leaned on his knees as he tried to catch his breath after jogging to the scene, "Man..." the officer panted, "You saved my life."

"Officer Bubba, glad you could join us. Remind me to seriously question signing you up on my intramural softball team. I'd have thought a little fear would have turned on the jets for you, but man, I almost got my butt shut off trying to buy you time," Penance chided.

"Sorry, I never was the fastest..."

"It's alright," Penance cut him off, "I'm glad you're okay. You were probably safe, though, Billy Bob Benson here..."

"Willie, sir," Bubba smiled, correcting the federal agent.

"Right, Willie, here is a pretty poor shot. His family probably has a squirrel-less freezer at home. Sad, really," Penance continued, shaking his head mockingly.

"You pompous Yankee son of a..." Benson growled, the outburst spiking the pain from the gunshot wound in his chest.

"Save your breath, Jethro, you've only got one working lung," Penance warned, rising from his makeshift seat as paramedics made their way to the exasperated perpetrator.

"Alright, folks!" Director Dixon shouted, clapping his hands, "Chief, if you've got the crime scene, we'll file our reports and get a ballistics report from Special Agent Penance."

"Sure thing, Dennis," the Sawyer Police Chief nodded, surveying the mess from the day's events, "Alright, guys, maintain the perimeter, we'll get the city clean-up crew in here."

The patrolmen nodded and retreated to their posts. Bubba paused and turned toward the FBI agents making their way out of the hardware store, "Agent Penance, welcome to Sawyer!"

"Uhh, yeah. Thanks, Bubba," Penance wore a mixed expression on his face, the kind when you taste something both sweet and sour. His personal affect around the situation of being transplanted in what he considered a pit of redneck purgatory tested against the genuine, naively innocent, kindness of the massive officer.

"People ain't so bad around these parts, eh, Special Agent Penance?" Director Dixon clapped him on the shoulders.

"Could have done without the squirrel comment, don't you think agent?" Assistant DA Hunt scolded disapprovingly.

"Just concerned about his family, that's all," Penance shrugged with a mischievous grin.

FIVE

The small federal office was buzzing with a fervor of energy as the agents returned. The Mayor had left the scene downtown to meet Penance first hand himself. A tall, stuffy looking gentleman in a surprisingly sharp suit trailed behind him.

Sighing slightly, Field Director Dixon painted on a broad smile, "Mayor Kittridge, I'd like you to meet Special Agent Penance."

Perturbed with the attention, Penance begrudgingly shook the mayor's hand.

"I understand you saved one of our patrolmen's life. Not bad on your first day in town, son," the mayor beamed, "We've been blessed to have FBI presence in our little town, rarely has it paid off so directly. Thank you, Agent…Penance, was it?"

Penance nodded, his gaze lighting on the man who entered with the mayor. The tall man wore a dour expression as he was sizing Penance up. Giving up nearly four inches in height, the agent squared up to the gentleman. His glare, breaking up the man's quiet stare.

Noticing the silent match, the mayor drawled, "Ahh, and this fine young man is our local District Attorney. One of the youngest our state has ever employed. Colton Jennings, Esquire."

"Pleasure, Special Agent Penance," Jennings declared holding out his hand.

As Penance reached to shake the DA's hand, the attorney gripped him firmly, with a scrutinizing eye warned, "Around here, Agent Penance, we generally try not to shoot the constituents, even the bad ones."

Moving his hand ever so slightly, changing the pressure point of his grip, Penance caused the DA to release his hand immediately, shaking off the acute pain Penance had sent shooting through his thumb and carrying all of the way up his arm. Penance cast his own wary glare, "Interesting analysis, though I don't remember you being directly shot at out there, Mr. Jennings. Though when we share such a moment, I'll be sure to take my time reflecting on your words."

Penance paused as he studied the D. A. The man's appearance didn't fit his environment. Almost over-attired and polished, much like Penance himself – but with a hint of southern drawl. He was uptight befitting a banker from the north, but with fabled southern aristocracy – an air of entitlement.

"I'm just saying we have rules to follow. No one in my district is above the law, no matter where your badge hails from," Jennings spat.

"I am sure when some redneck with a rifle has you dead in his sight, you'll read his Miranda rights or something..." Penance retorted.

"Alright boys, you can both clearly pee pretty far up the tree, I think we'll all agree. Agent Penance's work out there was exemplary," the mayor waved the two men off. "Wasn't it Ms. Hunt?"

The Assistant D. A. paused for a moment. Her cheeks glowed as she was pulled into the testosterone pissing match, "Under the circumstances, I believe Special Agent Penance reacted the way he had to, especially in light of the danger Officer Jeffries was in."

"Yeah, 'ol Bubba was up to his neck in it, wasn't he," Agent Roth grinned, "Agent Penance was the only out there with the stones to step up to the plate! Sorry, Ms. Hunt."

Begrudgingly, D. A. Jennings relented, "It sounds as though you are to be commended."

"There's no faulting his decision making," Director Dixon cut in, "Now, we just have to manage all that damned paperwork we'll have to file."

"I expect that in my office first thing tomorrow," Jennings demanded, "We like to keep our reports tidy."

"I imagine that is pretty hellish considering the literacy rate around here…"

"Now hold on a minute Penance, I know you're none too happy to be here, and maybe we aren't all Ivy-League hotshots, but these are good people here. We may seem backward to you, but I'll tell ya', there's more heart in this tiny podunk town than any one of those chaotic cities you like to imagine you belong in!" Director Dixon spat.

Taking a breath, Penance conceded, "Nothing personal boss. You're right. I am unhappy about the reassignment. Taking it out on you and the people here won't fix that."

"No, no it won't. But I'll tell you what will. Keep your nose clean…and oh, have the incident report logged an on my desk before you leave tonight," Director Dixon declared.

Looking at the stack of forms thrust into his chest, Penance called as his boss walked away, "Is there less paperwork if I kill them?"

"Welcome to Sawyer, Agent Penance, " the D. A. sneered as he turned to leave the office.

"Thank you for what you did today. I hope you give our little home a chance," A. D. A. Hunt said softly through pursed lips as she left to follow her boss.

"Hey, man," a voice boomed from the entrance to the office. Officer Bubba Manning stood grinning in the doorway, "We ain't so bad once you get to know us. Whattaya say to me fetching some grub while you get started on them reports. I gotta an in with the best kitchen in town."

"Oh yeah, which is that?"

"A little diner on Lafayette, my momma's place," the officer grinned.

Glancing at the stack of papers in his hand, Penance shrugged, "Sounds good, Officer Bubba. I could certainly eat."

"Great, hope you like chicken and greens!" the big man burst out of the office excitedly.

Penance shook his head at the exuberant officer. He couldn't resist a smile at the man's infectious spirit. With a sigh, he plopped into his seat and started sifting through the papers he had to file.

Six

Three hours wearily trudged by, leaving Penance preferring having been the one shot as opposed to completing this heap of paperwork. He hated redundancies in work, all of it already included in the case file, and then laboriously demanded three more times. As he signed the last line, he rubbed his eyes, barely aware of the previous section that he wrote. Slamming the pen down on the desk, he stuffed the mound of papers into a folder and tossed them unceremoniously on his new boss' desk. He turned to face the tiny office. His fellow federal agents had left about the time he started the reports.

Dutiful Officer Bubba Jeffries had made good with his promise to bring dinner. While not Penance's usual fare, he had to admit it was pretty tasty. As much as the federal agent didn't want to like *anyone* in this humid, bug-infested speck of lower America, he couldn't help but feel a twinge of kindness towards the officer. Though after forty-minutes of incessant questions about Penance – few he answered, none he wanted to – he had to ask Bubba to leave so that he could compile his reports.

Locking the office door and switching off the lights, Penance trudged out into the night. Though dark had set in hours before, the night air was still hot and humid. Cursing softly, he made his way to the ridiculous red sedan. Pulling a sheet of paper from his jacket pocket, he plugged the location Dixon provided him into his phone and followed the GPS trail through town. With his sense of direction innately honed, the tired agent knew the map on his phone was leading him astray. Driving down what he felt was every road in town, he begrudgingly gave up. Fishing another paper out of his pocket, he reluctantly dialed a number.

"Special Agent Penance, still hard at it?" the field director's voice boomed into the phone.

"Oh, the report is done," Penance sighed sleepily, "Just not sure I got the right address for the accommodations you graciously set up for me."

The phone erupted in laughter, "No, they're right. Sawyer is full of roads you won't find on Google or Rand McNally."

"Good of you to fill me on that, sir."

"Aw hell, where are you now?"

"Parked back at the city limit sign," Penance replied.

"Probably feel like crossing that one, I bet," the director smiled into the phone, "Turn back when you hit the little bridge that crosses the Chickasaw Creek, hang a left. Off to the right are about half a dozen houses. Yours'll be the one on the end where the road comes to a stop. I think you'll like it. I slept there a few times when the misses had enough of me."

"Alright, thanks, boss."

"Have a good night, Penance."

Hanging up the phone, Penance put the Ford into gear and whipped the car around, revving the old V-8 hard as it thundered down the road. His lights caught the piling of the bridge the director told him about, and he swung the car down a gravel road that followed the river. The homes were like a glimpse at old Americana, an image he might have seen in a textbook or how he pictured the houses when he read Sounder in grade school. Tidy bungalows with porches dotting the street. Hounds bellowed as he drove past, a few residents sitting on their porches stared.

Pulling into the last driveway, he found himself in front of the smallest of the homes, though despite the dark, it appeared to be the most kept up of them all. Pulling his bag from the car's trunk, he spied two teenagers making out on the neighbor's porch. As headlights approached from the road, the teens parted.

"Evening Mr. Doone," the boy said as he sailed down the steps past the man climbing out of a truck that had pulled in.

Ignoring the boy, the man stomped up to the porch. As the boy brought his Nova to life, his headlights illuminated the house. The man clad in overalls covering a shirt Penance could only assume was once white. The Nova took off in a shower of dust and gravel, just in time to avoid the tirade the man let into the girl.

"About how I would have imagined it," Penance shrugged to himself.

Trudging up his porch, he fiddled to get the key into the lock and let himself in. The door creaked open, flicking on a light, he revealed a flowing room. Sparsely furnished with a small, well-worn leather sofa, an aged television sat on a table opposite. Through an archway, Penance followed to the back of the house, finding a small kitchen. The appliances were old, but appeared to be clean. Just then, he realized he had not had time to stop at a store. He was even more grateful for Bubba's kindness in furnishing dinner.

Instinctively, he pulled open the refrigerator door. For what seemed like the first time in days, Penance felt like he had stumbled on good fortune. A six-pack of beer sat lonely on the top rack of an otherwise empty refrigerator. Attached to the top of one of the bottles was a sticky note.

Penance pulled it off and read, "Thought you might need this."

Nodding to no one, Penance grabbed a beer and snapped off the top. The cold liquid was bliss as it slid down his throat. Though it was a typical macro-brand, it was the best-tasting beer ever to him. It seemed to cut through the heat and oppressive moisture that hung mercilessly in the air. Noticing a door, he tapped on the exterior light and stepped outside. He found himself on a tiny concrete patio. In a corner, he found a pair of stacked resin chairs. Pulling one off of the stack, he plopped down in the chair.

Taking another sip of beer, he melted into the wobbly seat. The high moon overhead, bounced off of the narrow river as it tumbled by. Penance found himself strangely content. For a moment. Ignoring the swarms of mosquitos forming above his head and dive-bombing any exposed part of his body. Blocking out the occasional shouts from the squabbling next door. Ignoring the fact that he was a good fifteen hundred miles from what he deemed civilization, he was content. For a moment.

SEVEN

Alex Penance woke up a bit mystified. Initially, he was put off-center by the bed not being his own, the ceiling fan twirling overhead in the small bedroom – also not his own. Letting out a sigh, he internalized the second disheartening realization. His whirlwind plummet to the boondocks of the cotton belt was, unfortunately, not a dream. The early shafts of daylight streaming into the room were the wakening proof that he was living his personal purgatory out.

Relenting to reality, he assumed his usual routine. A quick drink fueled with vitamins and a blast of caffeine, he pulled on a pair of shorts and his sneakers, slipped his headphones into his ears and set off for a quick run. Penance blasted out of the house, following a crude trail that snaked along the narrow river. The terrain was rutted, but not terrible, frequent glances in front of him helped to prevent a turned ankle.

There were moments along his morning trek that he could almost admit were appealing—the river flanked by cottonwood and flowering azalea trees. The effect of the elements was old south; all that was missing was a large columned white house in the background. What wasn't missing were the occasional moving of branches likely caused by a water moccasin retreating away from his path or the splashes along the banks of one of the area's inhabitants heading down a gator slide.

The most appeal diminishing spots were those involving the locals that skulked along the riverbanks. Whether fishing or eyeing him from their hovels nestled deep in the thicket, Penance found their stained white shirts, hole infested overalls, cheeks puffed out with wads of tobacco and distrusting stares unnerving at best. He could only have imagined what characters lurked off the paved roads in these parts. Undoubtedly, he would visit a few of them in the course of what he hoped would be a short tenure.

As he clicked off what he figured to be five miles, he whirled around and retraced his steps. Occasionally, he would divert off-trail and pumped out a dozen pull-ups on a low hanging branch. He would drop to the ground and belt out a hundred push-ups. In between, he would increase his speed back towards the house, cranking up his cardiovascular system. He found the already steep heat and stifling humidity an added challenge to his work out.

In short order, he was at the house that Field Director Dixon had arranged for him. He was surprised to see a car waiting in the driveway. He could see the silhouette of a man inside, the windows rolled up, and the car left running. Penance reached the driveway, the car door opened. The federal agent found himself face to face with District Attorney Jennings.

Jennings waved a file folder in front of him, "Agent Penance, I had a couple of questions...."

"Good morning to you, Mr. Jennings. You didn't have to come all of the way out here just thank me for getting that done so quickly," Penance retorted and with a crooked grin he added hopefully peering through the windows of the D. A.'s BMW, "Since you did, you didn't happen to grab breakfast did you? Haven't had time to stock up, you know, ridding your town of deranged folk and all."

Ignoring the agent's jabs, Jennings continued dryly, "I find a few things in your report, how should I say it, convenient?"

"Hmm, I'll try to make them less so next time. What pray tell specific would you like to quiz me about? Wouldn't mind running that through over the shower, would you? I kinda have a timeline I was on today, counselor," Penance asked.

"I do not take these matters lightly, Mr. Penance," Jennings snapped.

Penance stopped and spun to face the DA head-on. Squaring up, he returned, "*Special Agent* Penance, counselor."

Ignoring him, the taller man pushed forward and began to pull on the front door. Penance dipped his shoulder to nip Jennings in the arm as he brushed by, despite his small frame, the agent packed considerable muscle in his well-defined build. The impact was just enough to knock the D. A. off-kilter, causing him to put his arms out to steady himself subconsciously. As he did, Penance grabbed one of them with a slight twist and thrust Jennings forward using the D.A.'s shoulder to force the door closed.

"I don't remember inviting you in, counselor. Not sure how you do things down here in Dixie, but where I come from entering a man's home without permission affords legally justifiable aggression," Penance barked behind Jennings' ear, "Now, I don't know what your problem with me is. Still, I promise you; you cannot toss your appointment at me and expect me to cow tail to your overcompensation of whatever insufficiencies you so obviously harbor. I don't want to be here anymore than you appear to want me to be here, so we've got that. But while I am here, you *will* treat me with respect!"

"I'll have you brought up on charges!" Jennings slurred through lips that still pressed against the frame of the door.

"For what? Preventing your unlawful entry into my private dwelling? Come on counselor, you'd lose your bar over that one," Penance scoffed, pulling Jennings away from his door, he spun him around and released his grip, "Skip the crap, what's your problem with the report?"

"In one section, you say that Benson had a direct shot at you when your weapon was not in your grip, right after that is when you shot him. Care to explain how you pulled off that magic trick?"

"Sure," Penance grinned. "I saw Willie tighten his grip on the trigger of his rifle – he had a clean little tell, he would flinch his right eye and the veins on his forearm would protrude – when I saw that, I spun my Beretta from the trigger guard into a firing position and squeezed off a clean shot before he could."

"All before he could complete the pull of the trigger?" DA Jennings scoffed, "How do you *know* he was going to fire? Maybe you didn't have to shoot him then; maybe it wasn't a justifiable shoot."

Penance grinned as he shrugged, "Well, he *did* tell me he was going to shoot me. And don't forget the whole forearm-left eye thing…we can go to the infirmary right now with a rifle, I can show you what I mean. I'll have him point the loaded gun at you, this time, of course...."

"Alright, fine. What about you shooting Benson twice? Your first shot disabled his right hand, was it necessary to shoot him in the chest?"

Taking in a deep breath, Penance barely refrained from rolling his eyes. Studying the D. A. for a moment, he suddenly lashed out striking Colton in the wrist. Jennings let out a howl, glaring at the agent.

"Yeah, I know, that hurt. Probably don't want to squeeze your hand right now," Penance conceded, "But you didn't drop your file immediately?"

The DA looked at his sore hand that was still gripping the manila folder.

"Benson didn't release his gun right away. No way he was firing with that hand, but he could still have transferred it. From what I could tell, he couldn't hit the ground if he was aiming at it, but even a bad hunter gets lucky every once in a while. Maybe he'd get lucky and get me before I dropped him for good, or maybe he'd hit Officer Bubba...or Assistant D. A. Hunt...."

Rubbing his sore wrist, DA Jennings soured, "Fine. A good shoot. Your report holds up. I don't like your kind, Agent Penance. You think your actions in the field are justified, no matter how far you push them. There are still protocols and procedures to be followed. In these parts, everyone knows each other. We go to the same churches. We sandbag the dikes together. We *like* our quiet, simple ways. We don't need someone who doesn't understand us kicking in our doors, making light of our plights, taking advantage of our wholesome ways."

Stifling a laugh, Penance smiled, "Nice speech, not sure what the heck you are talking about. I saved one of *your* cops. Your neighbor, your brother. Maybe if one of your hayseed police officers knew what the hell they were doing, they could have handled the situation. If you prefer, I'll acquiesce to your fine police force. By the way, counselor, it was Assistant D. A. Hunt that invited me along to the little town soiree anyhow...or...is *that* what bugs you? Some damn Yankee had to swoop in and save the day in front of Miss Hunt. Is that what's really needling you, counselor?"

"What bugs me is your egotistical attitude, Agent Penance!"

"Another thing I believe we have in common, Jennings," Penance returned, "Now, if you're done, I need to take a shower. Gotta new boss to impress, you know!"

Despite his best efforts, the squeak of the front door announced his presence. "Glad you could join us, Penance!" Field Director Dixon declared, glancing at his watch.

Stifling an irritated grimace, Penance responded as cheerily as he could muster, "Sorry, boss. Had a pleasant conversation with this town's wonder attorney…is that how it works around here? Business associates just showing up on my doorstep?"

"We *are* real friendly around here," Dixon admitted, somewhat tongue-in-cheek, and then more seriously asked, "What did Jennings want?"

"Scraping my report with a fine-tooth comb, trying to poke it for holes," Penance stated flatly.

"Humph," Dixon scratched his chin, "Probably spreading his peacock feathers. You make him nervous."

"From my experience, those who are nervous have something to be nervous about."

"Aw, I wouldn't read too much into it. Around here, the roosters get all riled up anytime another eligible bachelor swings into town," Dixon chuckled.

Snapping into a puzzled look, Penance asked, "So, why is there an FBI office in the middle of nowhere, Mississippi anyway…I mean other than to disarm crazy rednecks in hardware stores?"

Dixon nodded, approving of the question despite the sarcasm, "Back in the sixties, about the time of the Civil Rights movement, things were pretty heated around here. This is the hometown of Lionel Frakes, an upstanding, genuinely hard to dislike black man who was kind of the backwoods version of Martin Luther King. He was well respected, and his family accepted by most of the folks in

Sawyer. A few from the outskirts didn't get to know the man, just the shade of his humanity. They started some trouble. Our little town garnered some national attention: a few threats, a burned church, that sort of thing. Well, over the local authorities' ability to control, so they set up this little fed office. Once things settled down, the Bureau feared what the optics might be like if they yanked the office, so they reduced heads and pretty much forgot about it. A purgatory for too big for their britches Ivy League types like you," Director Dixon grinned.

Laughing with him, Penance couldn't resist a grin, "Thanks for that."

"Despite yesterday's excitement, there's not a whole lot of action running out of here. Serving warrants, combing the swamps for the occasional drug drop, assisting the locals…pretty much your law enforcement paradise," Dixon shared.

"So, which of those fun-filled tasks are on tap for today?" Penance asked.

"Well, might as well break you into Sawyer's most challenging citizenry, the Whatcom family," Dixon tossed a thick file in front of Penance.

Placing a hand on the folder without opening it, Penance asked, "What's the gist?"

"Family of roughnecks, basically been that way for over a century. They are one of the main reasons we have this office here. They are connected to a lot of the shenanigans against the town and the Frakes. Through the years, they have escalated and waned in everything from moonshine running during prohibition to weed this most recent century," Dixon declared. Flipping the folder open, a current warrant was paper-clipped to the jacket cover, "Butch Whatcom, oldest of the boys busted up some farm boys at the bar in Natches. Culminated with him throwing one of them through a plate glass window, but not before clubbing him in the head a few times with a Jim Beam bottle."

"Sounds like a local cop sort of issue," Penance shrugged.

"True. In most locales, you'd be right. Here, *we* get it. The locals are either afraid, too close or…uh, the Whatcoms still don't treat our African-American friends and brothers with the respect they deserve. We could force the issue, but the can of beans has been kept on simmer for the better part of a while, we just as soon keep it that way if we can," Dixon admitted.

"So, I can't bring Officer Bubba along? He's a big fella…"

"I'm going to send Timmy with you. He's familiar with the family and vice versa. If you are polite, shouldn't have too much problem. When you get there, talk to Delvin. He's the patriarch. While he is not a fan of authority, he has managed this current generation respectfully, if not completely within the margins of the law."

"Sounds like a treat," Penance pursed his lips slightly, grabbing the file, called to Agent Roth, "You ready to go?"

"When you are!" the young field agent beamed, snapping his badge to his belt.

Watching the young agent jump from his desk and scramble to the door, Penance stifled a laugh and mumbled, "Well, he's eager…"

"Yes, he is, Special Agent Penance. Try and use it to your advantage if you can figure out how," Dixon smiled.

As the agents exited the office, Roth gleamed at Penance, "I sure am excited to work with you. Don't think you'll find this one too exciting. The Whatcom's are a little rough around the edges, but they try to get by like anyone else."

"That's good, I guess. How often have you had to serve them?"

"Oh, a few times a year, I suppose. Mostly stuff for fighting, sometimes Billy and Butch get mixed up in some minor drug stuff," Roth shrugged.

Penance paused as they reached the two police interceptors. Rolling his eyes at the prospect of running around in either of them, he quipped, "Why not a black and white cruiser with blues and reds, maybe a big banner that says police?" Choosing to get a bearing on the town himself. As his co-pilot climbed into the passenger seat, Penance continued the conversation, "Director Dixon mentioned something about meth?"

"They've been busted a couple of times mixing up with small-time dealers. Not sure if they are a middle man from a group in another county or just got a hold of it themselves. They have been known to play Robin Hood a bit," the young agent shared.

"Robin Hood? I don't understand."

"Well, say runners use the back roads around here to avoid the police. They catch wind of it. It is rumored they hijack 'em. Take the shipment, destroy it, they've even turned some of them into us."

"Hmm, how civic-minded of them. From a business standpoint, sound practice to maintain weed as the cash crop. Not sure that's how I remember the Robin Hood story, but..." Penance stopped at an intersection and looked at his young partner.

"Oh, hang a left. The Whatcoms are a little bit out of town. Just inside the swamp. Sawyer's borders the northernmost of edge of the Louisiana line," Roth pointed.

Penance followed the junior agent's directions until they were winding down a rutted dirt road. As they rounded a tight bend, Penance slammed on the brakes. A pair of shotguns were aimed at either side window of the sedan. Penance considered his actions, whether he should draw or not.

Peering in the window, a large man with a red flannel shirt cut off at the shoulders to reveal massive arms, inspected the occupants.

"It's alright, boys. He's our new federal agent," a pleasant-looking man called as he appeared in front of the sedan. Smiling through the windshield, he waved, "Soon as we saw that interceptor coming up the drive, we knew it was either an old man lost coming home from church or a cop. You ain't no old man and it ain't Sunday. Come on up to the house. We can settle matters there."

Instantly the boys that had sprung from the bushes lowered the shotguns. The largest man glared menacingly in on Penance, but slumped his shoulders, dejected.

Pushing open an iron gate, the old man hopped into a vintage WWII Willy's Jeep, and his boys piled in the back. Grinding the old four-wheeler into gear, he led the agents up to a large old house. To Penance, it looked like it might have once been a grand place. Massive white columns were linked by a double porch that stretched along the entire façade of the old house. The posts which served sentry must have been elegant in their glory, now worn and sullied by years of neglect.

"Sorry about our introduction. Livin' out here in the swamps, well, you just gotta look out for your family. We see someone unexpected; the boys'll check them out. You gentlemen comin' out here to call on Butch, well, that wasn't unexpected. I teach my boys to take responsibility for their actions…," the Whatcom patriarch shared.

The conversation halted as a young lady bustled through the room, tossing a massive smile at the newcomers, "Why Agent Roth, who's your friend?"

"He, he…uh..," Roth stammered as he fought for words, or even blood anywhere near his brain to convey a message to his lips. His face flushed as he stared up at the woman.

Penance scowled at his young partner, who wore a ridiculously smitten grin. He could see why. The girl was beautiful. Pure blonde hair strung down beyond her freckled shoulders, which were barely covered by thin straps supporting a slinky blouse that bore her midriff. A tight strip of shorts left only the smallest amount of her to the imagination as her tall, well-tanned legs seemed to flow endlessly towards the floor.

Covering a hand to her mouth, she drawled, "It's *him*. He's the guy who took out Willie Benson out at the hardware store."

"Yes, Shannon. Now, we have things to discuss, and Agent Roth is challenged to keep his jaw off of my floor when you're near. Run along," her father shooed and then paused as he took in his daughter's attire, "Haven't we talked about those skimpy clothes?"

"Oh, Daddy, I was just sunnin' on the back porch, I didn't know we were havin' company over," Shannon sighed in response to her father, but meeting his no-nonsense glare, she acquiesced to her exit, "Pleasure Mr...I didn't catch your name?"

"It wasn't given," Delvin snapped, "Now git!"

The girl scampered off, and Delvin tried to shake off his glower of disapproval. "Sorry for the interruption. You have business with my son. You need us to sign somethin' or ..."

"I'm afraid with his record; the law requires us to take him in. He'll be processed, spend a night or two in county, and then you can post bail for him," Agent Roth answered, his tone revealing his discomfort with the reality.

"Come now, Agent Roth. You know we ain't running nowhere. I done told you he'll face his repentance," Delvin Whatcom declared.

Roth put his hands up defensively, "I know, I know. I'd like that to be the case, but Colton says we need to bring Butch in this time."

"Hmph! Jennings, I don't like that boy...," Delvin muttered. Penance couldn't resist a cough in agreement.

"Aw c'mon! I got plans. I can't be wastin' my time in jail!" Butch shot up from his seat.

Penance launched himself from the edge of the sofa, his hand flashing at his side, unhitching his firearm.

"Butch! Sit down!" bellowed the Whatcom patriarch, eyeing the FBI agent warily, "Whooee! That boy got some quicks in him!" Delvin and his youngest son burst into laughter, admiring Penance's speed getting into position.

Butch just glared at the agent, willing him to make a move on him. His father broke his thoughts, searing him even further, "Boy, I believe you'd have a hole in your head before you could draw up an inch. I know you don't like it, but you better go with them. You did the deed, you've got to make your amends."

"But Daddy...," Butch whined.

"Enough! Billy will take care of your business. You do what these men say," Delvin demanded.

Reluctantly, the big man nodded. Penance pulled a zip-tie from his pocket and walked up to Butch.

"That's not necessary, is it, sir?" Roth cut in.

"It is in *my* car," Penance declared tautly. Pulling Butch to his feet, he spun the big man around and forced his wrists together, drawing the cord tightly around them.

"You'll call when we can post bail?" the patriarch asked.

"Yessir! As soon as we can," Roth agreed.

Avoiding further drama, Penance led Butch out of the house and into the backseat of the Interceptor. The heat of the day made the old Ford sweltering. Despite his full suit, Penance took his time putting the air conditioning on, though the sentiment seemed to faze him more than the large man in the backseat.

Arriving at the tiny federal office, Alex wiped the sweat off of his forehead and switched off the engine. The hot, thick air outside of the car was no better than the sweat-box he had created inside the Interceptor. Sighing, he straightened his shirt, which had begun to stick to his body, and opened the rear door.

Staring at a silent and sullen Butch Whatcom, Penance relented to his heat-infused crankiness, "I can leave you in there a while longer if you like…"

Grumbling, Butch shuffled his legs out of the seat and swung them out of the car. Glaring up at the FBI agent, he rose to his massive full height and shoulder Alex, knocking slightly back. Butch tried to hurl himself forward, but Alex was able to plant his foot and use the big man's momentum against him, swinging him face-first into the roof of the sedan. The agent grabbed him by his bound wrists.

Leaning into his captor, Penance whispered, "Try anything like that again, you'll spend the afternoon in my trunk."

As they walked into the building, Agent Roth paused in the doorway, "That's not good."

Instinctively drop his hand to his weapon, Penance glanced at the agent, "What?"

"Hear that? No hum. A.C.'s broke down again."

Relaxing his grip on his Beretta, Penance pushed Whatcom into the building. "That's too bad. Hey Roth, where's the holding cell?"

"Oh, it's just the back room, not really a cell," Roth shrugged.

"You mean the one on the west wall getting hammered by the afternoon sun?"

"Yeah, I suppose..."

"Man, sorry about that, Butch. I'm sure you'll only be here most of the day for processing before going to county," Penance grinned as he walked to the back of the office. Pulling open a door, he revealed a small ten-by-ten room that housed boxes of printer toner, reams of paper, and an assortment of random office supplies. "This'll do," Penance approved, giving Butch a quick shove and shutting the door.

As Agent Roth twisted a key in the lock, a muffled Butch screamed from behind the door, "You can't do this!"

Roth shot Penance a concerned look.

"Make sure he gets a cool cup of water every thirty minutes. Have someone cover you when you do, he's going to get pretty cranky," Alex warned his colleague.

Roth nodded reluctantly, conveying that he understood the instructions.

EIGHT

Alex Penance spent much of his morning surfing for vehicle requisition forms while ignoring the angry wails of Butch Whatcom in the holding room. The agent could almost feel sorry for the brute, as the sun was furiously assaulting the building. Penance found himself frequenting the water cooler about every twenty minutes himself. He knew Whatcom would have to be sweltering. Shrugging, he figured the beast was used to the heat.

As he closed in on the form he was seeking; Chief Dixon burst into the office. The screeching of the front door encouraged more bellows from the storeroom. Dixon paused for a moment, and then smiling strode towards his office. "This morning's errand was successful; I take it?"

"No problems," Penance reported as he strolled to the printer.

"We usually take our prisoners to county for holding. An arrangement we have since we are short on facility resources," Dixon said flatly. Noticing Penance returned to his desk with the sheet from the printer, "And you can forget about the requisition. Not in my budget."

Wincing, Penance crumpled the paper and tossed it in the wastebasket.

The screech of the front door announced a visitor. Penance looked up to see D.A. Jennings walking purposely toward the agent, assistant D. A. Hunt trailing behind him. "Where is Butch Whatcom?"

"He is in holding, as demanded by the warrant that your office sent to us," Penance declared proudly.

"In holding *where?*" the D. A. began as Whatcom waged renewed protest from the back room. "Chief Dixon, I wasn't aware your station had a holding cell."

"I was just explaining to Agent Penance about our relationship with the county lock-up," Dixon replied.

"Let me see Butch, now!" demanded Jennings.

Penance stared blankly at the D. A. until Chief Dixon intoned, "Penance..."

Sighing, the FBI agent pushed away from his desk and grabbed the keys. Ignoring Jennings, he looked at assistant D. A. Hunt, "And how are you on this fine summer day?"

"I am fine, thank you, Agent Penance. How was your visit with the Whatcoms?"

Leading the attorneys to the storeroom, he paused as he replied, "Interesting family. Kind of reminded of The Godfather, except a few less teeth."

"They have had their troubles, almost the lot of them. Butch here has recently been the hardest case as of late. Delvin seems to be trying to enforce a quieter, almost civil status these days," Hunt offered.

"Enough chit chat. Open the door, Penance," Jennings moaned as wiped sweat off his brow.

Without any sign that he heard the D.A., Penance stopped with the key halfway in the lock, "You say the lot of them. What seems to be your take on the family business?"

"Well, it's no secret they have had their hands in the drug market, simple stuff like marijuana, mostly. They have had their share of domestic violence issues, disorderly conduct, racial harassment…"

"You sound kind of nonchalant about their deeds."

"Well, they're a tough bunch, don't get me wrong. Overall, I don't think the boys mean harm, just old, backcountry Mississippians. Haven't quite evolved out of their legacy quite yet."

"Sounds more like rednecks…"

Impatient of the exchange between Penance and his assistant, Jennings urged, "Just open the door, Penance!"

Pleased that he had successfully raised the ire of his newfound nemesis, the agent opened the door. They were surprised to see a slumped over Butch Whatcom, leaning against the wall of the storeroom. D.A. Jennings pushed past Penance to Whatcom's side.

"Look what you did, I'll write you up on charges!" Jennings spat, checking the fallen man's pulse.

Quietly wary, Penance replied casually, "Give me a break Jennings, he was given water every thirty minutes. I wouldn't…".

Before the agent could finish his sentence, Butch uncurled his body and snaked an arm around the attorney. "No one moves, or I'll snap the counselor's neck!"

"Easy there, Butch, you don't want to do anything stupid…well stupid for you at least," Penance warned.

"I'm warnin' you!" Butch snapped, pulling his captive in front of him as a shield.

"I think you better take him serious, Penance," Jennings gasped, his face turning a darkened shade of reddish-purple.

Putting his hands up, Penance backed slowly out of the room, giving the men space. As Butch shifted his weight, Penance's right hand shot to his side. In one fluid motion, he flicked his holster release with his thumb and snapped his Beretta out in front of him, squeezing off a round without hesitation.

Whatcom reeled backward, releasing his grip on the D.A. Penance leaped forward, yanking Jennings out of the way. Stepping in between the two, the agent casually holstered his handgun. Folding his arms, Penance looked down on Butch with a disapproving stare, ignoring the big man's howls of pain.

"Butch, I thought we had been through this. It's not nice to grab people, at least not the good guys."

"You shot me! I...I need to get to the doctor or somethin'!"

"Oh, quit your whining. I'll admit, a .40 leaves a bit of a hole, but that's pretty superficial. Probably didn't even hit any muscle, not that you don't have some to spare," Penance scoffed, "We'll get you a doctor, but you'll be fine."

"Is everybody okay in here?" Dixon appeared in the doorway, his face a bit more pale than usual.

"Yeah, we're okay..." Penance began.

"No, we're not. He nearly shot me!" bellowed Jennings.

"He *did* shoot me!" wailed Whatcom, "He tried to kill me."

"I *saved* you, Jennings. Butch...you're an idiot. If I wanted you dead, which assaulting and threatening a federal prosecutor would justify, you would not be a part of this conversation," Penance dismissed.

Dixon looked around at the bunch, who was now joined by Assistant D.A. Hunt and Agent Roth. For a few moments, it seemed as though he struggled to come to

terms with what had just occurred in his office. Finally
regaining his wits, and color, he spoke, "Agent Roth, how
about you take Butch to County, stop by the clinic and get
him cleaned and dressed. Call Bubba to go with you.
Jennings, how about you and our fine new agent come into
my office, and we'll sort this out."

Roth gingerly maneuvered Butch back into cuffs
and led him out of the storage room. Penance and the D.A.
followed Dixon into the Field Director's office.
Exasperated, he plopped into his chair, which let out a loud
squeak as it supported him. "Now, what in the heck
happened in there?"

"Well, as you know, your agent mishandled his
suspect by locking him in a supply room…"

"If a facility does not have a cell or available cells,
alternative locations can be utilized provided they are safe
and secure," Penance spat out.

Preventing the imminent argument from Jennings,
Dixon confirmed, "He's right."

"Okay, but he endangered *my* life when he took that
shot, that unnecessary shot at Butch!" argued the D.A.

"You were in no danger. When Butch shifted his
position, he left a window…at least three inches wide. More
than I needed for that shot. As for unnecessary, Butch is a
big boy. He could have snapped your neck in a split second.

He had already tried to attack me in the parking lot, which Agent Roth can attest to."

"Sounds to me like Agent Penance might have saved your life," Dixon assessed.

Jennings looked like he was about to boil over, "You know Butch. He's an idiot, but he wasn't going to kill me..."

"You said to take him seriously, counselor. So, I did," defended Penance.

"It was a good shoot. Perhaps a little over the top...," Dixon conceded, "Now, one more thing. I don't know what it is between you two. Both circling the other like mad roosters, vying for the top bird of the hen yard...it needs to stop."

"You be the cock, I'll be the alpha," Penance grinned at the D.A.

Jennings just held his hands towards the agent, motioning to Dixon, who was at the core of the problem.

"I'll handle Agent Penance. You mind your manners, Jennings. You have *both* been at it," Dixon scolded. As Jennings got up to leave, the station chief added, "Oh, by the way. If you have a problem with one of my agents and want to interrogate them, you come to see me. You don't track them down at their homes."

"Aw, I was just checking to see how he was settling in," Jennings smiled.

"Save your line of bull for the courtroom, Jennings," Dixon snapped.

With a sniff, the District Attorney turned and exited the office.

With the hostilities settled, Dixon addressed his newest field agent, "Son, I'll admit, Jennings can be a pain in the rear. He's a good man and a good attorney. To be honest, I think most folks around here are going to be a bit wary of you. You don't exactly fit with the culture."

"With all due respect, sir, I have no intention of fitting in with the culture. Serve my time and be on my way," Penance replied, his voice cool.

"You don't get out of here without my signature. In case you think you can get my John Hancock by pissing me off, you're wrong. You have to show accommodation. That might take one year, might take five. In the short term, you aren't going anywhere," Dixon cautioned.

"Yessir," Penance nodded.

"Now, about shooting all of our townsfolk," Dixon scratched his chin, "Someone's gotta talk to Delvin about his boy getting shot. I sure the hell don't want to do it. Roth is with Butch, so I guess that leaves you."

A dejected Penance nodded once more, "Yes, sir."

As the agent wandered toward the door, dreading another trip into moonshine country, his director called out,

"And have your weapons discharge and suspect wounded report on my desk by the time you leave tonight!"

Penance shot a quick wave of his hand over his head to signify he understood and opened the door to the blasting heat. Walking across the blacktop to his burgundy Interceptor, he could feel his shoes stick slightly to the melting tar. Opening the car door felt like opening an oven. Sticking the key in the ignition, he turned the car on and let the AC run through for a moment.

Taking unfound solace under the wispy branches of the Magnolia tree, he waited. Whining to himself about how much he hated being stuck in Sawyer, a vehicle running in the parking lot. Self-consciously, the agent straightened up a bit as he recognized the driver of the little Chrysler convertible.

"Why Agent Penance, seems you've been stirring up trouble again!" the assistant D.A. grinned.

"Just doing my job, ma'am," the agent grinned back.

"Trying to figure out who's gonna come harder on you, the Whatcoms or Jennings," Assistant D.A. Hunt prodded.

"Not sure I'm overly concerned about either," Penance replied defiantly.

Annie walked up close to Penance, her big brown eyes locking with his own, "I don't think I would underestimate either of them. They are both a little bigger than the small-town characters they appear."

"I can handle myself," Penance declared curtly.

"I'm sure you can!" grinned Assistant D.A. Hunt, her face hovering inches from the agent's for a few moments, "I'll see you around."

Letting the car run for another minute, Penance watched Annie Hunt stroll back to her car and drive away from the tiny office. Something was different about her. Something refreshing. She was sharp, genuine. Easily the best part of Sawyer.

As Penance wheeled the sedan into the rutted drive, a pair of guns aimed at either side of his window once more confronted him. Instinctively, he unclasped his holster strap. "Hi, guys! Remember me?"

"We ain't been told about you having no more business up here!" one of the men shouted, spitting a wad of tobacco juice on the ground in front of him.

"Wow, that was a lot of double-negatives," Penance muttered and then smiled at the gunmen, "Could one of you let Devlin know I need a quick word with him?"

"I got this, boys," Shannon Whatcom said as she strolled down the driveway. Her long, tan legs stretched out from her tight denim shorts. A mischievous smile, hanging slightly crooked on her otherwise pretty face. Next to her was a muscular dog who stayed in a perfect heel position. "It's alright. Special Agent Penance is our guest. Come on, Mr. Penance, you can walk me back to the house. Come on, they'll take care of your car."

"Well...I..." Penance began, mulling agency protocol and then glancing back at the maroon sedan shook his head, "You know, I really don't care. Okay."

Shannon smiled as she patted the dog who was eyeing Penance suspiciously, "This is Rexie. He'll tear your face off if told to. Don't worry. I *like* your face."

"Nice doggie," Penance forced a crooked smile, his hand nudging his pistol.

"So, Mr. Special Agent, what brings you back to our little ranch so soon," Shannon asked.

"I have business with your father."

"Oh, you can tell me. I don't care much about what the boy's dealin's are," Shannon looked up at the agent, "Is it Butch? What'd he do now?"

"He...uh, kind of got himself shot," Penance decided he'd try the news out on the sister before broaching the subject with the patriarch.

"He did? Is he alright?"

"He's fine. A little flesh wound, that's all," Penance replied bluntly.

"*You* pulled the trigger on him, huh? What'd he do to deserve that?"

"He threatened to kill the D.A."

"You mean that stiff guy? I don't like him much," Shannon shrugged, "Did you *mean* to graze him, or are you just an awful shot?"

"The only path other than that one was through the D.A. himself," Penance declared, "I was fifty-fifty in my decision making."

"You don't like him much, neither?"

"I don't know," Penance answered.

"Something about him…"

"Like he wears his underwear a size or two too tight," the agent surmised.

The comment caused Shannon to laugh out loud, "I like you, Special Agent." Reaching the door, she called, "Daddy, we've got company!"

"Thanks for getting me down in here in one piece," Penance said.

"Anytime, Special Agent," the young Whatcom girl twirled around him, suggestively, "Anytime."

Standing like a statue enduring the provocative gesture as the Whatcom elder came in the room. "Looks like my daughter has a shine on you," Delvin said almost cheerily and then snapped, "That's not a good thing."

"She seems like a nice girl, sir."

"No. No, she's not, well at least she'd like not to be. All Shannon's had to grow up with were her brothers and male cousins, not the best role models for a young lady," Delvin admitted, "Now what is it that rewarded us with your presence this evening?"

"I am sorry to report that there was an incident with Butch in custody. He attacked the D.A. and subsequently got shot," Penance declared and then quickly added, "He's okay, just a scratch. Getting patched up at the County infirm."

"Who shot him?"

"I did, sir," the agent admitted.

"A good shoot?"

"Yessir, it was."

"Alright then, I suppose thank you for coming to tell us in person?" the Whatcom family head answered a bit bewildered, "Suppose you could have just called…none the matter. See, we kind of like to keep private out here…"

"I have noticed."

"Well, since you're here, there may be a matter that you could look into. I'm not sure what you've heard about us, and I've no doubt some of it may be true, some not so true. We may have our beef with the government and some of their rules, but by in large, we try and leave Sawyer peaceful. I have…friends in town that suggest some shady characters have been stirring up problems, bringing drugs and stuff in – not harmless stuff, but the crazy things you think of being city issues. Meth and whatnot."

"Have you spoken to the local authorities?"

"Are you kidding me? Them boys wouldn't know how to handle a skirmish between old ladies at Friday Night Bingo. We need someone who knows what they're doing. Whattaya say? Will you look into it? Talk to Henry at the bar. He'll be able to point you in the right direction," Delvin conferred.

"I'll see what I can do," Penance agreed.

"That's about all I can ask," Whatcom replied.

"I'll see myself out," Penance said, turning away from the Delvin. Without turning around, he knew the patriarch was watching him intently. Judging him, trying to determine how much trouble he was going to be his family. The truth was, Penance was wondering the same thing.

Pulling up to the little house, a very tired and weary Alex Penance trudged up the steps, slapping at countless mosquitoes, chiggers, and who knows what else lurked out of the swamps at night. As his mind reeled with all sorts of wicked night creatures, enough to give himself a chill, he noticed a different kind of night creature.

On the neighbors' porch, the daughter and her boyfriend fully involved in a romantic interlude. Penance noted the Nova parked in the driveway. A rebel flag proudly displayed covering the back window. While wanting to avoid the display altogether, something made the agent pause.

"Come on, baby!" he heard the boy plead.

"He'll be home any minute!" the girl responded.

"Then let's go for a ride!"

"I have to be here, or I'll be grounded again!" she responded.

The brief argument was broken up by the sound of a V8 engine gunning down the dirt road. "Aw man!" the boy spat and released his embrace of the girl who quickly began straightening herself up. As headlight from the approaching vehicle swept closer, the boy caught Penance taking in the scene and sneered, "What the hell are you lookin' at?"

With the imminence of the pick-up grumbling down the dirt drive, the boy couldn't be afforded a reply. Racing down the driveway, he slipped in through the window of the Nova and fired the engine up, "See ya, tomorrow, babe!"

Pressing the throttle, the kid sent the Nova backward and then rocketing down the street in a spray of dirt and gravel, just avoiding the arrival of the girl's father. The man hopped out of the truck with a steel lunch pail in hand and ambled towards his porch. In moments, he and his daughter had launched into a fiery discussion about the driver of the Nova as they disappeared through a screen door with a miserably squeaky hinge.

Shaking off the scene, the agent disappeared into his own house. As he pulled a cold beer out of his refrigerator, he scoffed at his neighbors. He wondered how a father would have such poor controls with a vulnerable teenage daughter. But then, seeing the condition of the house, yard, and even their disheveled appearances, he assumed it was par for the course. Just a different lifestyle, and another reason, he couldn't wait to find his way out of Sawyer.

NINE

Bubba Jeffries bounced cheerily into the small bureau office, a box full of homemade biscuits under his arm. Before he could utter a word, Chief Dixon's voice rang through the air, "Biscuits? You gotta love your mama, Bubba!"

Penance shot Roth a look at the neighboring desk who shrugged, "Man's a bloodhound."

Bubba just grinned, "I do indeed love Mama, Chief Dixon!" Brushing past Penance's desk, he brought the box to the back of the office and set it on the chief's desk. Next to the box, he spied the report on Butch Whatcom.

"I heard about what happened yesterday," Bubba began, testing the receptivity to the conversation, "Boy, Jennings, was hot. He does not like you much, Agent Penance."

"That's alright, not too sure what I think of him either."

"And Butch Whatcom, shooting him in the shoulder, wow. How'd the clan take that?" Bubba continued.

"Klan or clan?" Penance chided.

"Somedays one and the same with a few of 'em, I think."

"The family took it better than I thought," Penance admitted, "Delvin asked me to check into some new faces that are stirring up trouble."

"What kind of trouble?" Bubba asked, his brows raised curiously.

"Most likely cutting into the family business albeit with a lot nastier stuff," the agent surmised, "Said checking in with a bartender named Henry."

"Henry would know. Not much passes through this town without Henry knowing about it," Bubba nodded.

"Want to look into it with me?"

"Sure, sounds more like city jurisdiction kind of stuff anyway," Bubba agreed.

"You driving?"

"I don't know, with my black and white, I don't think we'd sniff within a mile of them," Bubba frowned.

"Right, with my Police Interceptor, they'll never see us coming."

The bar was every bit the picture of what Penance had in his mind - shoddy building in bad need of repair. The smell of stale beer and cigarettes impaling his olfactory sense within ten feet of the front door.

Glancing at his watch, he looked up at the police officer, "They going to be open?"

"Not so much for drinking time, but Henry's usually here during the day. He has a manager that works the night shift," Bubba answered.

Penance and Bubba pushed their way into the bar, the room was dark and empty. A jukebox crooned a gritty country song, obscuring the noises of their entry. A tiny stream of sunlight leaked through cracks in the painted-over windows while the neon of the juke, a doorway behind the bar glowed.

"Office?" Penance's question met with a nod from Bubba.

As they approached, the door swung open violently, revealing a silhouette of a man and the unmistakable shape of a shotgun aimed straight at them. In a flash, Penance had his firearm released from its holster and at the ready.

"It's alright, Henry, it's me, Bubba, and an FBI agent."

After a tense pause, the man lowered the shotgun. "Damn it, Bubba, you nearly gave me a heart attack...could've got your head blown clean off!"

"Sorry about that, just wandered in."

"Don't suppose you came in for a cocktail…" the bar owner assumed.

"No, sir. We just have a few questions for you," Bubba replied.

"Alright, have a seat at the bar. Sure, you don't want anything?"

"I'm sure, Henry," the officer answered.

"This about those Yankees poking around in town?"

"So, you do know something about them," Penance asked abruptly.

The bar owner stared quietly at the agent for a moment. Bubba spoke up, "I'm sorry, Henry, Mama would've smacked for my manners. This is Agent Penance. He's working with Dixon and Roth for a bit."

"Delvin Whatcom thought that you might be in the know of things that are going on around here," Penance offered.

"Gotten to know Delvin already, huh? Oh wait, you're the guy who shot Butch! And Willie Benson," Henry's wrinkled mouth widened into a grin, "You sure know how to make an impression."

"I suppose I do."

"Not surprised Delvin is concerned. I'm only surprised he hasn't already sent his boys to deal with them. S'pose you can't go smack at hornets 'till you know whether

you're messin' with the whole nest of 'em or not," Henry
elucidated.

"What do you think, Henry, a few hornets?" Bubba
asked.

"Seems like it so far. You know how bees are. They
send a few sentries out to find goodies to bring back to the
queen or a new place for a nest."

"How many?"

"Just two. One real slick, the other seems like the
heavy. Big guy, like you, Bubba. They've come in here for
drinks a couple of times," Henry replied.

"Probably sizing up the clientele. How well do you
know your night staff?" Penance asked.

"It's a small town, we're all family," Henry shrugged,
"I trust them enough. Why?"

"Likeliest hub to enter into a new market –the town
bar or…," Penance trailed off, "If your staff won't let them
run business through here, then the next most likely place
would be the schools, or wherever you find kids hanging
out."

"This time a year, that'd be the swimmin' hole out
on Jameson Creek. Sometimes have to break up parties with
underage drinking and such," Bubba snapped his fingers.

"Gentlemen, that's about all I got for you. If
anything crosses my eyes or ears, I'll give you a holler,
Bubba," Henry offered.

After thanking the man for the information, Penance squinted as they entered the sunlight, "Where's the nearest hotel?"

"Why, not happy with the place Dixon set up for you?" Bubba asked.

"If you're a thug from out of town, you have to sleep somewhere."

"Oh, right. Sawyer has just one place, the Cottonwood Inn. Pretty small, nice owners. I'll take you there."

"Let's go."

Swinging the maroon sedan into the small parking lot, Penance parked just outside of the office. Following Bubba's lead, he entered the motel reception area.

"Hi Marjorie, how's business?" Bubba asked in his usual cheery demeanor.

"Can't complain, what can I do for ya?"

"Marjorie, this is Agent Penance," Bubba introduced to the petite woman behind the counter.

"I heard we got us a new agent. Funny, they keep staffing that place in our little town. Guess they gotta waste taxpayer money somehow," Marjorie said and then looking up at Penance, "No offense, we're glad to have you here, nonetheless."

"No offense taken. I've asked the same question myself," the agent smiled.

"We are looking for a couple of guys who are new to town," Bubba said.

"Little rat looking fella and a big guy?" Marjorie asked.

"That's them," Penance snapped excitedly.

"Well, them boys were here for a night. Acted real nervous like and then packed up and left the next day," the innkeeper declared.

"Get any information on them? License plates, credit card slips, phone calls...anything like that?" the agent asked.

"Nah, they paid in cash – two rooms and then gone. I'll be honest, 'round here, we're just glad to have paying customers."

"I understand. Thank you for your time," Penance said.

"If I hear anything, I'll give you boys a call," Marjorie promised.

Bubba thanked her and followed Penance out to the car. "I'll see if the Sheriff's department will help me keep an eye out. If they're still around here, someone's got to know about it."

"If they're window shopping, it's possible they very well might have moved on. Pretty small base here, and even if they play with different merchandise than the Whatcoms it's still competition that shrinks an already small market," Penance surmised.

"Yeah, probably long gone," Bubba conceded and then suggested, "Let's swing by Mama's, we can grab a bite."

"Love to, but I've got lunch plans already."

"Wow, you sure do move fast…," Bubba grinned.

Penance found Assistant District Attorney Hunt already seated at a table at the little restaurant on Main Street. One of a handful of tables lining the sidewalk outside of the restaurant, she faced the agent. The walk from his car allowed Penance to admire the A.D.A. from a distance. She wore a light yellow sundress, its thin straps revealing her tan shoulders. Her hair shone like honey in the noonday sun, pulled into a loose ponytail. With sunglasses covering her eyes, he couldn't tell if she reciprocated the analysis or was intent on studying the menu.

"Ms. Hunt…," the agent called as he approached the table.

"Agent Penance, thank you for joining me," Annie Hunt smiled. She pulled her sunglasses on top of her head.

"I couldn't pass up a lunch date, how else am I to make friends," Penance smiled, taking the seat opposite the A.D.A.

"I didn't think you cared to make friends in our hovel little hicktown," Hunt teased, and wrinkled her nose, "Which is a good thing, 'cause I don't think you're doing a great job in the friends arena."

"I'm here with you, now, aren't I?" the agent asked.

"As a colleague," Hunt assured. "Pretty dubious on the friend part, Agent Penance."

Beginning to twist a bit with the exchange, Penance put the conversation to its intended direction, "So, what did you want to see me about?"

"Well, to be honest, the fact that you *don't* have a lot of friends and history here…I was hoping that might be advantageous for a case we have had a hard time getting traction on."

"I see. What is this case of yours?" Penance asked, half disappointed lunch was more than social.

"Have you heard of *Los Ppiratas de la Caracas?*"

Penance looked at her warily and answered her slowly, "Yes, why?"

"We believe they have taken root throughout remote sections of Mississippi and Louisiana, most likely taking advantage of lower on the radar areas that have been hit economically after the hurricane and levee failures," Hunt replied.

"What would they be doing here?"

"Supply lines. Quiet, rural areas that are economically depressed are a perfect way to pick up some of the lesser morale neighbors who are desperate for cash. Access to the Mississippi River, state routes that aren't monitored and patrolled as well as the interstates…just like in the old days, whether it was sugar and cotton or moonshine during prohibition, this area makes for a logistical hub. Whatever the *piratas* are or aren't involved in, our county is packaging and distribution, not the customer. There just isn't money here," Hunt filled Penance in and slid a file across the table.

The agent quickly flipped through the file, he doubted the validity of much of the contents, but if the *piratas* were really in Sawyer, it could be the case that would represent his ticket out of there.

He tapped the file absently on the table as he stared away, trying to formulate a plan. As he did, his mind told him something his eyes were taking in seemed out of place. He focused his attention and located the anomaly. Parked amidst the dusty pick-ups and sedans, a shiny Porsche Cayenne gleamed in the sun. Just over the hood of the Porsche, on the opposite sidewalk where he and the A.D.A. were having lunch, he spied three men. Like the German

SUV, two looked out of place for the area. These two were polished, looking far more urban than the typical Sawyer resident. In the sunlight, a medallion gleamed between one of the men's shirt collars.

"What do you think?" Hunt asked on the other side of the file folder.

"What?" Penance asked, a bit absently as he continued looking past her and at the three men.

"The *piratas*…are you listening to me?" Hunt asked, raising a brow.

"Wha…yeah," Penance snapped back into focus, "Who are those guys right there?"

A little annoyed, she followed the agent's gaze, "That's Jimmy Nickels. Resident sleaze running pot mostly. Typically afraid to get into the hornet's nest of any big-time operation. We've locked him up a few times and gotten him to snitch a bit. The other two, I don't know."

"He snitched about anything lately?"

"No, been real quiet, why?"

"I think he thinks he's changing leagues," Penance replied thoughtfully, rising from his seat, "Would you excuse me? Thank you for lunch."

"Where are you off to?" Hunt asked, sounding perturbed.

Already at the sidewalk, Penance answered, "Getting my new company car…"

The men had concluded their business, as Penance crossed the street, the Cayenne pulled away from the curb and whooshed down the road, Penance took note of the "New Jersey Garden State" tags on the back of the SUV. Nickels had started down the sidewalk. Penance followed the snitch from a distance. Moving cautiously, the agent expected Nickels to glance over his shoulder occasionally, but he never did. Penance surmised he was either confident that he was not in trouble or was just not terribly bright.

As the agent thought about it, he was likely right on both counts. The handshake looked like satisfaction of preliminary agreement between the two. Moving through town rather casually, Nickels ducked into Henry's Tavern. Slipping in after him, Penance selected a chair in the dimly lit portion of the bar. With a quick wave of his hand, he signified to Henry not to overtly acknowledge him.

As the agent watched Nickels, he noticed him tap nervously on the bar. Receiving a shot of whiskey, the smalltime drug runner slammed it down and ordered another from Henry. After tossing the second back, he threw a few bills on the bar and moved toward the exit. Giving Nickels a brief head start, Penance too, made for the door.

Nickels rounded the corner and stopped outside of his economy car. Before reaching the driver's door, he spun and confronted the agent. Lunging at the wiry agent, he grabbed at Penance's jacket, trying to twist him against the exterior wall of the bar.

With a quick sidestep and downward blow of his fist, Penance dismissed Nickels' attack and delivered a quick shot to his assailant's throat, causing him to gurgle and gasp. As Nickels tried to regain his breath, Penance kicked his legs out from under, planting him on his butt on the sidewalk.

"Who are you, man, what do you want with me?" Nickels spat as he began to gather his breath.

"I'm a Federal Agent, who you just attacked by the way," Penance stated, "I have a few questions for you, Jimmy."

"I got nothin' to say to you."

"I think you do," Penance pressed firmly.

"Hey man, you can't mess with me, I ain't done nothing," Nickels whined.

"Maybe, but you're about to, aren't you, Jimmy?" Penance shrugged, "Certainly explains why you attacked me…"

"I didn't know who you were, just saw you at a bar not drinkin' nothin' and then following me out here…" Nickels swore.

Penance paused, hovering over the drug runner, "So tell me, do the Whatcom's know you're working into their world, or how about the *piratas*? Man...that takes balls, gonna get you killed, but serious stones, my man."

"How do you... they can't...." Jimmy spat nervously.

"I do, and they probably do too. What's up with slim shady, your buddy from Jersey?"

"I gotta cousin doin' time in Allen, he set me up. Told me he could land a score so big it'd get me outta this crummy town," Nickels admitted.

"Not that I don't understand your incentive, that score is going to get you killed. I tell you what. I am going to help you. And you are going to help me help you." Glancing in the direction of his grossly apparent Bureau car, and deciding a different tact, "You drive..."

Sitting in the back seat, immediately behind Nickels, Penance endured a cramped, bumpy ride. The trip took the pair off of the highway and up a deeply rutted dirt road. The agent thought for sure that the little Dodge was going to break apart.

"Sure, this thing can handle it?" he asked from the back seat.

"No," Nickels responded, and then trying to spy Penance through the rearview mirror, which abruptly broke off the windshield, bouncing off the dash. He asked, "What are you gonna do with me, man?"

"If you get out of line, I'll probably shoot you," Penance replied, "If you behave, I'll turn you over to the county prosecutors, might even forget about that whole assaulting a federal agent thing."

"I knew I shouldn't have listened to Billy Ray," Nickels whined.

"I do make it a point *not* to listen to anybody with two first names," Penance grinned, "That your cousin?"

"Yep. We used to run together, but he got mixed up in some stuff and got busted."

"That it up ahead?" Penance asked, spying a small building nestled in a patch of Sumac trees.

"Yeah, that's Flander's huntin' cabin…"

"Alright, stop right here, slide in along these bushes," Penance instructed his asset, who was becoming increasingly nervous, "I'd have you introduce us, but I have a feeling that wouldn't go over so well." Pulling a pair of zip-ties from his pocket, the agent snaked his arm out and catching Nickels by the wrist, lashed him to the steering wheel.

"What the…you just gonna leave me here? What if they get away? They'll kill me!" Nickels protested.

Slipping out of the car, Penance just muttered in response, "Well, guess I better make sure they don't get away."

Pulling his pistol from its holster, Penance made sure he had a round in the chamber. He repeated the process with his back up gun as he slithered through the thick growth. For a moment, the variety of lethal creatures that lurked under his footsteps in the Mississippi wilderness crept into his mind. Releasing a quick chill, he focused on his objective.

Nearing the tiny cabin, Penance spied the Porsche. Despite being a capable SUV, it looked strange and out of place in the backwoods. Turning his cast on the building, he paused behind a tree, searching for any activity. From the thin walls, he could hear a pair of voices.

The side of the cabin the agent was approaching from was windowless, allowing Penance to advance with little worries. As he moved forward, he picked up on a tiny shimmer just off of the ground. Looking closer, he found a line of monofilament stretching to a pair of posts rising inches off of the earth past either side of the cabin. Atop the pillars were little bells. Hunters and campers would often use these crude setups to warn of snooping bears and other critters.

Gingerly stepping over the monofilament, Penance slipped up to the side of the old shack. Inside, he could hear a voice lamenting accommodations.

Another voice snapped, "Quit your whining, Lenny. Another day or two, we'll have made our in-roads, and we can be the hell out of here. These people are so pathetic. We'll own this distribution route in no time."

"But there's nothin' to do here. No T.V...," the one named Lenny continued to complain.

"Shut up, Lenny. With the stuff we'll be able to move through these hick towns, you'll be able to buy a thousand flat screens."

"Let's go for a hike," Lenny suggested.

"Go for it, one of us has to stay with samples and the manufacturing template."

"Alright. I don't know who would find it way out here, but whatever, " Lenny sulked and made his way to the door.

Penance listened to the floorboards creak with every step. Readying his Beretta, he rolled along the wall to the corner closest to the door. With a loud groan, the door swung open one of the men Penance had seen in town stepped out and looked around, deciding which way he wanted to go. Selecting the natural path of the dirt road as opposed to the critter plagued thicket, the man referred to as Lenny headed straight for Penance.

Seeing the agent, Lenny jumped back in alarm. Before he could utter a noise or twitch a muscle, Penance sprung at him. The agent struck with his left hand, wrapping it around Lenny's mouth and applied enough force to twist Lenny around. Pulling the startled man back behind the wall, Penance buried his Beretta into his ribs and hissed, "Shh!"

Needling the pistol further into Lenny's side, Penance was able to elicit a nod of understanding. With his gun leveled just past his ear, the FBI agent cajoled the suspect forward. As they rounded the corner, the door flew open, and a flurry of shots fired in the direction, one clipping Lenny on the shoulder.

Lenny bellowed in pain as Penance pulled him back around the corner. Penance shoved his captive to the ground as bullets peppered the hunting cabin, many punching through the thin walls.

Kneeling by the corner, the agent hoped the support the structure would afford greater protection from the spray of bullets. Noticing a brief lull in the barrage, Penance knew it was his opportunity. Rolling out from the cover of the cabin, he located his target. A leg and shoulder just cleared the cover of a stump. Figuring the shooter was hunched over reloading his weapon, Penance took careful aim. With scarcely two inches of exposure, his shot had to be perfect. Letting out a breath, he squeezed the trigger twice.

The first shot met the drug dealer' shoulder; the second clipped his calf. Knowing his shots were not debilitative, the agent raced forward, just in time to see the shooter collect himself and redraw his gun towards the agent. Hurtling himself over the stump, Penance landed full-force into the suspect, driving him into the ground. The impact knocked the gun loose, which Penance snatched off of the ground as he wheeled into a kneeling stance, his own gun already aimed squarely at the blood-spattered suspect.

"Don't move!" Penance warned, now wielding both guns directly at the suspect, "I'm a federal agent. As you might have guessed, you and your buddy Lenny, are under arrest."

"Man, you could have been anybody. I was defending myself. You didn't declare yourself!"

"I'm pretty sure I did."

"No, you didn't!"

"Yeah, I'm going to go with I did - sooo much easier in the paperwork that way," Penance mused and with a wave of the pistols, "Now get up. We need to make sure Lenny didn't wander off, especially with that nasty wound and all. He might be a little angry at you for that. Personally, I thought it was hilarious!"

Finding Lenny curled in a ball, moaning about being shot, Penance tended to his wounds. Satisfied his prisoner wasn't going to bleed to death, he zip-tied each man's ankles and wrists and called in for support.

Lenny glared at his partner for shooting him.

The scene was frenetic with local police, paramedics, District Attorney Jennings and A. D. A. Hunt, Agent Roth, and Field Director Dixon. As each surveyed the scene, they observed the two men being treated for gunshot wounds and the very grumpy Jimmy Nickels, who was sore from being tied to the steering wheel for so long.

"Agent Penance, why am I not surprised to see you at another "shots-fired" scene?" DA Jennings chided.

"Because you let too many criminals walk the streets in your jurisdiction?" Penance quipped.

As Director Dixon approached, the D.A. shot him a stern look and nodded toward the agent. Dixon wore a peeved expression on his face. "Three days, three shootings. That must be some kind of record."

"I was fired upon, Chief Dixon. And really, I just winged that guy," Penance shrugged and then grinning, he nodded toward Lenny, "I didn't shoot *that* one!"

"Or me!" called Nickels.

"You are just one reckless son of a ..." Jennings began, standing in front of Penance's face, "Chief Dixon. You've been a fed for what, twenty years?"

"Twenty-three."

"How many people have you shot?"

"None, counselor," Dixon replied begrudgingly.

"Roth, how 'bout you? Shot anyone in your time as an agent?"

"Uhh, no," Roth answered thoughtfully and then perked up his head, "I thought about it the other day when Willie went all wacky in the town square."

"That's my point. Some hotshot, who got demoted in order to wind up on this detail, comes in bitter. Trying to make a statement like some sheriff in an old western!" Jennings beamed, feeling very sorry for himself.

"If I wanted to make a statement, I would have gone with the fuchsia shirt like you, Jennings. Now *that* makes a statement.!" dug Penance, thoroughly enjoying the screwed expression in the D.A.'s face.

"He did just single-handedly break up a burgeoning drug ring," a cheery voice called from behind them. A tall, well-dressed man in his early sixties strode up to the group.

"Maybe, but tell met this, Agent Penance, did you follow protocol?" Jennings spat, "Where was your back-up?"

"Based on the intel I received, I felt I had to act swiftly. I did so with prudence, I followed my lead to assess the situation, but was assaulted before I could call it in."

"About that intel, do you mean Jimmy Nickels? Who you, by the way, lashed to the steering wheel of his car – for which I demand an official reprimand for endangering and mistreating a captive suspect!" Jennings snarled, his face and neck glowing red.

"Come now, Jennings. Nickels was hardly in danger; it could be argued that Agent Penance kept the informant *out* of danger. And let's be clear, given the situation, Nickels was a flight risk," the newcomer countered.

Smiling squarely at the D.A. and then turning to his new defender, "You have a keen sense of the situation, Mr...."

"Doyle. Lonnie Doyle, Magistrate," the gentleman held out his hand to the agent, "A pleasure to meet you. You've made quite a splash around here during your meager stay."

"Yes, sir. I suppose I have been a little busy," Penance conceded.

"Well, I'm sure things will settle down, and you'll see just how quiet our little hamlet can be," Doyle said, turning to Jennings, "If you have dirty laundry, Mr. Jennings, I suggest you air it in closed quarters. Belittling a member of the justice community in public, never mind in front of a cache of suspects doesn't seem to me as the best route."

"Yessir," Jennings acquiesced meekly.

"Agent Penance, my wife and I are hosting a social this weekend. We'd love for you to attend, welcome you properly." With that, Judge Doyle spun and walked away, appearing satisfied.

"Well, *he* seemed to like you," a voice called from behind Penance.

"Ms. Hunt, welcome to my crime scene," Penance grinned.

"Shot another one, huh?"

"Oh, yeah, well, he shot first…"

"Of course," Hunt agreed sarcastically, "So, this is why you ran off during lunch?"

"Sorry about that, had to strike while the iron was hot."

"Lunch, what lunch?" Jennings popped in.

"I was asking Agent Penance to cast his opinion regarding one of my cases," Annie replied.

"If we want the opine of the FBI, we will requisition through Field Director Dixon," Jennings snapped.

"Jennings, put a sock in it. You have come to my agents on a regular basis, now all of a sudden you have a lust for protocol?" Dixon snapped back.

"Your agent is a loose cannon that needs to be reeled in before he does real harm to innocent people!" a beleaguered Jennings stormed off, his shuffling feet making little dust devils along the dirt road.

"He hasn't shot anyone innocent yet," Dixon quipped. Turning to his agent, "Penance, I'll see you at the office. And try to stay out of trouble."

"Sure thing, boss!" Penance grinned happily.

"Oh…" Dixon began, his finger pointed in Alex' direction before his agent cut him off.

"I know, a report by tomorrow morning," Penance sighed.

Watching his superior walk away and knowing just how much his career had sunk in just a week, gave him pause. Penance kicked lightly at the dirt.

"It's hard not to justify the shootings, but a bit harder to see just why you like to rile those two up," A.D.A. Hunt said softly.

Shrugging, Penance looked at Hunt and quit playing with the dirt, "Dixon's alright. I think he likes the forgotten office here in...in..."

"Sawyer."

Nodding, Penance continued, "Jennings...that guy is strung *way* too tight."

"He takes his role very seriously. He's a good man," Hunt reported.

"I suppose, if you like that uptight sort of thing..."

"Agent Penance, I think it would do you well to open up a bit to the people around here. They are real, genuine people. Maybe not as polished as the Ivy League-Martha's Vineyard crowd, but I'd put my faith in them any day."

Scratching his chin, Penance replied, "Martha's Vineyard is nice."

"You're impossible!" Hunt declared and spun to leave, "Please let me know what you think about the case I showed you."

"I will," Penance agreed, the first hint of seriousness in his tone the entire afternoon, then a quick return to cheeky, "You going to Judge Doyle's? Maybe we could go together."

Annie rolled her eyes and walked off.

When Penance walked into the office, Roth and Dixon were just packing up for the night. As Dixon walked by, he plopped the stack of papers on his agent's desk, landing with a resounding thud.

Running his thumb through the now-familiar stack, "Seriously, is there less paperwork if I just kill them?"

A disapproving pause at the door was Dixon's only offering.

With a sigh, Penance dutifully slid the first sheet over and began filling out his report. He had no idea how long he had been filling in redundant information about the incident at the cabin, but he saw that it was dark when a colossal figure pushed his way into the tiny office. A Pavlovian growl emitted from his stomach as the aroma of chicken wafted to his desk.

"Bubba, you're are a tremendous sight, *literally*. But you're accompanied by an even better smell. What have you got there?"

"This is Mama's spicy chicken and black beans," Bubba beamed, "It's one of my favorites."

"Bubba, no matter what anyone else says, I think you're the best," Penance salivated over the offering.

Bubba frowned, "What do other people say?"

"Nevermind."

"There's a lot of talk about you around town these days. Some people think you're crazy, or maybe that's just how Yankees are. Some of the womenfolk are in a fluster over you, that just makes the men dislike you more," the police officer announced.

"Yankee…more of a Red Sox fan," Penance mumbled through a mouthful of chicken and beans.

"I knew them boys from Jersey were no good. Didn't think they'd stay too long though, no one ever does," Bubba said.

"Can't imagine why," Penance jabbed to an oblivious Bubba.

"Aw, there just ain't much money here. Some farms and such. We kind of cater to pass-through traffic, the land-based tributary of the Mississippi."

"I think that's why the Jersey boys liked it here. Out of the way, but on the way."

"That makes sense," Bubba nodded thoughtfully, "Well, I'll let you get back to your paperwork. I know it's not much fun."

Penance nodded quietly as the officer made his way to the door. As Bubba reached the exit and pushed the door forward, Penance called out, "Thanks, Bubba! I really appreciate it!"

As the officer left, Penance tapped his fork against the container that Bubba had brought him. Staring towards the door, he felt a bit unsettled in how flippant he was to the exceptionally kind man.

TEN

When Alex Penance finally left the office for the evening, he was pleased to be met with the first cool air he had felt since he arrived in Sawyer. Driving to his little house by the river, he let the rolled down windows invite the cooler night air. The drive was pleasant enough that he had forgotten to be annoyed at driving the burgundy Interceptor.

Pulling in front of the house, Penance noted the now-familiar Nova parked next door. Another late evening for the father, he assumed. As he walked to his porch, activity in the old Chevy alerted his instincts. Noticing the steamy windshield, he quickly averted his attention, feeling somewhat awkward at spectating a romantic interlude.

Penance closed in on the door handle. One word gave him pause - "Stop!"

Now more attentive, he noticed the commotion increase in intensity and once more, "Stop! I'm not ready!"

"Come on, baby... you know you want it!" resonated between the two properties.

That was enough to spring Penance into action. Gliding across the scrub crabgrass yard, the agent reached the Nova. Through hand streaks down the side window, he could see the boy holding the neighbor girl down by pushing her face and leaning his body into her. His free hand was trying to snake its way through under the tail of her shirt.

Without hesitation, Penance reached out with his sleeved forearm and smashed through the driver side window. In a single, fluid motion, Penance grabbed the boy by the seat of his pants and yanked him out of the car, forcing the boy to bend at the waist, so both his top half and bottom half fit through at the same time. Flinging him onto the gravel driveway, the agent menaced from above, "She said 'no'!"

Wiping blood from his forehead, the shocked boy stammered, "What...who...this ain't none of your business!"

"Protecting innocent girls is every *real* man's business," Penance snapped, "I'm a federal agent. If I see you near this girl again or treat any other girl in this town that way, you'll be on the other end of that same deal but with some dude named Roy in a jail cell."

The boy's feigned cockiness faded into the fear that had consumed him. Helping the neighbor girl out of the Nova, Penance stared at the boy, "Do we understand each other?"

With a weak nod, the boy climbed back into his car. The seat crunched under the glass shards as he settled in behind the wheel. Bringing the engine roaring to life, the boy rolled the Nova out of the driveway and speeding down the dirt road.

Sliding off his suit coat, he wrapped it around the tearful girl and gently led her to the porch. Hesitating for a moment, unsure of the next proper step, he asked, "Is anyone home?"

Nodding, the girl replied through a curtain of sobs, "My little brother."

"When does your father get home?"

The girl shrugged, "I don't know. We never know."

Penance hummed disapprovingly. "Can you call you him?"

Shaking her head, the girl answered, "Our phone got cut off months ago, we ain't allowed to call anyway, he gets in trouble."

Sighing, the agent's ire for the situation grew. "I tell you what; I am *right* next door. I promise, if you need anything or anyone gives you guys any trouble, I'll hear it. I'll come right over. Alright?"

With a nod, the girl opened the door and entered her house. The deadbolt slide into place satisfied Penance as thoroughly as he was going to get that evening.

Ambling up the porch steps of his bungalow, the agent's weary body found its way to the kitchen and pulled a beer from the otherwise empty refrigerator. Wanting a shower and a quick trip to bed, he instead settled in one of the plastic chairs on his tiny back patio. Through the whisper of the river and the insect songs, he was comfortable that he could hear if the boy or anyone else came down the gravel road.

As he allowed the cold liquid to pour down his throat, the last week of his life flashed before his eyes. From hero and the closure of the most significant case of his career, and his imminent promotion to Deputy Director of a D.C.-based field office shattered by a morally and cognitively fault riddled evening, an angry senator and his trip to...to...he still struggled with what forsaken backwoods pit the agency remanded him. The events of the past three days, taking out the idiot at the hardware store, Butch Whatcom, the Jersey thug - did he have to shoot them or was Jennings right? Was he running a little hot and loose?

He didn't have time to answer, not that he would have come up with one. The sound of tires on the dirt road raised him to alert. Setting down his beer, he moved to the corner of the house. Peering out, he watched the neighbor's pick-up pull into the drive. The disheveled man climbed out of the old truck and stomped towards the house. The man paused as he tried to survey the driveway and the shattered glass. With a loud creak of the screen door, the man disappeared inside.

His vigil over, Penance returned to his beer. This time, his mind was quiet in its exhaustion, tilting his chair back, so it was resting against the house. If it wasn't for the frequent visits from biting bugs, he reasoned he could almost sleep comfortably in that spot.

Drifting into a numb world of river and nocturnal insect lullabies, the agent relaxed in peace. He didn't know how long he had been in his half-slumber when he heard the sound of footsteps approaching. Snapping to attention, he readied for the intruder. Rounding the corner, the neighbor man appeared with two beers in his hands.

Offering one to Penance, he opened his own and motioned to the vacant chair opposite the agent. Nodding, Penance opened his beer and studied the man. The neighbor quietly drank his beer for a long moment, staring down at the ground.

Taking another swallow, the man sat looking out towards the river that he knew was out there somewhere in the darkness. Finally, he spoke.

"It's been hard since Mary died. She was always there for the kids. And me. I'm probably not equipped to raise them myself, but I'm all they got. I try," the neighbor admitted, taking another drink from his beer.

"I may not look like much, my house is in shambles, I work too much...wasn't always that way, " the neighbor stopped himself abruptly, "You don't want to know about that. I guess I'm just a long way to sayin' thank you for steppin' in with Maggie."

The neighbor stood up to leave, having said his peace.

"I'm Alex Penance," the agent offered, standing up with his hand held out.

"Mr. Penance, a pleasure. I'm Frank Doone. Mags and Danny...they're my kids."

"Thanks for the beer, Frank. I doubt you'll have any problems with the Nova boy anymore," Penance said.

"No, doesn't sound like it," Frank conceded, raising his near finished beer in the air and pointing the tip of his bottle towards his neighbor's.

Penance watched the man walk away. He could tell that Frank was a proud man, yet a man precariously near defeat.

ELEVEN

Penance left the house with a new-found exuberance. Guiding the burgundy sedan down the dirt road, snaking alongside the river, he made his way towards town. Driving past the Bureau office, he followed the printed instructions for the county impound.

Pulling in next to the guard shack, he hopped out carrying the requisition papers. Handing them over to the tech, he tossed the Interceptor keys on the counter. "You take care of this too?"

"We can arrange it. Want it back at the office?"

"Oh, no. I think it's headed for the boneyard," Penance replied, a mock look of dismay on his face, "Resting time for the old girl. She's served me well."

The clerk looked up, unmoved, "Sure."

Punching a few more keys on the computer, he finally looked up, "Alright, she's all yours, space twenty-three. Sheriff Day is going to be disappointed. It was going to fetch a lot at auction."

Snatching the keys and approval form, Penance walked through the door the clerk buzzed open and made his way to space 23. Pressing the button on the key fob, he opened the door to the Porsche Cayenne SUV he had spied the day prior with A.D.A. Hunt. The "Start" button brought the engine to snarling life, its 400 horsepower singing through its exhaust ports. Settling into the forming leather seat, he stroked the buttery steering wheel approvingly. Opening the sunroof, he shifted into gear and pulled out of the parking space.

Waiting as the chain-link fence wheeled open, he pushed the throttle as soon as it was clear. With a burst of speed, the agent turned the Porsche sideways onto the street and sped toward the FBI office. For the first time in days, he felt civilized, basking in the German engineering.

Wheeling into the parking lot, he noticed he was the first one there. Unlocking the office, he made a pot of coffee and settled in behind his desk. Opening up the file that Annie Hunt wanted him to look into. Taking a swallow from his mug, he conceded to himself that he was beginning to enjoy the coffee fortified with chicory root.

Shuffling through the papers, he realized that he wasn't engaged with the Assistant District Attorney when she asked him about the case. A slew of teenage girls had gone missing from towns throughout Sawyer and neighboring parishes. The first case in the file was two years old. The rate of girls disappearing had steadily increased and had reached over a dozen. A second stack paperclipped together revealed another dozen girls from Louisiana and Alabama had also gone missing during the same timeframe with a similar pattern of escalation.

Rubbing his chin, he muttered to himself, "It certainly seems as though *something* nasty is going on."

The door opening shattered his thoughts. Field Director Dixon and Agent Roth both burst through. Roth pranced in like an excited schoolchild. "Nice rig, Penance! Is that thing yours?"

"That the same SUV that was at the crime scene yesterday? It seems to me it was scheduled to be loaded on a flatbed for County," Dixon asked, a stern note in his voice.

"That guy from Jersey won't need it for...oh, I don't know twenty-five to life," Penance replied.

"Doesn't mean you can just take it," Dixon scolded.

"I didn't. I had a lot of time filing papers last night. Found a nifty expedited requisition form a field agent can use to confiscate and use an impounded vehicle from a current investigation," Penance beamed.

"I don't recall you being on a current investigation. You closed that one yesterday."

"Well, yes. The report is on the desk, but you haven't closed it yet. Therefore..."

"Agent Penance, that is an abuse of the situation, don't you think?" Dixon fumed, picking up the approval from his agent placed on his desk, "Really, Penance? This says for covert operations."

Shrugging, Penance grinned, "It could be..."

"Drive that little European sports car back to county and grab the Interceptor. Shoo," the field director waved dismissingly with his hand.

"Ah," Penance grimaced, "Last I saw, it was being hauled away. Parts salvage, I think. Besides, you told me to fit in better with the locals. What's more backwoods than a four-by-four?"

"A pick-up maybe. That flashy German metrosexual SUV is not what I had in mind!" Dixon snapped, retreating to his office, angry but defeated.

Roth looked at Penance, "Expedited requisition, huh?"

"Don't even think about it, Roth!" Dixon growled from his office. Roth's face fell like a child who just watched their balloon float away.

Penance started to walkway, but his superior officer's voice yanked him back. "Perfect time to toss this at you," the Field Director handed Penance a pink slip of paper.

The agent's face screwed as he read the letter, "Psych eval? Really?"

Dixon smirked, "Kind of happens when you shoot three people in the first three days of an assignment. Especially where no one has been shot out of this post in over twenty years."

Penance fumed, crumpling the paper.

"You can find her at the county building, she's expecting you."

Penance stormed out of the office, bringing the powerful SUV to life. In a fury of wheel spin, he gunned the Porsche out of the parking lot and down the road. Gliding his vehicle in and out of traffic, he pressed the SUV hard on the way to the county building. Pulling into the spot marked for Sheriff's Deputies' vehicles, Penance climbed out. Pulling the crumpled paper from his pocket, he read the psychologist's name once more and stomped up the steps of the building.

As he entered the main hall, he found a very buttoned-up woman waiting on a bench. Her hands politely folded against the file in her lap. "Agent Penance?"

"Yes," Penance grunted out his reply.

Standing, she motioned to an open doorway, just beyond the bench. "We can use this conference room."

Closing the door behind them, the psychologist held out her hand to the agent. Receiving a half-hearted hand in return, she introduced herself. "I am Mary Watson, counselor for the Bureau. Please, have a seat."

Penance plopped in a stiff chair at the table and drummed impatiently with his fingers.

"You have had quite the week," the counselor smiled.

"I suppose I have," the agent admitted.

"Why don't you tell me about it."

"I'm pretty sure you already know. It's all in that file, right?" Penance retorted.

"It is. I was hoping to hear it from you. You were on your way to a Director role in D.C., and now…you're here. How do you feel about that?" the counselor asked.

"Couldn't be happier. A backward career move, backward people…what's not to love."

"So, you *don't* like the people here," the counselor pressed, pressing her glasses against the bridge of her freckled nose and making a notation in her notebook.

"Some of them are alright, I guess," the agent shuffled in his seat. "Just because I'm unhappy, doesn't mean I have turned trigger happy or shot people unnecessarily. That's ridiculous."

"I'm not saying that's what happened, Agent Penance. It is odd that in a place where I had to go all the way back to the seventies to find an FBI field agent shooting a suspect, you have shot three in the very first week of being here," the psychologist waved Penance's file.

"In the first three days," Penance corrected.

"Indeed," Watson acknowledged the correction.

"Did your research happen to note how many non-FBI agents were shot during that time span? It seems to be no shortage of criminals firing off rounds, just a noticeable absence of good guys willing to step up to the plate and fire back," Penance reasoned.

"Stepping up to the plate and out on a limb are two quite different scenarios. It is my job to determine if you are fit for your role."

"I don't need a shrink, what I *need* is for people to quit shooting at me, and then I'll do my part in not shooting *them!*" Penance declared, his tone showing his agitation.

"They were apparently good shoots, that has been declared by your superiors in the reports," the psychologist looked at the agent squarely. "What we need to understand is if you are putting yourself in positions that escalate situations unnecessarily."

"The bad guys have guns, Ms. Watson. Do you put yourself in front of a gun barrel to protect other people? Until you do, don't pass judgment on me. If I didn't shoot the bad guys, myself or other people would be dead. And yes, I'll gladly take the life of a bad guy instead of my own and most certainly to protect a civilian. But does your report say that I put my life out there to spare others? These yokels are in over their heads. If I didn't step in, do something that someone like you might feel is a bit dangerous, perhaps even foolish, good people would have gotten killed," Penance fumed.

"Your behavior, while perhaps admirable, has not met the Bureau's protocols for a field agent in those situations," Watson declared.

"The guys in their cubicles writing those protocols, haven't been here this week. I'm alive. I sleep well at night because I know my actions were the right thing, not because of some damned protocol."

"In more than one case, you put yourself squarely in the line of fire, Agent Penance. That's not brash or heroic, that's dangerous. It incites a situation where the outcome derails to a shooting," the counselor pressed.

"A madman waving around a gun and taking shots at police and civilians incites an outcome that involves a shooting."

"If a madman is waving a gun, why step in front of him?"

"Because I knew I could disarm him."

"How could you know that? You could have, should have, been shot yourself."

Penance got up from his seat and walked up to within inches of the startled psychologist. "Slap me."

"What?"

"Slap me. As hard as you can," the agent slid his hands in his pockets.

"I will not..."

"You want to understand me better, I am trying to..." Penance stopped short as a hand flashed out through the air. Despite his restricted movement, he had enough time to free his hands, gently clasping her's inches from his cheek. "You are right-handed, yet all of your movements and gestures have been with your left. Your lips pull even when you have taken notes, and you even grabbed your things with your left hand. You have an injury to your right side, your elbow, or shoulder, probably for about a week or two. Plenty of time to begin to compensate, but not enough time to get used to the pain. Your hands are soft, and while you are in lovely shape, I presume it is the result of eating well and genetics, not from working out. By all rights, you should have been able to slap me with my hands in my pockets, but using your non-dominant hand was just retarded enough in its movement – both in delivering a tell as your shoulders shook prior to striking as well as in the weak delivery itself."

Still holding her hand gently but firmly in his own, he looked into her bright green eyes through her glasses,

"I'm not crazy. I don't have a death wish. I am good at what I do."

Watson swallowed hard, a soft breath releasing from her lips as she stared into the agent's eyes. "Uhm, you...you can let go now," she whispered.

Agent Penance opened his hands apart. "Are we done?"

The counselor nodded silently.

Without another word, Penance turned and left the conference room.

As Agent Penance left the county building, he tossed the pink paper into the trash. Descending the steps, he noticed a county sheriff hovering by the agent's car, wondering what he should do.

"Hey, you're parked in a..."

Penance flashed his ID, "Federal Agent."

The deputy still looked confused as Penance put the Porsche in reverse and backed out of the parking spot. Before he put the SUV in gear, Penance noticed the Bureau psych watching him from the county building door. Shoving the gear lever into place, the agent drove off.

TWELVE

Realizing he was a block away from the courthouse, Penance thought of Annie. He was feeling sheepish for his lack of attention paid to the A.D.A., especially in the face of the seriousness of the case she presented. Besides, he liked the idea of visiting the defiantly attractive southern belle.

Swinging his newly acquired Porsche into the next parking lot, he grabbed the case file from the passenger seat. In typical antebellum fashion, the courthouse was a massive piece of architecture adorned with tall pillars. The ornate structure was in contrast with the simple facades of most buildings in the town. Poking his head down random hallways, he found Ms. Hunt's office on the top floor.

Finding her office empty, he continued to roam the hallways until he heard her voice. Following it, not far from her own office, Penance stood before an office with no less than three placards noting the owner - Colton Jennings, Esq. Walking straight in, he was met by an excited young lady who positioned herself in his path.

"May I help you?" she asked. A glance at the reception desk told Penance her name was Nancy Blevins.

"No, I'm good," the agent replied, his voice ringing dismissively.

"Uhm, District Attorney Jennings is in a meeting," Ms. Blevins replied meekly.

Looking past the receptionist, Penance could see Annie Hunt's legs through the open doorway. "I know, that's why I'm here."

"Is he expecting you? I don't recall..."

"My meeting isn't with Jennings, but rather Ms. Hunt," Penance declared, stepping around the woman.

"Sir..." Nancy began before her boss appeared in the doorway.

"What is all the como...oh, it's you, Agent Penance. What are you doing here?" Jennings asked curtly.

"Came to talk about the case with Ms. Hunt."

"Well, we are in a meeting, perhaps you can make an appointment?" Jennings suggested.

"Is your meeting more important than the welfare of a pair of young girls?" Penance snapped.

"So, *now* you are interested in my case," Annie popped into the reception area.

Instead of allowing himself to be flustered, he flashed a coy smile, "Ms. Hunt, I am truly interested in every word you care to utter."

Ignoring an impressed murmur from the receptionist, Penance continued, "I apologize for having to tend to that other matter that broke up our lunch meeting. Today, I am all yours."

Pleased with his candor, the Assistant District Attorney smiled, "Well then, let's see about finding those girls. Colton, we were done, right?"

"Well..." Jennings started before Agent Penance cut him off.

"Alright, shall we, Ms. Hunt?" Penance held out his arm for the A. D. A., who looked at it for a moment but elected to decline and walked passed and into the hallway.

"I'm glad you came by. I think we need somebody with your experience on this case," the Annie conferred.

"I'm glad to do what I can," Penance replied as they walked, "You're pretty sure the girls didn't go willingly? It seems like they hailed from trouble homes, according to the case files."

"I know, believe me, we covered that angle well, and you're right. Even if so, there seems to be an element that is leading them away."

"Sounds like fox guy from Pinocchio, Honest John," seeing his analogy met with a questioning glance, he waved his hand, "No, follow me here. You have these lost souls, easy prey for someone to pick on, and gather for their own nefarious dealings."

"I get it, just a weird way to put it."

"Oh," Alex thought to himself for a moment and nodded, "Probably right. At any rate, count me in. I'll talk to Dixon."

"I already did!" Annie grinned.

Penance opened his mouth to speak, but was interrupted by the A. D. A.'s cellphone. After a brief exchanged, she looked up at the agent, "You want to soak up more of the local color?"

Offering a passive shrug, "Sure, what's up?"

"Local drunk tends to have a weekly tiff with his wife, this time, it sounds like he's in a bad way," Annie replied.

"What kind of bad way?"

"Shotgun toting kind."

"Gotta love the south...," Penance muttered as he followed the A. D. A. out of the courthouse.

Hearing rapid footfalls behind them, Penance glanced at the windshield of a parked car that they were passing. The reflection showed a determined D.A. Jennings closing ground. "Babysitter..., " the agent mumbled.

"Hmmm?" Hunt cast a curious glance at Penance, and then out of the corner of her eye; she realized what he was referring to, "Ah. Jennings, care to join us?"

"Well, Satchel Jones is a repeat offender, he was on my docket last, so I feel kind of responsible," Jennings declared and then intoned, "Besides, need to make sure the agent doesn't kill any of our good citizens."

"Greatly depends on how many of your citizens try to kill me," quipped the agent.

"Since we're all together, we might as well ride in one car," Hunt said, jingling her keys.

"Shotgun!" Penance spat to a roll of the DA's eyes.

"I have other business to attend to, I'll drive myself," declared Jennings.

"Let's go," Hunt huffed, visibly annoyed with the posturing men.

After a short drive, just outside of the town, they pulled into a dirt driveway. As they got out, Penance and Hunt joined a growing mass of people gathering on the street. The crowd hunkered behind a row of cars that buried in the growth of weeds as they surveyed the scene.

Bubba and a pair of his fellow officers were trying to console an irate Mrs. Jones. "Just shoot the son of a bitch!" she yelled.

"Ma'am, we don't want to shoot anybody," Bubba cooed in his customary calm demeanor.

"Well, I want you to!" Mrs. Jones declared.

"Here's the new FBI agent," an unknown voice from the growing crowd announced, "*He'll* do it!"

"Hey, Agent Penance," Bubba smiled, "Gotta little situation here. It seems Mrs. Jones threatened to walk out on her husband."

"I didn't threaten, ah'm doin' it!"

"At any rate," Bubba continued, "Seems like Mr. Jones pulled out his shotgun and suggested that he might shoot himself with it."

"He ain't got the guts! Too bad if you ask me," Mrs. Jones snapped.

"I'm assuming you got all the useful information from her that you could?" Penance asked, largely ignoring the woman's inflammatory remarks about her husband.

"I think so," Bubba nodded.

"Know what kind of ammo he carries in that thing?" Penance asked.

"Uhhh," Bubba began.

"Birdshot, not that he could hit the side of the barn with it!" Mrs. Jones elucidated.

"Thank you, Mrs. Jones," the agent said cordially.

"You can call me Alice," the woman said, stroking her long twists of gray hair.

"Yeah," Penance grimaced, "Officer...Bubba, why don't you have one of your boys escort Mrs. Jones..."

"Alice!" the woman reminded.

"...Alice, somewhere she might be more comfortable," the FBI agent suggested.

Bubba nodded and motioned for a fellow officer to remove the belligerent woman from the scene. "So, what do you think, Agent Penance?"

"Have you guys had positive contact with the objective?"

Bubba frowned, "What...oh, Satchel. We came to the door, but he said he'd shoot himself or us if we pressed him."

"It's not the first time we have had to respond to the Jones', nor the first time a firearm has been used in a conflict," Annie Hunt admitted.

"Uhh, this time seems a little different," Bubba said, wiping sweat off of his brow.

Almost as if on cue, a voice slurred from the house, "Pull!" followed by a blast. Several crows rose excitedly from their perch on the roof, and the windows shook.

From the passenger seat of a patrol car Alice Jones screamed, "That's another of my grandma's dishes!"

"He must be *real* angry this time," Bubba whistled.

"Well, our choices are this: we can let him shoot up the house, maybe pass out...maybe shoot himself. Or we can go in and get him, which might encourage him to shoot at us or incite him to crank one into his own chin anyways," Penance offered.

"Why don't you just go in guns blazing cowboy? You haven't fired your weapon yet today," District Attorney Jennings dug, "At least, not as far as I know."

"Say something, counselor? I swore your lips moved, but all I got was the scent of a horse's ass. Must have been your breakfast, you guys eat that around here?" Penance volleyed, as he sat against one of the rusting cars.

Chewing on his lip in silence, his eyes lit up. Addressing the crowd, the agent asked, "Anyone of you have some liquor on you?" At first, his question met with confused silence. "Aw come on, I'm not asking to bust you. Here, I'll pay twenty bucks for a bottle of something hard."

Holding up a twenty-dollar bill, he waited. After a few moments, one by one, at least half a dozen members of the crowd pulled a flask or pint bottle out of their pockets. Selecting the fullest one, he turned and called out to the house. "Hey, Satchel! You getting dry in there? I've got some good stuff for you!"

Holding the bottle up in the air, "Not even opened up yet. Maker's Mark, yeah, that's the stuff!"

A minute later, the door opened up. A haggard Satchel Jones stumbled out onto the porch. His shotgun swung erratically around, causing the people behind Penance to duck and take cover. "Hey, I know you don't want to hurt anybody. Why don't you put the gun down, we'll talk over a glass of whiskey?"

"You...you're that crazy Yankee feller they been talking 'bout," Jones slurred.

"I suppose I am," Penance admitted.

"I ain't talkin' to no Yankee. I ain't talking to no one!" Jones yelled. Taking a shaky, wobbly step backward, he motioned wildly with his gun for the agent to walk away.

"Come on now. I'm not supposed to shoot anyone today. It's almost noon, so I'm doing pretty good," Penance pleaded.

"I *want* you to shoot me!" Jones complained.

"That's what Mrs. Jones said too...," Penance frowned.

In a fury, Satchel raised the gun up towards the agent. The action made him stumble backward as he squeezed the trigger. The blackbirds that fled from the rooftop, scattered from the nearby tree they had taken refuge. As soon as the first shot fired, Penance snapped his arm forward, sending the pint bottle in his hand flying at Jones, hitting him in the head. The impact, with the state of his drunkenness, sent him cascading to the ground, a second shot peppering the roof of his porch. By the time he landed, Penance was already bounding up the steps lighting next to the inebriated man. Squatting, he grabbed the shotgun and wrenched it from the crumpled man's hands.

Bubba and a fellow officer rushed in grabbed either side of Satchel Jones, lifting him off the porch, they drug him down the driveway towards a patrol car. "Penance, you're crazy. You could have been shot!"

Glancing at Annie Hunt, who had been chewing her lip nervously, Penance replied to the big officer, "I wasn't too worried. In his condition, he was sagging on his back foot, and his grip was weak. He had given himself a raspberry on his cheek from not managing the recoil. Both of those suggested he would probably shoot high."

"What if he didn't?" Bubba pressed.

"He wasn't going to hit me," Penance stated boldly and looked around for effect, "Those birds in that tree over there...I was worried about them. Oh, they're okay, they flew away with the first shot. One of them might have crapped themselves...hard to tell. They're birds. They tend to do that."

"Wow, a situation without a casualty. Impressive," Jennings mocked.

"Uh, not too sure about that. Jennings, isn't that your car parked under the bird tree? I wasn't kidding about the bird crap," Penance winced. The D.A.'s BMW was speckled with white splotches. "Aw man, is your sunroof open? Yuck. Sorry about that."

Jennings looked at his car in horror and stomped off to it in a huff, pulling a handkerchief from his pocket.

"I am trying to figure out whether you are crazy or really that good," A.D.A. Hunt said thoughtfully.

"What are you leaning towards?" Penance crooned.

"Crazy."

THIRTEEN

Penance pressed greedily down on the accelerator, causing the Porsche SUV to kick its back end out as it burst onto the dirt road. The evening sun shone brilliantly through the open sunroof as the cockpit filled with an invigorating breeze.

In spite of himself, the agent was in very high spirits. He found it remarkable that he was arriving at his temporary home with daylight left to spare. With a meal supplied by Bubba on the floorboard of the passenger seat, he only had to crack open a beer and watch the river drift along.

Pulling into his driveway, he retrieved his dinner from the passenger side. A slight squeak told him of a visitor, turning on his heel, he found the neighbor boy sitting on his big wheel trike. Penance greeted him with a raised eyebrow.

The neighbor boy, Danny, looked up with a severe expression sewn on his face, "Hey mister, are you gonna beat up Maggie's boyfriend?"

The agent paused, studying the boy while hiding is humor at the question and staid tone, "Only if I have to. My hope is your sister will associate with boys who respect her."

Reflecting on the response, Danny stared up at Penance, his eyes intent and thoughtful. Seemingly approving the answer, the boy nodded and pedaled back to his house.

With the boy's back to him, Penance finally released a repressed grin. Gliding up his front steps, he entered the bungalow, shed his suit in exchange for a pair of jeans and a T-shirt.

Grabbing a beer, he opened up his back porch. As he took his first step, he froze. Reclining in the little resin chair, a smiling Shannon Whatcom looked up at him. "It's about time Agent Penance, it's *hot* out here," the young girl feigned a scowl and fanned her blouse, revealing a glimpse of her sweat gleamed chest, then he eyes brightened, "Is that for me? I could sure use a cold one. Why don't you run along and get one for yourself and join me?"

Penance frowned, "Are you even old enough to drink?"

"My ID is in my back pocket, you can fish it out if you want to check it," a wicked grin flashed across the girl's face.

"That's okay," Penance muttered and pinching the bottleneck between two fingers he extended his arm out and offered the beer.

Relenting, the agent shuffled to the kitchen and retrieved his beer. Returning to his back patio, he slid the other resin chair away from the wall and sat down. Leaning his elbows on his knees, he rolled the bottle gently as he looked out towards the babbling river. He took care not to look at the girl directly, but studied her through his peripheral vision.

"So, what do I owe the pleasure?" Penance asked caution in his tone.

"Pleasure, I like that word. It can mean so many things. It can be peaceful, it could be your drink of choice at the bar, it can be a night of exhausting, sweaty lovemaking," Shannon smiled and tilted her bottle towards the agent, "I'm partial to that last one."

Taking in a swallow of her beer, she let her words sink in for a moment. "It's muggy tonight. I love how cool the air feels coming off the river. Come on, Agent Penance, walk with me along the river."

Seeing the agent's hesitation, she groaned, "Not like I'm askin' for a date, just a walk..."

"I suppose it can't hurt," Penance agreed, jumping up from his rickety chair.

"I know a little path just past the bridge. We can look for lightning bugs and listen to the crickets!" To Penance, those were the first genuine words he had from the girl. For a very brief moment, the Whatcom girl displayed a sweet innocence that rang more attractive young belle than backwoods southern harlot.

As they neared the river, the smells from the foliage change greeted them – from the cottonwoods to the cattails. The hot evening was moderated slightly by the warbling brook, mixing in with the burgeoning calls from the frogs and the crickets. Penance had to admit the walk was quite enjoyable.

"So, is there a Mrs. Agent Penance?"

"No."

"Mrs. in waiting?"

"No."

"Huh," Shannon sounded pleased with this discovery, and then her face twisted, "Not gay, are ya?"

Penance shot her a disgruntled look, "No."

"Just checking. You don't dress like the boys around here," Shannon shrugged. Cocking her head at her companion, "Ain't you going to ask me?"

"No."

"This is not a very exciting talk."

"I don't remember inviting anyone tonight," Penance retorted curtly.

"You Yankee boys don't have much by way of manners," Shannon reeled, "Why don't you like me, Agent Penance? Don't you think I'm pretty?"

"Oh, you're pretty alright."

"But..."

"But your family is the backwoods version of The Godfather."

"Ouch, you don't hold back much, do you?" the girls winced at Penance's brutal reply, "I'm not exactly in the family business. They don't see it as women's work."

Penance walked in silence. True, with the golden haze cast from the disappearing sun, the girl was radiantly beautiful, but he remained stoic in his response.

"You know, I'm not staying around here forever. I haven't figured out how yet, but I'm getting out. I bet we have that in common, huh, Agent Penance."

Unable to resist a laugh, "Yes, you're right about that."

"So, how'd you end up down here anyway?"

"I made a poor choice. It pissed the wrong person off. This swamp is where they send fallen agents, I guess."

Shannon chewed on that statement for a moment, taking a wider berth on the path to avoid an alligator slide. "It was a girl, huh?"

Sighing, the agent admitted, "Yeah, it was a girl."

"That's why you're not into me," Shannon declared, "There don't have to be strings, you know." She moved closer to Penance, her shoulder nudging the outside of his arm. Swirling her bottle, she lamented it being empty and flung it towards the river. In a flash, Penance stepped down on a stick, launching the other end in the air. Snatching the makeshift bat, he struck at the bottle, knocking it down to the bank.

Frowning, he strode over and picked up the discarded beer bottle. Shannon looked at him, bewildered, "Littering fall under the jurisdiction of the FBI?"

Ignoring her remark, he noticed the light of day fading. "We should probably get you back."

"Aww, it's early," she complained.

"We have to walk back."

"The fireflies are just coming out, look," Shannon pointed to the bank along the other side of the river. A quartet of tiny flashes blinked in the twilight.

"I didn't see a car, how'd you get out here?" Penance asked.

"I hoofed it."

The agent cast a scrutinizing eye.

Shannon grinned, "Alright, I hitched a ride most of the way. Not everyone is so blind to my offerings."

"Does your family know where you are?"

"Heck no, but they never really do. Long as I'm not underfoot and into Daddy's business," the Whatcom daughter replied.

"Let me drive you home then," Penance offered.

Slithering directly in front of him, Shannon placed her hand on his chest and leaned in. Penance could feel the warmth of her breath. The scent of mint gum mixed with beer and perfume. It was a strange formula that gently tugged at him.

"I was hoping we could hang out at your place a little longer," Shannon whispered, her voice hoarse.

"That's not going to happen."

"Dang, you're a tough one!" Shannon cursed. Deliberately running her nails extra rough down his chest as she pushed away, "You might want to stop a little short of bringing me all the way up to the house. Some of the boys aren't too happy with how you handled Butch. "

"You aren't mad at about that?"

"He's my brother, but he ain't the sharpest one of the bunch. I know how he gets out of hand. In my opinion, he needed to be taken down a notch," Shannon replied dryly.

"I think I can handle your family bringing you home."

"Yes, you probably could, Agent Penance," Shannon agreed and shot the agent a meek glance, "But I can't."

FOURTEEN

A lex Penance wasn't particularly interested in local politics or the slightest bit concerned in ingratiating the powers that be. He didn't mind, however, the opportunity to spend a little off duty time with Assistant District Attorney Hunt.

He wheeled the Porsche SUV to the address Annie had provided him. He was dressed in his usual business attire, having selected one of his favorite suits. Glancing at the address one last time, Penance rapped on the door.

For a few moments, there was no reply. The agent began to triple check the address and glance at his watch to ensure he had the right place and time. Before he could lament any further, a call came from deep within the house, "It's unlocked, come on in. I'm almost ready."

Penance tried the handle and found the door to be unlocked. The moment he entered the house, a cat streaked out to greet him. The fuzzy pet stopped just short of an arm's length and studied him. Scanning the Hunt abode, he found the trimmings simple and nicely appointed. Atop of the attractive furnishings was a scattering of clothes draped haphazardly, and files fanned out on the dinner and coffee tables.

Annie came hurriedly down the hall, fastening an earring in place. "Sorry I'm running a bit behind, I kind of get lost in things sometimes," witnessing the condition of her own home, she suddenly stopped and reddened, "Oh, wow, my place is a mess. I don't get many guests, just Mickey and me."

"Mickey?"

"My cat."

"Oh, right. We met."

"You're in for a treat, Judge Doyle throws a heck of a bash," Annie smiled, "He seems to have taken a shine to you. I'm not sure if that is good or bad."

"Me neither, guess we'll see how it plays out," Penance held the car door for her.

"Nice move on the requisition. I'm sure you don't mind another thing for Jennings to complain about in regards to you," the A. D. A. said as Penance slid into the driver's seat.

"To be honest, I don't care what he thinks. He *is* pretty easy to get all riled up," Penance shrugged, shifting the SUV into gear, "Not sure what his problem is."

"Jennings takes his role very seriously. He is very much 'by the book.' He sees you as a bit of a rogue."

"How about you?"

"A rogue," Annie giggled, "Could be a good thing or a bad thing. I guess we'll have to see how it plays out."

At the end of the meandering, poplar-lined drive, a pair of valets waited for Penance to pull up, "Are you kidding me?" he muttered to himself.

"Nice ride," the attendant said as he held the door.

Penance nodded and collected Annie on the other side of the car. "Guess he is serious about his parties."

"Gotta keep the image up," Annie whispered, "Thanks for being my date…uh, not date…bringing me."

"Would it be that bad to be on a date?"

"Wouldn't be good," Annie winked.

Ignoring her blast, Penance led the way into the party. A smiling woman, lavishly attired and adorned in sparkling jewels, welcomed the pair and ushered them into the backyard. Music filled the air as guests mingled with Juleps, wine spritzers, and glasses of bourbon in their hands. Over in one corner, Jennings sipped water from a glass, watching the crowd grow. His face fell when he saw Penance walk in with Annie.

"Aw, he looks so lonely over there," Penance said as he tugged gently on Annie's arm, "Let's go the other way."

"You two boys are ridiculous," Annie declared, winning the arm tug-of-war leading them to Jennings.

"Afternoon, counselor," Penance offered a fake smile.

"Penance."

"Look at you two, becoming friends. I like that," Annie beamed.

"It's your cupid's touch Annie," Penance declared.

From across the massive patio, a voice boomed, "There he is!" Judge Doyle peeled away from the group he was speaking with, "Come on, boys, I want you to meet someone."

The magistrate approached with a cadre in tow, "This is Agent Penance. He has been here, what a week? And he has already dispatched with several hooligans. I believe he's wrought more justice than we had in the past year in his brief tenure. Isn't that right, Jennings?"

"Well, last year we closed..." Jennings began.

"Aww, I'm just making a point," Judge Doyle snapped, "Penance is just who we need to iron out the few blemishes our parish has, if you know what I mean."

"Say, why don't you join us on the hillside balcony, we were just about to shoot some skeet," one of the gentlemen suggested.

"Shoot skeet before, Alex?" another man asked.

"Kind of."

"Joe's the resident expert, he's won the state tourney three times and placed second in nationals," another of Judge Doyle's friends filled in quietly.

The man named Joe took a gun out of a case that had been resting by the Do-All trap launcher. A series of clay discs were loaded in the chamber as one man controlled the fire button that would release the airborne targets.

Joe carefully loaded a few rounds into his shotgun, and, as he pulled his sites up, he called to Penance, "This is a pretty fast, tight load, you have to be real accurate, or you'll miss the pigeon. The spray is real narrow, at this distance, maybe a foot or two at best."

Nodding to the launch controller, he called, "Pull!"

Within seconds the clay Frisbee was hurtling out over the lawn, CRACK! A shell fired and the disc shattered. A second pair of targets rifled into the air with the same result to the applause of the onlookers.

"Jerry, hand Alex one of Lonnie's rifles, give him a wider load," Joe suggested, "I'm sure you have experience with a tactical shotgun, same principles, just a running target with a little distance to it."

Nodding in understanding, Penance called "Pull, Pull, Pull." Jerry anxiously tried shoving the judge's shotgun in the agent's hands. Instead, Alex stepped back as the three discs had taken flight and were escaping the kill zone. The crowd looked on in bewilderment, several urging, "Take the gun!"

In a flash, Penance's hand slipped behind his jacket and retrieved his .40 caliber pistol. In the same fluid motion, he snapped the gun in front of him. With three quick pulls, the clay pigeons were shattered and scattered all over the lawn. The agent holstered his firearm to a chorus of cheers.

One man called out, "Hey Joe, what's the spread on a .40? It's a little tighter than a foot or two, right?"

The skeet marksman took the ribbing in stride and patted Penance on the shoulder, "About half-an-inch, I believe. Nice shootin' boy. I'm glad those boys in Washington still teach our guys how to shoot."

"Thank you, sir," despite his overt display; Penance delivered a humble tone.

One by one, the men shared their pleasure in meeting the agent, each to the chagrin of D.A. Jennings. When all the fawning over Penance ceased, Judge Doyle put a hand on his shoulder, "Anything you need, you just call. I know around here, things seem pretty simple, and as a federal agent, you are tasked with some rather mundane local affairs that frankly, fall outside of your jurisdiction. That synergy between fed and local is essential for our little area. We're glad to have you aboard."

"What was all that about?" Annie asked when back in the car.

"He was ranting something about synergy and for me to fulfill the need to iron out a few blemishes, whatever that means," Penance shrugged.

"Who knows, Lonnie is a great guy, but as you might tell, he has some of that good ol' boy club in him," Annie acknowledged, "So what was with the little shooting expedition? Taking out the local hero and state champ like that? A little showy if you ask me."

"So, noted. I couldn't resist. The lesson and the purposeful detuned rifle they wanted me to use as opposed to his dialed-in rifle was too much not to give a little back. The rifle was choked for widespread with a low fps load…"

"What does that mean?" the ADA broke in.

"It means it was tuned to loose, but if the shooter got lucky and nicked them all, the ultra-wide pattern was a built-in excuse "favoring the novice." The reality is, the load will fall short and late, significantly limiting the chance for contact. I think 'ol Joe knew the gig was up and tipped his hat. Everybody wins," Penance replied.

"And here I thought all that fancy shooting was just to impress me."

"Did it impress you?"

"No," Annie declared flatly, pushing her sunglasses tighter on the bridge of her nose, and settled back into the seat for the ride home.

Having been turned down for an offer to dinner or a post-party drink by Annie Hunt, Agent Penance was left to fend for himself that evening. He was strangely enthusiastic when the call from Bubba Jeffries came in. Agreeing to meet the officer at Henry's tavern, Penance drove towards the center of town.

Still in his finest suit, he stood out among the crowded bar. Most clad in denim and t-shirts, a few wore plaid button-downs. Even most of the women fit the standard for attire, though several found ways of folding, rolling, and tieing their clothing in ways to be me more revealing.

The tune ringing from the jukebox was a gritty country song. Penance scanned the bar looking for his friend. With a glance, it was clear he had beaten Bubba. Ordering a Southern Prohibition beer, he found an open spot on the corner of the bar to lean – a natural vantage for the agent which provided him a clear view of the entire bar.

Penance's eyes automatically noted the inhabitants of the bar as he sipped his beer. He watched as a romantic couple in the corner entangled in conversation oblivious to anyone else in the tavern. Four large men traded shots, a bottle of tequila sat on the table between them. A pair of ladies, each tried to outdo the other by adjusting their tops to clear the most cleavage while tempting were half a dozen grisly men scattered throughout the bar.

Aside from a few sideways glances at his attire and a couple of giggles from the cleavage girls, no one paid him any attention. By Penance's third sip, he saw Bubba amble through the door and stride happily towards him.

"Get you something, pal?" Penance asked.

"A Coke would be nice," Bubba nodded.

"You on the payroll tonight?"

"Huh?"

"On patrol?" Penance restated.

"No, not tonight," Bubba replied, "I don't drink much. I don't like the way it makes me feel."

"Fair enough, but why suggest we come here?"

"It's the only place open."

"Ah," Penance nodded, sipping from his beer, he asked, "So, is there a potential Mrs. Bubba out there?"

Blushing, the big police officer raised his hands, "No, I mean, I hope somewhere, just haven't met her yet."

Tilting his beer towards him, Penance offered, "No rush there, friend."

"I had a girlfriend when I was in college, but she wanted to stay in New Orleans. I wanted to come home."

Scratching his head, Penance looked thoughtful, "Uhm, not much of a pool around here. I mean, you've got the cleavage twins over there…"

"Oh, that's Sandra and Sally. Mama says their trouble," Bubba nodded towards the pair of giggling women.

Penance could swear as each had another set of glasses in front of them, the two ladies had managed to free even more of their feminine attributes. "I'd have to say your mom's right about that one."

Bubba smiled and slurped his Coke though a straw.

"Tell me about this girl," Penance prompted.

"We were at Tulane. She was Pre-law, I was Criminal Justice, boy, she was something," Bubba's mind wandered off into a realm of mental photographs.

"You alright there, pal?"

"Wha…oh, yeah. Sorry. She was beautiful and sweet. We'd go to church every Sunday together," Bubba said.

"Just couldn't convince her to come to …where are we again?"

"Sawyer."

"Yeah, Sawyer."

"No," Bubba sighed, "And can you imagine me in the city?"

"Only as an Offensive Tackle."

"I tried that. The coach said I wasn't aggressive enough."

"A giant, friendly Gummy Bear."

Bubba shot the FBI agent a questioning look.

"Nevermind," Penance shrugged.

Penance's attention pulled to the group of shot slamming men, whose voices grew louder with each empty glass slammed back down on the table. The muscular foursome began ranting about UFC fighters and boasting about how they would fare. One snatched the tequila bottle off the table he held it over a glass. Shaking it upside like a ketchup bottle, he was dismayed when no liquid came out. Slamming it to the table, he staggered to the bar.

"Hey Henry, another bottle!" he stammered.

Henry looked at the customer and then at Bubba. Reluctantly, Henry shook his head, "Can't do it. I think you boys have hit your limit."

"What?" the big man cursed, looking menacingly at Henry and then shooting Bubba a glance, "Why, because Sambo over there might bust you? It looks like he's busy sipping on his little soda. Isn't that right, Sambo?"

"My name is Bubba. Henry is right. It's his call," Bubba said softly.

"I don't give a rip what your name is *boy*. You're the town idiot with a badge."

"Hey now, fellas. There's no need to get uptight, you've had fun," Bubba tried to quell the situation but only served to lure the other three men into the mix.

"You telling us what to do, boy?" one of the drunk's compatriots sneered.

Surrounding the officer and largely ignoring the much smaller Penance, the foursome closed in. The initial instigator gave Bubba a push. "What's it gonna be, Opie, you gonna make us leave?"

"It's Bubba. It's up to Henry if he would like you to leave. And if you won't, then I will help you leave."

"Let's just say he did ask us to leave, and we refused."

The man lunged a massive fist at Bubba. Penance stepped in, deflecting the blow with the palm of his hand and slipped between the mild-mannered police officer and his foes. "*I'm* telling you to leave," the comparatively diminutive Alex Penance snapped, his voice cold and calm.

The four inebriated men looked down towards their new threat, scoffing at their undeniable size advantage. "Hey there, little fella, you don't want to be mixed up in this. This is man talk."

"Leave," Penance demanded coolly.

The largest of the group took a half step back before throwing a haymaker in the agent's direction. Sliding away from the blow, Penance grabbed the man's arm. Using the momentum of the missed punch, he forced the man into one of his buddies, sending both of them into a group of empty bar stools.

The other men split up, one laying into Bubba, while the other wrapped Penance up from behind.

"Put your hands up to protect your face, use your forearms and elbows to deflect shots to your ribs!" commanded Penance.

As Bubba complied, the other two had recovered and stampeded headlong for Penance. As they neared, the agent raised his legs, planting his feet on the chests and heads of the charging opponents, "running" up to them, allowing him to flip over the man who was holding him. His arm wrapped around the neck of the man who grabbed him from behind, he braced himself as the charging pair ran headlong into their friend.

The first three tied up in their collision, Penance freed to come to the aid of Bubba. Being ruthlessly pummeled, Bubba absorbed blow after blow from the enraged man. Penance delivered a quick, bone-crunching kick of his leg to the man's shin. The drunk collapsed to the ground writing in pain.

"Come on, man, you've got to fight back," Penance glowered.

"I'm alright," Bubba whimpered.

Spinning, Penance faced the three remaining attackers. Fed up with the situation, the agent launched three, lightning-quick, decisive attacks. Grabbing the first of his opponent's oncoming fist, twisting it, wrapping it behind the man's back and slamming him into a thick wooden post. Simultaneously, he struck out with his foot catching the third man on the chin, snapping his head back, landing him unconscious on the floor.

Facing the third head-on, Penance eyed the primary instigator, "Sure you want to do this?"

A sloppy punch answered the agent's question. Penance casually blocked the punch, and then another. With a flash of his fist, he delivered a blow to his aggressor's nose. Blocking another flurry of punches, Penance again lashed out with another blast to the man's nose, followed by a precise flurry of his own.

Pausing his attack, he watched as the bloodied man stared blankly at the agent before wobbling and finally collapsing to the floor of the bar. With a deep breath, Penance released all of his aggression and adrenaline. "You alright?"

Bubba nodded, looking over the chaos of the four strewn bodies. "They were a *lot* bigger than you."

"And you, them," Penance replied, "You're a peace officer, not a police officer. That's okay. We need them too.

But there are times the only way to arrive at peace is through fighting for it."

Bubba nodded solemnly.

"Let's clean these guys out of here for Henry," Penance suggested, dragging one man by the arm, dumping him by the curb.

FIFTEEN

"Agent Penance," Chief Dixon called from his office as the agent entered the bureau, "Now we add bar brawls to your concise resume in our parish?"

"Man, doesn't talk long for word to spread in this town," Penance muttered.

"That it doesn't. Surprise you?" Dixon replied, "Sounds like you gave those boys a good whooping. Eh, probably deserved it from what I hear, but you did put one in the hospital with a broken leg."

"There were four of them, each outweighing me by at least a hundred. I had to immobilize one," Penance shrugged.

"Bar brawl, huh?" a lighter voice came from near the coffee maker, "Sounds like you are fitting right in."

Penance looked up and grinned, "Good morning, Ms. Hunt. What brings you to our little office, can't be the coffee, it's terrible."

"Came to collect *you*. There has been another missing girl. I wanted to take you to her home," the Assistant District Attorney informed.

"That's even more terrible, let's go. You can fill me in on the way."

Annie Hunt's expression was severe as she drove her convertible through town. Penance couldn't help but find her visage of consternation particularly attractive. The Assistant D.A. nibbled anxiously on her bottom lip as she navigated her car towards the crime scene.

The drive took them several minutes outside of town, to a cluster of small, poorly maintained homes. "This is the second girl from this neighborhood," Hunt informed quietly.

Penance scanned the area, noting the collection of rusty vehicles and appliances strewn throughout the yards. The jungle of weeds failed to demarcate where the various properties ended, and the other began. Some of the houses were missing shingles from their roofs and even glass from windows. In front of two of the houses, late model sedans stood out to him. As the agent and A.D.A. approached, a trio of dogs abandoned their naps to converge on the newcomers. "You always take me to the nicest places, Ms. Hunt.," instinctively, Penance tapped his holster.

"You aren't going to shoot them…," Hunt cursed under her breath, stepping gingerly towards the path to the house.

Shrugging, Penance smirked, "Only if I have to."

Eyeing the dogs who continued to circle and snarl at them, they made their way to the front steps of a home. Penance noted one of the newer sedans parked along the overgrown walkway. After a few raps on the door, a disheveled woman peered through a crack she allowed.

"Mrs. Hollis? We're here to speak to you about your daughter," Annie declared.

"I already spoke to the Sheriff's deputy, ain't like you're gonna do anything for a girl out here," the woman snapped.

Hunt cast an expression of dismay, "I assure you, we will do everything we can to help. I'm Assistant District Attorney Annie Hunt and this FBI Special Agent Alex Penance. The disappearance of your daughter is my number one priority."

"Well, you *are* here, aren't you," the woman opened the door. Instinctively Annie and Penance took a half step forward, but instead, the woman pushed by them and stood on the porch. Pulling a half-smoked cigarette from the banister, the woman lit it as she studied the visitors.

"I can only imagine how tough this is for you…," Hunt began.

"Aw, Hailey's been trouble since day one," the woman spat, "But I guess the fruit don't fall too far from the tree, now does it?" The woman gurgled and coughed as she sucked in another drag.

"Has Hailey gone missing before?" Penance asked, his eyebrows raised.

"Since she turned thirteen, it has been an almost weekly occurrence. But she's always come home...," the woman's voice trailed. Her steely eyes showed emotion and concern for the first time.

"You think she's in trouble," Penance filled in.

The woman nodded, "I do."

"Tell me about this incident."

"We had a big fight, she said she wanted to leave...she said that before. I suppose this time she meant it."

"Any idea where she might have gone?" Penance asked.

The woman shrugged, "N'orleans, Florida..."

"Thank you. We'll be in touch."

"What he means is we'll find her, Ms. Hollis," Annie corrected.

"Please do, that girl's got a whooping comin' for sure," the teary eyes Ms. Hollis wore revealed the falseness in her gruff statement.

As Ms. Hollis retreated into her dilapidated home, Annie faced Penance, "What are you thinking?"

"You said another girl was missing from this area?"

"Yes, right over there. I interviewed the family a couple of weeks ago. The girl had already been gone fourteen days before I got involved."

"How'd the interview go?"

"About like Ms. Hollis. Troubled child, fractured parental relationship, the girl had run away before. This time, never came back," Annie shrugged.

Penance studied the shiny vehicle in front of the house Annie had indicated. "Run their DMV records?"

"No, why?"

"Strange, in a place where people use garbage bags to replace windows and tarps to patch roofs, that the two homes with missing children have newer vehicles," Penance said.

The A. D. A. kicked herself for not having made that connection herself, "I'll have them run right away."

"Find out when they were bought and how much and how they paid."

The ride back to the office started quiet. Annie Hunt's lip chewing had become fierce frustrated. Penance glanced over, "You know, with the propensity of people around here to drive cars that cost more than their homes, not too hard to miss that one. I mean, look over there, late model Mustang, immaculate. Parked outside a trailer with plywood in place of a missing panel of siding."

"You don't have much positive to say about the people down here, do you?" the A. D. A. asked.

"I like *you*," the agent grinned, his face falling as his comment was met with a disapproving furrow of Hunt's brow, "Look, it's just not my cup of tea."

"I'm not sure you would know," Annie replied as she started to get out of the SUV.

Shooting a questioning glance across the car, Penance asked, "What do you mean?"

"You haven't given it a chance," Annie said coolly, "I'll let you know what I find when I run the plates."

"Whoo boy!" a voice bellowed through the office as Penance walked in, "You sure put a lickin' into those boys!"

"Judge Doyle," the agent acknowledged.

"A few of them boys have seen the inside of my courtroom," Judge Doyle commented.

"Yeah, well, they didn't need to treat Bubba that way," Penance replied.

"Careful Penance, you might actually make a friend down here," Director Dixon scoffed.

"Ah, Alex is going to make lots of friends here, this is a great place to be!" Judge Doyle gleamed, wrapping his arm around Penance's shoulders, pulling him roughly. "Speaking of making friends, what's with the case you're working with Ms. Annie?"

"Some missing kids, several girls in roughly a one hundred mile radius," Penance reported.

"Sure, they're all related?"

"No, we're following a couple of hunches to verify that they tie together," Penance replied and then snapping his fingers, "We need to poke through some financials of a few families..."

"Send my office the names, consider it granted," Doyle offered.

Agent Roth, who tried to ignore the conversation, scooted back from his desk, "I can run those financials for you...free you up to put your skills to better use."

"You know, I'll take you up on that Agent Roth. "

"Glad to help," the agent responded, grabbing a list of names from Penance.

SIXTEEN

Annie Hunt was sitting in her car, pouring over papers when Penance walked by. Only the rustle of paper alerted him someone was in the driver's seat. "Annie?"

The Assistant D.A. wrinkled her nose and pushed her papers against her steering wheel.

"If I had to share an office with Jennings, I'd probably work out of my car, too," the agent quipped.

"I just needed a quiet spot."

"Roth is reviewing the financials of the victims' families."

"Good. I probably should have..."

"Quit beating yourself up. The vehicles, while new, haven't changed for several years, other than the taillights, you couldn't know if they were five years old or purchased yesterday. What engine does your car have?" Penance asked.

"What...I don't know..."

"What cars were in the driveways?"

"I don't know, I kind of noticed they were cleaner, but that's about it," Annie admitted.

"That's my point, not your area of expertise. Let it go," Penance consoled.

The A. D. A. looked up at the agent. Her brown eyes expressing real warmth, "Thank you, Agent Penance. I appreciate you backing me."

"I'm just telling the truth," Penance replied, returning a grin, "But yes, I have your back."

Letting out a massive sigh, Hunt slid the file on her dash. "So, what now?"

"If you were a young girl, troubled home, wanting to stretch your legs a bit, where would you go?"

Pulling on her lip, Hunt thought for a moment, "If I wanted to be seen, probably Centreville, just one county over. There's a bar there where the kids hang out discretely...but could be anywhere – family hunting cabin, school grounds."

"Let's stick to the static option - the bar," Penance suggested, "What are you doing now?"

"Taking you for a ride to Centreville."

As Agent Alex Penance and Assistant D.A. Annie Hunt pulled alongside the curb outside the shanty bar, the agent whistled, "Nice place."

Hunt nodded, "It's pretty rough."

"You have a picture of the girl?"

The A.D.A. flipped open a manila folder and handed him a photograph. "The kids are usually in the back. There is supposed to be a secret speakeasy sort of room they get into."

"Do me a favor, walk into the bar and hand the bartender the photo and ask about the room," Penance requested.

Annie shot a confused glance.

"Trust me. He'll blow you off. When he does, just leave, get into your car and drive around the block."

Nodding, Annie made her way into the bar. Penance watched for a moment and then slipped down the alley. Finding the back door, he backed against the wall and waited.

Inside, Annie Hunt made a beeline for the bar. Ignoring the catcalls from a few of the patrons, she kept her focus straight ahead. Squeezing between a pair of men, she slapped the photo on the bar. The barkeep glanced at it and rolled his eyes, "Whataya want me to do with that?"

"Tell me what you know about her," the Assistant District Attorney demanded.

"Why would I know anything about a child, this is a bar, lady. 21 and over."

"Because out back, you have an entrance for customers you can't have seen in your bar," Hunt snapped, "This girl was here, and now she is missing."

"Sorry to hear that, but she ain't been here. What you see is what you get, no secret clubs or nothin'. Now, unless you gotta warrant..."

"I'll be back," the ADA said abruptly, snatching the photo and spinning to leave.

Annie walked as coolly as she could, though she was wholly unnerved as she left the bar. The sidewalk and her car door couldn't meet fast enough. Climbing into her car, she quickly turned the key and wheeled away from the tavern.

Penance didn't have long to wait. A couple of minutes after he left Annie's car, the deadbolt clicked, and several teenagers streaked through the door. Striking his hand out, the agent collared one and slammed him against the wall. As a second brushed past, the agent snatched a flailing arm and joined him with the first. In a flash, he had the two handcuffed together. Kicking out their legs, they landed in a heap at the base of the wall. Spinning, Penance caught the last straggler. With a quick kick, the young man darting out of the building crumpled into the doorframe. Gasping for breath, he held his side before the agent gruffly shoved him down by the first two.

"Where're you going, guys? Oh, the barkeep got spooked and ejected you guys, that's sad," Penance mocked. "I'm not particularly interested in the whole underage drinking thing, that's more up to the Centreville police who don't appear up to the task. But, let's see who we have here."

Starting with the last one he apprehended, he shuffled through his pockets. "Hmm," he snorted as he pulled out a baggy. "Seems you guys are up to more than underage drinking."

One by one, he went through his prisoner's pockets, retrieving more drugs and IDs from two of them. Studying the boys at his feet, he advised, "We have a dilemma here. You three are in a lot of trouble. I can take you all in for underage consumption and possession."

The three stiffened, and Penance paused, allowing the prospect to sink in. "Truth is, I have more important issues to deal with. I think you can help me. If you do, you might just be forgiven for your young crimes. Will you help me?"

The first two nodded their heads. The third, the one who lacked ID, refused to look at Penance. "I'm going to guess you have the most to help me with," the agent said, kneeling beside him. The sullen man suddenly lashed out at the agent with a knife he slid from inside his waistband. Snatching the boy's wrist, Penance twisted the arm, freeing the blade immediately. The agent's other hand shot out, catching the man's chin, driving his head back into the cement block wall of the bar.

A glance at the man's wrist revealed a tattoo. Penance heeded a closer look. An image of an old Spanish pirate marked the boy's skin. "Ah, *Las piratas*. You are *definitely* the one who will be working with me."

Turning to the other two, he flashed the photo of the missing girl. "That's Hailey!" one of the boys blurted. The other nudged him. Disgruntled, the boy who spoke jerked away. "I've been worried about her. She was partying with one of those drug runners. We haven't seen her since. I'd do anything to help, but I just don't know where they took her. Ask him!" With his un-cuffed hand, he pointed to the man with the tattoo.

"Shut up, fool!" the tattooed boy spat.

Penance smiled. "I guess I know who I need to have a deeper conversation with," the agent rose. On the street along the alley, he could see the nose of Annie Hunt's convertible. "Come on, friend, you and I are going to get to know each other better," Penance drug the man up from the sidewalk and shoved him forward.

"Hey, what about us?" one of the boys who were still shackled together pleaded.

"I said *I* would forgive you. I do. Whether or not the County Sheriff feels the same way...," Penance offered a little shrug and walked away.

A chorus of "You can't do this, man!" followed the agent and his suspect down the alley.

Ignoring the calls, Penance prodded the tattooed boy towards Hunt's car.

"Successful I take it?" the Assistant District Attorney asked.

"Yeah," Penance nodded, "You have any friends here in Centreville?"

"Sure, I suppose," Hunt responded, cocking her head.

"There are a couple of kids handcuffed in the alley that might need a stern talking to."

"I see, I'll get right on that. And who is this?" Hunt asked.

"He is a pathetic pirate who is going to fill us in on what is going on around here."

The young man struggled against the agent's grip, "Man, I ain't telling you nothin'! *Las piratas* will kill me, then you."

"You - I believe. Especially when I gift wrap you for them."

Watching the exchange unfold, Annie got out of the car, "Uh, how about I call my friends for the alley boys and you take your little friend there and do what you need. I can't imagine this is good for my career."

"Suit yourself, won't be long. Where can I meet you?" Penance asked, shoving the boy into the passenger seat.

"There's a little diner in town. They make a killer shoofly pie and terrible coffee. I can hang there."

Grinning from the convertible's driver seat, Penance waved, "See you soon!" With the roar of the strained engine, the agent pulled away. Making a point to drive through town in a way that attracted plenty of attention, he finally wheeled down a dirt road that followed a river.

Slamming on the brakes, he slid to a stop alongside a bridge. Hopping out, he crossed over to the passenger side and opened the door for his suspect. Grabbing his collar, he yanked him out of the car. "Let's go for a little walk."

As the young man's feet hit the ground, he took off in a mad dash. "Seriously?" Penance groaned. Breaking into a sprint himself, he quickly caught up to the fleeing suspect. With a quick kick of his foot, he sent the man sprawling face-first onto the gravel road.

"Now, how is our conversation going to work if you act like that?" the agent scolded.

With a nudge of his foot, he flipped his suspect over. "Alright, I am not really in the mood to mess around. I know you're a *Las Piratas*. I know you've been running drugs and using local kids to dip into the local market. How are your bosses going to feel about that anyway? The product runs through here. You've been skimming to make a few quick bucks with the local riff-raff. About right?"

The tattooed young man just glared at the agent.

"I see. Big tough gang boy routine. I got it," Penance reached down and grabbed the boy's ankle. Dragging him towards the bridge, he looked back at the boy, "You know what creeps me out in this place? You might think the rednecks, and well...you'd be a little right. But it's all the nasty creepy crawly things. Every species of poisonous spider and snake that we have in the U.S. has some representative example. Some of the snakes are probably down in the river there."

Penance stopped as he reached the middle of the bridge. "And then there's the gators. Oh man, are they crazy. See those streaks along the slope. Those are slides. Definitely some gators here. Wonder if they are in the water right now? Probably." With a heave, the agent swung the boy in the air and draped him over the side of the bridge, his hand clamped around the suspect's ankles.

Penance had to stifle a laugh as the tough, tattooed character shrieked in a high pitch squeal.

"The *piratas*, now they're scary, huh? Couple gators are probably nothing for a tough guy like you."

"Get me down! Get me down!"

Penance craned his neck over the side of the bridge to see the gangster looking back, his eyes as big as saucers and full of tears, "You mean down on the bridge or...down there?"

"You son of a..." the boy screamed as he squirmed.

"Easy there, buddy, all your wriggling around, I might lose my grip," Penance warned. "Now, I don't recall you giving me any useful information. Remember, girl in trouble...all that stuff. That will keep you from being gator bait. Up to you."

"*Las Piratas* are using this area as a transport hub. Cheap, dumb labor. Lots of backroads. Easy airdrops and gobs of ways in and out! Now pull me up!"

"The girl?" Penance reminded.

"Man...nothing was supposed to happen, just some fun. Halfway in, she got a conscience. Suddenly, she wanted to jet. That meant she was a risk."

"You?"

"I couldn't. Freddy took her. I didn't want to know. I didn't want to know...," the now entirely still suspect said, his voice genuinely morose at the end.

Penance hauled the young man over the rail and released him hard on the deck of the bridge. Without reverence, the agent yanked the boy to his feet. "Where do I find Freddy?"

"Freddy will..." the young gang member looked at the agent.

"Freddy isn't here. I am," Penance snapped. "Accidents happen out here all the time. Wonder if the gators drown you first or if they start chomping, and you bleed to death. What do you think, lungs bursting as you gasp for breath sucking in gallons of water or your intestines being pulled out of you while you're still alive?"

The thug paled. "Freddy Sanchez is in New Orleans, Club Thibodeaux. He smells you comin', and we're all dead, man!"

Penance smiled, "Somehow, I'm not real concerned."

SEVENTEEN

"New Orleans?" Dixon mulled. "Why don't we just call in a couple of suits to bring him in? They have a lot bigger office than we do."

"They'd get to them faster, too. Less chance of someone tipping them off," District Attorney Jennings suggested.

"Now, who's going tip anyone off?" Penance scoffed.

"I have an old poker buddy down there. I'll give him a call and clear the way with warrants and whatnot," Judge Doyle offered. Pulling a sticky note off of Penance's desk, the judge asked, "Who are we after?"

"Freddy. Freddy Sanchez," Penance replied.

"Dirty Sanchez? He's bad news!" Agent Roth exclaimed.

"You've got to be kidding me!" Penance choked incredulously. "Doesn't *anyone* around here think about names before they use them?"

"What? That mean something in Spanish?" Roth asked.

"Dirty Sanchez. It's…it's a kinky thing. Nasty. Involves uh…defecation and cellophane."

Dixon roared, laughing, doubling over, holding his stomach. "Dang gang–bangers just get dumber and dumber!"

Bubba had been quietly eavesdropping on the conversation. He looked at the agent wide-eyed, "Why'd anyone want to do that?"

"Beats me. Ask that Fifty Shades lady, sounds like something she'd be into," Penance shrugged.

"Who?" Bubba asked.

Penance shook his head, "Nevermind, you don't really want to know."

"Stupid name aside, he's serious business," Roth warned. "He's the real deal from the Mexican cartel world."

"All the more reason to bring 'Dirty' in," Penance replied solemnly, Dixon again broke out into hysterics at the use of the drug runner's nickname.

"Want me to go with?" Agent Roth asked.

"I think I've…on second thought, yes. You can ride shotgun," Penance declared.

"When do we go?"

"Right now," Penance said, instinctively checking his holstered weapon as he headed for the door.

The two-hour drive south towards the Gulf coast was quiet. The two agents would occasionally exchange words, but most of the time, they were silent in their preparation. If this guy was everyone claimed he was, they weren't going to be able to waltz in and extract him easily. Penance had hoped to keep it as quick and quiet as possible. At the same time, he intended to send a message - he didn't fear the Mexican drug cartel.

Agent Roth, on the other hand, looked nervous. He had checked his department issue .45 at least half a dozen times. Roth wiped his forehead, beads of sweat seeping atop his furrowed brow.

Penance noticed his partner's trepidation and silently chewed on it. He would take control of the situation. He just hoped Roth could maintain a suitable backup. "Just don't be so nervous you shoot me in the back, alright?"

"Wha- why…," the young agent started and then realized he was being made fun of, he laughed. "No, I'll be fine."

Penance barely blinked and kept his head straight on the road ahead. The agent allowed his mind to drift away with the highway until they reached causeway crossing Lake Ponchatrain. Here he knew he was closing in on New Orleans. His senses and muscles began their pregame warm-ups, making sure they were ready for anything that was to come.

Arriving in the Crescent City, Penance slid the Porsche into a parking garage near the Superdome – mixing in with the vehicles from the local law offices and Tulane professors. "From here, we're on foot." He told his partner.

Roth looked momentarily stunned, "We're going in *now*? I thought we were going to grab Sanchez when we had secured back up? Later tonight, tomorrow?"

"The more bodies thrown at them, the more heads up they get." Penance replied.

A final weapons check, and they left the SUV and made their way onto the streets of the Big Easy. Taking a cable car to the French Quarter, it wasn't difficult to mix in with the eclectic mix of the revelers. Walks of every imaginable life and even some unimaginable made up the crowd filtering through the hotspots. From the famous hurricane and Zydeco clubs to the burlesque shows and drag clubs, people moshed together, most carrying beverages to their next stop.

Penance and Roth weren't the only suits wandering the streets. Some off for their favorite pile of crawfish, others to their night-time call to throw money at ill gains before they went home to their wives. The agent didn't care which people thought he and Roth were, as long as they vanished among the sea of bodies.

The agents were suddenly exposed as they turned down an alley. Not only had the crowd become thin, onlookers were painfully aware that they were the only Caucasians in the lane. Two large African-American men and a muscular Latino stood vigil at a windowless door where a half-dozen Hispanic males were showing their IDs. One of the bouncers looked up and saw Penance and Roth heading right towards them.

Penance picked up his pace, taking several strides ahead of his colleague. Confidently and swiftly, the agent made his way uncomfortably close to the bouncer that eyed him. The six-foot-five bouncer dwarfed Penance. So much so, the other door attendants ignored him as a non-threat while they continued to process the line.

"I think you're in the wrong alley pal," seeing Roth making his way tentatively forward, he wrinkled his nose, "Definitely the wrong place. You're looking for Calle del Maine."

"I don't think so. This is Club Thibodeaux."

The bouncer snapped to attention, "Where'd you hear that?"

"A friend. He said this was the place."

Hearing the club's name spouted by the little Caucasian in the suit brought the attention of the other two at the door. The Hispanic pushed forward, "You're in the wrong place. Scram if you know what's good for you."

"Angry little Hispanic strutting like he's in charge, exclusive clientele in some dingy pile, no, this is *definitely* the place," Penance declared defiantly.

"Sorry, *gringo*, but you're gonna end up floating alongside the *Natchez*," the door attendant spat. Snapping his fingers, the two giant bookends of bouncers grabbed Penance.

Curling his shoulder, Penance spun away from the grip of one, bringing his knee into the diaphragm of the one who still held him. As the bouncer doubled-over, Penance drove his elbow downward, striking the big man at the base of his skull, dropping him limply to the ground.

Deflecting a lunge from the other large bouncer, Penance kicked his leg backward, using the big man's stride against him. The agent hooked his foot into his assailant's, sending him off balance, catching himself on one knee. Spinning, Penance delivered a blow to his opponent's knee, the sound of shattering bones and ligament. Wailing in pain, the bouncer held his leg and reeled in agony on the ground.

The Hispanic man who seemed to be in charge watched the scene unfold so quickly in front of him. He could barely grasp what was happening. Seeing the second of his men go down, he reached for his semi-automatic handgun. Before he was able to free it cleanly from his waistband, the agent in the alley had already drawn his weapon and had a round chambered, ready to deliver it between the door attendant's eyes.

Smiling calmly, Penance declared, "Sanchez. I'm here to get Sanchez, and then I'll be on my way. Will that be a problem?"

Then attendant wanted to say yes, at least to the Beretta that pointed his way, but he knew what was inside, and he knew that it was his job to keep people like this white guy in a suit out. "You're crazy, gringo! They will never let you within 100 feet of him!"

"Like you and your buddies there?" Penance motioned to the grumbling bouncers who were being trussed by Agent Roth. "You see, the thing is, you're going to bring us to him."

"No way in hell I'm..."

Before he could finish his sentence, Penance squeezed off a round, just slicing into the right triceps of the door attendant. The man reeled back as though he were shot in the chest. Gasping, he looked at the agent, "What'd you do that for?"

Out of the corner of his eye, Penance could see his partner looking almost as shocked as the thug. "You still had your hand on your weapon," the agent replied, "And I need you to understand you don't have a choice in this matter. Now, hand your gun over to me."

The attendant tried to do as he instructed but stopped as he winced in pain. "I, I can't move my arm, it hurts too bad."

"Yeah, people don't realize how much they use their tris until they hurt them. Use your *other* hand, numbnuts."

Fumbling with the weapon, the attendant finally tossed the gun at Penance's feet. Looking over at his partner, Penance ordered, "Drag those big boys over behind those dumpsters. Cuff and gag them!"

"But…" Roth tried to protest.

"Do it, Agent Roth. Protocol will get you killed right now. We're about to poke a stick into a massive hornet's nest."

Three men suddenly appeared in the alley. The scent of their oversaturated cologne almost announced their presence before their footsteps. Waving his gun, Penance shouted, "Club's closed fellas! Apparently, it's infested." The men paused and then decided they wanted no part of the scene; they collectively withdrew themselves from the alley.

"Ready pal?" Penance asked the club door manager as he placed a hand on his shoulder and directed him towards the steel door. "Quicker you get us to Sanchez, the more likely you are to live through this."

Reluctantly, the man nodded.

"Roth, stay in the alley with your friends. Keep anyone else from entering. In ten minutes, you take off for the car. Whether I'm back out or not, if you get there before I do, start driving this way, but I wouldn't put the car in park, if you know what I mean."

The young agent nodded and trained his attention on the two men he had zip-tied at his feet.

Wasting no further time, Penance prodded the doorman forward through the front door of the club. A strange mix of Mexican *Son*, Country-Western, and techno thumped through the walls. Sticking close, Penance followed him into the Club Thibodeaux.

Placing one hand on the man's shoulder, the agent prodded him forward. In his other hand, he kept his Beretta at the ready. The noise of the club was both a help and a hindrance. On the one hand, Penance and his "host" could travel through the halls undetected, but on the other, Penance had no idea where trouble might be lurking. He reasoned in a place like the Club Thibodeaux; trouble could be anywhere.

The attendant turned, his face was pale. Penance was unsure whether it was from the graze of the bullet or from being nervous about Sanchez' reaction. "He...he'll be in that room in the back," the attendant nodded towards a room at the end of the hallway. "You can go on ahead, knock, and they'll open up. I'll just see myself to the hospital now."

Penance scowled, "Okay. Two things. First, you don't need a hospital. Clean your shoulder with some peroxide and bandage it up. You're barely bleeding. Second, you aren't going anywhere. I know how you guys work. I bet if I knock on the door, they know something's not right. They probably just level a shotgun blast right through the door, am I right?"

The doorman stared at the agent. Finally, he nodded solemnly, "Yeah, something like that."

Weaving their way through patrons who were busy ogling over the only two women in the club, Penance and the door attendant were able to reach the door.

A man appeared from a door behind them on the side of the hallway. Since he had an apron was in his hand, he figured he was the club's bartender. *Bano de Caballeros* scrawled across the door.

Penance shifted his gun hand, so it was out of sight. Staggering into the doorman, the agent slurred in a loud voice, "Ah, here it is amigo. Thank you." Scowling, he faced the bartender who was zipping up his fly. "Hey, which one's the men's room?"

The bartender just scoffed as he walked away, tying his apron, "You figured it out, gringo."

The hallway emptied, Penance nudged the attendant forward. "Alright, slick. Do your thing."

Lifting the door to the fire alarm lever, the attendant stabbed at a button. A moment later, the door clicked open. As soon as a crack revealed, Penance kicked it open, slamming the wooden door into whoever was opening it from the other side.

The door bounced back after a voice cried in pain on the other side. Penance shoved the doorman forward, hoping he had pushed the man hard enough that his sprawl to the floor would spare him the bullets volleyed his direction.

Spying a man on his knees just inside the door, Penance, he reasoned that was the victim of the door breach. Hoping he was a high enough rank that Sanchez might want to spare, the agent swooped down and hooked an arm under the man's chin and pulled him up, ceasing the onslaught of bullets.

"Afternoon," Penance smiled, quickly surveying the room. He counted five men, not including the doorman and his current human shield.

A man in a linen suit sat calmly in a leather chair at the end of a long table. Flanked on either side by a pair of men who held a variety of handguns trained on the agent. Without any inflection in his voice, the man in the chair asked, "And who the hell are *you*?"

Recognizing the man as his target, Freddy "Dirty" Sanchez, Penance focused his attention on him. "I am your new traveling buddy," Penance replied.

"That so? I don't think so. I choose who I travel with, and you...you aren't on my list," Sanchez said.

Penance shrugged from behind his human shield. "I was afraid you might think that way, but I can be very convincing."

"Ha!" Sanchez spat, "Unless you can convince me from your grave, I don't think you have much of chance."

With the slightest nod, the men with the guns in their hands stiffened. As the first pleas rose from Penance's shield, bullets began flying.

The agent had little choice but to leave the man buckling as his companions peppered him with holes. In one fluid sweep, Penance dove below the table line, bullets slamming into the dense wood and raining onto the floor all around the agent. Allowing his momentum to carry him, Penance slid along the floor, the length of the table. Skidding to a stop at the feet of Sanchez, his Beretta slamming into the groin of the drug cartel lieutenant.

In a shriek, Sanchez called for his men to stop firing.

From under the table, Penance looked up. "Ready to go, travel, buddy?"

Sanchez inched his crotch away from the nose of the pistol. "Man...gringo, you got a death wish!"

"I've been told," Penance nodded. Making his way out from under the table, his gun trained at the thug's genitals, Penance circled the leather chair and moved the pistol to the base of Sanchez' skull.

"Since I see how you treat your friends," the agent nodded towards the body riddled with bullet holes near the entry, "I think I'll rely on the only thing you seem to value-yourself."

"You are *dead*," Sanchez spat.

"Strange thing for a man to say with a bullet less than three inches away from his brain. Less of course, small enough for me to miss at that distance," Penance cajoled.

Hearing a small army making its way down the corridor towards the backroom, the agent glanced around. "Any good drug den has a back way out. How about you have one of your boys open the way for us," the agent said.

With a nod, one of the gunmen walked to the back of the room and slid back several bolts and twisted several locks on a heavy steel door. With a heave, the door gave way to the alley.

Agent Roth looked stunned to see Penance and Sanchez march out of the club. "What...How did you...Nice work, Penance," the young agent said.

Sanchez and Roth shot each other a glance that melted into a snarl from Sanchez.

"We should probably go," Agent Penance declared, nudging the crime boss forward.

"You're both dead!"

"Yeah, yeah. We already covered that," Penance replied nonchalantly.

As Penance jostled Sanchez down the alley, he noticed that Roth hesitated. Pausing, he turned his head back. Roth held a gun out towards the agent.

"I can't let you do this."

"What are you doing, Roth?" Penance grabbed Sanchez by the arm as he turned to face Roth directly.

"I can't let you take him in."

Sanchez sneered, trying to pull away from Penance only to have the Special Agent tighten his grip.

"What does he have on you, Roth?" Penance asked.

"I don't want to hurt you, Penance. I just can't let you take him," the agent pleaded.

"It's not going to happen. You know the things this man has been doing. Using children...," Penance replied.

"Agent Roth, need I remind you of the consequences," Sanchez warned.

"What is it, Roth? What can be so bad that you would have this man unleashed in your community? Your friends' children."

"That's just it. They handed me a photo. Las Piratas were standing over my girlfriend's bed while she was sleeping. They promised to leave her alone, and our town if, I just shared some information, kept him out. And if not..."

"If not, they grab your girl," Penance nodded. "Roth, this ends now."

The young agent relented, lowering his weapon.

"I'm going to need you to drop your clip and unchamber."

Roth removed the clip from his weapon and tossed it to Penance. Ejecting the round in the chamber, Roth threw the bullet away.

"Let's go. I'll have Bubba swing by and pick up your girl," Penance assured.

EIGHTEEN

Penance wheeled the Porsche into the lot of the County Sheriff's office. "We're home, Sanchez," he called to his passenger, who responded by forcefully kicking the seat.

Unlocking the rear door, he had secured with the child safety locks; the agent unbuckled the gang leader. Pulling Sanchez out by the cuffs, he led the way up the steps to the County Corrections officer. "Special Agent Penance, Director Dixon, should have alerted you."

Nodding, the desk officer, confirmed, "He did. Here is the paperwork."

Penance accepted the documents. Looking around the station, he frowned, "I would have expected a bit more...attention for our friend here. No additional detail?"

"Nah, he'll be fine," the deputy shrugged.

"So, the Sheriff himself is going to be responsible for the security of the leader of the most ruthless gang..."

"Thanks," Sanchez called, appreciating the comment as a compliment.

"No problem," Penance replied and continued, "The most ruthless gang in Louisiana, perhaps ever?"

"Agent Penance, I'm not in charge. I understand your request was considered. Beyond that, I don't know. They probably have a plan to add detail with shift changes."

"Here," Penance slapped the paperwork down on the desk. "I'll at least stay for processing and place him in his cell."

"I'm sure that's not necessary."

"I'm sure that it is," Penance snapped sternly.

"Aw, all this fuss for me," Sanchez sneered.

"You should see the paperwork had I shot you. Staying a little longer is nothing," Penance replied.

Eventually, additional deputies arrived to take Sanchez through processing and ultimately secure him in a cell separated from any other guests of the county. Penance was disappointed with the level of security, but his complaints ran as much of a course as they were going to.

Relenting, he fired up the Porsche and headed home. He didn't realize how exhausted he was until he sat in the driver's seat.

Rolling down the windows and blasting the SUV's exceptional stereo, he let the throttle out and allowed the vigor of the sports car to give him a second wind.

Sliding into his driveway, he cut the engine and walked up to the house. Exhausted, he walked to his fridge, realizing he hadn't taken any time to restock. Some condiments and an empty six-pack holder were the only things the refrigerator kept cold.

He considered driving back into town but realized nothing in the town would be open at that hour. Sighing, he gave into just getting ready for bed.

A knock on his door stopped him. Cocking a curious head, he strode to his front door.

"Mister, uh, Agent Penance?" his neighbor called through the screen door.

"Alex," Penance corrected.

"Alex," Frank Doone fixed, "I saw you drive up, thought maybe you'd like a beer? I know it's late…"

"You know what? I really could. Come in, we can sit out back," Penance said, opening the door.

Finding their familiar seats on the small back patio overlooking the creek, Frank held a can of Coors Light out to the agent.

"It's probably not as good as the stuff you like, but it's what I have," Frank shrugged.

"Tonight, it's perfect," Penance grinned, taking a long sip, finding it strangely refreshing. "I'll admit, I came home and realized I hadn't gone to the store since I got here. Guess I need to do that."

"Are you hungry? We brought home leftovers from church. Some fried chicken and macaroni salad."

"I would love some chicken. Sure you don't mind?" Penance asked.

Shaking his head, Frank set down his beer and dashed off for his house.

Penance settled back in his chair, enjoying his beer and the sound of the creek and crickets. He took in a big breath and thought about his experiences since coming to Sawyer. The people he met, aside from maybe Annie Hunt, didn't fit with his usual repertoire of associates. He found them plenty backward, even annoying at times. But he couldn't help but appreciate their kindness and sense of community.

Frank returned with a plate of chicken thighs, handing it to the agent.

"Oh man, this hits the spot, Frank. Thank you so much," Penance said, eagerly digging into the plate.

"Think nothing of it. The church is kind enough to send me home with leftovers, only right to share it with others," Frank replied.

"How're things with your kids?"

"Well, they didn't fuss going to church. That was good," Frank said.

"You guys go pretty regular?"

"Used to. Tougher to these days with work and whatnot. But after Maggie's dealings with that boyfriend of hers…"

"Ex, I hope."

"Yes, ex-boyfriend. Figured we as a family needed to make the time. Be good for all of us. Be with good people. Let the kids make friends with the kinda parent would approve."

"Makes sense. Surround yourself with the kind of people you want to be, and you are more likely to be that way yourself."

"Let your daughter hang around with hoodlums and…"

"And they begin dating hoodlums," Penance mused.

"That they do," Frank laughed.

Falling into silence, the two men settled into enjoying the songs of the critters and the creek.

NINETEEN

Despite a very late night, Penance arrived at the office first. He was pleased to see a package on his desk. Tearing into it, he pulled out the contents and set them out on the counter in the back of the office. Scurrying around the office, he put his purchase to work as Director Dixon arrived.

"What is that?" Dixon bellowed.

"Real coffee. Here, have a cup," Penance beamed, holding a cup intense Italian roast to his boss.

"Where did you find that stuff around here?" Dixon asked.

"Amazon."

"Careful, you are starting to settle in."

"Just ensuring I can operate at top performance," Penance replied.

"Hmm, well, this is pretty good," Dixon lofted his cup. His face turning more stern, "Internal Affairs will be here around ten this morning to indict Timmy. They'll want to depose you."

"I figured as much. I'll spend the morning banging out the report. Can you see if the Sheriff heeded my request for added detail to Sanchez while he's holed up there?"

"Concerned about something?" Dixon asked.

"He was pretty adamant that his crew would be paying a visit."

"And you think they will?"

"Cartels tend to not like being showed up. They will find some way to get the last word. Save face," Penance suggested.

"What're you thinking? A jailbreak?" Dixon asked.

"I don't know. Maybe. Something for sure. That I have no doubt."

"I'll call him," the Deputy Director assured.

"Thanks. Where is Roth, anyways?"

"He'll be here. I told him to get his things in order. Feel comfortable his house was in order and to report by nine a.m."

"And you think he won't run?"

"He won't," Dixon assured.

"What about his girlfriend? I would encourage her to visit relatives or something," Penance suggested.

"Probably right, at least until we know what the *Las Piratas* are planning," Dixon nodded.

"She could be the very retaliation they are considering."

"Could be. I'll talk to her. I've gotten to know her a bit, especially waiting for you guys to return last night."

"Good. One less thing the *Las Piratas* can use for leverage," Penance acknowledged.

Roth arrived at the office at 8:45. He had a small duffle of personal items and a handful of FBI equipment to turn in.

"Coffee? Agent Penance brewed up some fancy stuff," Dixon offered.

"Uh, yeah, sure," Roth nodded. Turning to Penance, Roth looked sullen as he began to speak.

Penance cut him off. "You did what you did. At the moment, probably what you thought you had to. Own it. Carry on."

Nodding, Roth replied, "Yes, sir."

"We're going to suggest to Stephanie that she leave town for a while. Is there anyone she can visit?"

Roth nodded, "She has family in Tennessee."

"Good. I am sure she'd be fine, but taking one concern off your plate should allow you to concentrate on what you need to."

Penance's phone pinged. Checking the message, he shook Roth's hand. "Good luck, Agent Roth."

Dixon called out from his office, "Where are you going? Internal Affairs'll want to speak with you."

"I'm sure they will. Everything I have to say is in the report. I have other things to attend to," Penance said and left the office. He was glad the text came in. He didn't have the stomach for an overdrawn IA deposition.

Heading into town, Penance parked the Porsche outside the café.

Poking his head inside, he scanned the tables. In a back corner, he found Assistant District Attorney Annie Hunt. She looked up from her notes and flashed a quick smile at Penance.

Almost as if to correct herself, her expression snapped to a staunch professional countenance, "Thank you for meeting me. We didn't have time last night to talk."

"I had to get Sanchez locked up as securely as the County Sheriff's office provides."

"You did an amazing job. I can't believe Agent Roth...."

"People do what they feel they have to, especially for those they love," Penance cautioned. "They still need to be held accountable."

"Yes, as a federally appointed attorney, I have to agree. Still, it's unfortunate."

"It is. Is that why you asked me here?" Penance asked, looking directly into Annie's eyes.

"Well, no, I, uh…" Annie stammered, somewhat relieved when the waitress came up, extending a coffee pot.

Flipping their cups over, the waitress filled them up and sat down a pair of menus.

Taking a sip, Penance winced, "You should have come to the office. I have a nice pour-over of Italian roast. It's quite good."

"Now you tell me," Annie grinned over her coffee cup. "So, I appreciate what you did in New Orleans. Taking on the *Las Piratas* like that. Single-handed...."

"Well," Penance looked sheepish, "I didn't realize I was going in there, single-handed."

"But you had a suspicion," Annie pressed.

"I did. The only way to be sure was to put him to the test."

"With your life on the line," Annie scowled.

"My suspicions allowed me to prepare for either outcome," Penance defended his decision. "Sometimes groups like this, situations like this, hitting them decidedly and directly is best. They don't expect anyone to go after them that way."

"What's next?" Annie asked. "What about the girls?"

"Taking down the head of the snake will at least stop the flow and keep additional girls from falling prey to the *Las Piratas*. We need to see what we can get out of Sanchez."

"You think this will stop now?"

"For the moment. The *Las Piratas* have layers. The cartel will just insert their next lieutenant, and the cycle will start again. Almost to spite the system, show their relentless strength. This is the start. If we can get Sanchez to roll on the operation, we may be able to go and shut it all down. One thing I am sure of, I need to get him to lead us to the girls that are already gone."

"How are you going to do that?" Annie asked.

"I'm glad you asked. I'm going to need your help. And maybe Jennings' as well."

"What do you need?"

"When the time comes, I am going to need to, uh, borrow Sanchez for a bit."

Annie looked horrified.

"I'm not going to beat it out of him or anything like that. As much of an idiot as he is, he wouldn't have risen to his position in the cartel if he wasn't tough. He wouldn't give up what I needed by physical incentives."

"Then what?"

"I need to find other incentives."

"Fair enough, I'll let you keep those cards, for now," Annie consented and then jumped. Reaching down to her side, she grabbed her phone. "Ugh, it looks like Butch is in trouble again."

Tossing some bills on the table, Penance stood up, "Well, let's see what we can do to help."

When Penance and Annie arrived at the scene, the parking lot of the Piggly Wiggly was in chaos. A police officer and pair of deputies circled the big man, trying to gain an effective angle. One officer lunged, Butch spun, catching the officer by his shirt and flinging him against a parked car. The other two advanced, each slamming into an arm, the big man wrenching them both in headlocks, smacking their heads together.

Menacing, Butch spun in three-hundred and sixty degrees, looking for the next threat to face him.

Bubba pulled up in his patrol car and hopped out next to Penance and Annie. Behind him, Chief Pruitt showed up with Jennings screeching to a halt right behind.

"Butch, you've been in enough trouble, let's talk this one through," Penance tried to reason.

Butch squared up on the agent and snarled, "You!" Rushing headlong, the big man lunged at Penance.

The agent sidestepped the blow, deflecting most of it as Butch careened by. What little did connect was enough to send the much smaller Penance stumbling back. Somehow Butch was able to adjust and grabbed a fist full of Penance's shirt and yanked him to the ground.

Penance rolled with the force of the assault, tucking his shoulder and ending up crouched on his feet, relatively unharmed. Steadying for another attack which Butch was already launching, both men were surprised with a flash of police uniform cut off the attack. Bubba launched himself and levied a textbook tackle on Butch just before landing a blow on the agent.

An enraged Butch Whatcom wrestled away from the officer, bellowing, he returned to his feet, spinning away from Bubba and glowered at Penance. The agent had positioned himself following Bubba's tackle and delivered a quick palm strike to Butch's chin, snapping his head back, temporarily cutting off his oxygen supply.

Staggering, Butch teetered. Before he could regain himself, Penance snatched a tazer from one of the original responding officers and whipped his trigger hand up, releasing the electrodes into the big Whatcom boy. Keeping the trigger squeezed until Butch final dropped to a knee, and his body ultimately gave into the shock, sinking onto the pavement.

Letting go of the tazer, Penance motioned for the officers to pin and cuff Butch. The crowd that had gathered began to cheer as the Butch was taken into custody, laughing at the effect the tazing had on Butch's bladder.

Among the crowd, Butch's brother Billy and Devlin, the Whatcom family patriarch emerged, scowling at the crowd that quickly dispersed in their presence. "Was that really necessary?"

"Ask Officer Dewey with a broken nose, Officer Peters with a sprained wrist, and I believe he broke that car's mirror with his back," Chief Pruitt said.

"What was Butch being charged with?" Penance asked.

Officer Peters stepped forward, "Nothing, at least not at the time. I stopped him for a rolling stop."

"And he got out of his truck?"

"Well, no. I asked him to get out."

"Standard protocol for a traffic infraction like a rolling stop?"

"No, not typically."

"Why did you do it in this case?"

"It's Butch. Probable cause…"

Officer Dewey said, "Officer Peters called the Sheriff's office and me in for support."

"I began searching him, and he got belligerent. We went to restrain him, and all heck broke loose. And then you came."

"I put this on you and your officers Chief Pruitt," Delvin Whatcom said, waving a finger at the police chief. "And embarrassing him on top of it!"

"You can't blame his pants issue on us," Penance cautioned. "The over the top traffic stop can be addressed."

"My family walks on eggshells around here. Sure, my boys ain't perfect, but this ain't right."

"He assaulted my officers…"

"Your officers assaulted my boy…"

"Deputy Byers, take Butch home, we'll sort this out."

"I've had it, Pruitt," Devlin shouted, "We've long fought hard to get along, I think those days are gone. The Whatcoms aren't for your officers or this town to use as a running joke. "

"Devlin…." Chief Pruitt called.

Devlin ignored the chief and warned before ushering his boys away from the scene, "You stay away from my family. All of you, or there'll be hell to pay!"

"He's got a point," Penance shrugged as the Whatcoms disappeared.

"You pulled the tazer on him," Jennings pointed out.

"After he bashed the faces in of most of your town's police force. I didn't taze him for a rolling stop," Penance countered.

"Fair enough. We might agree on this one," Jennings relented, "Chief, I expect you to manage your staff appropriately."

"What about the Whatcoms?" Annie asked.

"Overzealous traffic stop or not, that does not justify assaulting police officers. I have no choice but to charge

Butch for these crimes on top of everything else he is already on the hook for," Jennings announced.

"That will throw gas on the fire between the Whatcoms and the town," Chief Pruitt said.

"It is my job to carry out justice, not appease grudges by overlooking serious crimes," Jennings replied. "It is this tendency for leniency that allows these behaviors even to be considered."

"It's your call," Annie conceded.

"Boys, in my office," Chief Pruitt demanded of his officers, "After you visit EMS. Bubba, you're on patrol."

"Yes, Chief," Bubba answered.

"Nice tackle," Penance held out his hand for the officer.

"I was worried Butch would get the best of you. You're tough, but he's a my-size boy," Bubba said.

"He did knock me off balance a bit. I'd have been alright, just the same. I appreciate you being there."

"Anytime, Penance," Bubba grinned.

"I've got your back too, my friend," Penance smiled. His kind words for the officer taking him, and the other around him a bit by surprise. "Alright, gotta get back to work, and you're on patrol."

Penance shuffled away from the scene before anyone gave him any grief or thought he might be getting soft on the town. Before he could make a clean getaway, the patter of feet sounded behind him.

"Uhm, you're my ride," Annie reminded him.

Penance turned, looking sheepish, "Right."

Opening the passenger door to the Porsche for her, Annie climbed in.

She grinned at him as Penance slid into his seat. "Admit it. You're starting to like it here."

Penance looked irritated. "I kind of, sort of like *some* of the people here."

"Who else do you kind of, sort of like?" Annie pressed.

"My neighbor, Frank. Hard-working guy. Brings me chicken. In fact, *both* of the people that I like in this town bring me chicken," Penance announced, and then turned toward the windshield. "I still don't like it here," he declared emphatically pressing the start button roaring the engine to life.

TWENTY

Much to his chagrin, the moment he entered the FBI office, a man in a dark suit stepped in front of Penance. The man swabbed at his forehead with a tissue. "Agent Penance, I am Ned Schefter, with the Bureau Internal Affairs office. I believe we are overdue for a lengthy discussion."

"I'm sure we are. Fortunately, I have written comprehensive reports that should drastically reduce the need for any long talks. Perhaps you can email a list of questions you have, and we can move this along much more efficiently," Penance quipped. He stifled a smile at the impeccably dressed man wilting in the overwhelming heat.

"I'm afraid it doesn't work that way. I need to verify some of the details within your reports. Details can be tough to recall after...uh, operations like the one you completed. Especially when it involves a fellow field agent," Special Investigator Schefter declared.

"Ok. How about a nice walk, afternoons around here are..."

"No," Schefter instinctively wiped his tissue across his brow. "I have arranged that we can borrow Director Dixon's office."

"Great! I get the good chair!" Penance beamed and pushed past the IA agent heading towards the director's office. Sliding behind Dixon's desk, he leaned back in the leather chair. He laced his fingers behind his head. "Let's do this. I have a prisoner to question."

"Your prisoner will have to wait, though I appreciate your diligence," Schefter noted, his tone dripping with annoyance.

"Where should we start? At the beginning?" Penance asked. He knew protocol was to ask questions from the report in a non-linear manner so that stories were more difficult to craft and maintain flow.

"Let's start with your trip to New Orleans," Schefter directed. "Who made that call?"

"I did, with Director Dixon's approval. The *Las Piratas* have been going after kids in this town. Drug parties, and maybe worse. We tracked it to their local boss down in New Orleans, so we went after him," Penance shared.

"You and Agent Roth," Schefter pressed.

"Yes."

"You had no indication that Agent Roth was dirty?"

Penance looked at Schefter squarely. "I had a suspicion that certain crime elements passing through this town were getting a bit of a pass. I wasn't sure if I was right or who it was."

"And yet, you returned to Sawyer with Agent Roth in handcuffs…"

"Not exactly. In custody, yes. In cuffs, no."

Schefter frowned, "I do believe transport protocol would require some sort of restraint."

"Humility can, at times, be a useful restraint."

"I see," Schefter replied, scribbling notes furiously on a notepad. After what Penance felt was an egregiously long time of note-taking, Schefter looked up from his page. "Infiltrating the den of a drug boss without a back-up team or local support, that seems a bit brash."

"You think?" Penance frowned. "Sounds like my job."

"We build protocols for a reason. Protect the community, preserve evidence, keep our agents safe, even you-Agent Penance. "

"I went in the way I did, because if any additional presence were broadcasted, they would have fortified quickly and it would have been a much more dangerous situation," Penance stated.

"How did you manage to get out of there without bloodshed?"

"I had leverage."

"Leverage?"

"I was able to get to Sanchez quickly, positioning him between his men and me," Penance declared.

"I see. You used the suspect as a hostage…"

Penance wrinkled his nose, "Not a hostage…more like a meatshield."

"I'll be sure to put that in the notes," Schefter stated, his voice absent of humor. "How can we be sure that *you* are not also involved in protecting the drug trade?"

Penance choked, "Seriously? Arresting my alleged partner would probably not work in my favor if that were the case. Since I have only been in town a couple of weeks, that would be impressive to inject myself into what is a fairly established situation, even for me."

Schefter pursed his lips and nodded absently, making more notations. "Let's shift gears a bit. As you state, you have only been in town a couple of weeks, and yet you have fired your weapon numerous times and shot at least four people that we know of. You're on pace to match the entire city of Chicago by year's end."

Penance gave the Internal Affairs agent a sideways glance, "Agent Schefter, I believe you made a joke."

Schefter refused a change in his expression.

"In each case, there were very bad guys with very real guns pointed at people...or me. Director Dixon has classified each at a justified shoot."

"District Attorney Jennings has reported that you assaulted him."

"Hmm. Did Jennings tell you that he had unlawfully entered my residence at the time?"

Schefter bit at his lip, "No. He did not mention any such action."

"No, I suppose he wouldn't," Penance retorted.

The IA agent stared at his notes for a long time. Opening the folder, he turned each page of its contents slowly. Tossing it on the table, he looked at Penance. "I am not sure if I have had a case quite like yours, Agent Penance. You have an unusual mix of truly excellent fieldwork laced with borderline physical treatment of suspects, a historically high number of shootings, and a pattern of reckless decision making."

"Aw come on, Schefter. What reckless decisions?"

"Well, your very first day in town, you shot up a hardware store, put yourself directly in the line of fire, and ultimately shot the suspect," Schefter reported.

"All true. With a local policeman in the line of fire and a police force that was over their heads to manage the situation, I did what I did so that Officer Bubba wasn't splattered all over the road," Penance defended.

"The report says that," Schefter nodded. "And Butch Whatcom?"

"Had the DA in a compromised position. I *un*compromised him."

"At the cabin?"

"Crazy drug dealers who started unloading their weapons at myself and another suspect," Penance answered.

"And the bar fight?"

"Protecting Officer Bubba and the property of the tavern owner," Penance said.

"It seems you have an answer for everything."

"I have a *reason* for everything," Penance shot back.

Schefter rubbed his chin, "You can certainly represent it that way. By the same token, you have over one hundred arrests throughout your career in Boston and not a single suspect shot. No bar fights. You were exemplary. What changed?"

"Nothing changed. Circumstances are different."

"Your co-workers suggest you aren't happy with your current situation," Schefter pressed.

"What's not to be happy with? One minute I am headed to DC, next I am reassigned because of a cranky senator. I'm probably black-balled for my career," Penance spat.

Schefter looked pleased with evoking a reaction. "I see. Does this change make you angry, Agent Penance?"

"Angry, sure. I'm mad as hell that a politician can be a complete douche and yet ruin people's lives at whim. Does that make me shoot people unjustly? That's ridiculous," Penance replied.

"Alright. I think I have enough for now. I am recommending that you be placed on probation. Another incident will result in a suspension pending a hearing. I do think you are a good agent. I am not sure you are currently equipped to maintain your duties without significant oversight," Schefter said.

"Oversight? How about you follow me around, and when some yokel is ready to light you up, we'll see how you prefer I respond," Penance spat.

"Aggressive. Yes, that's it. That is the word I would use to phrase your responses," Schefter largely ignored Penance.

"Are we done?" Penance asked.

"You can be dismissed. I will have a few words with Director Dixon, and we will address the situation with Agent Roth. He'll be leaving with me, consider him released to my custody," Schefter declared.

Penance slid his chair out from the table and walked out of the room. Pausing by Agent Roth as he walked past the Director's office, he slapped the agent on the shoulder. "You take care of yourself."

Nodding quietly, Roth watched Penance maneuver his way out of the FBI office and disappear into the fading daylight.

Instead of heading home, Penance found himself pointing the Porsche towards town. The setting sun cast an ethereal crimson glow across the town's sky. Parking at the edge of town, the agent strolled aimlessly down the sidewalk. He had no destination in mind, was just restless.

Walking past shops that were closing for the night, he slipped into deep thought. Thinking about Roth and the position he had been in, wondering what would ultimately come from the investigation. He also thought of Dirty Sanchez and his gang of hooligans. He knew how these things worked. The gang would retaliate; he wasn't sure how or how strong that attack would be.

Watching the folks wave as they shut their stores for the night, he couldn't help but feel for this community and that even in this part of the world, drugs and predation on kids was an issue.

He was so deep in thought; Pastor Carson Roberts had to call his name twice and ultimately ran up and tapped him on his shoulder.

"Alex, you look like you could use a beer. Let me buy you one," Pastor Roberts offered.

Penance looked confused for a moment. "You can do that?"

Pastor Roberts laughed. "Sure. You know, the whole water to wine thing…"

"Oh, right. You know, that sounds pretty good," Penance nodded, following the pastor into the tavern's patio.

Holding up two fingers to the waitress, Pastor Roberts led Penance to a table.

"Great night. The way the sky rolls red over the town is…impressive," Penance declared starting down Main Street before turning his attention to the pastor.

"That it is. I'm glad you find some positives in this town of ours."

"Well, yeah. I do. It's not where I would choose to be, not for myself, but I am beginning to see certain merits to it," Penance said.

"Ever believe things happen for a reason?" Pastor Roberts said as the waitress placed two beers in front of the men. "Thank you, Jenny."

Tilting his glass ever so towards Penance, the pastor said, "Cheers!"

Returning the glass tilt with a nod, Penance took a sip of beer and studied the pastor. "Do you mean some sort of grand plan? I don't think I'd be so sure that a stupid mistake landing me here was part of some design. How could it?"

"Some pretty tragic things would likely have happened if you hadn't shown up," Pastor Roberts suggested.

"Maybe. Maybe me coming stirred up the pot, maybe I was a catalyst for some of those things."

"Could be. It seems to me most of those events were in motion before you arrived," Pastor Roberts offered.

Penance shrugged as he took another sip of beer, "I guess so."

The two men shared a few quiet moments as they enjoyed their beers.

Suddenly, Penance blurted, "I don't go to church very often!"

Pastor Roberts took a sip and replied coolly, "I didn't ask."

"Well, I…okay," Penance stammered. "I used to as a kid. My mom liked to go."

"That's good. What kind of church?"

"Regular, I guess," Penance shrugged.

Pastor Robert laughed, "Funny, that happens to be the kind of church that I lead."

Penance studied the pastor and realized he was being made fun of a bit.

"I didn't ask you to beer to make you come to my church, though you are most welcome – Sunday Service is at 10 am," Pastor Roberts replied. "I just wanted to see how you were doing. You have been through a lot in a pretty short time. It's got to take its toll."

"I appreciate that. It certainly hasn't been as quiet as advertised in Sawyer," Penance said, swirling the froth in beer.

"You have made quite the impact around here, that's for sure. I think you coming has been like sending a dog into the bushes, you've kind of scared up what has been hiding right under the town's foliage."

"I guess that's a way to look at it," Penance said.

"Shine a light into dark places, and critters tend to scurry out. It is not a bad thing. It presents what it is you have to deal with," Pastor Roberts said.

"Yeah, I suppose you're right. The town have any idea the stuff that has been going on?"

"Some of it, I suppose. Nowhere near the degree that you have unveiled." Pastor sipped his beer. "So, you have recognized a spectacular Main Street evening sky. Anything else about the town you have liked?"

"Well, sure. Southern hospitality is a real thing. Everyone who hasn't pointed a gun at me has been real nice. Maybe not the D. A. so much, I don't think he cares for me much," Penance shared.

Pastor Roberts laughed softly, "You're two alpha males. He has peed in every corner of this town, and you stomp through giving it no credence, and I'm not saying you should, mind you. That and you have replaced him as the most intriguing eligible bachelor, which in a town our size, is kind of a big deal."

"He can relax about that. I am on a bit of a hiatus," Penance declared.

"Probably can't blame you there. Still, I don't think Colton will be so easily convinced," Pastor Robers mused.

The men seemed thoughtful as they enjoyed their beverages. Annie Hunt's car pulled up to the curb, and the A. D. A. stepped out, not initially seeing them.

Pastor Roberts observed as Penance noticed her.

When Annie approached, she saw Pastor Roberts and Penance. A bright smile crossed her face as she called "Gentlemen."

"Ms. Hunt," both men returned in unison.

"Well, Agent Penance, I'm glad to see you have taken to proper company. Pastor Carson, you might have your work cut out for you with this one," Annie teased.

"Just two friends enjoying a glorious Sawyer evening," Pastor replied.

"Indeed," Annie eyed the pair.

Penance shifted in his seat, "Care to join us?"

"I'm, I'm meeting a friend myself," Annie replied. "I'll leave you boys to it."

"Enjoy your evening," Penance said and watched her briefly as she went to find her table. A man Penance hadn't seen before raised his hand, waving her over.

"That is another area of potential tension," Pastor Roberts said.

"Hmm?" Penance looked confused.

"You and Colton Jennings. He covets Ms. Hunt as well. He just hasn't found the path around her being his subordinate," the pastor declared.

Penance blushed a little, "I, uh, we work on cases together…"

"No shame. She is a lovely woman. Blessed by God's hand."

Penance started to protest.

"I know, you're on hiatus. You're still human."

Penance couldn't resist a grin with his new friend. "I suppose so."

TWENTY-ONE

Penance was on a mission when he awoke. He wanted to get useful information from Sanchez as quickly as he could.

Arriving at the courthouse, he made his way to the prosecutor's offices. Nancy Blevins quickly greeted Penance.

"Nice to see you again, Nancy."

"Mr. Penance," the assistant acknowledged. "I believe Mr. Jennings would like a word."

"Annie said you would be stopping by. Look, you have to understand, this case is tenuous. How you apprehended Sanchez, his connection is not exactly conclusive…I have never seen this many lawyers involved…," Jennings said.

"He has information that can lead to where those missing girls are," Penance insisted.

"I know. We'll try to get information from him, but his lawyers…"

"I can be pretty convincing," Penance assured.

Jennings stopped. He looked genuinely conflicted. "I'll be honest with you. I *want* you to go in there. I'd hope it would take you knocking the tar out of him. I have no doubt he deserves it and more. *I* can't."

Penance' frustration was boiling, but reading Jennings' demeanor, he could see the intent. He wasn't stonewalling Penance as part of their grudge. He felt as though he had no other choice. Letting his anger subside, Penance tried to reason with him.

"Look, he won't talk, certainly not with his lawyers present. And honestly, while it would be fun to knock him around a bit, you only get false answers that way. I need leverage. The system has very little information on him. I need to find what is inside his messed up head and puny little heart to find what matters enough for him to talk," Penance pleaded.

Jennings waved him off, "I get it. I do. My hands are tied. Maybe something will turn up from the raid in New Orleans."

"Maybe," Penance shrugged. "If I could..."

"We're done, Agent Penance," Jennings said. "I'm truly sorry."

Penance wheeled around, unsure what to do next, knowing any further interaction with the prosecutor would not likely go well. A shadow slipped in beside him as he made his way to the elevator.

"I'll work on him," Annie promised as the doors closed.

"You heard."

"I was listening," the Assistant District Attorney nodded.

"A guy like Sanchez will only give information if you twist whatever is near and dear to him. Even sociopath drug lords have something they care about behind the curtain. We just need to find out what it is," Penance said evenly.

"I know. We'll work something out," Annie assured. "It was good to see you and Pastor Roberts visiting."

"Surprisingly fun guy to have a beer with," Penance admitted. "How about you? Who were you visiting with?"

"Mark? Knew each other since high school. He owns the town grocery store, family business."

"I didn't know you were seeing anyone. High school sweethearts, that's nice."

"We aren't dating. It was just dinner."

"You sure that is what he thought?"

Annie looked confused, "Well, I ... what if it was? Would that matter to you?"

The two studied each other for a long uncomfortable moment. The elevator reached the bottom floor, the doors slid open, granting them much needed relief.

"I'll let you know as soon as we figure out a way to get to Sanchez!" Annie called, watching Penance leave the building as the elevator doors closed shut.

Thwarted with direct access to Sanchez, Penance set to work on other angles on *Las Piratas* and their lieutenant that he had in custody. Hoping that Jennings was right and the New Orleans raid at the club revealed useful information, he stopped at the Bureau to get the update.

"You alright?" Dixon asked as Penance entered the office.

"Should I not be?"

"Got a call from Jennings' office that you might not be thrilled with his decision to provide you access to Sanchez and that you might find ulterior means of forcing your hand," Dixon revealed.

"I'm not upset at Jennings for that. Still needs to happen, but he's not wrong," Penance conceded.

Dixon cocked his head, "Hmm. Good to see you two being reasonable for once."

"Don't get used to it. And it may still not end well. If I can't find information on where the cartel is taking those girls…" Penance warned.

"I get that," Dixon nodded. "You may not like the report from down south then."

"Oh?"

"The FBI team out of New Orleans raided the club as soon as you filled me in. The place was cleaned out. I mean, the club out front was still intact, and the stench of all that, but the office in the back where you nabbed Sanchez, picked clean," Dixon shared.

"They are serious players. They have contingencies built for things like this. I'm not surprised," Penance looked away.

"What are you plotting in that head of yours, or do I want to know?" Dixon asked.

"You may not want to know," Penance said. "I'll leave you in the pleasantness of plausible deniability."

"Fair enough," Dixon acknowledged. Focusing on the piece of paper in front of him was a sign to Penance that the conversation was over.

Penance parked the Porsche SUV in front of the county lock-up facility.

The moment he entered the building, he was met briskly by a corrections officer. "Special Agent Penance, uhh, we were given strict orders to not let you near anywhere near your prisoner."

Penance flashed a smile, "It's okay, I'm not here to see Sanchez. You guys have the kid that I busted in Centreville?"

The guard looked confused, turning back towards his partner behind the terminal who shrugged, replied, "Yes, we have him. He has been arraigned and is pending transfer to Jackson."

"I assume there are no commands that prevent me from seeing him?"

The guard shrugged again, "I guess not."

"That's who I am here to see," Penance declared.

The guard nodded to his partner, who buzzed the agent through.

"Down the hall to the left. The hall guard will let you in to see Gabriel Martez. He's the kid you popped in Centreville. Not really a kid, he's nineteen," the guard shared.

Nodding, Penance thanked the guard and headed through the door. Following the instructions that the guard provided, the agent found the hall guard at his desk.

"Here to see prisoner Martez," Penance flashed his badge.

Pushing up, the guard nodded, checking his tablet, he pressed a button which was followed by an audible buzzing.

"Double locks, electronic is controlled by the tablet. PIN on the cell door trips the final lock. For serious prisoners, like the one down the opposite hall, has a third electronic lock that is manned by the mainboard," the guard shared as he led Penance toward the cell where they young gang member was being held.

Punching in the code, he slid the door open for the agent to walk through.

"I'm good," Penance said, his voice flat as he passed through. "Give me fifteen."

The guard nodded and shut the door behind him.

Penance leaned against the door jam; arms crossed; he studied the prisoner. "Remember me?"

"I remember you," Martez spat sullenly.

"Your cooperation in helping to bring in Sanchez has been noted," Penance shared. "Probably get you a lighter sentence, if you live."

Martez' eyes went wide, "What do you mean?"

"Well, you know how these things go. Cartels like *Las Piratas* have greased palms and moles in the system. That is how the bosses above Sanchez' pay grade avoid getting busted themselves. The thing is, lieutenants like Sanchez are high enough in the ranks that they get certain protections. The cartel is going to find out that the word came from you," Penance declared.

"You, you guys can protect me, right?" Martez trembled.

"Sure, once you get moved to Jackson or further into the federal system. But here in County, this place can't stop a group like *Las Piratas*," Penance added.

"But, my lawyer said they're moving me," Martez said defiantly.

"Sure, you're on the docket. Soon as my office approves the transfer," Penance said.

Martez' head fell, "What do you want? I sent you to Sanchez. Now you're telling me I need to do what, or you're going to let them kill me?"

"I didn't *say* that. Though the sooner we process that request, and you gotta see the paperwork we have to go through for these things..."

"What do you *want*?" Martez pleaded.

"The girls. That's all I want, Martez. Where does Sanchez' crew take the girls?" Penance demanded.

"I don't know. My only contact with *Las Piratas* was at the bar. I don't know nothing, man."

"You called them in, right?"

"Yeah, sure."

"Who did you call? Who picked them up? What vehicle did they take them away in? Did you hear them talk about where they were taking them? These are the types of answers that encourage expedited paperwork," Penance said. "How long do you suppose it will take for them to respond?"

"I don't know, man. It's not like they give me a business card or nothing."

"Phone number."

"They took my phone in evidence. The lock screen is 'p'."

"A 'p'?"

"You know, the dots on the screen. Make a 'p'."

"Big or little?"

Martez, scrunched his face, "I don't think it matters. Anyway, the contact is "honey"."

"Cute. So, what do the guys who pick up the girls look like?"

"Darker skinned than me. I think they are from Mexico or Columbia or somewhere. They aren't American. There are usually two of them. A bigger guy and a little shave-headed guy."

"Bigger guy...like tall big or..."

"Fat big. Not real fat, but heavy. He's got a gold tooth. Sort of sticks out when he licks his lips," Martez shared.

"They both sound charming. How long does it take for them to arrive when you call?"

Martez shrugged, "Forty-five minutes or so. We just keep feeding the girls drinks while we wait."

"The vehicle?"

"Like a beer van."

"So, frequent visits to the back of bar look like a regular business," Penance noted.

"That's all I got, man. You gotta get me out of here. The Piratas are going to kill me."

"No one's going to kill you. Your new friends in the pen might, though, even those scumbags don't like pervs who bag young girls," Penance warned.

"But, you said the files..." Martez sputtered.

"Files are sealed. The only way the Las Piratas would know anything is if they bought the federal prosecutor, your counsel, or one of my team. The guards don't even know your connection to Sanchez," Penance said.

"You're a jerk. You had me scared to death," Martez said.

"You should be scared, Martez. Just not of Sanchez and his men," Penance said. Glancing at his watch, his ears met with the buzzing sound and the footfalls of the hall guard. "If you somehow get through all of this in one piece, make some new friends. You don't really seem Las Piratas material."

The door opened and Penance walked out. As he left the secure area, he was surprised to see Magistrate Doyle, nearly running into each other as they rounded a corner.

"Judge Doyle," Penance acknowledged.

"Agent Penance, good to see you," Doyle declared.

"What brings you to Sawyer's finest?"

"Well, you might as well know, I'm here to release Butch Whatcom," the judge replied.

Penance frowned, "Release him?"

The judge made a sour face before he answered, "This whole business with the traffic stop, getting the Whatcoms all fired up...you've got to understand, there is some long, serious history here."

"I'm sorry, history changes the law, how?"

"It doesn't change the law, but it shapes how we judiciously apply it," Doyle said. "You see, these are old families here. Most go back before we were a nation or around thereabouts. Wars have been fought against each other, alongside each other. Families have feuded, mixed in marriage, and feuded again. The Whatcoms are one of those families. Their reach goes beyond Delvin and his brood. As a whole, they have had their nasty past. With Delvin, at least in his later years, peace has more or less been the tale. Sure, his boys get into their malfeasance, but in another way, they have kept out worse elements that would try and unleash a plague in our fair corner of the world."

"Long story short, you'll bend the law to keep the Whatcoms at bay," Penance said.

"Keep the peace as long as they don't stray too far off the moral trail," Doyle corrected.

"I thought justice was supposed to be blind. Legal lines aren't meant to be fuzzy," Penance stated.

"They've *always* been fuzzy, son. Even in the FBI, intent has to play a factor in how you manage the criminal element," Doyle pressed. "Delvin's boys might be idiots, but Delvin intends to keep the peace around here. As long as the lines they cross don't make that fuzzy turn blatantly crooked and they on the wrong side of it, I'm going to suggest keeping the path that promotes peace amongst our neighbors."

The judge paused as he observed Penance's reaction to the statement.

"Now, if you don't mind, I've got to get to it," Doyle said and continued down the hall.

Stepping out of the elevator, Penance pulled out his cellphone.

"Special Agent Penance, I hope this not a call to post bail for you," Deputy Director Dixon called through the phone.

"Why would I need bail posted?" Penance asked.

"I was concerned that you might be weaseling your way into Sanchez' cell."

"I'm not going to lie, that was plan B if I didn't get anything out of plan A," Penance admitted.

"Oh? And what was plan A?"

"That young wannabe gang banger from the next county over. I used Sanchez' chapter and the Las Piratas reputation of tracking down squealers for a little leverage."

"I see. You told him it was public knowledge who led you Sanchez and that only the federal government could protect him," Dixon guessed.

"That's about right," Penance admitted. "Got a description of two Hispanic males, stationed within forty-minutes or so of that dive bar they were using as a bait trap. I'll send you descriptions. Also, a bolo on a beer truck in that forty-minute circumference with faded logos of Mississippi Mud, I think he called it."

"Mississippi Mud Black and Tan. Good beer, I'll have your fridge stocked with some," Dixon declared.

"Sounds good," Penance said. "Hey, did you know about Judge Doyle releasing Butch Whatcom?"

"He give you the historical families and keeping the peace speech?" Dixon asked.

"Yeah, pretty much."

"Southern justice can be a bit nuanced. Kind of like a backwoods version of the old families in the northeast – the Kennedys, Rockefellers, Vanderbilts…I promise you, if crime outside of murder crossed their paths, the system would treat them a bit differently than you or I in the same situation," Dixon shared.

"I suppose," Penance acquiesced. "Do you trust Judge Doyle?"

The line quiet as Director Dixon weighed his answer, "Doyle means well. But his family goes back as far as anyone else's, which means there are a lot of crossing paths with the other families. As long as Delvin limits the Whatcom's enterprises and keeps the boys under wraps, there are a lot of sins that will be forgiven."

"Alright, Judge Doyle can do things his way, I'm going to continue mine...the right way," Penance declared. "Let me know if the bolo returns anything."

TWENTY-TWO

Penance had just pulled the Porsche into the parking lot when the call came in that the All-Points-Bulletin on the van had a hit. Deputy Director Dixon burst out of the bureau doors, making a beeline for the SUV.

Rolling his window down, Penance leaned across the console.

"Normally, I'd be sending Timmy with you, but under the circumstance, I'm all you got. Let me in this obnoxious thing," Dixon called.

Penance looked warily at his boss. "When's the last time you've done fieldwork?"

"I go out to calls all the time," Dixon replied.

"Standing with the police chief in the back row. This is front line stuff, it could get ugly," Penance warned.

Dixon looked offended, "Don't you worry about me, I can handle myself."

"Just make sure you check your crossfire," Penance grinned as he gunned the engine and pulled out of the bureau parking lot.

Penance pulled up to the Sherriff's SUV. Casting an awkward glance at the Porsche before recognizing Dixon in the passenger seat, he frowned, "This what the bureau is supplying you guys with these days, Dixon?"

"Only when my rogue agents figure out how to goose requisition papers after a convenient drug bust," Dixon replied. "Sheriff MacReady, this is Special Agent Alex Penance."

The Sherriff shook Penance's hand, "I've heard about you. You are making quite the splash in Wilkinson County. No big surprise they dumped the van over on the Louisiana side of the big crick. Staties and County fellas kind of stuck at the bridge based on their jurisdiction. We see it all the time on one side of the bank or the other."

"I see a badly charred van, but the scene seems to be absent of Central American drug and human traffickers," Penance observed.

"Not one much for small talk, is he, Dixon?" Sheriff MacReady noted.

"All work and no fun this one," the FBI Director replied.

"That's alright. We can get to the point. Van was found fully engulfed by some flat bottom fishermen on their way to the mangroves. Called it in. By the time we got here, it was smoldering rubble," the sheriff replied.

"Don't suppose there are any highway cameras between here and Sawyer?" Penance asked.

"There ain't any highways between here and Sawyer," the sheriff replied. "We got calls out for anyone who might have seen it, but they dumped it here because it is not very well-traveled."

Penance surveyed the scene, carefully scanning for anything that might present a clue to find the Las Piratas gang members. Dixon and the sheriff joined him, each with their chins near their chests as they combed the ground.

"No additional tire tracks, so they were likely picked up by a chase vehicle that never left the road," Dixon declared.

Penance studied the area. Suddenly, he left the roadside nearest the van and crossed the street. Kneeling, he inspected the tall grass along the side of the road. "Or, they were met by a boat. It looks like something or someone walked this way towards the river."

"That sure ain't a gator path," the sheriff acknowledged, joining Penance. "Unless they swam, they would have been picked up in a small Jon boat. It is way too shallow to get anything else closer to the bank here."

"That should serve as another clue as to where they might be holing up," Dixon declared. "We can map out the bar, response time, and river access as well as this dump point."

"It's something. There is a lot of harsh ground to cover on both the Mississippi and Louisiana side. Swamps and dense forest," Sheriff MacReady said.

"We'll have the van flat bedded to New Orleans and see if there is anything forensics might find from the truck, though after firebombing it, I am not too hopeful," Dixon shared. "And then, we'll start working the map. Maybe see if the techs from Jackson can come in with drones and see what they can see."

Penance nodded as he stared out at the river separating the two states.

TWENTY-THREE

"So, Bubba tells me you're the one that got him out of trouble with that Willie Benson fellow. And then into trouble with them rednecks at the bar," Mrs. Jeffries said, her voice even as she looked across the table at Agent Penance.

"And out of trouble once again, Mama," Bubba corrected.

Mrs. Jeffries studied the agent for a long minute. "I like a man that sticks up for his friends."

Penance nodded, "Your son is a good man. Heart of a lion."

"I wanted him to go to business school. Learn how to turn our diner into one of those franchises," Mrs. Jeffries stated. "Not chasing criminals, especially here in Sawyer. They know him too well here, and his size don't affect them."

"You know, ma'am, sometimes talking people into being reasonable is a better course of action. I think I used to carry on a bit more like him. Besides, your recipes are amazing. Worthy of far more than a franchise," Penance said.

"That's sweet," Mrs. Jeffries said. With a raised brow, she asked, "So what changed?"

Penance looked confused, "Ma'am?"

"What changed that moved you from peacekeeper to law reckoner? Just curious if over time my boy might swing that way," Mrs. Jeffries pressed.

Penance swirled his iced tea and watched the ice cubes dance around in a tiny whirlpool. "Probably a couple of things," Penance admitted. "I was in an incident where terrorists were going to kill tens of thousands of people. I caught one of them. I knew I didn't have time and had to act. I got him to talk in a somewhat unconventional manner."

"Did you save those people?"

"Every one of them."

"I don't see the downside, yet."

Penance paused, "That action, breaking protocol won me accolades. Riding that high, I made a lapse in personal judgment. That lapse brought me here."

"I believe *God* brought you here, Mr. Penance. If you had not been here on the day Willie Benson was shooting up downtown, my Bubba might be dead. Sometimes you can't understand the story that He is writing on your behalf, but you were called to be in the right place at the right time," Mrs. Jeffries said sternly.

The agent struggled to know how to respond, merely agreeing, "Perhaps."

"Why don't you boys clean up from supper, and I'll see if the rhubarb-cherry pie is ready," Mrs. Jeffries suggested.

"That sounds like a fair deal to me, if not a bit in our favor," Penance grinned.

Sliding his chair out, he began collecting the dishes while Bubba grabbed the serving bowls.

"Thank you for inviting me for dinner, Bubba. Your mother is as wonderful as her cooking," Penance.

"She is. After my daddy past, we make meals together a priority."

"That's nice. Not sure families do that enough these days," Penance admired.

"Momma says there'd be less crime and divorce if more families did so," Bubba added.

"Love to be out of a job because families encouraged one another. Until that day comes, I guess we have to keep doing what we do," Penance said.

Penance left the Jeffries house as content as he had felt since arriving in Sawyer. There was a solidness to match the generosity and kindness that emanated from Bubba and his mother. The duo made a strong impression on him.

Rumbling the Porsche SUV up the gravel drive towards his house, his headlights picked up the slightest reflective gleam from the bushes. The momentary flash caught the agent's attention. His senses were on alert with a concealed vehicle with only his house and the neighbor's left on the street.

Forcing the automatic lights off, he coasted to the edge of his driveway. Quietly opening the driver's door, he stood against the SUV, his hand resting on his firearm. Penance eyed where the vehicle was parked and then studied his own house, knowing he had already made enemies amongst the criminal element in Dixie.

His eyes flashed from window to window, the edge of the house to edge of the house looking for light, shadows, or movement. The sound of glass breaking followed by a shriek brought Penance into a full sprint towards the neighbor's house, his service weapon drawn.

Pulling up alongside the front window, his back to the siding, Penance peered into the house. Framed in one of the far windows, he could see two shadows moving towards the center of the room, followed by the sound of quick footsteps. The footfalls sounded light, springing Penance into action.

Leaping up onto the porch, Penance aimed a single, powerful kick against the front door, right above the handle. Penance pounced through as the door burst open. He found himself between the young neighbor girl and a pursuer that had just reached out to grab her. Recognizing Penance in the dim evening light, she flung herself into his arms, with her pursuers redirecting their path past the girl and through the open door.

Penance tried to pull away and chase after them, but the girl clung tight with deep sobs as she pushed into his chest. Relenting to console the girl and ensure there were no other surprises in the house, he stayed and allowed the offenders to get away. He heard the sound of an engine clacking to life and gravel strewn along the dirt road.

"Are you okay?" he asked.

The girl nodded silently against him.

"Where's your brother?"

"At a friend's house," she choked.

"Was that your boyfriend?"

Penance could feel her shake her head, "No. They had accents. I haven't seen him since you pulled him through the window."

"That's good. How about your father? When will he be home? Can you call him?" the agent asked, his investigative instinct wanting to take over.

Understanding her fear, he had her place her arm around his waist so that his arms remained free. Snapping on his flashlight, using his forearm to steady his firearm, he swept the small house. Satisfied that the two were the only ones threatening the girl, he guided her to his own home.

To ease any remaining fears, he did a quick sweep and led Maggie to sit on the sofa. Holstering his firearm, he finally freed his cellphone and called it into the local police.

It was nearly a half-hour before the patrol unit showed up. Chief Pruitt and Bubba arrived in tow. Penance eyed Bubba, who was in street clothes.

"Are you on duty?" Penance asked.

"I heard the call come in. I wanted to be here," the officer replied.

"Thank you, Bubba," Penance acknowledged. Recounting the events of the evening, as the sheriff and his deputies joined the small Sawyer contingent, Penance led the team to the neighbor's house and pointed to where the vehicle was parked.

"I didn't see it, but it was a Chevrolet, likely a V6," Penance declared.

"If you didn't see it…," one of the officers began to ask.

"Chevrolets have a distinct start and cam. The exhaust wasn't throaty or as rhythmic as a V8. Probably a passenger van or another commercial decoy," the agent replied.

"Any ID on the perpetrators?" Chief of Police Pruitt asked.

Penance shook his head, "Not clear. They ruled out the victim's former ex. Both assailants were roughly five-ten. The girl said they spoke with an accent."

"What kind of accent?"

"Hispanic."

"Well, not a lot to go on. We'll see if they left prints or anything else behind," the chief said.

Penance watched as a pickup drove up and parked in line with the police cruisers outside of the neighbor's driveway.

"Excuse me," Penance said and walked toward the truck.

"Frank!" the agent called. "She's at my house with an officer. Come on. She'll be glad to see you."

"You saved my little girl once again," Frank said, his voice declaring his exasperation.

Penance tried to soften the moment, patting Frank on the shoulder, "Just being neighborly."

Assistant District Attorney Annie Hunt burst into the Bureau office minutes after Penance had arrived himself.

She beamed as she strode with determination up to the FBI agent's desk. "I got it! I convinced Colton to let you take a shot at Sanchez!"

"Nice work," Penance smiled in approval. Cocking his head, he asked, "But...there are conditions..."

"There are conditions," Annie confirmed. "He wants to be there with you during your inquiry."

"Of course, he does," Penance grimaced. He knew trying to apply leverage with the District Attorney present; he would have to play it by the book.

"We have a window from nine to ten this morning. Colton will meet us there at ten minutes before to go over ground rules."

"Sound like fun," Penance retorted.

"It sounds like you had an eventful night. Related to our case?" the assistant district attorney asked.

"Maybe. At first, I thought it was the ex-boyfriend, but it turned out sounding a lot like the *Las Piratas*," Penanced conceded.

Dixon burst into the office. Like Hunt had moments before, he made a beeline towards Penance's desk. "Special Agent Penance, why is it that I have to my phone blown up by local law enforcement to hear that one of my agents was in the middle of foiling an attempted kidnapping that might be related to one of this office's federal cases?"

Penance wrinkled his nose, "It was unclear whether it was a local or federal thing until the situation unfolded. By then, I didn't see any reason to disrupt your evening."

"Agent Penance, I appreciate your courtesy, but let me be clear. In the future, as long as you are an agent under my purview, I want to be alerted anytime you pull your badge, lay your hands on someone or draw your weapon, are we clear?"

Penance hesitated and then relented, "We're clear...sir."

"Okay, then. On the bright side, it sounds as though you saved a girl, though the perpetrators got away," Dixon continued.

"That is correct," Penance conceded.

"According to Chief Pruitt, you broke up the assault and terminated the baddies in order to console the girl," Dixon recounted.

"That too is correct." Penance admitted.

Dixon studied his agent thoughtfully, eyeing A. D. A. Hunt, who was a bystander to their conversation. "It would seem to me, Agent Penance, you made an unusually correct call on this one. Ensuring the victim's wholeness over chasing the bad guy. Nice work. Only next time, I'd rather hear from you than the locals."

"Understood," Penance agreed.

"Now what blessed us with Ms. Hunt's presence this morning?" the Bureau Chief asked.

"I came by to tell Special Agent Penance that our office has agreed to allow him to interrogate Sanchez, under specific conditions," Annie shared.

"Those conditions include Jennings hovering over my agent's shoulders, I presume," Dixon suggested.

"They do," Annie nodded.

"Why don't I come along too?" Dixon suggested. "I tell you what, how about you two go ahead, I'll spring for coffees, be right behind you."

Penance shrugged, "Alright."

"Want to ride together?" Annie asked Penance.

"Sure," he grinned, picking up the Porsche keys, "I'll drive!"

Heading towards the county holding facility, the Assistant District Attorney studied the FBI agent for a moment. "You put aside your hero tendencies, to look after a frightened young girl."

"Yeah, so?" Penance asked as he turned the SUV onto Main Street.

"Kind of belies the shoot first action hero we have come to know since you arrived in Sawyer," Hunt observed. Poking the agent, "There is a genuine human being underneath that badge."

Penance cast a disgruntled glance at the ADA, "What did you expect?"

"Oh, come on. You were tasked with a decision – pursue the bad guys or stay with a girl who was scared, but otherwise fine at that time," Hunt pressed.

"It was a tactical decision, recover and maintain the victim, hunt the bad guys down another day. Battles are often won by deflecting the skirmish and assembling an organized, subsequent attack," Penance responded.

"Sounds like military training."

"My Dad. Special Forces, spent much of early childhood at the doorstep of enemy lines," Penance shared.

"Ah, commando by blood," Hunt raised an eyebrow.

"He was a field medic. Never fired a weapon," Penance corrected. "The day I was born, he promised my mother he would retire when his tour was done. Became a private practice doc so he could be home with my mother and me."

"I see."

"He wasn't so much leading me to be a commando but to be a patriot," Penance said, wheeling the SUV into the county corrections parking lot.

"So much to learn about you," Hunt mused.

They sat for a moment, after the SUV 's engine went silent. The Assistant D.A. turned to the agent and asked, "How about you come with me to church on Sunday? Maybe grab lunch afterward, my treat?"

Penance studied Annie before nodding slowly, "Sure, why not?"

"Great! Service starts at 10, so pick me up by 9:30," Annie smiled. Grabbing the handle, she opened the car door, "Let's go find Colton."

The District Attorney was waiting for Penance and Annie just inside the metal detectors. "Special Agent Penance," Jennings acknowledged.

"Jennings," Penance nodded.

"Let's walk, and I'll tell you how this is going to work," Jennings held out his hand for the two to proceed down the hallway. "No touching the prisoner…at all. No threats to him or his family. No discussions about deals, as you have no authority to make any. Do not discuss particulars of any case outside of his own. No referencing what his future holds, as the case has not yet been determined, and we do not know what his future holds. I'll set the ground rules and let you have the floor, but know I will have to step in if you violate any of those conditions."

"I should have brought him some flowers and chocolates. What do you suppose we use to get him to talk?" Penance quipped.

"That is your area of expertise, I suggest you use whatever *legal* and approved means of questioning you have learned in your FBI training," Colton suggested evenly.

Pressing the button for the elevator, the D.A. checked his watch, "They should be ready for us."

As the three stepped inside, a voice called from down the hall, "Hold the door guys, after all, I have the coffees!"

Bureau Chief Dixon held a tray with four coffees as he hustled down the hall after them. Sneaking into the elevator, carrying the beverages close to his gut.

Agent Penance freed his arm from the elevator door sensor and allowed the doors to shut.

"Fine day for an interrogation, ain't it?" Chief Dixon smiled. "Made sweeter with a little caffeine, I thought."

Dixon held the tray with one hand and doled out the coffees with the other. "Here you go, Ms. Hunt. Honey and almond milk latte. Agent Penance, a Chicory au lait. Kinda like the Starbucks of the bayou. Colton, I got you and me chicory straight up."

Dixon held the cup in front of the DA. As Jennings reached out, the cup exploded, showering him with hot coffee. "Aw nuts, I'm sorry Colton, the lid must have been cockeyed."

Jennings stepped away from the cup in his hands, which was dripping brown liquid onto the elevator floor.

The damage was done as coffee showered him and his suit. As the doors opened, Jennings adjusted the lid and headed for the restroom. "Let me clean up real quick, and I'll be right behind you before we go in."

The trio nodded as Penance shot Dixon a knowing glance. The Deputy Director produced an innocent shrug as he took a sip of his coffee, a grin wiping across his lips.

"Officer Samuels, watched Johnny on the mound the other night, kids got a cannon-like his daddy," Dixon smiled as they walked up to the secure meeting room.

"Naw, he's *better*. But thanks, I'm real proud," the guard replied. "Waiting for District Attorney Jennings?"

"We don't have to wait, he said he'd be right behind us and catch up," Dixon smiled, nodding towards the door.

"Alrighty," the guard said. Punching in his code and nodding into the monitor for the main office to cue their pin. A buzz followed by the locks clanging into place freed the door.

"There you go."

"Thanks, Samuels."

Dixon, Penance, and Annie strode into the meeting room as the door clanged shut.

Sanchez looked up at the three. "I ain't got nothin' to say to you, especially that gringo. He's a dead man anyway."

Penance patted himself. "I don't feel dead. I tell you what, though. I'll try to make you a sweetheart deal. And when you're out, you are welcome to find me and draw on me…anytime."

Sanchez just glared at the agent.

"Ms. Hunt, will you go find Jennings…just to help him find the right room. Dixon and I will get acquainted with Dirty here. Dirty Sanchez…" Penance burst into laughter, saying the *Las Piratas* lieutenant's nickname aloud.

The cartel member cocked a confused look at the FBI agents' laughter.

"You know, I should check on Colton myself. I feel awful about what happened with his coffee," Dixon said, holding the door for Annie.

As the door shut and it was just Agent Penance and Sanchez, Penance sat on the edge of the table close to the gang leader. Leaning in, he whispered hoarsely, "To be clear, I don't make deals with scumbags like you, so I am afraid you will never get your shot at me. Too bad really. It would be a fun four seconds before your eyes got that surprised look as you realized you were shot and moments away from crumbling to your death."

Sanchez scowled, "If you didn't come here to bring me a deal, we got nothing to talk about."

"See, I think we do. A deal gets you protection at the cost of our country's hardworking taxpayers. The *perception* of a deal gets you shivved in prison," Penance argued.

"You got nothing. My people will never believe I rolled," Sanchez spat.

"No, I think they will. Aside from the drugs, I know about your sex trafficking of little girls," Penance eyed Sanchez and added, "And probably little boys."

"What are you saying?"

"I am saying the news of Heckle and Jeckle, who drove the beer van to Centreville and nabbed kids from the underage club in the back. I'll let it leak that information on the part of the *Las Piratas* enterprises came from you. There is little enough public and documented, that I can fill any name on the "source" line. I was thinking Dirty Sanchez, *Las Piratas* drug lieutenant shared a little info on the other operation to save himself some time off the clock," Penance said.

"Or...or you can provide me with some useful information that campaign and I will see to it that you are protected. You know as well as I do, if the *Las Piratas* even *think* that you breathed a word, you'd be dead by breakfast your first full day in lock up," Penance eased back and let his words percolate in the gangster's mind.

The now-familiar buzzing followed by clanging of door locks announced that the entourage was rejoining him.

As expected, Jennings burst through, "Special Agent Penance, stand down!"

Penance calm waved his hand in the air, welcoming the intrusion, "It's alright, District Attorney Jennings. I was just explaining to Mr. Sanchez here, that the government would be willing to ensure his safety in prison if he were helpful with the investigation. Mr. Sanchez was just about to fill me in on the human trafficking department in his organization. Weren't you, Mr. Sanchez, or would you prefer I call you 'Dirty'?"

"I...I," Sanchez scowled and then dropped his head. "You can protect me?"

The foursome exchanged glances, and Jennings nodded, "We can."

"Alright. The cartel divides the duties. There are the seeds. They create scenarios that draw the kids to the operation. They party for a bit, call it in and then the pick-up crew comes. They transfer to the stash house until transfer comes. After that...I have no idea.," Sanchez shared.

Penance stared hard at the gang lieutenant. "What happens when the situation is compromised? The bar is shut down. What now?"

Sanchez breathed a deep sigh before he replied. "They will fill up the final transfer and then head south until they receive new instructions."

"Fill up?"

"Our contracts run half a dozen at a time. If the collection point is jacked, they'll go street sweeping or doorbell ringing."

"How full is this final transfer?" Penance pressed.

Sanchez laughed in a snarl, "I don't know, gringo. You've had me in here. Could be full, could need a couple more."

Penance shot glances at the others in the room. "I foiled the attempt last night. They are probably still on the prowl."

"Well, let's go catch these creeps before we lose more girls," Dixon declared.

Sanchez leaned forward across the table, "You're gonna protect me, right?"

The foursome turned without saying another word and buzzed to leave the room. As they stepped out into the hall, Sanchez wailed behind them, "You promised me protection! You need to protect me!"

"Jennings, thank you for putting this little soiree together. Agent Penance and I have got some work to do," Dixon said.

"Hey, do you want to open the car and get the air running? I want to go over a plan of attack with Dixon," Penance said, handing Annie his car keys.

As Penance and the Deputy Director walked down the hall, Penance whispered, "You squeezed the coffee cup, didn't you?"

Dixon looked aghast as he swiveled to face his agent, "Why would I do a thing like that?"

Penance grinned and pressed the call button for the elevator.

TWENTY-FOUR

Alex Penance felt a twinge of nervousness that caught him by surprise, and he could not explain. He straightened his tie and checked his collar for the third time as he studied himself in the mirror.

Facing his superiors, entering a crime scene, or facing off with a criminal, were virtually automatic for the FBI agent. This day felt different, but he couldn't put a finger on why. He liked Annie Hunt, but he had liked women before. Conversations with her were so comfortable. He had been to church before, and Pastor Roberts was comfortably relatable. Something else was knocking on the door of his subconscious. He just didn't know who or what.

Shaking his head, he grabbed his car keys and headed towards the door. He paused for a moment as he patted his holster, wondering if it was somehow blasphemous to take it, but a check of his watch told him he had to go.

Walking towards his SUV, he looked across at his neighbors, who waved.

"Heading to work?" Frank asked the agent.

"Church!" Penance replied.

"Alright, then," Frank beamed. "We'll see you there!"

Turning the key in the ignition, Penance fired up the Porsche and pointed it down the dirt road.

"Well, Agent Penance, you look like…well, if I'm honest, you look like you do every day," Annie Hunt declared. "But, that's not so terribly bad."

"Well, you, Ms. Hunt, look…well, you are a vision," Penance said. "But today of all days, it's Alex. Not Agent Penance."

"Very well, Alex."

"Shall we?" Penance held the door open for her.

"I love Sunday mornings," Annie shared. "It's kind of like Christmas, the world seems a little bit sweeter, a little calmer."

Penance held the door for her and closed it behind her.

"I think the world could use a little bit of sweeter and calm," Penance admitted. "Thank you for inviting me."

Annie grinned, "I wasn't sure you'd come."

Penance slipped his glasses on and started the SUV. "I wasn't either."

Pulling into the church parking lot was like attending a town meeting. Most of the town turned out for the service. Police Chief Truitt stood talking with Magistrate Doyle and District Attorney Jennings.

His neighbors arrived and met up with another family with children roughly the same age.

Pastor Roberts stood in the doorway, greeting every parishioner as they entered the church.

Penance was surprised to see the Whatcoms arrive. Devlin wore a vest over a striped shirt while Butch and Billy wore cleaner versions of what they usually wore. Shannon Whatcom walked a few steps away from her family, in a flowing sundress. In her Sunday best, she wore an air of innocence. It was a look that escalated her natural beauty ten-fold. Mama Whatcom paraded ahead of the brood, pausing to make overly animated pleasantries with everyone she walked by.

"The queen and her court?" Penance frowned.

"It's kind of like tradition. Break the rules all week and act all proper come Sunday morning," Annie shared.

"The fun starts all over again on Monday?" Penance asked.

"By about the time Sunday lunch has been eaten," Annie corrected.

"I see."

"Well, well, Mr. Alex Penance and the beautiful Ms. Annie Hunt, looking as radiant as ever," Magistrate Doyle called as he spied the pair.

"Doyle, Chief…" Penance acknowledged, adding, "Jennings."

"I didn't see your car in the church parking lot," the District Attorney looked surprised. "Annie, is your car running right? If not, I could have ol' Jake at the auto shop give it a look."

Annie frowned, "My car is fine, Colton. I invited Alex to church. He offered to drive me."

"Nice to see you can train a northern boy chivalry," Jennings quipped.

Penance started to respond, but Annie cut him off, "Oh, he has been *more* than capable and adept at being a gentleman. Though, less discerning tongues might value a lesson or two."

Doyle smacked Jennings on the chest, "She got you on that one, Colton. Son, we're glad to see you here."

"Thank you, sir," Penance said, walking past Jennings his eyes square with the D.A.'s.

"I guess the truce is off," she whispered in Penance's ear as they walked towards the church.

"Don't look at me. I didn't start it."

"Penance, great to see you," Pastor Roberts stepped forward to shake the agent's hand.

"Good to see you, too, Pastor," Penance replied.

Inside the doors, Bubba greeted them. The big police officer wedged into a somewhat poorly fitting tan suit. He didn't show any discomfort as he wore a big smile seeing Penance and Annie. "My stars, Ms. Annie, you are something to behold."

"Why, thank you, Bubba. You're looking pretty sharp yourself," Annie replied.

"Penance, you came to church," the big man beamed.

"That I did. Good to see you, my friend."

Bubba's grin somehow grew even wider at the reference of friend. "I can sit you right next to me and Mama…if that's okay."

Penance nodded, "That'd be great."

Bubba led them to the pew where his mother sat.

"Hello, Mr. Penance." Mrs. Jeffries offered.

"Alex, ma'am. It's nice to see you again," Penance acknowledged.

"I was thinking of throwing together a little picnic after church if ya'll'd like to join us," Mrs. Jeffries offered.

Penance looked at Annie, who shrugged. "We'd love to come. What can we bring?"

Bubba's mother smiled, "You just bring that pretty thing on your arm."

Pastor Bob walked down the aisle, smiling and saying hello to anyone he may have missed on the way into the church. Pausing, he smiled as he observed the congregation. Nodding his approval at his audience, he began the service.

When worship finished and the church began to file out, Penance observed the Whatcoms not speaking to anyone as they left. Shannon, as she did on the way in, strayed a bit from her family.

Penance watched his neighbors work their way towards the door. Giving a slight wave as they left the church.

"Well, Bubba, Mama Jeffries, we'll see you in a bit," Penance acknowledged and escorted Annie out of the pew and down the aisle.

As they left the church, they found a crowd gathered around the police chief's car. Scrawled across the windshield, bright red paint "estamos llegando".

Police Chief Pruitt strolled up, "Now what the hell...sorry Pastor...is that?"

"We're coming," Penance said.

"You can read this stuff?"

"We had a few gangs in Boston. You tend to pick up a few words," Penance shared.

"What does this mean?" the chief asked. "Who's coming? For what?"

"I think the 'they' are the *Las Piratas* and they are coming for Dirty Sanchez at county lock up," Penance surmised.

"If they were already here to write that, why would it say they are coming?"

"Sanchez was a lieutenant. I think they intend to come in force," Penance said.

"To free him?"

"If they can. If they can't, make a statement."

"What kind of statement?

"A bloody one," Penance declared grimly.

Penance pulled the Porsche SUV into the parking area of the Lake Mary picnic grounds. "Hmm, this is kind of nice."

Annie Hunt looked aghast, "What? Did Special Agent Alex Penance just say something positive about Mississippi?"

"I'm sure there are a hundred things in and out of the water that want to kill me," he added.

"There it is!" Annie laughed. "You'll be fine. You should see Lake Mary from the air. It looks like a giant letter 'C'. Although occasionally, the Mississippi runs its banks and levels it."

"Explains the stilt houses," Penance observed.

"Oh yeah, that's the only way to have a house around here, it turns into a giant bayou."

"There is no shortage of places nasty little pirates can hide, are there?"

"I suppose not. Really have to have an informant or pick them up in town and track them. Once they slip into the lakes and swamps, forget about it."

"On that sobering note, let's enjoy a Sunday picnic," Penance said as Bubba and his mother arrived in her catering van.

Greeting them, they each carried an armload of food and picnic trappings to a table overlooking the lake.

"You picked a nice spot, Mrs. Jeffries," Penance said.

"It's lovely out here, for sure. Bubba's daddy used to love fishing off these banks. He always coveted them stilt homes, saying how nice it would be to roll out to the back porch and cast a line in," Mrs. Jeffries admitted.

"You ever come here with him, Bubba?" Penance asked.

"A few times in grade school. I didn't appreciate the fishing so much, but the time with him. Especially in between deployments," Bubba replied.

"Your father served?"

"Amry. Never expected to get sent to war," Bubba said.

"Iraq?"

"And Afghanistan," Bubba nodded. "That's where we lost him."

"Sorry for your loss and grateful for his service," Penance said solemnly.

"You ever serve, outside of the FBI, Mr. Penance?" Mrs. Jeffries asked.

"A few special assignments with a troop out of North Carolina, but nothing official. College brat, straight into the academy," Penance admitted.

"Bubba says you don't like it here much," Mrs. Jeffries pressed.

Penance shot a knowing look at Annie and wrinkled his nose, "Probably homesick."

Mrs. Jeffries studied him for a moment. "What got you sent down here to Sawyer?"

Penance looked surprised, but couldn't stifle a grin, "What makes you say something got me sent down here?"

"With all the places you *could* be, only a fool like Dixon who grew up in Mississippi would *choose* Sawyer," Mrs. Jeffries said.

"Well, you're right. I didn't choose to come to Sawyer, but this is where I am," Penance said. "I may not have been thrilled with the opportunity, but I'll admit, folks like you and Bubba and Annie have made feel especially welcome."

"I'm not one for coincidences, I believe you were called here," Mrs. Jeffiries surmised.

The confused expression on Penance's face encouraged her to continue, "I'm telling you, by God. He's got a plan for you, and he wanted you in Mississippi...in Sawyer."

"He saved my bacon, that's for sure," Bubba grinned, patting his friend on the shoulder.

A voice called from behind them, "Well, I'm glad my Sunday sermons have life in them after the pulpit." Pastor Roberts grinned.

"Pastor Roberts, I'm glad you could join us."

"Mrs. Jeffries, only a foolish man would ignore your invitation to supper," the pastor said. "Great day for a picnic."

"Great day, indeed," Annie agreed.

"Y'all ready to eat?" Mrs. Jeffries inquired.

"I'm not sure you really needed to ask, Mama," Bubba grinned.

"Pastor?"

Pastor Roberts bowed his head and blessed the food, Mrs. Jeffries, and the rest of the picnic-goers.

"Mrs. Jeffries, I'd say you outdid yourself, but you have already set the bar so incredibly high. You are consistently amazing," Pastor Roberts said, looking at the spread.

Mrs. Jeffries smiled wide, "Now, you see why I invite him."

As they sat down the eat, the pastor turned to Penance. "Well, what did you think? The sermon, I mean."

Penance sat his chicken down. "It was not exactly what I expected, though I am not sure what I expected. How you made the stories from the Bible practical and relevant to our lives today, I thought it was...compelling."

"We're not called to repeat what people can read on their own and then send them out the door. Our true mission is to build disciples," Pastor Roberts said.

"Disciples?"

"Others to share the Word, in *their* stories," Pastor Roberts replied. "To go out and to do good. Help people."

Penance squirmed a little in his seat.

Recognizing the agent's discomfort, Pastor Roberts added, "Let's say we're all wrong. All of us people of faith are wrong; that believe God as our Lord and Savior is not our salvation. We do good things on this earth as we go."

"Makes it hard to argue," Penance admitted.

"Do you believe, Alex?" Annie asked.

Penance picked at his food with his fork, "I...I don't really know. I mean, we celebrated Easter and Christmas growing up, went to church a bit..."

"It's okay, we don't need to grill you over lunch, I'm just glad you came," Pastor Roberts cut in, much to Penance's relief.

"So, what did you do for fun up in Boston?" Bubba asked.

Penance cocked his head for a moment, "This one shouldn't be so hard to answer, but outside of work, I didn't do much. I guess on the upward career track. Work was my life."

"You didn't do sports or nothin'?" Bubba asked as he slathered honey butter on this cornbread.

Penance brightened, "I went to the range a lot. I owned the marksman record at the academy for draw time and distance with .40 cal."

"Wow, you really know how to cut loose, don't you?" Annie teased.

"How about you, Annie? What do you like to do for fun?" the agent asked.

"Giggin'."

Penance looked perplexed while the rest of the table burst in laughter. "*What?*"

"Giggin'. My daddy used to take me giggin' down along the cricks and the rivers," Annie replied with a drawl as big as one as she had uttered since Penance met her.

Penance scowled, still confused.

"Maybe Bubba will take you after lunch," Annie grinned. "If we don't have giggin' poles, we can make some out of sticks. You just need a few sharp points, find'em frogs, and gig'em!"

"You puncture a frog with a stick. What on earth for?" the agent was incredulous.

"Some people eat them," Annie replied.

"Ooh, Mama can fry'em up real good," Bubba grinned.

"How about you, Pastor Roberts, you do any 'gigging'?" Penance asked warily.

Pastor Roberts laughed, "No. No gigging for me."

Annie burst into laughter, "I'm messing with you. I mean, my daddy *did* take me when I was little, but poking poor little frogs never became my thing."

"I'll still take you," Bubba offered.

Penance looked at his friend, "No, thank you. I'm okay missing that experience."

"So, what do you do for fun, Ms. Annie?" Mrs. Jeffries asked.

"Well, I like to go to the theater if there is anything good playing. And I tell you what I love, going to the stadium – baseball in the summer and football in the fall. The crowd, the community and, all respect to Mrs. Jeffries fine cooking, a good old hotdog."

"Mustard or ketchup?" Penance asked.

Annie grinned, "I kind of like mine with ketchup and hot sauce. How about you? You like a hotdog?"

"At Fenway Park, watching the Red Sox play, it is straight-up mustard. But I have to say, ketchup and hot sauce," Penance snapped his fingers and pointed, "That sounds like a great idea."

"Then maybe we'll catch a game in Jackson. Watch the Generals play," Annie suggested.

"Could be fun," Penance admitted.

The table conversation halted at the ring of Bubba's phone. Excusing himself, he pushed away from the table. In a few moments and explained, "I'm sorry, y'all. There seems to be an issue with one of the Whatcom boys. I've got to go."

"Butch?" Penance asked, scooting his chair back.

"Not this time, his younger brother Billy," Bubba replied.

"Seeing as you have ridden here in your mother's van, how about I drive you?" Penance suggested. "Would one of you be able to drive Annie back to her car?"

Both Mrs. Jeffries and Pastor Bob nodded.

"Thank you for lunch, sorry we have to run," Penance said, tossing his napkin over his plate.

"It's alright, boys. Be sure to be safe, baby! You too, Mr. Penance!" Mrs. Jeffries called.

"Will do, Mrs. Jeffries!" Penance replied over his shoulder as he unlocked the Porsche. To Bubba, he said, "Let's go get us a Whatcom."

TWENTY-FIVE

Penance brought the Porsche roaring up to the scene. The Centreville police and the Sawyer police bookending an old green pickup with a six-inch lift.

"Chief Pruitt, what's the sitrep?" Penance asked as he approached the Sawyer police cruiser.

"Billy Whatcom's been pacing back and forth waving that pistol around, threatening to shoot an officer if we approach," Chief Pruitt replied.

"How did this all start?" Penance asked.

"According to the Centreville police, Billy was swerving across the line. They pulled him over, he started accelerating, but then thought the better of it. But when the officer approached, Billy suddenly pulled the pistol. And here we are," the police chief replied.

"Anyone fired yet?"

"No."

"Know what kind of piece he's packing?" the agent asked.

"A Springfield 9mm, I think."

Penance watched Billy for a few moments. The younger Whatcom boy was pacing back and forth, muttering to himself.

"He usually this anxious and high strung?"

The chief shook his head, "No. Not usually. Probably pulled him over half a dozen times. Even arrested him once. Nothing like this, though."

Penance nodded. Unholstering his weapon, the agent strode out from behind the police cruiser. Holding the gun with his thumb, high in the air away from his body, Penance called, "Billy, I'm coming out to talk with you."

"I know that trick, Federal. You did the same thing to Willie Benson," Billy said knowingly.

"Yeah, that worked pretty well. Not for Willie, but for me…and justice," Penance admitted. Crouching down, he placed his gun on the roadway.

"See, I'm leaving it behind me. Just you and me talking," Penance added as he took a step forward.

Billy watched the agent warily.

"What's going on, Billy?"

"I ain't got nothing to say to you, I just want to be left alone," Billy snarled.

"I get that. It sounds like it was just a simple traffic violation, until you pulled the gun on a police officer," Penance declared.

"It, what? What for now? Look, if you just let me go, I'll come by the station, I swear."

Penance winced, "It's a little too late for that. Right now, I need you to put the weapon down. Can you do that?"

"I do that, what leverage do I have then?"

"Uh, Billy, you don't have any leverage either way," Penance announced.

Billy swung the gun in his direction.

"You don't want to do that. You just went from threatening a police officer to threatening a federal agent. That's worse," Penance warned. "Tell you what, swing the gun at the ground, or at least my feet, and I'll pretend you didn't do that."

Billy stared cockeyed at the agent but tilted the gun towards Penance's feet.

"Now what's *really* going on? You seem a touch amped today."

"Nothing, man. I gotta get home," Whatcom said.

"You been drinking? If so, it's not that big of a crime."

"No, not that much."

"Officer saw you swerve?"

"I dropped my phone. It slid under my seat. I was trying to get. Ain't no big deal."

"Wasn't a big deal, but sort of looks that way now," Penance said. "What's in your truck?"

Billy snapped his head up, "What do you mean?"

"Every time you pace *towards* your truck, you look at the backseat," Penance observed. "Look, unless you have a body stuffed back there, nothing is worse than threatening a police officer."

Billy looked exasperated, "I just *need* to go home."

"Run an errand for your father?"

"No!"

"Brother?"

Billy flapped his arms down and stomped, his face fallen morose, "No, man."

Penance took Billy's tantrum as an opportunity to strike. Having inched up the duration of the conversation, he lunged at Billy, driving his full force into his midsection while wrapping his arms tightly around Billy's.

The impact slammed Billy's chin against the cab of the truck. The big man reeled, blood streaking from his chin, slamming Penance into the passenger door. Penance lightened his grip slightly. Billy took the advantage to try and spin away and point the gun back at the agent. As he whirled, Penance snatched the weapon away, leaving Billy pointing his empty hands at him.

"I got it!" Penance said, as if the altercation had not occurred. "You have something in there you don't want your *family* to see. That is why you are so agitated. Well, let's have a look."

Bubba and the chief had rushed them as they tussled and were already on Billy, placing him in cuffs as the Centreville police joined from the other end of the roadblock. Penance directed them to the rear seat. The officer flipped the seat up, revealing a duffle bag. With a quick zip, several white bricks wrapped in cellophane gleamed in the afternoon sun.

"Billy Whatcom, transporting heroin. I thought your daddy swore the Whatcoms only dealt in natural stuff you can pluck from the dirt," Penance said. Wrinkling his nose, he surmised, "They don't know about this, do they?"

Billy stared blankly at him, his eyes wet with tears.

Penance's eyes suddenly grew wide. "*Las Piratas.* You got this stuff from the *Las Piratas.*"

Billy frowned, "The who?"

"Let me guess, a seedy little bar in Centreville, right?"

Billy nodded sullenly.

"Billy, you are working with a Mexican cartel," Penance announced.

"No, I got it from Lanny. Skinny little white dude!"

"Who is working for the Mexican drug thugs," Penance informed.

"Daddy's gonna kill me," Billy said.

"He might," Penance admitted. "I may be able to convince him and Jennings to go light on you. Let's get you off the road and somewhere more comfortable, like the county lock up. You and I are going to have a deeper chat about this."

Bubba corralled Billy into the Chief's car and climbed into the passenger seat. The Centreville officers called for a tow truck to haul Billy's vehicle to the impound.

Dixon had arranged for Billy to be held in an interrogation room upon his arrival. Meeting Penance out front, he walked into the building with his agent. "Whatcoms upping their game?"

Penance shook his head, "Young Billy going rogue, I think."

"That won't go over well with Devlin," Dixon noted.

"If Devlin was telling the truth about staying away from the harder stuff," Penance responded. "Harder and more profitable."

"Do you see the Whatcoms living the high life?" Dixon asked.

"Hard times lead to hard decisions," Penance replied, holding the door for his boss to enter the county facility. Looking back towards the parking lot, Penance spied a van with its engine running. Two men sat in the front seats.

"I'll be right in," the agent called. Penance strode directly towards the van. The vehicle quickly slammed into gear. Before Penance could close the gap, it sped out of the parking lot. Snapping a quick photo with his phone, he watched the van drive off.

Returning to the county building, he found Bubba and Dixon waiting for him. "I'll take you to Billy. Sheriff Day is processing him now."

A deputy nodded in acknowledgment as they reached the holding area and opened the door.

"Bubba, this could be a long evening. Would you get us some coffee and for you and the chief as well?" Dixon requested.

Bubba nodded and accepted the bills that the FBI Bureau Director handed him.

Entering the interrogation room, Dixon led off, "Alright Billy, there is a world of hurt coming, so let's make this quick and limit the damage."

"You don't scare me, Dixon. Neither does your new agent," Billy scowled.

"You don't need to be scared of us, Billy. The Las Piratas and your daddy, now there's reason to be afraid," Dixon warned.

Billy looked away for a minute and back to the FBI agents. "I didn't know I was working with the Mexicans."

"But you knew the stuff you were slinging wasn't part of the family business," Dixon pressed.

"Yeah, I wanted to make a quick score. Show Daddy and Butch what I can do on my own," Billy pouted.

"An impressive sight, to be sure," Penance smirked.

"So, what's it going to be, Billy? Help the Mexicans or help your people in Sawyer?" Dixon asked.

"Man, I ain't helping the Mexicans."

"Then help us. They are doing worse things to the people of Mississippi than selling heroin," Dixon advised.

Before Billy could speak, a loud knock banged on the door. Muffled voices escalated in volume before the door swung open. "He insisted on coming in, saying Billy isn't represented," the deputy said.

"That's alright, let him in," Dixon waved.

A very irate Delvin Whatcom appeared in the doorway. Scanning the room, he cast disapproving looks to both FBI men. With a fixed gaze on his son, Delvin's face glowed crimson, "What in the hell is going on?"

Billy, as though he had swallowed something wrong as he tried to speak, "I's just, I's just helping a friend, making a few bucks while doin' it, Daddy."

"That what you were doing? It sounds to me like you were violating a family rule, one with major penalties, Billy Boy!" Devlin snarled.

"The money…"

"To hell with the money, boy. You idiot!" Devlin lunged at his son. Penance wrapped him up and spun him towards the wall.

The elder Whatcom tried to wriggle away. Looking over his shoulder, he snarled, "And *you*…crossing the yellow line, was it? You'll do anything to harass my boys!"

"Centreville police, we had nothing to do with it, Devlin," Dixon replied.

"Let go of me, boy!" Devlin squirmed in Penance's solid grasp.

"I will if you calm down. The truth is, heroin from the Mexicans is the least of our concerns," Penance said.

"Mexicans?" Devlin relaxed his body enough that Penance let him free. Spinning to face his son again, he spat, "That who you're doin' favors for? The damn Mexicans?"

Billy shook, "I didn't know…"

"Who'd you think was producing that stuff? Your backwoods friends across the tracks? Boy, you and Butch are battling for the top spot on the dumb list, ain't ya?"

"What we want to know is..." Penance started before the door opened again. Police Chief Pruitt scanned the room cautiously before whispering in Dixon's ear.

"Well, shoot. That complicates things a bit," Dixon announced. "I hope you find this bit of bad news incentivizing for telling us what we need to know."

"Not one for keeping the Mexican's secrets, but why should he help you?" Delvin asked.

Dixon looked grim, "Because I think those Mexicans have kidnapped your daughter."

TWENTY-SIX

S hannon Whatcom had barely walked out of the shop with her ice cream. Taking a lick, she walked towards her car. As she dug in her pocket for her keys, a hand was clamped on her mouth as an arm wrapped around her and flung her into the open door of a van. A man waiting inside pinned her down and stretched duct tape over her mouth before she could utter a word.

The man who grabbed her slammed the door shut and raced to the driver's door. Putting the van in gear, he mashed the accelerator.

Shannon tried to wriggle free, the whole time, shrieking helplessly through the tape.

"Easy, *chica*. This will all go better if you just calm down," the man in back snarled.

Shannon rolled to the side, squirming away from the man. Reaching for the door handle, a pair of arms tackled her. The weight of the man pressed down on her.

"You got some fight in you, I like that," the man licked his lips as he righted her. Studying her for a moment, he lashed out, the back of his fist striking Shannon, knocking her to the floor of the van. "You're a gorgeous piece, too. You'll fetch top dollar, if we don't use you up ourselves first."

The instant Delvin Whatcom heard the news of his daughter's kidnapping; he lunged across the table at his son. His hands full of his boy's collar when Penance and Dixon pulled him off. "If anything happens to your sister, I'll whoop you myself, boy!"

"He won't be any good to us if you wring his neck first. Let us get the information we need, and then you can have at him," Penance suggested. Comfortable Devlin was properly restrained, the FBI agent queried. "What do you know of the operation in Centreville?"

Billy looked at the FBI agent, at his father and then back at Penance, "I deliver…uhh…herbs and vegetables to the club behind the bar. They pay top dollar. Lany told me I…we could make even more if I carry *their* stuff into Sawyer, especially if we add their products to our route sales."

"You decided to do this on your own?" Devlin leaned in.

"Just figured I'd try. Make a run or two, and show you the money," Billy replied.

"And how'd that work out?" Devlin pressed.

Penance interjected the family debate, "Following the path of the drugs is all well in good, and believe me, we plan on getting to that. But right now, I want to focus on the girl. How I can find your daughter, your sister."

"I don't know nothing about that. There were always pretty girls there. I didn't know they were kidnapped," Billy stammered.

"At that point, they likely weren't. Called by the lure of the party and a fix of their preferred substance," Penance replied. "The more dots we can connect, the better. The drugs, the bar, the people."

"Lany is the only guy I know. There were others around. The owner sometimes poked his head in…there were a couple of Mexicans around," Billy said.

"Tell me about these Hispanic fellas," Penance said, sitting on the edge of the table Billy was shackled.

"One was kinda cleaned up, spoke good English. The other, bigger fella, he didn't say much, when he did it was in Spanish," Billy shared.

"Anything particularly identifiable…tattoos, scars, anything like that?"

Billy thought for a moment, frowning like he was concentrating extra hard. "They both had tattoos. The little guy just had the one, matched the big fella's. The big fella had quite a few. And a row of what looked like scars on his upper arm."

"Death cuts," Dixon said.

"What?" Billy frowned.

"A knife cut for every life he's taken," Dixon said.

"About how many of those scars?" Penance asked.

"I don't know, six...many seven," Billy replied.

Penance turned to Dixon, "Get a sketch artist on a video meeting and get some mock-ups of Billy's little friends. Include the bar owner and Lany so that we can proliferate the whole works. Make sure to get as many of the tattoos as Billy can remember."

"Where are you headed?" the Bureau Director asked.

"Last known, work my way from there. Have the Centreville police watch the bar, report any movement in or out as well as the owner and Lany," Penance suggested.

"I'm on it," Police Chief Pruitt nodded.

"Bubba, you're with me. I could use someone with the lay of the land," Penance said.

Bubba looked at his chief, who nodded.

Devlin Whatcom stepped in front of Penance. Squaring up, he looked Penance in the eye. "I appreciate any efforts you put forth to get my baby girl back. You see to it your actions don't get her killed," Devlin snarled.

"If anything happens to Shannon, it's on your boy," Penance declared and walked out of the room.

Penance drove the site where Sawyer police located Shannon's car. Penance wheeled his head around, pointing at nearby businesses, "Pull whatever security camera footage we can from these shops..."

Bubba paused as he studied the FBI agent, "Uhm, this is Sawyer, Penance. Ain't no one with cameras."

Penance nodded absently, "Well, let's see if we can't round up some witnesses. I'll start here at the ice cream shop. That building and the parking lot has a good vantage. You try over there."

"I'm on it," Bubba agreed and headed towards the coffee shop across the street.

Penance leaned against the walk-up order window of the ice cream shop.

"What can I get you, mister?" a young voice called to the head peering out of the shop window.

"I am a federal agent. I was hoping that you might have seen something this afternoon," Penance replied.

"The van that pulled out of here. Skinny feller and a husky feller. Eyeing Shannon Whatcom walk to her car and then pulled out here like their butts were on fire," the ice cream shop employee said.

Penance cocked his head at the young girl, "You didn't think to call the police?"

The attendant looked confused. "For what? Two guys eyein' Shannon and driving away quick?"

"Did you notice that after all that looking and fasting driving, Ms. Whatcom's car was still parked in your parking lot?" Penance pursued.

"I did," the attendant drawled. "While a bit odd, I've taken to stay out of the Whatcom family's affairs."

"That, I can understand," Penance admitted. "What can you tell me about the van?"

"It was kinda old and faded. Had some sort of car parts logo on the side."

Penance nodded, "Okay, that's good. I can use that. What color was the van?"

"Grey…dirty white? The car parts were orange and blue," the attendant said confidently, smiling at her recollection.

"Thank you," Penance said.

"You sure I can't get you an ice cream? Law officers get a free cone…"

Penance looked over towards the florist shop where he saw Bubba preparing to cross the street. "Sure, why not? Do you have swirl?"

As Bubba reached Penance, who was standing alongside the Porsche, the FBI agent held out the ice cream cone.

"For me?" Bubba grinned, his typically deep voice rising a few octaves.

"How'd the florist shop go?"

"They kinda saw a van and Shannon Whatcom and the van pull away quick-like. And then saw Shannon's Jeep was still there," Bubba reported.

"And?"

"And they said they tend to stay out of the Whatcom family's business," Bubba said.

"Yeah, I got that one, too."

"Now what?" the Sawyer police officer asked.

"We head towards Centreville unless we get a call that steers us otherwise," Penance said, opening the driver's side door. "Mind finishing that before you get in?"

Bubba looked at the cone and back at the FBI agent. With a grin, he shoved the ice cream, cone and all into his mouth and climbed into the Porsche.

Penance and Bubba pulled up alongside the bar in Centreville. Bubba looked at the FBI agent, "This ain't my jurisdiction."

"It is mine," Penance said. "Let's go."

Walking around to the back of the building, the FBI agent approached the private room door. No one was manning it. Checking the door handle, he found it locked. Placing an ear against the door, he listened intently but did not hear any sounds from the room on the other side.

"Look over there," Penance said to Bubba. The officer turned his head, unsure of what he was to be looking at. With a quick kick to the door handle, the door splintered away from the frame. "Hmm. Seems to be open."

The room was dark. It was filled with stale odors but seemed to have not been in use for days. Walking through the room, the agent scanned what he could. "Look for papers, receipts, matchbooks, food containers…anything that people might discard," Penance said to Bubba.

The officer nodded and began poking around the room. Making a note of anything referencing fuel, entertainment or food, but finding nothing else of use, they made their way to the door for the main bar.

Penance gave it a heave, surprised to find it swing open freely. Finding themselves in the back room of the bar, they were surprised to come face to face with the bartender.

"What the hell…"

"You should check your locks, they don't seem to be working," Penance said.

The bartender looked confused as to how he should react to the intrusion.

"Take it easy, we just need to ask a few questions," Penance tired to put the bartender at ease.

"Is this about the club in back? As you can see, I put an end to it after your last visit. I realized being ignorant was no excuse for allowing that b.s. on my property," the bartender protested.

"I see that, and I'd agree with you, it really is no excuse. But, I'm glad to see that filth shut down," the FBI agent acknowledged. "Now, we're not here for you, though I am happy to take down anyone associated. How helpful would you like to be?"

"It's like I said, I took a little cash to look the other way. Part of the deal was not asking lots of questions. I don't know how much I'll be able to offer," the bartender said.

"What do you say we give it a go just the same," Penance suggested. "Someone came into your bar and said, how about you open your back room for some cash, don't ask don't tell."

"That's about right," the bartender nodded.

"Who?"

"Local greaser named Johnny T. Said it was just going to be kind of like a speakeasy, nothing too bad," the bartender shared.

"Did you know they were luring kids?"

"Not at first, but I'd see the…uh, clientele go by and figured. By then, Johnny T. warned me that pulling out would be bad for both of us."

"Did you further know that a lot of those kids ended up on the backs of milk cartons?" Penance asked, getting heated in the conversation.

The bartender looked confused, "What do you mean?"

"The underage drinking and drugs was the cheese for a kidnapping mouse trap. Most likely sold off as sex slaves."

"I've heard about stuff like that. You think that's what was happening?"

"Afraid I'm pretty sure," Penance nodded.

The bartender stepped back, shaking his head. "No wonder you came in here looking like you were looking for an excuse to lay into me."

"My tolerance is low," Penance added. "Where can we find this Johnny T.?"

"Word is, he has a little shack in Possum Holler," the bartender said.

The FBI agent looked incredulous, "Possum Holler, that can't be…"

"I know where it's at," Bubba piped in.

"Possum Holler…"

Bubba shrugged, "Possum Corner is the real name. Not far from the Louisiana border along the river."

"Yep, this place just keeps getting better," Penance said. "Let's go find this Johnny T."

Pausing on his way out, he turned, "If I find you had any more to do with this, rest assured, I will hunt you down, and this conversation will go very different."

With Bubba's help, Penance guided the Porsche SUV down a rutted dirt road not far from the Homochito River, just east of the Mississippi. The myriad of crossroads deep within the brush caused the FBI Special Agent to shake his head. "I don't know how we will find anything in this mess," Penance said. "Don't suppose you have access to a helicopter?"

Bubba shook his head, "No, but I have a few ideas. Places where a van can go and ruling out places I know a van couldn't make it, too swampy."

Penance nodded in approval, "Alright. I'll follow your lead."

For two hours, the pair crisscrossed through the Possum Corner back roads and brush. They would stop at cabins, check tire patterns on the roads and continue to narrow their search. Finally, they came to a remote cabin that looked like it had been lived in recently. Penance noted the number of fast-food containers in the steel drum that served as a trash can.

Weapons drawn, they approached the cabin. Penance motioned for Bubba to stop short as he pressed close to the single window in the front of the cabin. No voices or movement could be detected. Holding up his cellphone, hit the video record button and positioned the phone so just the tip of the camera breached the frame of the window. The FBI Agent slowly turned the phone in a one-hundred and eighty-degree arch and pulled it back down.

Hitting play, he didn't see any activity in the cabin. Sliding the phone back into the breast pocket of his jacket, he readied his firearm and swung over to the door. With a quick turn of the handle, he launched inside the cabin. Penance's eyes followed the tip of his Beretta as he scanned the room.

Lying in that back of the room, he spied a body crumpled under a small table, a clean hole through the man's forehead. As Bubba approached from behind him, Penance waved for him to cover the door and watch the driveway. Moving throughout the cabin's one additional room – a bedroom just past a small galley kitchen that was open to the rest of the cabin, he holstered his weapon, "We're clear."

"That our guy?" Bubba asked, nodding at the body on the floor as he called the scene into the County Sheriff.

"I am afraid so," Penance said. Checking the man's pockets. His wallet was missing, but his phone was in his pocket.

Penance fumbled with the cellphone, stuck on the lock screen. Hitting a button, he lifted the lifeless man by the collar, holding the phone's camera up to his face. In an instant, the phone turned on. "Gotta love facial recognition," the agent mumbled to himself.

"This is Johnny T," Penance confirmed. "Let's see what we can learn from him." Scrolling through the text and emails, there was little other than cryptic notes, presumably from his Las Piratas contact, and the usual social gibberish a lowlife would communicate to his similar friends.

Scrolling through the apps, he clicked on the map tool. Penance pulled up its history and smiled, "I'm sorry we weren't able to visit with you, Johnny T., but I think you have given us something to go on."

With his own phone, he dialed Deputy Director Dixon, "I'm going to send you a map history off of a dead guy's cellphone. You think you can add it to the other area data points that Annie and we have collected regarding this case? We might be able to center in on a prime area where our sleazebags are holding the girls."

"Sure thing. I'll plot it out. You coming back into the office?" Dixon asked.

"Yes, unless you call with coordinates for our next step," Penance replied hopefully.

"I'll see what I can do," the Deputy Director said.

Slipping his phone back in his pocket, Penance eyed Bubba, "Let's poke around, see if there are any other clues, and get out of here."

Bubba wrinkled his nose, "What about Johnny T.?"

Penance shrugged, "He'll be fine. Not going to get any more dead before county gets here."

The agent studied the dead man. Pointing to the back of the head. "Double-tap." Using a plastic fork that was on the table, Penance carefully moved Johnny T's hair out of the way. "See the bullet hole here. It starts nice and round up top and then curves in a bit to make another nice circle. Like a tiny little two ball snowman. Two bullets. Killed execution-style."

The police officer looked at Penance, "What does that mean?"

"It means the *Las Piratas* at least teach their thugs proper execution technique."

TWENTY-SEVEN

Finding nothing to expressly point to where the *Las Piratas* may have been hiding the girls, Penance urged Bubba back to the SUV and sped towards the FBI office, making quick work of the dirt roads in the four-wheel-drive Porsche.

Annie Hunt and Deputy Director Dixon were pouring over a large map they had tacked to the far wall. Oversized thumbtacks dotted the map, both Annie and Dixon worked highlighters to draw large circles around the thumbtacks. In two places on the map, several of the large rings met, leaving a dark orange area where the green and pink highlighter colors mixed.

"I see you're making progress," Penance said.

Dixon and Annie both jumped a little at the voice, both concentrating on their work.

"Remind me to put a bell on the office door, you've clearly learned to avoid the squeak," Dixon muttered to Annie. "We have three zones that intersect the various points from the phone, from witness accounts and the various activities that we currently know these guys have operated in."

Penance studied the map. "Not this one."

Annie looked at where Penance was pointing and then turned, "Why not there?"

"Too much travel on the main roads. If they are transporting the girls and get pulled over for a simple traffic violation, it would be game over. Too much eye witness potential too," the FBI agent replied. Leaning in close to the map, he inspected the other two locations.

"It's gotta be in here," Bubba tapped a space on the map.

"Jackson Point," Dixon nodded. "That'd be a good place to lay low."

"Jackson Point?" Penance asked.

"It's this area where Mississippi juts out towards Louisiana. Mostly ghost towns and hardwood swamps. Some rough roads veined throughout," Dixon replied.

"Looks like a big area," Penance said, studying the map.

"I'd start here around Kienstra. Might be some structures intact enough you could clean them out and use as a holding shelter," Dixon added.

"You'd have access at the river to go by boat or connect through the dirt road to US 61," Bubba said.

"Alright, we're going to need support—four additional teams. We can head through Jackson Point from the south, have another team head in from the north, have two opposing teams on the Louisiana side, and one running the river. We'll either find them or flush them out, hopefully right into one of the teams," Penance directed.

"I'll make the calls," Dixon said, making a beeline for his office.

Before the Deputy Director could make his first call, his phone rang. "Penance!" he called. "Witness reported seeing the van. Passed through Woodville heading west less than five minutes ago."

Without a word, Penance sprinted towards the door with Annie and Bubba in tow. "You two stay with Dixon, set up the southern team. I'll meet you as soon as I can."

Racing to the Porsche, Penance fired up the engine, slammed it into gear, and pressed the sensitive throttle to the floor, rocketing the German SUV out of the parking lot and screaming through Main Street. Weaving around the modest traffic of town, he kept the accelerator punched.

Beyond the limits of the town, Penance had the gas pegged. With the speedometer dancing around 140 mph, he closed the distance very quickly. Passing through Woodville, he saw the Sheriff's deputy on the side of the road.

Guiding the Porsche to a stop, he rolled down the window. "That the witness who saw the van?"

"It is," the deputy nodded.

Holding up his phone, Penance showed the picture of the van that he took outside of the county holding facility, "This the van you saw?"

The witness leaned close to the passenger window to see the phone and nodded.

"Thank you," Penance said. Slipping the Porsche into gear, he mashed the accelerator, pulling away with a chirp of the tires.

Watching the map on the GPS, he guessed the route that van might head. Pushing his SUV to its limits, he sped along, turning the trees to a blur outside of his window. Around a large bend, just miles before an access road for Jackson Point, Penance spied a vehicle in his windshield.

At the speed he was pushing the SUV, the vehicle changed from a speck to a fully perceivable van. Shooting past, Penance slammed on the brakes. The well-tuned car held a straight line until it slowed enough and Penance yanked the wheel, careening the Porsche into a one-hundred and eighty-degree turn. Facing the van, he could hear the squeal of brakes as the van snaked its way to a stop.

Two men with semi-automatic weapons jumped out, each screaming at Penance. "What the hell's wrong with you, gringo. You best move along."

"I'm a federal agent. I need you to put your weapons down," Penance called.

The driver laughed, shooting a look to the man opposite him. With a nod, the passenger raised his weapon. Penance squeezed the trigger on his Beretta, placing a slug in the gunman's shoulder, knocking him back and causing him to drop his gun.

Swinging the gun in the driver's direction, Penance saw the barrel of the semi-automatic trained on him. Diving into the ditch along the side of the road as bullets peppered the pavement. As the driver made his death-triangle walk around the nose of the van, closing in on the federal agent, Penance flattened his stomach to the ground and eased his eyes above the blacktop. Squeezing off a round, he sent a bullet into the driver's ankle. As the driver fell to the ground, Penance fired a second shot catching the gunman in the chest.

Penance launched himself up and kicked away the semi-automatic from the passenger who had recovered and was trying to determine how to steady the gun with his non-dominant hand. Pointing the Beretta at his head, Penance said, "I only need one of you alive. Wouldn't you like that to be you?"

The man looked up at the FBI agent and relented a sullen nod.

"Now, I'm going to handcuff you to the door handle. I like these older vans. Most newer cars don't have handles like these anymore. I've gotta use a tow-hook on the bumper…I've even used the little holes on the chassis where the jack goes, you know, like when you blow a tire. Not convenient…or comfortable, I imagine, but real sturdy," Penance informed the gunman as he shackled him to the van.

"Now to see about your friend," Penance declared. Walking around the van, he found the driver gasping for air, laid out on the pavement. Even in his state, he tried to reach for his weapon as he saw the FBI agent approach. "You have bigger problems than trying to shoot me. Keeping at least some of your blood inside your veins, for instance. Let's concentrate on that."

Penance scooted the man's weapons out of reach and began working on his injuries. Slapping the driver lightly on the cheek, the agent commanded, "I need you to stay awake. I'll dress your ankle, but you are going to need to continue to apply pressure to your chest. That's the one that will kill you."

The man struggled and gurgled as he moved, staring at Penance.

"Pretty sure I winged your lung, I wanted to make sure I missed your heart. Uncomfortable to breathe, I know, but you'll live," the agent said and added, "Most likely."

Collecting the weapons, he carried them to the back of the van. Using the keys he took from the ignition, he opened the rear of the van to find Shannon Whatcom bound, gagged and duct-taped inside of a refrigerator box.

Gently gliding the Whatcom girl out of the box, Penance began working on her restraints, starting with the gag around her mouth. Tear and mascara stained eyes stared at the FBI agent.

"It's okay. You're going to be alright," Penance said. Before he could finish removing her bindings, she leaned into his chest. Sighing, Penance wrapped his arms around the girl and held her tight, trying to comfort her after her tortuous ordeal.

TWENTY-EIGHT

Sirens closed in from a distance. Wilkinson County sheriff's deputies and EMTs rallied around Penance.

Penance provided a brief situational report to the deputies as EMTs began working on the *Las Piratas* gunmen. The driver was quickly loaded in the back of an ambulance and carted off.

As rescuers tended to the passenger, Penance waved the EMTs off, "This one's with me." The FBI agent led him back to the van and locked him once more to the door handle.

Penance glared at the gang member. "The girls."

"I ain't telling you nothing, *puta!*" gunman spat.

Penance frowned, "I know enough Spanish to know that's naughty."

A Ford SUV pulled up to the scene. Deputy Director Dixon and Assistant DA Annie Hunt got out and spied the FBI agent.

Penance pulled away from the *Las Piratas* member to confer.

"So, what's the deal?" Dixon asked.

"Shannon Whatcom is safe. She's over with the EMT's. The driver was shot…a couple of times, nothing life-threatening, probably. He's already been transported by ambulance. He had a passenger who is currently handcuffed to their van," Penance informed the two.

"Any word on the rest of the girls?" Annie asked.

"I was just getting into that conversation," Penance said.

"What happens now?" Annie pressed.

Penance declared, "We don't have much time. These two would have been expected within a certain window. If that window isn't met, they'll pack up shop."

Annie "What about the girls?"

Penance looked serious, "They'd kill them or move them as far away as fast as they could. Either way, they'd be lost forever."

The Assistant District Attorney looked Penance in the eye, "Then we better find them, and quick."

The FBI agent nodded. Without another word, he pulled the van keys out of his pocket and strode quickly to the driver's seat. Slipping the key into the ignition, he gave it a twist. Slamming the driver's side door shut, he slid the transmission into gear.

"Uh, Mr. Agent! Aren't you forgetting something?" the gunman said, still tethered to the passenger side door handle.

"Depends, you got anything to tell me?" Penance asked.

The man looked confused, "Look, if they know the information came from me; I'm a dead man."

Penance stomped on the accelerator, causing the tires to chirp above the roar of the engine lurching the van forward. The gunman leaped with it.

"You're crazy, man!" the *Las Piratas* henchmen screamed.

"Crazy is thinking it is okay to kidnap girls and sell them for…whatever you are doing with them," Penance said. Returning his focus on the windshield, he pressed the gas.

The gunman made desperate strides to keep up with the van. Looking out of the open passenger-side door, Penance asked, "Cardio's important. How long you think you can hang in there?"

The thug let out a string of Spanish-infused profanity.

"I'll tell you what, all you have to do is tell me left, right or straight. How'd that be?" Penance offered, pressing the accelerator harder.

Coming up to an intersection, the FBI agent looked towards the gang member, "Well...time to do your job."

The gunman studied Penance and then the road, in between pants, he gasped, "Left!"

Penance wheeled the van to the left, the gunman momentarily catching air while the van turned before returning to his sprint alongside.

The man looked close to exhaustion, struggling to maintain his pace. Penance slammed on the brakes, causing the man to drag on the passenger door. Penance slowed to a stop. Looking at the gang member, he said, "I was thinking, wouldn't this be easier from inside the cab?"

"Please...," the gunman gasped.

"To be clear, if I let you inside, you will tell me exactly how to find those girls as efficiently as possible, or I promise, you will be handcuffed to the bumper and I'll see how this thing does in the swamp," Penance declared.

"Alright. Alright," the man conceded. "I think you are crazier than the *Las Piratas* anyway, man."

"Great!" Penance said with a cheerful grin as he hopped out of the driver's seat and walked around the van and unlocked the handcuffs. "Let's go!"

Shoving the man inside the van and re-handcuffing him to the interior handle of the van.

Driving north on rural roads through the St. Catherine Creek Wildlife Refuge, they headed for the outskirts of Natchez. Calling it in, Penance demanded that the first arrivals observe and wait. He did not want the girls to be caught in the crossfire, or worse, sacrificed by the *Las Piratas*.

Butch Whatcom rolled a cigarette on the hood of his truck outside of the town police station. He and his father arrived to receive updates on Shannon. In addition to the police department, Devlin had his small army of workers doing their own investigation.

Devlin knew two things; he had to find his daughter alive and well, and the culprits would pay dearly. Not much happened in Wilkinson County without his knowledge and approval. He was confident that his people would outpace the police, but he didn't want to leave any stone unturned.

Joining his son in the parking lot, he asked, "Anything from the boys?"

Butch shook his head, "Not yet. They are aware of the *Las Piratas* and are following up with Billy's contacts." He licked the paper and smoothed the cigarette tight. "Anything inside?"

Devlin shook his head. "Nothing they would share. Not like I expect anything from that lot. Our boys had better pull through, however."

"They will," Butch assured.

Devlin glared, "You didn't know anything about these thugs?"

Butch shrugged, "I knew they existed. I was told they stayed out of our business."

"And your brother?"

"I ain't his babysitter. I figured he was seeing a girl in Centreville or whatever," Butch deferred.

"Time for you to grow up and keep better tabs on what is going on in our organization, boy," the Whatcom patriarch snarled.

"I guess that means little brother Billy, too, huh?" Butch scoffed.

Before Devlin could respond, a Cadillac Escalade pulled up between them and the police station. Both front and rear seat heavily tinted windows rolled down. From the back window, a 7.62mm machine gun pointed at the pair. Devlin's anger flared, but a bob of the rifle barrel froze him in his tracks.

In the front passenger seat, a *Las Piratas* Lieutenant looked at the two Whatcom men, "Little Billy is in custody. You need to shut him up before we do it permanently. *Las Piratas* can reach anyone, anywhere." Flinging a piece of paper out of the window, he added, "We can reach your whole family."

Without another word, the Escalade roared off, kicking the paper they discarded into the air. Butch snatched it and angrily handed it to his father.

Devlin grabbed the sheet and studied it. Shannon bound in the back of the van, tears streaking from horrified eyes stared at the camera.

"Find that Cadillac," Devlin snapped.

Butch nodded and began broadcasting the word through their network.

Penance stopped the van a half a mile from the transport site. The Las Piratas gunman described it as an abandoned general store and service station between the towns of Cloverdale and Natchez. Several Wilkinson County sheriff's deputies pulled alongside him.

"The staties are en route. They have an entourage with a S.W.A.T. team," the deputy who pulled up alongside the van said.

"What's their ETA?" Penance asked.

"Probably about fifteen."

"Call off the S.W.A.T. Have them pull off somewhere nondescript and bury themselves. The *Las Piratas*, for as evil as they are, are smart. They have lookouts. If someone sees S.W.A.T. coming, those girls are as good as dead," Penance instructed.

The deputy nodded and made the call.

As two more deputies arrived, Penance got out and addressed the group. "Here's the play before the staties mess things up. Have them come in behind us and play mop up. I'll get my deputy director to enforce it in case you catch flack."

Casting a glance towards the *Las Piratas* gang member, the FBI agent hatched his plan. "They are expecting this van with two gang members and hostage. That gets us to the front door. We need to get their attention out front while the girls in the house are secured. I need one of you as a driver, maybe another in the back, if nothing else, to have your gun trained on the back of that man's head.

I need the rest of you to follow the assault from the tail. We'll have maybe forty-five seconds before they realize the things aren't right. You can join the fray then."

"And the girls, sir?" a deputy asked.

"I'll get them. When you drive the van up, do so at speed. Lay on the horn a bit, but be ready to fight. It should draw them out, give me the time I need to insert myself into the building and locate the girls," Penance declared.

"You don't want back up?"

"That part of the operation requires stealth. Once stealth is lost, be prepared for a battle. I want that battle out front," Penance replied. "Let's drive up. Let me out. I'll slip through the woods and up to the house. Give me ninety seconds and bring the van."

Nodding, a deputy climbed in the van. Penance stood on the bumper and held onto the back-up mirror to stabilize himself. The Sheriff's deputies in their cruisers held back as the van drove forward. Just before the general store, the van pulled over, allowing Penance to hop off and jog through the woods.

Watching his footfalls carefully, he avoided branches, twigs and leaves the best he could. He was so focused on his task, he even forgot to fret about the snakes and other critters that wanted to bite, sting, or chew on him as he slid through.

Closing in on the defunct store, he saw a puff of smoke billow from behind a tree. Lining his own body against a tree, he watched. The left shoulder of a man appeared on the edge of the tree. Using extreme stealth, he slunk toward the tree, keeping an eye on movement on either side while sweeping the area for other bodies.

Penance breathed softly and carefully approached the tree. Watching intently, he waited for the person on the other side to move slightly more left or right. As another burst of smoke billowed, the man shuffled just to the left of the tree.

Striking with viper-like speed, Penance sprung at the man, hooking his left hand around the tree, catching the man by his throat, slamming the back of his head into the tree. From the right side of the tree, Penance grabbed the man's right arm, which was already reaching for the semi-automatic rifle slung on his right shoulder. Clutching the weapon himself, Penance curled around the left side of the tree, his hand on the man's throat so that he could not scream. Bringing the man's gun around, the FBI agent slammed the butt into his temple. Guiding the man by his throat, he gently let him melt into unconsciousness at the base of the tree.

Making a quick scan to ensure no one witnessed the takedown and there were no more *Las Piratas* nearby, he crept towards the derelict store.

Crouching behind the bushes, Penance could see more activity. All four corners of the building were manned. Most of their attention was out front, which the FBI agent planned to use to his advantage.

As the *Las Piratas* van driven by the Wilkinson County deputy careened wildly down the road and screeched into a four-wheel drift just short of the general store, each *Las Piratas* posted instinctively moved towards the van. Splitting the two rearward guards, Penance sprinted to the storeroom door.

With a quick strike with the gun he retrieved, Penance freed the padlock from its hold and swung open the door. The storeroom was the best place to hold the girls, with the exception of a rear entry. Penance did a quick scan of the half dozen girls surprised by his appearance. Motioning for them to be silent and stay low against the side walls of the room, he quickly dispatched the *Las Piratas,* who burst into the storeroom from the front of the store. From the dark storeroom, the men silhouetted from the light streaming into the front room. With two quick shots, both men were down before their eyes could adjust to the dark.

Gunfire erupted from the front of the store. Penance crept to the door to inspect the men he shot and secure their weapons. From the vantage of the door, he saw a man with a long gun trying to snipe the deputies out front.

"Hey!" Penance yelled, with his Beretta trained in the sniper's direction.

Swinging the gun towards the FBI agent's direction, the gunman was quickly put down before he could sight Penance.

Light suddenly flooded the storeroom. One of the Las Piratas rear guards stood in the doorway with a Molotov cocktail, readying to toss the incendiary into the room. With a quick shot, Penance shattered the bottle, leaking fluid all over the gang member who sighted Penance in the doorway of the store. His right side bursting into flames, the man raised his gun hand.

Penance squeezed his trigger in rapid sequence sending the burning man flailing backward, falling on the ground behind the store.

Sufficient flaming liquid leaked onto the decaying wood floor of the storeroom, setting the room quickly ablaze. Penance burst into the store, scanning for more *Las Piratas* before urging the girls to follow him through and way from the flames.

A glance out of the store windows told Penance that the deputies, now joined by the state police, had the situation outside under control. Ushering the girls outside and safely away from the fully involved building, Penance positioned them between two state patrol cars, having them sit or squat low. At the same time, he and the responding officers ensured there were no residual gang members that would pose them a threat.

The swarm of police officers began a thorough search of the surrounding woods to ensure *Las Piratas* gang members hadn't slipped away from the scene. Penance turned his attention to Bureau Chief Dixon and Assistant District Attorney Annie Hunt, who arrived on the scene with a pair of women.

Surveying the scene, Annie spoke directly to the two women and approached Penance.

Eyeing the burning building, gang members either receiving treatment or awaiting the coroner, she quipped, "Not hard to find one of your scenes, Agent Penance."

The FBI agent made a quick scan of the area, "They're not all mine. That one…right there, I didn't shoot *him*. And those two being checked by the medic, clearly not my work." Staring at the fully engulfed service station, "I did kind of do that," he admitted.

Annie laughed despite herself. Casting a glance at the girls he had rescued, "Nice work. Were you…able to get them all out?"

Penance nodded, "I did. What happens to them now?"

"The social workers will bring them to Jackson. Allow the state police and FBI to get their statements, but more importantly, determine where their homes are and see if they can't get them headed the right direction. They'll get the care that they need as well. I can only imagine the trauma they have endured," Annie said. "You saved them from a much worse fate."

"I'm glad we were able to get there in time," Penance nodded. "They were on a kill order, if anything went wrong. A guy was about to toss in a Molotov cocktail when he decided to wear it instead, after I shot him. By then, the state and county guys had enough of the situation out front in hand. I was able to get them to safety."

"Solid work, Agent Penance," Deputy Director Dixon chimed in. "Where does this leave us?"

"We've certainly disrupted their supply line in western Mississippi and eastern Louisiana. We don't know how many girls lives they've ruined or how many in other locations need saving," Penance replied.

"I'll get our team in Jackson to see what they can get from the *Las Piratas* we have rounded up," Dixon suggested.

"Question I have, is will they humbly reroute their distribution, or will they react? They targeted Shannon Whatcom to send a message," Penance declared.

Annie wrinkled her nose, "What do you mean?"

"Smaller rings will break up and disappear when confronted. Maybe they pop somewhere else. Maybe they lick their wounds and go into another line to make a living. Larger cartels don't like to be pushed around by anyone, and they aren't afraid of anyone," Penance cautioned and shrugged, "I guess we'll see. On the other hand, we have exposed this marketplace under Sanchez and his men to be inept. The cartel will likely route through another pipeline – Florida or the southwest."

"We'll put those districts on high alert. The Jackson team is here. They can perform clean up with the state and counties. Give their lead your perspective and then head home, you had a long day," Dixon declared to his agent.

Penance nodded and began to head towards the recently arrived FBI contingent. Annie followed him a few steps and gently grabbed his arm. The weary agent spun to face her.

"I was hoping we could catch up tomorrow and debrief. I appreciate you taking on this case. It was far more involved than I had ever imagined," Annie said.

Nodding, Penance agreed, "Sure. At your office or the bureau…?"

"I was thinking, maybe more at my house? I could make dinner," the Assistant District Attorney suggested. Hearing her own words resonate out loud, she quickly blurted, "Just less distraction. Besides, there is a lot to cover. I just figured it would be more comfortable."

Penance grinned, "I'm sure your home would be more comfortable. Only, you don't look comfortable yourself right now."

Annie frowned, "No, I mean…I'm fine. Yes, just want to be clear my intentions are professional, of course."

"Of course. That would be fine, professionally," Penance nodded. Taking a stride towards the Jackson FBI team, he paused. "It's a date then."

Whisking away, he left Annie to fume at her sophomoric handling of the appointment. "It's not a date!" she mumbled to herself.

TWENTY-NINE

Alex Penance was glad to park the Porsche in front of the cottage. Walking through the front door he didn't even wince when he mumbled to himself that he was happy to be "home". The day was a long one both in duration as well as physical and emotional drain. He knew Shannon Whatcom's life was in his hands. He wasn't at all sure how that was going to turn out. He had an even worse prognosis for the rest of the girls that were being held by the *Las Piratas*.

All in all, he was pleased with the net result. It was a good day for the good guys.

Entering the kitchen, desperately hoping he had a beer left in the fridge, he froze. An object on the counter caught his attention. Taking a quick scan around the house, he freed his service weapon. Poking his head into the bedroom and then the bathroom, he peered around the corners, ensuring he was indeed in the cottage alone. Moving to the back porch, he scanned the yard towards the river. Opening the door, he stepped out, listing for footfalls. Satisfied he was alone, he placed the gun on the counter.

Studying the out of place item, he found a card underneath it. Slipping the card out it, he read, "Agent Penance, our daughter is a treasure. We are grateful for your effort in her safe return. Delvin Whatcom."

Placing the card down, he picked up the gift that one of the Whatcom's men had broken into his house to place. It was a wooden box. Lifting it, he felt that it had some heft to it. Sliding the box lid open, it revealed a bottle of Pappy Van Winkle whiskey.

Not being a big whiskey drinker, he set the bottle back on the counter. Checking the fridge and finding it bare of refreshment, he shrugged and returned to the bourbon whiskey. "I might as well give this a try."

Pouring two fingers into a glass, he stepped out on the back porch and sat in one of the resin chairs. Just getting off of his feet felt like a luxury. Leaning back, he pulled the glass to his lips. The caramel and smoke tones of the golden liquid smelled intriguing and yet odd to Penance. Tilting the glass back, he took a sip.

The flavors hit the back of his throat while the alcohol rose through his sinuses. Wincing, he studied the glass, realizing he couldn't see much of it in the dark.

Penance was startled to hear a giggle among the harmony of crickets and frogs.

"You shouldn't cringe when you drink the good stuff, Pappy's the best," Shannon Whatcom laughed as she strode forward onto the porch.

"Shannon?" Penance declared. "What are you doing here?"

"I came to thank you, but I now I see you need *my* help," Shannon drawled. "Here, let me guide you through the finest of southern experiences. Mind if I get a glass?"

"Help yourself," Penance relented, swirling his glass in the air.

In moments, Shannon returned and pulled the other resin chair close to his.

"When you're new to whiskey, it's like…jumping in the creek in early Spring. You stick a toe in, you go real slow, it's got a bite to it," she breathed as she grabbed the bottle and poured two fingers for herself. "Sometimes it's just better to jump in."

Shannon pulled her glass to her lips and slammed the whiskey back. Swallowing the contents in a single gulp, she held her glass out as she savored the experience. "Let the heat draw you in, envelope you." Pouring another two fingers, she held her glass up. "And then you're ready to sit back and sip every drop down," she cooed.

Penance was drawn by the young Whatcom girl's presentation. It belied her rough edges and demonstrated a sultry, mature delivery that was undeniably impressive.

"Well, go on," she prodded. "Shoot it!"

Penance did as he was instructed and slammed the liquid down his throat. It had a slight medicinal quality, but was smoother than the sip, knocking off the rough edges. The alcohol still rose through his sinuses, yet provided an oddly pleasing complement to the warming of his throat as the liquid traveled down its path.

Shannon poured another dram into his glass.

Penance followed her suit and returned to sipping the beverage. It retained some bite, but the girl was right, it was more pleasant following the shot. Leaning back in his chair, he raised his glass, "I'm glad I was able to find you."

"I was scared as hell," Shannon admitted. "But when I heard your voice outside, I knew I was going to be alright. I just didn't want you to leave me. I felt safe."

"You heard about the other girls?" Penance asked.

Shannon nodded, "I did. I heard you thrashed those boys a good one."

"Most of them got what they deserved, as much as can be doled out on earth, I suppose," the FBI agent nodded.

"To the hero. To *my* hero," Shannon raised her glass and met it softly against his and took another sip.

"Isn't your family worried about you running around the countryside after what you went through?" Penance asked.

"Daddy would be beside himself if he knew I was out. I told him I was exhausted, which wasn't much of a lie, and I needed to go to bed," the Whatcom daughter replied. "They're grateful for what you did. But they're still pissed at all ya'll L.E.O.s and how Billy and Butch been treated."

"Billy was part of the reason the *Piratas* grabbed you," Penance scoffed.

"I know it. Daddy knows it too. He just figures Whatcom justice is a better way to resolve it," Shannon informed the agent.

"I see," Penance said, taking another sip. The longer he spent with the strange liquid, the more comfortable with it he was becoming.

Shannon leaned in, the whiskey from her breath mixing with his. "How about it, hero…can you help me feel safe?"

For a moment, Penance froze, his thoughts and emotions clouded with impulses and intrigue. He allowed Shannon's soft lips to linger against his. The whiskey on her lips and in her breath more intoxicating than the drink itself. Closing his eyes, he leaned back into his chair, pulling away. Taking a sip from his glass, he studied the attractive girl from Mississippi.

"I get it. All work and no play," Shannon said, settling back into her chair. "I still like you, though."

The pair drifted into silence, allowing the chorus of nocturnal singers to carry the moment as a soundtrack to the bourbon. As they consumed the third glass of tidy pours, the air on the back porch was as thick as the humid Mississippi night itself.

"I should get you back. If your family found you gone, they'd lose it," Penance suggested.

"Probably shoot the first person they saw near me," Shannon grinned.

"Probably," Penance admitted. "Even the more reason to get you home."

Shannon rolled eyes, "Alright. Just let me know when you want another lesson in fine southern delicacies." Licking the remnants of Pappy Van Winkle from her glistening lips, she sighed. Reluctantly, she accepted Penance's hand as he offered to help her up.

Letting the FBI agent's grip pull her up, she allowed her body to flow all of the way to his. Once more, she allowed her lips to hover close to his. "Thank you again for saving my life, Agent Penance." Planting a solid kiss on the agent, she pulled away. "It's okay, it was just a thank-you kiss, *this* time," she giggled.

"Let's go," Penance instructed, collecting the glasses and bottle, placing them inside the door.

THIRTY

Penance was the first to arrive in the office. Making a fresh pot of coffee, he settled at his desk and began working on his field report from the previous day's events. He sifted through the facts and witnesses, the searches, and the chases. He was judicious about explaining his interrogation of Shannon Whatcom's kidnapper, which ultimately led him to the holding facility that housed the rest of the missing girls.

Detailing the firefight and rescue at the abandoned general store, he looked up as Dixon walked in the office, his cellphone against his ear. Motioning to his agent, he had Penance follow him into his office.

Placing the phone down, Dixon settled into his chair, "That was Jackson."

"They get anything from the Las Piratas?"

Dixon looked stern, "I'll give them boys credit, they are a loyal, tight-lipped group of bastards. The only thing the agent in Jackson could get out of them is that they swear the *Las Piratas* will get their retribution, whatever that means."

"Forensics come with any evidence that might lead us towards any other girls?" Penance asked.

"No. The gang might be a bunch of hooligans, but they run a tight ship," Dixon admitted. "Their vehicles were clean, the store, as you know, was completely burned. I'd suggest they handcuff one to a van and see how much they could get from them driving down the road, if that wasn't just an alleged interrogation technique."

"Pretty sure that is not in the interrogation rule book, sir," Penance said calmly.

"No, you're probably right," Dixon nodded. "Think there is anything else we can squeeze out of Sanchez?"

Penance shook his head, "I doubt it. He's definitely drunk the Kool-Aid. Like the reports out of Jackson, he just muttered that the *Las Piratas* would be coming."

"Do you think they keep records of that stuff? Trafficking girls and where they sent them?"

"I don't. I think they have some way of communication so that they can notify their buyers when they have distribution – whether that's code or direct, I don't know. We've got to get one of them to talk," Penance looked off for a moment. "The thing is about these guys, is that they don't care about anything. They barely care about themselves. It's hard to get leverage on them. Anything on Sanchez' history?"

Dixon shrugged, "Not much. Like a lot of the cartel, they sort of just show up one day."

"See if his home country has anything on him. Do one of the family tree DNA kits for all I care," Penance said, getting up.

"Where are you going?"

"I'm going to go talk to the only *Las Piratas* member we have in our local custody. See what you can dig up and call me if you get anything."

"And if I can't?" Dixon asked.

"Then I guess I will have to be creative," Penance said, leaving the office.

Dixon had Sanchez waiting for Penance in the interrogation room. His hands shackled securely to a bar on his side of the table.

Alex Penance leaned back in his chair and set his heels on the table across from the gang leader.

"You still alive? Heh, not for long *puta*," Sanchez spat.

"You keep saying that, yet here I am. Your men tried to snatch the Whatcom girl...that didn't work out in their favor either. In fact, your entire Mississippi operation has been dismantled...by *me*," Penance answered.

"That just means *Las Piratas* got something special coming. They were coming for me, now, they'll come for the whole damn town," Sanchez warned.

Penance shrugged, "Their business here is dead. There is nothing for them here."

"They won't be coming back to do business. The cartel will torch this town to the ground to send a message to the next location they decide to set stakes in. I just hope they come and get me first. I want to watch you and this town burn."

Penance brushed the gangster's rhetoric off, "Yeah, yeah, I know...the big bad pirates. Very scary. I kind of hope you are right. It will save us from a bunch of extradition headaches."

Sanchez's face split into a wicked sneer, "Be careful what you ask for."

Returning to the office, Penance found Deputy Director Dixon with Colton Jennings and Annie Hunt. Bubba walked in close behind him.

"Well, the gang's all here," Penance said, "No pun intended."

Recounting his visit with Sanchez, the FBI agent shared the warning.

"I don't think it is just hot air," Dixon shared. "We are starting to get reports from Shreveport, Mobile. Baton

Rouge and Memphis that *Las Piratas* members have been picked up."

"They're coming from all sides," Jennings said.

"If they are catching that many, how many are getting through?" Penance asked.

"They'll be closing in fast," Dixon offered. Waving his hand for them to follow him, he walked over the large screen in the back of the office. Tied into his computer, he pulled up a series of photos. "I think this is what they mean by retribution. Here is what they left in their wake in a town not far from Victoria…and here just outside of Juarez when the Mexican police and army tried to make a stand."

The images on the screen seemed like they were out of war documentary. Buildings and cars were on fire. Human carnage littered the streets.

"In both incidents combined, over 483 people were slaughtered. Every building in both towns was deemed uninhabitable," Dixon declared.

Annie gasped, "That's half of Sawyer's population. More than half in Sawyer proper."

"They couldn't do that here," Jennings scoffed. Looking at the concerned expressions on both FBI agents, he recanted, "Could they?"

Penance looked serious, "If they bring enough men with them and the right firepower, they could do the people of Sawyer some serious harm."

"I've already requested assistance from other bureaus and the Mississippi state police, it will take them some time to get the necessary approvals, assemble and get here," Dixon stated.

"Approvals?" Jennings spat.

"It is a mere threat and a theory at this point, though the gang members being picked up by patrols suggests the threat is credible," Dixon said.

"Bubba, have Chief Pruitt set up patrols at every major intersection coming into Sawyer," Penance instructed.

Bubba nodded, "Chief Pruitt and the boys are out on patrol now; that's why he sent me to synch with you."

"Good. What frequency do you use, we should all synch to that one," Penance declared.

With Bubba's input, they all set radios to the same channel.

"Have the Sheriff's men secure the lock-up, that will be one of the first places, the *Las Piratas* try to hit," Penance suggested.

"What do the rest of us do in the meantime?" Jennings asked.

"I don't know…anyone up for a bite to eat?" Penance shrugged.

Despite grabbing a duffel bag full of shells and a shotgun, along with a pouch of extra magazines for his pistols, Penance left the bureau office casually. Dixon stayed back to man the phones, and Jennings declined the dinner invitation. Holding the passenger door to the Porsche open, Penance helped Annie in.

"Where to?" he asked.

Annie studied him for a moment. "How can you be so nonchalant with effectively a war coming our way?"

"We'll be okay. I'll make sure of it," Penance promised. Inside, he did not know what type of assault the gang was capable of in America. The fact that members had been picked up from multiple different directions had him concerned, but he did not want to worry Annie.

"I threatened you with dinner at my place. I suppose I should uphold my perilous offer," Annie said.

"Alright. I can be sous chef, I'm handy with a knife," Penance agreed and started the engine.

"So, what are we making?" Penance asked as they settled into Annie's kitchen.

"The first thing you are making is the cork in that wine bottle relieved of its duty," Annie replied, setting a cutting board out on the counter and sliding a wine screw towards the FBI agent.

Penance smiled as he went to work on the wine bottle, "Can do."

Accepting a glass, Annie took a solid sip. She looked across at Alex as she played with her drink, "You seem pretty calm."

"Is there something I should know about your dinner invitation?"

Annie looked aghast, "Oh, no. Nothing like that. I mean with the *piratas*."

Penance shrugged, "I'll deal with that problem as it comes. Who knows what they will bring. The thing about terrorists is if you can continue living your life...sharing a glass of wine with a beautiful woman, making a meal together...they lose."

Hoisting her glass in the air, "Then I guess we win."

Penance raised his glass with hers and smiled.

"You do make me feel...oddly safe," Annie shared.

"Oddly? Do you not usually feel safe?" Penance asked.

"Well, from a crime-perspective, yes. From spending time with a man perspective, no. Though there is a little voice screaming at me from the back of my head, suggesting that I shouldn't, I trust you. I do feel safe with you," Annie said. "I mean, you can be a bristled, opinionated pain in the rear...maybe a bit too honest at times. Maybe that's the comfort. I don't have to guess with you."

Unwittingly, the two leaned close to one another as they talked and played with their wine glasses. Annie stared intently at Alex' eyes. Feeling as though she may have lingered a bit too long, she abruptly snapped her head away. "We had better get this meal cooking. We have no idea what kind of night we are going to have," Annie declared.

"Oh?" Penance shot her a mischievous look."

Annie rolled her eyes, "I meant the *Las Piratas*."

"I know," Penance grinned. "Let me give you a hand.

Annie laid two catfish on the cutting board. "Think you can prep these, sous chef?"

Rolling up his sleeves, Penance approached the counter, "You bet."

When they finished their meal, Penance got up to gather the dishes. Annie stopped, "Leave them. I'll get to them later. I want to enjoy the evening. Come on, bring the wine."

The Assistant District Attorney picked up her glass and led her guest to the front porch. Sitting on the porch swing, she nodded toward the spot next to her, urging Penance to join her.

Complying, the FBI agent settled in next to her. "Beautiful evening," Penance said, taking a sip of his wine. "Thank you for dinner."

"Thank you for your help. It was fun," Annie admitted. "You are handy in a kitchen."

"Quantico knife skills finally came in handy," Penance grinned. "It was delicious. Do you always cook like that?"

Annie laughed, "For myself? No. Glass of wine and a hot pocket is a more common meal for me. I wanted to treat you to a taste of Mississippi – catfish and blue crab. A taste of home."

"Not bad…not bad at all," Penance admitted.

"This is nice," Annie whispered. Leaning in, she placed her head on Penance's shoulder.

Shifting his head slightly downward, he kissed her softly on her forehead. Looking up, Annie brought her lips square with his. Their eyes locked, they hovered for a long moment before leaning slightly forward, closing the tenuous gap between them.

Penance could feel the heat of her breath against his as their kiss was imminent.

Before their lips met their marks, Penance's phone rang. And then Annie's phone rang. Understanding what the interruption meant, they relented to pulling apart.

"Penance," the agent said into his phone. "I see. Understood."

Hanging up, he looked at Annie, who had just hung up her phone. "One of Sheriff Day's deputies got hit out on Highway 61. He was able to call it in. They aren't sure what condition he is in."

"Police station south of here was firebombed," Annie declared.

"Time to go. Lock up and head to the FBI office," Penance instructed. "I'll join you there as soon as I can."

Annie looked up at the agent to question the direction, but understanding the seriousness of the situation, nodded and got up to do as he had suggested.

Penance paused for just a moment, grabbing the Assistant D. A. softly by her arms and kissed her on the cheekbone. Without another word, he bound down the steps and raced to his Porsche SUV. Wasting no time, he fired up the engine and spun the tires as he pulled away from the curb.

Agent Penance could not prepare himself for the brutality of the scene. Seeing the police cruiser, he pulled his SUV to the side of the road. Bullet holes peppered the patrol car. The body of the deputy splayed out on the hood of the police car caught him off guard.

Penance surveyed the scene. He could hear sirens whaling in the distance, closing in. On a whim, the FBI agent jumped into his SUV and drove ahead of the incident. His instincts were rewarded. Parked off to the side of the road, nearly one hundred yards away was a green sedan concealed in the bushes. Continuing forward until he had rounded a bend, he pulled over.

Getting out of the car, Penance drew his weapon and doubled back to the scene with the cruiser. He moved with caution as he approached the hidden sedan. Searching the vehicle and area carefully, he was alerted by the sirens closing in on the scene. Penance slid behind a tree as the Sheriff's Interceptor and the EMS van slowed to a stop.

As Sheriff Day opened his SUV's door, several figures emerged from the nearby brush, each armed with an automatic weapon. Penance squeezed his trigger twice and then twice more, dropping the two men closest to the Sheriff. Two others spun to face the FBI agent, returning a volley of shots his direction.

The Sherriff re-emerged with his shotgun in hand, firing at one of the remaining men while Penance shot the other. Cautiously, the two law enforcement officers surveyed the area until they were confident they had dispatched the last of the Las Piratas.

Converging on the deputy's cruiser, Penance held back and allowed the Sheriff to manage his discovery.

Sheriff Day shook his head as he studied his employee's body. Looking away, he collected himself before nodding to the EMT van. As they approached, he shook his head solemnly, noting that they needed to recover a body and not tend care to a victim.

"I'm sorry, Sheriff Day," Penance offered.

The sheriff waved him off, "Just help me and the town deal with these bastards."

"I will," Penance acknowledged. "Look, this is just the beginning. They set this ambush to whittle down what few resources we have in town. Kind of the leading band of a hurricane, it is just the light winds before the real storm hits. We have very little time to get the town to batten down the hatches and allow as many as we can to evacuate to safer ground."

The sheriff looked over at his deputy gently transferred to the EMT's gurney.

"We'll mourn our losses, but first, we need to get back to town and keep them safe," Penance encouraged.

Nodding, the sheriff waited as the EMT crew loaded their van and headed back towards town. "What about these guys?"

"They wanted to leave a warning for us, let *them* be a warning for the *Las Piratas*," Penance shrugged.

THIRTY-ONE

When Penance arrived at the FBI district office, he found a full house. Dixon was leading the charge with Annie and District Attorney Jennings looking on. Bubba and Chief Pruitt were hovering along with Mayor Kittridge and Judge Doyle.

"Agent Penance," Dixon looked grim, "There was another attack at the north checkpoint. Sheriff Day is on route. He and his deputies will be wary of an ambush this time."

"What happened out there?" Chief Pruitt asked.

As Penance filled the audience with the details of the southern checkpoint and the attempted ambush, Dixon slipped into his office to receive a call.

By the time the FBI agent had recounted the events along the southern highway, Dixon reappeared. His face appeared even more concerned than before. "The routes along highways 24, 33, 61 and 98 have been cut-off…burning cars, fallen trees, bridges blocked," Dixon reported.

"What does that mean?" Annie asked.

"It means help isn't coming, but the fight is," Penance answered. "And it is not far away."

Chief Pruitt turned to Bubba, "We have to get our team ready."

Penance looked towards his boss, "Can you work with Mayor Kittridge, find a place where the women and children of Sawyer can hunker down – storm shelters, bomb shelters, anywhere that could provide them with safety?"

Dixon nodded, pulling Mayor Kittridge aside and began making plans. Jennings and Judge Doyle joined them.

"Chief…Bubba…can you two rally up any help you can find? Former vets, hunters, anyone who can shoot straight…I know it is a lot to ask of civilians, but we are going to need them," Penance instructed.

Leaning towards Annie, he whispered, "I need you to go with the mayor. Do what you can to keep the people in the shelters calm."

Annie peered deep into his eyes before nodding and joining the shelter crew.

As the Mayor and Jennings had the crew put together for getting the shelters up and running, Penance pulled Dixon away.

Pulling a map and satellite views of Sawyer up on the presentation screen, the FBI agent rubbed his chin.

Suddenly he pointed with his tactical pen, tapping the screen, "Here, here and here…these are chokepoints into the town. We will want sniper positions and protected ground placements with avenues to fall back. If we can force the *Las Piratas* to funnel through these zones…"

"They come right through a kill chute," Dixon nodded in approval.

"What is the most defensible building in Sawyer?"

"I'd say the bank, or the courthouse and the jail," Dixon replied.

"Courthouse is too far out, on the outskirts. Let's move our operations to the bank. It is right down on Main in the center of town. The furthest from all directions the *Piratas* would have to travel, the most centralized final fall back position," Penance declared.

"I'll start moving the communications hub and grab what weapons and ammunition we have there," Dixon acknowledged.

Penance pulled his keys out of his pocket and opened up the munitions locker. Grabbing a large duffle, he selected a combat shotgun, a scoped rifle and an extra handgun. Scooping up ample ammunition for each, he slung the bag over his shoulder.

"Where are you headed?"

"To the first place the *Piratas* are going to go," Penance said.

On his way to the car, Penance pulled out his phone. Dialing the number for his neighbor, he pressed send.

"Hello?" Frank answered.

"Frank, are you at work right now?" Penance asked.

"I am...why? Is everything okay?"

"Everything is fine, right now. Are your kids at home?"

"Yes, Maggie is looking after Danny for me."

"Listen, you are not going to be able to make it home tonight. You might not even be able to make it tomorrow, and it will be too dangerous for you to try. I am going to and pick up the kids now and ensure they are somewhere safe," Penance declared.

"What is going on?"

"A cartel member is being held at County. The entire gang is converging on Sawyer, and they intend to upend the town," Penance replied.

"Oh, my God. I need to get home!" Frank shouted.

"Frank, listen to me. I get it, I would want to do the same thing, but the roads into town are blocked, and there is no way of getting in. I will get the kids myself, and I will let you know where they are and that they are safe," Penance promised.

"I get it. If there is a way for me to get to them, let me know as soon as possible," Frank requested.

"I will," Penance hung up and tossed the duffle into the hatch of the Porsche.

Starting up the car, he sped towards his neighbor's house. Keeping a keen eye for activity along the road, he pushed the accelerator hard. As he neared the bridge by his drive, he saw a figure duck behind a truck while another waved him down as though there was a problem. Tucked in the shadows on the opposite side of the road, Penance could just make out the profile of a man with an assault rifle.

Instead of slowing down, Penance pressed hard on the throttle, launching the SUV forward. The men were surprised at first and then reacted. The man waving his arms suddenly stopped. Reaching behind his back, he produced a handgun, firing shots at Penance. Ignoring the frantic, poorly placed shots, Penance rocketed directly at the gunman, forcing him to dive to the side of the road. Hitting the bridge, Penance cranked the wheel, putting the Porsche into a spin. Hitting the automatic windows, he freed his handgun, squeezing off shots towards where he saw the figure duck behind the truck and as the car rotated, towards where the man in the shadows was waiting.

The car came to an abrupt stop, and Penance leaped out, rolling behind the truck, looking up at gunman. With two quick shots, Penance dropped him. Using the vehicle for cover, Penance peered out as an automatic assault rifle peppered the truck. The man who had been waving his arms peered over the piling of the bridge, trying to square up a shot, but Penance saw him first, delivering a bullet to the man's forehead.

Circling the truck, which was still fielding a barrage from the assault rifle, Penance crept to the driver's window. Slipping the vehicle into neutral, he leaned into the a-pillar and pushed the truck into motion. Using the truck for cover until he neared the spot of the third gunman. Waiting for the sound of an ejected magazine, Penance stepped out from the truck and leveled a controlled shot towards the gunman. Nervously trying to cram a new magazine into place, he watched as Penance calmly aimed and delivered two clean shots at the man.

Checking the contents of the van and surveying the surrounding area to ensure there were no lingering *Las Piratas*, Penance bolted back to the Porsche and sped towards his neighbor's house.

Kicking up a trail of dust along the dirt road, he pushed the SUV hard, sliding as he reached the neighbor's driveway. Using momentum to slide the rear end around, he stopped the vehicle pointing roughly the right direction for a quick getaway.

Hopping out, he raced up to the porch to see the kids burst out, each carrying a small bag.

"Daddy called and said you were coming and to be ready," Maggie said.

"Nice job, guys!" Penance beamed in praise. Taking their bags, he tossed them in the back with his duffel and allowed them to pile into the vehicle.

Checking on his passengers, he called, "Buckle up!"

With a spin of the tires, he sent the SUV hurtling back towards town.

Thirty-Two

As Penance neared the entrance to Sawyer, he noticed activity around one of the arteries he and Dixon had identified as a natural chokepoint. A pair of dump trucks and a garbage truck barred the path. A glance through the windshield, Penance spied a pair of men perched on the rooftops on either side of the barricade with long rifles surveilling the roads.

A worker who was setting concrete dividers down alongside the trucks recognized the FBI agent and waved a man in the garbage truck to back out of position and let him in.

Nodding his appreciation, Penance guided the Porsche through the checkpoint. Driving to the bank, he found the crew of the bureau office reconvened at the secure building.

Jennings escorted Penance and the children inside.

"We have three shelters, one in the basement of the school, one under city hall and the other the old American Legion building, both of the latter locations have bomb shelters. All three are stocked with first aid, food, and water," Jennings reported.

"Sounds good, Jennings, nice work," Penance acknowledged.

"With all due respect, I am going to take off and tend to my own family now that we most of the innocents as safe as we can get them," Judge Doyle declared.

"You going to be good up there, Judge?" Penance asked.

"Just so happens that my wine cellar serves as well fortified storm shelter. I got weapons and ammo for days, too," the judge shared.

Looking at the kids and then back towards the judge, "Wouldn't have room for two more small mouths, would you?"

Judge Doyle clapped a hand on each of the children's shoulders, "I think we can manage."

"Good. As soon as I can, I will get their father up to them," Penance said.

"Don't worry about a thing; they are in good hands," the judge replied. Wheeling the children out towards the door, he said to them, "In the back of the wine cellar is a little hidden room, in it, is an arcade. You two like pinball and video games?"

Penance watched them as they left, grateful that the kids would have a safe place to hole up while the town was under siege. "Jennings, why don't you go with them. I would sure feel a lot better," Penance said. Pulling his back-up pistol from his waistband, he handed it to the DA.

Jennings studied the gun.

"Just make sure the dot by your thumb is red, point, and shoot," Penance offered.

Nodding, Jennings wheeled out behind Judge Doyle and the kids.

"All the patrols and checkpoints up and running?" Penance asked.

Dixon nodded, "They are, checking in with fifteen increments."

"Good. How's this place looking?"

"Well, we have two layers of protection, not including the vault. You have behind the counter and the glass, the offices which are behind security doors and then, of course, the vault, which has oxygen feed and CO_2 release," Dixon said. Waving his hands behind the counter, "We have two-stage communication. Primary is behind the counter. Secondary is in the offices. We have cameras atop the roof fed to a monitor in the offices."

"Any word from the bureau?"

"They are bringing guys in, but they are likely hours away," Dixon said.

Penance looked cross, "How about helos?"

"Air support? With budget cutbacks, they aren't releasing choppers until bullets are flying," Dixon scoffed.

"Tell the deputy this isn't an *imminent* threat. The sheriff and I killed four cartel members down south, and I killed another three up by my house. This is an active threat," Penance said.

"I think they…" Dixon was cut off by his radio chirping.

"Director Dixon, this is Deputy Banks at County, three vans are coming in hot!"

"Hunker down and hold tight, I got guys coming to you!"

"Bubba, let's go!" Penance called.

Bubba chased after the FBI agent. The officer had barely shut his door before Penance had the SUV screaming out of the parking lot and streaking through downtown.

"Should we call for more back up?" Bubba asked.

"How was the town recruitment?"

"We have four guys at each checkpoint, two at each shelter and four at the bank," Bubba replied.

"No more?"

"That's all we could rustle up," Bubba admitted. "Along with the Sheriff, Chief Pruitt, the two officers and I, that is all we got."

"No, that's great work," Penance acknowledged. "Between the guards at county and us, we are going to have to deal with them. How many do they staff?"

"Four."

"How many targets?"

"Says looked like six in each," Bubba said, looking worried. "Eighteen cartel members versus six of us."

"I know," Penance grinned as he floored the accelerator. "Hardly seems fair, does it?"

Reaching the parking lot of the county building, Penance turned off the lights and slipped the Porsche in to neutral, allowing it glide quietly towards the vans. From the SUV, they could see the men circling the building, trying to find a way into the secure site. When none of them could gain access, one waved the others back. Reaching in his jacket pocket, he pulled a small object and tossed it towards the front door.

Penance knew what it was prior to it reaching its destination and took advantage of the pending calamity. A flash followed by a loud explosion filled the air as the front door buckled. Using the cover of the bang and the subsequent shower of glass and shrapnel that had the men concentrating on the door and ducking to avoid being struck by debris, Penance dispatched the two trailing Las Piratas gang members.

The men up front didn't notice, intent on storming the county building. Penance raced behind them, urging Bubba to trail him. Following the men into the building, he watched them navigate through the security station and divide to find their incarcerated comrade.

Penance motioned for Bubba to follow the men who went left while he took the right. He did not want to leave Bubba on his own, but he knew he didn't have much of a choice. Deciding to strike quietly, but decisively, he sprinted after the men. Sliding over the security table, he reached the first man from behind, just as he was about to descend the stairwell. With hand over the man's mouth, he wrenched the crook of his elbow against the man's throat until his body went limp. Spinning him face down, Penance laced his hands together in a pair of zip-tie restraints.

Hopping up, he ran to the stairwell wall and peered around the corner. He could hear footfalls ascend the steps. Quietly, he followed suit until he heard gunfire exchange at the top of the steps, knowing the guards had engaged. Penance took advantage of their focus and the noise to bound up after them.

The sound of gunfight intensified. Positioning himself behind the seven men in the stairwell, he leveled his firearm and yelled. The men were startled to hear a noise behind them, half turning towards the sound and half wary of turning away from the guards. Two men tumbled downwards with the guards taking advantage of the distraction. Two men swiveled their weapons to face the FBI agent. Penance quickly put them down with double trigger squeezes each. The remaining three ducked below the line of fire from the security guards and focused on Penance. Leaping backward, he landed on the ground floor and rolled out of sight.

Pulling the tactical shotgun he had sheathed to his back, he thrust the barrel up the stairs and pulled the trigger twice. One *Las Piratas* tumbled to his feet while he heard another whaling on the steps. Switching on the tactical light attached to the shotgun barrel, he thrust it once more towards the stairs. Firing once blindly, he stepped out. Seeing a man at his feet with a blood-splattered chest trying to raise his assault weapon towards the FBI agent, Penance stepped on his forearm while lining a clear shot for the last gang member who was trying to determine whether he should go up or down.

"Indecision on the battlefield will get you killed," Penance declared, squeezing the trigger and felling the man, sending him tumbling down the steps.

Penance studied the man at his feet. He was pale and choking on his own blood. "I'm sorry pal, I don't think you are going to make it." The agent gave the man mercy with a shot to the head from his handgun.

Hearing shouting from the far end of the upper hallway, Penance sprinted up the stairs. As he reached the top floor, he waved the guard who had engaged the *Las Piratas* at the head of the stairs to follow him.

Sheathing his shotgun, he grabbed an assault rifle dropped by one of the cartel gunmen and raced down the hallway. Two men stood on either side of the second stairwell while two more men we staring down the stairs. They had Bubba pinned at the base of the stairs. Penance was about to even things up.

In a full sprint, Penance ran down the hall, as the first man saw him and raised his assault weapon, Penance dropped to his knees, sliding below the man's aim while firing several burst shots from his assault rifle. The guard dropped the second sentry as Penance dove towards the stairs taking out the legs of the two staring down towards where their men were trying to flush out Bubba.

Using the wall to stop his slide, he used the momentum of his soles, hitting the concrete wall to catapult him to his feet. With a quick swipe of his assault rifle against the head of one man, he rammed the barrel against the chin of the other and let out a burst.

Using the limp body, he sent it hurtling down the stairs towards the remaining four Las Piratas. The collection of bodies tumbled down the steps, landing in a heap at Bubba's feet, who towered over them with his tactical shotgun levied at the mass of them. One man on the periphery tried to slide his assault weapon towards the officer, but Bubba caught him, slamming a heavy foot on the man's hand and then delivering a vicious blow to his head.

Penance and the guard joined him, separating the *Las Piratas* from their weapons. Quickly, they went to work assessing the men for injuries and zip-tying those not destined for a body bag.

"Bubba, collect all of their weapons," Penance instructed. Kicking over a garbage can, he discarded the used bag and reached into the can for the collection of unused bags the janitor stored in the bottom and handed them to Bubba.

"Other than Sanchez, any priority prisoners?" Penance asked.

The guard shook his head. "Gather the rest of your men and the guys you have in lock up. If they are in for something non-violent, cut them loose. Hell, recruit them if you trust them. Otherwise, get your team and meet up at the bank in Sawyer. I'll take Sanchez in myself," Penance ordered.

The guard nodded and ran up the stairs to gather his team and the prisoners. "Keep your head on a swivel," Penance said to Bubba, who was busily stacking cartel assault weapons. Penance paused to pick one up and ejected its magazine. Giving it a check, he slid it into his waistband.

Mounting the steps, he followed the guard to the small block of the county facility. He could hear Sanchez sneering and whaling from his cell. As they approached, Sanchez had his hand wrapped around two bars, and his face smashed up between them. Sanchez spit at the guard as he walked by.

Penance smashed the butt of his assault rifle through the bars and against Sanchez' forehead, sending him rearing backward in his cell. "Open it up," the FBI demanded. The locks buzzed, and the door unlatched.

"You can go quietly or quietly," Penance scowled.

"My men…where…" Sanchez stammered.

"Your men are not very good at their jobs. So far, we're up twenty to one, and I am very pissed off about that one!" Penance snarled at the gang leader. "So which form of quiet is it going to be? By choice or your limp body?"

Sanchez glared, as if trying to divine a retort but then relented.

"Turn," Penance demanded.

Sanchez stood and turned away from the agent. Penance zip tied the gang lieutenant's hands together and marched him towards the door.

The guards had gathered the prisoners that demanded watch and allowed the others, mostly held on drug charges, free to join the community in the fight or flee to safety. Billy Whatcom was one of the prisoners released.

"Let's go," Penance said, maneuvering Sanchez down the hallway.

THIRTY-THREE

The bank was a busier scene than Penance had expected. Men and women with personal firearms were deputized by the Sheriff and given specific instructions that their roles were for defense only.

Dixon looked up from the gathering and took notice of Penance and the county guards. "I see you brought friends."

"If you mean the gentlemen with the county badges, then yes," Penance said. Giving Sanchez a shove forward, he added. "If you mean this trash, then no."

"Got a plan for them?" the FBI director asked.

"This place have one of those rooms where people visit their safety deposit boxes?"

"Yeah, down the hall to the left. It has one of those iron gates, would be perfect," Dixon acknowledged.

Sanchez twisted and tried to pull away, "I ain't going there, *putas!*"

"You're right," Penance agreed. "I have a much better place for your ugly mug."

Dixon shot his agent a questioning glance.

"Basement?" the agent asked.

"Past the safe deposit room at the end of the hall. Here's the key," Dixon tossed Penance a key ring.

"You'll like it down there. Make friends with the rats, probably have lots in common," Penance steered Sanchez down the hall and into the basement.

Testing a steel pipe for its durability, he tethered the Las Piratas lieutenant to it with both hands linked through cuffs. "Reinforced concrete walls, no one will hear your bellyaching. Not me, not your cartel friends," Penance declared, surveying the dark and dingy room. "It's going to be a long night. You'll notice your cuffs allow you to slide all the way down to the floor so that you can sit. Nice and comfy, right?"

Sanchez smiled wickedly at the agent, "This is gonna be your *last* night."

"Maybe," Penance admitted. "I promise there'll be a whole lot fewer *Las Piratas* members too. Good night, Sanchez."

The agent retreated from the basement, ignoring the string of shouts and obscenities lobbed at him by the gang member. Taking a quick look over his shoulder, he closed the basement door, inserting the key, rotated the lock. As satisfied as he was with the sturdy hold for his prisoner, he was more satisfied with the silence that followed the closing of the door.

Returning to the main lobby, he reported the scene from the county lock-up to his boss.

"So, these guys are serious," Dixon mused.

Penance nodded, "They are. Well-armed, moderately trained."

"Where do you want me now, boss?" Bubba asked the FBI agent.

"We have positions manned at the checkpoints. We have sniper roosts at several outposts around town, including here at the bank. It sounds as though the Sheriff will have his newly sworn militia maintaining a perimeter here in the center of town. Why don't you stick with me?" Penance suggested.

"What is our role?" the officer asked.

"You and I are the reaction team. Kind of like fighting a forest fire, we'll be in charge of managing the hotspots," Penance said. He expected his friend to wear a look of concern at the direction, but he was impressed when Bubba met him with a dutiful resolve.

Penance slapped Bubba on the shoulder, "For now, try and relax. Get something to eat."

The agent led his friend to a table that had water bottles, nutrition bars, and other essentials. Knowing he may not have many chances to fortify his mind and body through the evening, he helped himself to a bar and a banana.

The two leaned back, watching the nervous townspeople check their weapons as the instructions and their placements were detailed to them by the sheriff.

"You did good work at County," Penance acknowledged.

"I got myself penned in," Bubba shrugged. "Didn't even pull the trigger."

"But you didn't get yourself shot, and you helped stop a paramilitary unit hell-bent on killing us. I'd put that in the solid "win" column."

"I guess. You sure you want me as your back up tonight?" Bubba asked.

"Nobody I'd trust more to have my six," Penance declared.

Agent Alex Penance perched on the roof of the bank building. He mindlessly disassembled and reassembled his sidearm as he scanned the horizon. "Kind of a pleasant night," he muttered.

"It is," Bubba nodded despite Penance remaining fixed on the landscape ahead of him.

"Your mother tucked away safely?"

"She is," Bubba acknowledged. "She is with my aunt in Baton Rouge."

"Easier to focus when you know those you care about are safe," the FBI agent said. At that moment, movement on the street caught his attention, "What the…"

Pushing away from the edge of the rooftop, Penance bounded towards the stairs. Bubba trailed, not seeing what got the agent riled, but rested his hand on his sidearm as he followed.

Making a beeline for the door, Penance pushed through the entrance. Reaching out, he grabbed his target by the arm, rolled them both into the shadows of the side of the building. "What are you doing here?'

"Everyone was settled in the shelters. I wanted to see if I could be more help here," Annie Hunt pleaded. "I know everyone is tense, I kind of didn't expect it from you," she giggled.

Penance let her arms go. Turning, he paced along the sidewalk, sighing as rubbed his chin. He didn't want to admit what had him riled. He felt somewhat relieved, more focused thinking she was in one of the shelters.

"It isn't safe here," Penance said, turning back to face the assistant D. A.

"You're here. There are plenty of civilians, even a handful of ladies," Annie pressed. "So, what's so bad about me being here?"

"I...uh...I needed you. I wanted you to keep the people calm. Be our source inside the shelter," Penance stammered.

Annie cocked her head, trying to discern what was going through the agent's head. "Well, I'm here now. The people in the shelters are fine. They have board games, beverages, snacks...like a cozy town sleepover. So, you might as well put me to work right here."

"Fine," Penance relented. With his hand gently against the small of her back, he led Annie towards the bank. As he turned, he was almost startled to see Bubba waiting for him by the front door. Not noticing the large man behind him was another sign that Annie's presence was a bit distracting. "I did tell you to stick with me, huh?"

"Got your six, Penance," Bubba grinned.

Penance guided Annie into the bank. "I'll tell you what, if you must stay here, I have the job for you."

Annie shot him a look.

"We need someone to monitor the airwaves. Help Dixon manage point," Penance said, leading Annie to the executive office where they set up the radios and monitoring equipment. "You'll be safe in here. There are two layers of secure doors and the office door itself is a steel core door with fortified strike plates."

"I feel like you are trying to quarantine me," Annie pursed her lips.

"You and Dixon, both," Penance admitted. "I need someone to lead the troops, be our eyes, and...work with the cavalry when they do arrive."

"What do you mean?"

Penance looked serious, "Mop-up depending on exactly how things turn out."

"Don't say that," Annie frowned.

"We need to be prepared for anything," Penance said. "Can I count on you to man your post, please?"

Annie grinned as she shot him a salute, "Yes, sir. You can count on me."

With a roll of his eyes, he started to leave the room but then paused. "I'm not glad you're here. But I am happy to see you."

Walking down the hall, he looked for Dixon, who was exchanging plans and instructions with Sheriff Day and Chief Pruitt. "We all set?" Penance asked.

"As much as we're going to be," Dixon sighed. "The bureau confirmed a team is being assembled and on standby."

"I'm not sure what body count they are waiting for, but we'll feed you what information we can from the field. I have Annie stationed in the executive office we are using for comms. I need you with her," Penance stated.

"I thought I was the Bureau Director," Dixon quipped. "You know, the one that gave the orders?"

"You want to head out with Bubba and leave me to run point?" Penance pushed back.

"Fair enough. I will run comms and protect Ms. Hunt with my life," Dixon promised.

"Let's hope it doesn't come to that," Penance said. His attention strayed as a man dressed in black carrying an AR-15 walked into the bank. The agent had to blink as his eyes translated the image to his brain.

"Pastor Roberts?" Penance called in disbelief.

The pastor looked at the agent and noted the surprise in Penance' gaze.

"What? The armor of God is a necessary tool to protect His flock," Pastor Roberts shrugged. "So, how do you use these thingies?" he asked, fumbling with the AR-15 to the horrified look of Penance.

Penance lunged to assist before the pastor quickly and effortlessly checked his magazine and primed the charging handle. "Just kidding," Pastor Roberts grinned. "I've shot thousands of rounds through this, just never at a living thing."

"I'd just as soon not put you in that position tonight," Penance declared.

"We'd all prefer that. Just the same, people we love and care for are in danger, and we must protect them, with God's guidance and blessing," Pastor Roberts agreed. "Where do you want me?"

"Right here in the bank, behind the teller stand and in the secure hallway leading to the executive offices," Penance instructed. "Director Dixon and Annie are in the bank president's office manning the comms and running point. You will be their last line of defense that hopefully does not get tapped."

"Understood and understood. I don't want to but am ready if I have to," Pastor Roberts said.

"Prepare for the worst, hope for the best," Penance nodded.

The pastor put his hand on the agent's shoulder, "Do you mind?"

Penance looked confused.

"I'd like to pray for you, for everyone."

Penance scoffed, "I don't mind at all. In fact, I'd very much appreciate it."

Not a moment after Pastor Roberts prayer, Penance's radio crackled to life. A voice Penance only vaguely recognized as one of the police chief's officers called out, "Car coming in fast on the south end checkpoint!"

The officer's voice strained, the stress of the event was taking its toll on the people of Sawyer.

"Bubba, we're up!" Penance called, grabbing his duffle over his shoulder and grabbing one of the Colt M4 carbines he had pulled from the FBI weapons locker.

Sliding into the driver's seat of the Porsche SUV, he lowered the windows and opened the massive sunroof as Bubba climbed into the passenger seat. The agent wanted his wanted full input to his senses as well as to have full access to react.

Putting the SUV into gear, he rocketed towards the south checkpoint. The sound of gunfire echoed through the night air. "Stay low, keep a barrier between you and outside of the barrier," Penance instructed to a nervous but nodding Bubba.

Penance's eyes swept the area, matching what visuals he could with the sounds. The men on either sniper nest at the barrier were engaged. In contrast, the two ground level men nervously tried to spy action from behind the concrete dividers and construction vehicles that separated them from the road into town.

"Stay here by the car. I'll see if I can gauge the threat and engage. Keep your radio handy," Penance said, sprinting towards the barrier the town had placed.

Following his instinct, he ran to the building adjacent to the right-side sniper's building. He wanted height, but from an angle that would allow him to assess the scene without a direct line to the action. Sprinting to the building, an antique shop on the ground floor with apartments on the top floor, he launched himself from an ornate bench and reaching up, grabbed the edge of the antique shop's awning. With one smooth movement, he lunged with his upper body, flinging him on top of the canopy. Using the awning like a trampoline, he sprung himself upward, grasping the floorboards of the wrap-around deck of the second-floor apartment. Working his way to the edge of the balcony, he kicked a foot in between the iron spindles of the porch and reached up with his right hand.

In moments, he was on the wrap-around porch. Skirting the shadowy edge, he crept to the back of the building. From his vantage, he could see the exchange from both sides of the firefight. Five *Las Piratas* fanned out along the street below while the Sawyer officer and civilian tried to hone in from their perch atop the buildings along the barrier.

Penance was confident that the five gangsters were all that had shown up so far, the sedan that two of them were using for cover fire would only seat five.

As he surveyed the action, one gang member trying to make a wider sweep and flank the shooters left the cover his tree for another. He let out a yelp and dropped to the ground. He was hit.

Leaving four men, currently to dispatch, Penance crept to the back end of the wrap-around porch. Lowering himself over the side, he jumped down to the ground below.

Using what little moonlight shone down to do his best and avoid twigs and branches that would snap underfoot.

He crept within a clear shot of the closest gang member, hiding behind a tree, occasionally taking shots at the town's snipers. Penance knew as soon as he fired a shot, the two at the car would have an easy bead on him. Even if he were able to drop one, the other would be in a position to fire on him.

Penance had to remove the first man, and then he would have a shot at taking both of the gunmen behind the car. Moving deftly forward, he took a deep breath and set the M4 at his feet. In one smooth movement, he closed the gap wrapping his right forearm tightly under the gunman's chin while using his left arm to exert maximum pressure. Before he collapsed, the *Las Piratas* member fired a slew of random shots in the air that blended into the chaos of the firefight before slumping at the agent's feet.

Tossing the man's assault rifle into his duffle, Penance retrieved his M4. Lining the two shooters at the car up in his sights, he pulled the trigger twice, dropping the first gang member and then twice more dropping the other.

With the heat of exchange off of them, one of the snipers found their aim true with the fifth member of the attack. The night fell suddenly silent. Penance waved the two men on the ground level over. "Retrieve their weapons, stow them behind the barrier," Penance called.

"What about the bodies?" one of the men asked.

"They aren't going anywhere," Penance responded coolly.

Leaving them to their task, the FBI agent returned to the gang member he choked out. Lacing the man's hands and feet in zip ties, he tied a gag around the man's mouth and pulled a roll of duct tape from the duffle, completing his task. Rolling him down the slight decline and into the briar patch, he muttered, "I've got to try to remember to get him in the morning."

Bubba's voice was heard, calling to the agent from the edge of the barrier. "Penance, call from the radio. The Jackson side barrier is under attack!"

"Get the car started, Bubba. I'm on my way!"

Penance tossed his duffle back over his shoulder and raced back towards his vehicle. As he got there, Bubba started to climb out of the driver's seat. "We don't have time for that, you're driving," Penance directed.

Nodding, the officer put the vehicle into gear and spun the tires as Penance closed his door. The calls from the radio were frantic as the Jackson side entrance had been breached and the four townspeople, one deputy and three civilians, were being attacked from both sides.

"Floor it right towards the barrier and then lock it up one block prior," Penance said, checking his mag.

Bubba did as directed, rocketing the SUV towards the new gunfight. They could hear gunfire and see muzzle flashes from the street level. The snipers focused outward while the two on the ground level were struggling to repel the threat from the breach.

Penance pushed up from his seat and leaned his upper body out of the sunroof. Training the M4 ahead, he lined up where the town's shooters were firing from and vectored in on the first *Las Piratas*. With a double squeeze of the trigger, he dropped one of them as Bubba sent the Porsche into a sideways skid.

"Stay on this side of them but watch for crossfire. The last thing we need is to get picked off by a friendly," Penance said. "Use that building for cover. Don't shoot until your aim is true, or you're as likely to get one of ours."

The car barely stopped and both were sprinting to either side of the street. Penance found a large planter box to use for cover. From there, he could see a man on Bubba's side of the road. The man's head swiveled, trying to locate on Bubba while checking his shot with the ground level barrier crew.

Penance wished that scope had night vision or thermal, but he had to rely on the dark mass of shadow in his sight. He breathed deep, let the air out, and fired a shot.

The gang member flipped to the ground like a ghost had tackled him. Headshot.

Taking the distant nighttime shot, Penance had to concentrate intensely. He was startled to see Bubba pointing his gun towards him. The muzzle flash caused Penance to duck instinctively. A hanging plant shattered a dozen feet away from his as a man dove away from the falling debris.

Rolling onto his back from his prone shooter's position, he drew his sidearm and fired off two shots, landing them into the man Bubba deterred with the planter. "Nice work, Officer Bubba," Penance whispered to himself. Taking a moment to ensure he did not miss any other gang members beyond the breach, they pushed towards the barrier.

Using care, they crept along either side of the street. The ground crew had turned their attention roadside, suggesting Penance and Bubba had handled the breach. Joining the ground crew, Penance had Bubba spell one of the men's positions so that the agent could score a quick field sitrep.

"A car and van came up fast. Stopped about a football field away. Two advanced while four others laid cover fire, and then they swapped until they were on both sides and through the barrier," the man said, his voice quivering with stress.

"You sure there were six, exactly," Penance pressed.

The man stammered, "Sure…I mean, I think so."

"Enough to bet our lives on it?"

"Well, no. I'm not that sure."

Recognizing he was having a conversation with a civilian with not training for an event like this, Penance backed down. "Alright, we will go with that and be cautious on our sweep in case there are surprises. Hang in there. We'll get through this."

The man nodded and returned to his post, where Bubba had fired several shots and was ducking down to reload.

Meeting back up with Penance, Bubba leaned in and asked, "What's the play?"

"Let's go the edges of the barrier, make them widen the amount of ground they need to target, and give them a few more angles of fire against them. I don't need to tell you, above all, keep your head down and your body concealed. Move around your shooting position so they can't hone in on your position by targeting your muzzle flash," Penance instructed.

"I got you, boss," Bubba nodded and maneuvered to the edge of the barrier while Penance moved to the opposite.

Using a sideways parked dump truck for cover, the FBI agent positioned himself between the cab and the bed.

Through the gap, he stood looking for motion on the other side. As no movement presented, he rolled to the edge of the truck bed. Peering out, he waited. As the exchange of gunfire continued erratically, he caught muzzle flash from the corner of the building closest to the gang member's cars. Letting his eyes adjust, he could see the man picked up on Bubba's last shot and was trying to draw a bead.

Penance did not have a clear shot himself to take the man down. He needed to angle away from the building, which would expose him outside of the protection of the dump truck. Noticing how much ground clearance the vehicle gave way to, he dropped to the ground. Rolling his body towards the outside edge of the barrier, he exposed enough of the gunman, just as he was readying to return volley towards Bubba. Firing a quick shot, the man reeled, clearly struck.

Himself exposed, Penance rolled back as a bullets peppered the ground where he had just laid. Whirling, he tried to catch where those shots were fired from but missed the opportunity. Blasts from the sniper nests followed with silence. They didn't miss.

Penance and the barrier team waited several minutes before moving away from their safe locations. Once again, Penance had the ground crew locate and retrieve the *Las Piratas'* weapons.

As the men scoured the road and surrounding area
for discarded weapons and ammo, Penance leaned against
one of the big trucks providing a barrier to the town.
Looking out at the cars the *Las Piratas* arrived in, he had an
idea.

Walking out to the vehicles, he opened their fuel
tanks. With his knife, he removed strips of roof liner from
the first car and stuffed each tank with a generous strand of
cloth. Slipping each car into neutral, he wheeled them nose
to nose, spanning the breadth of the roadway.

Satisfied with his rig, he returned to the barrier.
Calling up to the sniper nooks on either side of the road, he
asked, "What caliber are you running?"

".308!" the first sniper called out.

"556!" the deputy in the other sniper's nook
answered.

"We have a winner," Penance mumbled, digging in
his duffel. "You a good shot?"

The deputy shrugged as he looked down on the FBI
agent. "Yeah, pretty good."

With duct tape, Penance tied together three rounds
of ammunition and tossed them up to the roof. "Those are
tracer rounds. I opened the fuel doors and put some
combustible material stuffed in the filler. When the next
wave of Piratas come, light them up!"

"Roger that!" the deputy called.

THIRTY-FOUR

With silence once again enveloping the town, Penance and Bubba made their way back to the bank, converted to the siege suppression headquarters. With a body count that was rapidly escalating, Penance took solace that, while no death was a reason to celebrate, so far, the townspeople were spared and relatively unharmed.

Suggesting Bubba hydrate with water and fuel up at the grazing station, Penance joined Dixon and Annie in the comms room.

"We got the reports from the checkpoints," Dixon said.

"The stack of bodies fueling a response from FBI HQ?" Penance pressed.

Dixon looked grave, "They're 'working on it'."

"Right. This will all be over, and we'll have half a town left if we can hold out," Penance muttered. Shooting Annie a glance, he realized how his words must have sounded. "We'll be okay. Bureaucracy was never my strong suit. I get a little frustrated."

"I get it," Annie said. "What can we do to help?"

"I need you two to keep monitoring the wires and the reports. Keep me updated. Use text along with the radio. Depending on the situation, I do not always have it on," Penance reported. Turning to Dixon, he asked, "Think you can gather a three-man unit? Need to make sure the lines are refreshed with water, food, ammo...anything else they need to stay focused, ready, and as calm as they can muster."

"We'll put something together," Dixon nodded. Heading out of the bank president's office, he went to organize a crew to support the barrier teams.

"How are you holding up?" Annie asked softly.

The FBI agent turned to look at her directly. "This is bad business. I really don't like having civilians out there."

"I'm glad you are here," Annie said.

"I feel kind of responsible for the *Las Piratas* coming here to Sawyer," Penance admitted.

Annie frowned, "They were already here. They were filling our schools with drugs and luring girls into sex trafficking schemes. Left unchecked, how many kids would lose their lives to those monsters?"

"Maybe I took it too far. I turned a criminal incident into a war," Penance said.

"If you take two gang members off the street, what happens the next day?" Annie pressed.

"Two more take their place," the FBI agent muttered.

Annie looked defiant as she walked towards him. Sitting on the edge of the desk where he was standing, she looked up at him, "There you go. To get rid of the yellow jackets, you have to remove the entire nest. Sometimes they get riled up and try to sting people. If left there, they would *definitely* sting people."

"Remind me to have you represent me if things go sideways," Penance laughed.

"Things are *already* sideways. Besides, I am the one that asked you to take on this case," Annie replied. "And yes, I'd be happy to represent you anytime."

Penance enjoyed the moment looking into the assistant district attorney's eyes. He preferred to stay there, lose himself in those brown pools. Pulling away, he knew he needed to check himself and prepare for the next wave of what he knew would be a relentless evening.

"I should check with the troops and reload, myself," he said.

"Take of yourself, Alex," Annie said.

"Will do what I can," Penance promised.

Pausing, he placed his hand on the door jamb and looked back at Annie. "Take care of yourself. When…if things hit the fan, secure each layer of doors to this room."

"I will," Annie nodded and watched the FBI agent disappear down the hall.

In the lobby of the bank, Dixon was coordinating with Pastor Roberts and another man to build kits for the barrier crews. "Penance, you want to piece together ammo packs for the look-outs?"

"Sure thing," the agent nodded. He liked the idea of being busy rather than just waiting.

"Here. I have a list of the weapons they are carrying," Dixon said.

"Good. I'll redistribute the *Las Piratas'* weapons and ammo as well. I've got them in the hatch of the Porsche," Penance added.

"Good idea. Some of these fellas are using shotguns and hunting rifles out of their personal stocks. Could even out the field a bit better," Dixon said.

Penance paused as he began making stacks of ammunition. "You know what? I'll go with the pastor. I can walk them through the guns we grabbed. Tec-9s and AK47s. Short and medium-ranged gunners, so far. That's one reason we've owned the battlefield so far."

"So far. We saw from Juarez clean up, rocket launchers and fifty-cal rounds were used," Dixon warned.

"Copy that, chief," Penance nodded. Using file boxes from the bank storage room, Penance put kits together for each of the barrier units.

Stacking the boxes, he lifted with the bottom handle and nodded towards Pastor Roberts, "Ready?"

Pastor Roberts looked up and grinned, "You get to be my chauffeur?"

"Bodyguard, I think I'll have you drive," Penance said. "Bubba, I'll be back in a bit, and we'll stock up ourselves and go on patrol."

Following Pastor Roberts to the pick up loaded with water and snacks, Penance slid the boxes of ammunition in the back and closed the tailgate. Hopping in the passenger, he pointed towards the road, indicating that he was ready.

Pastor Roberts put the truck into gear and headed for the first barricade. "Pretty bad out there, huh?"

"It is," Penance nodded.

"How do you handle it…the killing?"

The agent scoffed, "Like anyone else, I suppose."

"Uhm…" the pastor started.

"Anyone else that has been trained and been through it," Penance corrected. "It's disturbing. The first man who died in front of me still tries to mess with my dreams. I try not to let him."

"Have you been through that a lot, deaths I mean?"

"My team was a special anti-terrorism task force. We managed a few situations the public may never know about. To save lives of innocent people and in some cases, our own versus those with very evil, ill intent, my team and I have had to do things," Penance said.

"Your reputation since you arrived, has been one of an irreverent trigger finger," Pastor Roberts noted.

Penance studied the pastor before replying. "I'll admit, I have had a...busy run since coming to Sawyer. Each of those incidents come home with me. Each of those I have to reconcile. I don't care about the reconciliation with the reports and my superiors, or Jennings for that matter, I mean with myself. Each of those shootings was just."

Pastor nodded as Penance spoke. Pulling up to the first checkpoint, he put the truck in park. "I can't imagine you have easy decisions when someone is pointing a gun in your direction."

"By the time they point the gun in my direction, the decision is pretty easy," Penance corrected.

"So, noted," Pastor Roberts coughed.

Penance looked up at the sniper locations as he walked to the back of the pick-up. Frowning, he unholstered his sidearm. Calling up to the sniper closest to his side of the truck, he waved his arm, "Hey, move a few steps that way... and shield your face!"

The nearby street light captured the man's frown. Pastor Roberts looked on with curiosity. When the sniper moved as the FBI agent had instructed, Penance squeezed off a shot to the alarm of the border guards. The street lamp shattered in a shower of glass. Pastor Roberts jumped a bit as the gunshot went off.

"Sorry, I just realized the light completely silhouetted you. Not a good place to be if baddies come rolling up," Penance declared. Turning his attention to the contents of the truck, he shrugged nonchalantly, "Well, now that I've got your attention, let's get you refortified for the rest of the evening."

Penance hauled the box of ammunition and four of the *Las Piratas* guns. He handed the ground crew Tec-9s while giving AK-47s to the snipers. "Good for about three hundred and fifty yards, give or take," he announced.

"How are you gentlemen making out?" Pastor Roberts asked. "Nice night, if there is such a thing, under the circumstances.

"We're good. Ready for action," one man chirped, tapping the Tec-9 he had just received.

"Be careful what you ask for," Penance quipped. "Look, gentlemen, this is likely to be a long night. If our analysis is correct, they are going to come hard. Your job is to keep them as far from your barricade as possible. They are typically stopping about one hundred yards away, within the range of the snipers. In one instance, they got through the barricade and started to flank...that's not good. If that happens, hunker down and call for reinforcements."

"So, you can flank their flank," another man grinned.

"Exactly. In the heat of battle, though, you have to be ready to survive with what you've got, the four of you," Penance added.

"Look, as I started saying, keep them at bay. Taking out a few gang members is not worth your life. Your absolute, number one job is staying safe. Hide, run, fire, and run and hide again. Stay safe. Stay alive," Penance instructed to bobbing heads.

"It's a shame Sawyer has to have this mark on her history. Let's make sure we are all able to get together at dawn's light. Bring our mothers, wives, and daughters back home...along with those who stayed behind to fight with us, and celebrate our town's survival. All of us," Pastor Roberts said. Bowing his head, he prayed.

Leaving their final delivery stop, Pastor Roberts put the truck in gear and headed back towards the bank. Penance watched as the quaint town rolled by his window. He feared for what the Sawyer might look like by morning, a fear he kept mostly to himself.

"You do well speaking to the troops. I think they find comfort in your knowledge and having been through stressful battles and come out the other side," Pastor Roberts observed.

"Yes, I enjoyed running a team. I was supposed to be running an entire program of teams had I not messed up," Penance said. As the bank came into view, he asked, "There's a lot about second chances in your stories. Is redemption really so accessible?"

The pastor looked over at the agent as he slid the truck into park. "Those stories are from one of two sources, either accounts from Jesus' walk in the New Testament or people that I have known through the years. Yes, redemption is accessible. Not always easy, but it is accessible."

Penance was lost in thought as he stared at the street lamp outside his window. "How do you start down that road?"

"First, you have to accept and forgive yourself," the pastor said. "Confess what is weighing on you to someone, out loud. Pray about it sincerely and let it go. Start walking down a new, more righteous path."

"You make it sound so easy, just put it in a bubble and let it go, huh?"

"Never said easy. Probably no more classic case in the scripture than Saul. He was a brutal and effective persecutor tasked with arresting Christians with impunity. When he saw the light, literally, he became Paul. Led the charge for the growth of Christianity as one of the most influential apostles in the times of the New Testament," Pastor Roberts said. "Anytime I have doubts in our ability as fallible humans on earth to change, that is the story I fallback to."

Penance looked deep in thought, trying to digest the message the pastor was delivering to him. "When this is over, let me buy you a beer, and we can go into that story in greater detail," the FBI agent said.

"Given the circumstances of the night, I might recommend sooner than later, but if it is to be that way, so it is," Pastor Roberts said, climbing out of the truck. "But given the night, might make that a bourbon."

"You sure you're ready for this?" Penance asked.

"I'd rather not, but if it comes down to protecting the innocent people of Sawyer, you won't have to worry about me hesitating," Pastor Roberts replied.

"You've got my trust in the final security between the outside and Dixon and Annie in the Comms Room," Penance declared to a nodding Pastor Roberts. "And you're on for that bourbon."

Thirty-Five

Special Agent Penance found Bubba and encouraged him to prepare for heading out on patrol the remainder of the night. Finding Deputy Director Dixon, the two pulled off into a room adjacent to the bank president's office.

"How are the troops holding up?" Dixon asked as slid an office chair around to sit.

Penance followed suit. "They're doing okay. Wide-eyed. Some too gung-ho for their own good, that will change when bullets start flying in their direction. It is a terrible thing to have civilians out on the street."

"I don't disagree. This is their home. They elected to stay and defend it. Have to respect that," Dixon said.

"I do. Good people at the heart of them. I am worried about them, though," Penance replied.

"It's healthy to worry. Prevents taking people for granted. They aren't just a tally mark like they can seem to be from Washington's perspective," Dixon said. "There are no acceptable losses in the real world."

Reaching behind him, he grabbed two glasses from the desk. Placing one in front of Penance and another in front of himself, he produced a bottle of bourbon. "Pappy Van Winkle. Found it in the president's office. Figured he wouldn't mind."

Pouring a dram in each glass, the director put the bottle away. "Salud!"

Penance grabbed the glass, swirling the liquid as he hoisted the glass high, "Cheers!"

Each man slammed the glass back and set them back down on the table.

"Any word from the boys in DC?" Penance asked.

Dixon looked grim, "They are assembling."

"Assembling?" Penance spat. "There is a war upon us, and they are assembling."

Dixon looked over his bourbon, "The kinds of bureaucratic stuff you had hoped to fix from the inside, huh?"

"Had I actually gotten there...," the agent scoffed.

"Who knows, maybe you still will."

Penance shot his boss a glance over his glass, "If it wasn't likely before, it sure as hell won't be now." Taking a sip of his whiskey, "The brass will consider this whole mess my fault."

Dixon laughed in spite of himself, "Well, you sure have brought a certain amount of excitement to our forgotten little town."

"Yeah," Penance nodded and looked a bit distant.

"Oh, come now. There were bad guys that needed arresting, a few of them needing to be shot. The point is, the bad guys were there. You just happened not to tolerate them once you flushed them out. That is not necessarily a bad thing," Dixon defended his man.

"Can I expect those to be your words in the report?" Penance asked.

Dixon beamed, "Hell no! I like my job too much."

Penance smiled at the director. Swirling the last trace of bourbon in his glass, he tilted it to his lips and slammed his glass down. "Well, might as well get back to it. Bad guys to flush and shoot. Might even arrest a few...but probably not."

The agent rose and looked back at his boss, "Be safe, Dixon. I'm just starting to like you."

"You be safe too, Alex," Dixon said and then grinned. "Not sure I like you a whole lot, though."

Penance bounced his grin back and disappeared down the hallway.

Alex Penance and Officer Bubba circled the town in the agent's Porsche. Cruising past the checkpoints, they were silent, listening for activity.

When they had made their third loop, Penance asked, "What is the highest point in town?"

Bubba looked thoughtful for a moment. "Water tower at the distillery."

"Right," Penance nodded. "Commanding view of town, too."

Making a beeline for the spirits distillery with its four-story brick building, the FBI agent stopped the car alongside the main entrance.

Getting out, they made their way to the fence enclosure surrounding the water tower. Tossing his long rifle over his shoulder, Penance led the way.

Finding the enclosure locked, Penance drew a set of tools from his wallet. Working the pins of the lock, they heard the mechanical release within seconds.

Pushing the gate aside, they reached the ladder. "Make it up there?" Penance asked.

"Now's not the time to ask me, we're here. I'll make do," Bubba said, and with a smirk added, "Save me a spot."

Taking the lead, Penance grasped the ladder and began scampering up to the platform ringing the base of the holding tank. Looking down, he watched as Bubba overtook several rungs, paused, and moved on to consume more in his path.

Convinced his partner would make it okay; the FBI agent looked out of the town of Sawyer. From this vantage, he found the town quite charming—neatly placed streets with rows of buildings, all lined with Magnolia and Angel Oak trees.

As a meaty hand surfaced on the top rung, Penance leaned over, grasping a fist full of the officer's shirt, pulled him up safely onto the scaffolding of the water tower. Taking a moment to catch his breath, Bubba sunk down on the metal grate and leaned back against the tower.

"I ain't ever been up here before. Kinda nice, really. The peacefulness...shame this night won't stay that way," Bubba said, taking in the Sawyer skyline.

"No, no it won't," Penance replied. "But it is nice, for now."

"What drives men to act this way? Take life and people for granted?" the officer asked.

Penance shook his head. Shrugging, he allowed his eyes to scan the night, "Power, desperation, money. That's the core of it. The ones at the top of it, at least. For others, the gang life becomes their family. The guys at the top, their patriarchs. They feed them, give them purpose, if a bit...if a lot messed up."

"Still, the taking of innocent life. Going after an entire town," Bubba sighed. "I just don't get it."

"I've been around this stuff for a long time, Bubba. I don't want to get it. I just want to stop those that intend others harm," Penance declared.

"At all costs?" Bubba pressed."

Penance frowned, "At all costs? No. But given the choice between an innocent life and someone intending to harm them, well, there really is no choice."

"Yeah," Bubba said thoughtfully, "But it still must be tough to pull the trigger…"

"I don't take ending anyone's life lightly, but when someone is foolish enough or evil enough to force that position, no. I don't have too tough of a time of a pulling the trigger," Penance said.

"Oh," Bubba said quietly.

"It's okay, even normal, to not feel very good about it. I've had intense training, experiences in the field, gone after people much like these *Las Piratas*. Nasty people bent on delivering tremendous harm to a lot of innocents. I wouldn't say the edges ever dull when it comes to taking a life, but the knowledge that my pull of the trigger is saving someone else's life, at times my own, releases any hesitation," Penance said.

The thoughtful Bubba nodded slowly, intent on the nighttime vista of Sawyer.

The pair sat in silence for some time before Penance inquired, "Tell me about your dad."

Bubba didn't speak right away. "My daddy…," he started. "He was a good man. A Master Sergeant in the army. We lived in Louisiana, at Fort Polk. 10th Mountain Division."

Bubba laughed softly, "Daddy was a big, commanding man. He didn't move for the world. The world moved for him. As a black man in the army, he had no problem with commanding respect. He was a hero. *My* hero. Tough as he was with his unit, I can only imagine how he would lay waste to the enemy, he always came home as my daddy. Not Master Sergeant Jeffries. To Momma and me, he was kind and gentle."

"Sounds like a good man. It's not always easy to be in a combat situation, return from deployment and reconnect as you were," Penance said.

"There were times we could tell he was fightin' it. But he never let it boil," Bubba acknowledged. "Then one trip, to some mountain in the Middle East, a mortar got lucky, found its way to his unit. That box…I hated seeing that box, yet somehow felt like he came home to us. I was in Middle School. The army took care of us for their allotted survivor terms, and we found our way back to Sawyer. Momma started her kitchen, and I helped."

"I'm sorry, Bubba. I'm grateful for his and your family's service."

"Yeah," Bubba said solemnly.

"Must have been tough, you were just a kid, and suddenly the man of the house," Penance observed.

"It was. I helped Momma around the house and at the restaurant. She still pushed me to do good at school and football. It just didn't feel the same for me without Daddy. I joined ROTC and was determined to get a unit myself and go overseas, like I could find the random fool who killed my Dad. Senior year I ruptured my patella tendon. Couldn't earn the commission I wanted by enlisting, but…"

"But, you could become a cop."

"Not exactly my Daddy's footsteps…," Bubba mourned. "You seen me. I ain't all that tough."

"Tough comes in many flavors, Officer. Being a hero's not all fist swinging and guns blazing the real ones aren't like that at all. The real ones know how to build people up. That's you. Your dad's a hero for what he did in Afghanistan or wherever he was. The bigger hero moment was coming home a husband and a father, leaving his baggage at the base," Penance countered.

Bubba shrugged, "Yeah, maybe you're right.'

"He'd be every bit as proud. You're a good man, Bubba. A good man and a good cop," Penance affirmed.

"Thanks, coming from you, that means a lot," Bubba gushed.

"I'm just a demoted FBI agent with a chip on my shoulder."

Bubba laughed, "That's what you want the town to think."

Bubba stopped short as he stared out at the skyline, "Uh…oh."

A firework that Penance had placed at one of the checkpoints shot into the air, exploding to bloom in the night air. It was a sign that a band of *Las Piratas* was approaching. Penance swung his long rifle in the direction of the checkpoint. Staring down the scope, he trained his attention on any movement beyond the barrier.

Bubba came alongside with the night vision binoculars. "Aw man, they are coming in force. Lead vehicle and probably…ten more behind it."

"There seems to be a guy in charge," Penance asked as gunfire exploded from both directions in that area.

Bubba scanned the *Las Piratas*, "There, a third vehicle, center of the road. Just ducked behind a door."

Penance fired a shot. Through the scope, he could see a keyed reaction a man down behind the car door. "Bad guys never have learned car doors are only good shield in movies and TV shows. Who's next?"

Before Bubba could respond, another firework rocketed up into the air, and then another. "Two more checkpoints are under attack!"

"Ok, let's give this one a head start, and we'll move on," Penance said. He shared the instinct to immediately bounce to the next threat, but he knew as outmanned as they were, they would need to be strategic, and they would not be able to defend all fronts at all times.

"Two more guys seem to be giving orders. Either side of the row, same, range," Bubba replied, concentrating on the scene well below the water tower.

"Alright, I've got them. Go ahead and get to the next checkpoint," Penance said, his voice almost a whisper as he controlled his breath and located his target. Firing a shot, he watched just long enough to see the target react before pivoting his aim and repeating the process with another shot.

Getting up from his perch, he circled the water tower scaffold until he found Bubba. "What do we have here?"

"Similar scene, ten or twelve cars, one guy in particular barking out orders," Bubba replied. "If it makes it easier, roughly the same location."

"Alright...I've got him," Penance declared, squeezing the trigger. Seeing the *Las Piratas* lieutenant fall, he asked, "Who's stepping up to the plate?"

"They uh, they seem confused. Maybe that guy by the van?" Bubba suggested.

"Good enough," Penance said, agreeing with a pull of this trigger finger.

"Let's move on to the next group," the FBI agent said.

Nodding, Bubba relocated once again.

They repeated the process, taking out the top *Las Piratas* members that they could identify. Ready to move on, the final checkpoints had launched their fireworks. The first group set off another of theirs, indicating a breach.

"There, quick!" Penance said.

Running to the side of the water that had a vantage on the breached checkpoint, they surveyed the scene. Several *Las Piratas* had made their way between the construction vehicles and were attempting to break their cover for deeper into Sawyer. Without hesitation, Penance squared up a shot, clipping one gang member in the shoulder. Without lifting the rifle, he pivoted it along the railing locating another target and fired a shot.

"Other side, two men are through!" Bubba called, his voice nearly a shout.

"Be my eyes in the sky; keep calling in the scene. I'm going down," Penance said, pulling a pair of gloves from his tactical bag.

Slinging an assault rifle over his shoulder, he grasped the rails of the water tower lower and dropped down, allowing the metals rails to slide though a loose grip of his gloved hands. Using the soles of his shoes, he pinched the metal rails, allowing him to control his descent until he was close to the ground and let go.

Not wasting any time, Penance ran through the shadows towards the checkpoint with the breach. In his earpiece, he heard Bubba dictate what he saw in the scene. "There are now four guys behind the barrier. The first two are about two blocks deep. The second two are lagging by one. You are right on top of the first pair."

Penance pressed his back to the wall of a building. Listening intently and spying for shadows, he slowed his breath. Just the tip of a shadow breached the triangle of visual space around the corner. Penance ducked low and spun out far enough where he could squeeze off a shot and wrap back into safety.

The screams from the other side of the wall told him he had hit at least one of the first two men. The barrage of bullets plinking the wall gave him an idea of where the second man might be. Taking a few steps back, he began making a slow, full arch, pivoting his way around the corner. Continuing the methodic triangle, he caught the slightest visual. Four inches of movement later, Penance had dispatched the second of the two gunmen.

As he moved forward, to find the second pair, his earpiece crackled. "Penance, we have another breach. West side, wait, and north end. They are now coming through the north end!"

"Call it into the bank. Which is worse?"

"North, definitely north," Bubba reported.

"Okay, have the bank send no less than a pair, tell them to be careful and retreat if they need to, I'll head north," Penance said.

Pushing ahead, Penance found the second pair. As one gunman sprinted to a new position, Penance gauged his sites a few steps forward, putting pressure on the trigger, he anticipated where the man would be and dropped him. The other scurried back towards the breach in the barrier.

Securing his gear, Penance moved as quickly as he could toward the north barrier.

"Penance, they got both of our guys on the ground at the north checkpoint. The snipers are pinned down," Bubba reported over the radio.

"I'm close," Penance whispered. Half a dozen men were progressing through the streets while another half dozen were on the snipers like a hound dog eyeing a treed cat.

The FBI agent crouched behind a cement planter. He wrestled between dividing them to lessen the advantage or keep them pooled in a position he could determine where they all were. If it weren't for the men in the sniper nests, he likely would have opted for divide and conquer, but that operation would take more time. He decided keeping them grouped was a more efficient option.

"Bubba," Penance whispered. "Take shots behind them!"

"Uhh…," the officer started.

"It's okay," Penance hissed. "You don't have to hit them, just make them real uncomfortable about going backward."

A second later and shrapnel from the asphalt showered the cone of light from the nearby street lamps.

"Attaboy, Bubba," Penance breathed to himself.

Taking advantage of the alarmed *Las Piratas*, who had just turned to sprint towards his direction, Penance sprayed the pavement in front of them. From his vantage, he called, "You are trapped between my sniper and my assault rifle! Lay down your arms or every one of you will be dropped!" the men hesitated as shots from Bubba's long rifle continued to pepper the ground behind them.

Finally, one nodded, and the others laid down their weapons. Penance carefully pulled away from his protected vantage and moved toward the group, kicking their guns aside and quickly went to work zip-tying their hands.

"Up," he demanded, the men slowly rose to their feet. Spying the butcher shop, he fired a burst from his assault rifle through the large window in front.

Motioning to the *Las Piratas*, he marched them through the rough glass opening he had created and into the shop. "In there," he waved the barrel of his gun towards the meat locker. Reluctantly the men followed suit. "Good news, if we win, you'll probably be saved. If we don't, your guys won't likely find you. I'm good either way," Penance said as he slammed the freezer shut.

Knowing the freezer had a door release from the inside, he twisted a heavy electrical cord around the outer hand and tied it securely to brackets on either side of the door.

"How are we doing out there, Bubba?"

"They keep coming and immediately sight on our posts," Bubba responded.

Penance curse to himself, "The lights!"

"Lights?" Bubba asked.

"The town's light guide the *Las Piratas* directly where to attack while our guys have gangsters appearing out of the dark!" Penance declared. Thinking for a moment, he asked. "Where is the Sawyer substation?"

"It's not far from the water tower, about a quarter-mile from where you are now to your south," Bubba shared.

"Roger that, I'm on the move," Penance said.

Making his way through town, he headed for the area Bubba said he would find the primary power connection to Sawyer. Looking around, he spied a row of landscaping equipment. Finding a gas canister, he tossed it over the chain-link fence amid the main transformers he followed it with inserting a tracer round into his chamber. He fired a shot into the gas can.

In seconds, the entire substation burst into flames, causing the transformers to arch. The whole town's electrical grid flashed. Sawyer went dark.

"They'll be mad at me tomorrow for that," Penance muttered to himself. "If we get to tomorrow, anyways."

THIRTY-SIX

"You alright down there?" Bubba called through the radio.

"Tiptop. Took away the cartel's advantage with the lights. Now its time to turn the tables. Call to the checkpoints to use their remaining fireworks as spotting flares. Let's light up the *Las Piratas* positions!" Penance said.

"Roger that!" Bubba said. "I know your hands are full, right before you turned out the lights, the south checkpoint was breached."

"I'm on it," Penance replied and darted through the streets towards the latest breach. As he approached, he could hear gunfire.

Peering through the cover of a grove of trees, he assessed the situation. He could see muzzle flashes surrounding the checkpoint. Suddenly, the sky was lit up, just briefly from a brilliant firework.

The flash highlighted two *Las Piratas* closing in on the ground crew at the barrier. Penance took careful aim, fired a burst shot, swung his barrel and fired a second round. As another firework lit up the sky, he found that he had hit his two marks, but there were two more in the shadows. He tried to get an angle but couldn't get a clean shot. The gunmen, however, had a bead on the checkpoint crew.

Sighing, Penance knew he had to act. Sprinting towards the checkpoint barrier, he covered half of the ground before he had the attention of the gang members. More importantly, he had changed his vantage enough that he had solid shots. He took the first man out. The second began firing in Penance's direction. Penance felt a hot sting burrow into his right thigh. Not giving in, he kept moving, getting off two quick shots, dropping the second gunman.

Rushing in, Penance couldn't fully gauge the threat, as a third man appeared in his peripheral vision. The man had a clear shot on him. Prepared for his own end, he was surprised when the man collapsed to the ground. Staring in the direction of where the shot came from based on how the man fell, Penance was surprised the bullet did not come from a checkpoint sniper.

Taking his second chance to value, he sprinted to a nearby alley and out of the open. He assessed his leg, which was openly bleeding. While unpleasant, he guessed by the severity of the injury, it was likely shrapnel and not a bullet.

Pulling a field roll of field dressing out of his pack, he quickly wound it around his leg and tied it off.

In between the occasional firework blast and subsequent exchange of gunfire, Penance heard a new sound as engines roared towards the checkpoint he had just helped defend. Suddenly an explosion rocked the barrier, and two light four-wheel drive technicals poured into town, mounted machine guns clattered to life, tearing up the sniper nests and anything else that happened to be in their way.

"Great!" Penance muttered to himself.

"Uh, Penance, we've got...tanks?"

"Technicals – vehicle-mounted machine guns," Penance corrected. "Either way, it's bad news!"

Moments later, a building a mere block away from the FBI agent exploded, spraying shrapnel throughout the neighborhood. Penance dove behind the wheel well of a car to avoid being hit by the debris. "And...we've got mortars."

"The technicals took opposite directions, circling the town," Bubba reported.

A mortar blasted another building closer to the center of town.

"The technicals are bad. The mortar is worse. Can you try and locate where the shells are coming from?" Penance asked.

As he got the words out, another building, not far from the bank, exploded. "They are zeroing in on the square, this is bad!" Penance noted.

"Got it. The mortar is posted just outside the southern gate the technicals crashed through," Bubba said.

"Good work, I'll see what I can do," Penance said. Maneuvering as quickly as he could, he made a beeline for the southern checkpoint. His only consolation was that with the mortars targeting downtown, the technicals would avoid that area. Once he dealt with the mortars, he would need to contend with them quickly, or they could shred the bank and everyone inside.

As he ran, he pressed, "Bubba, get everyone from the checkpoints to fall back to the marketplace square as soon as the shelling stops. Warn them to take cover, because the machine guns will arrive on their heels."

"Roger that," Bubba responded.

Peering out from the shadows, Penance could see a small, well-armed contingent defending the mortar with a two-man team tending to it. All in, he counted six *Las Piratas*, not knowing what was on the other side of the barrier.

The four guards were well spread, covering decent angles, each with cover. Penance breathed deep, determining a plan of action. Before his brain could complete a strategy, one of the guards abruptly dropped. A moment later, a second one fell.

Not hesitating, Penance sprung into action, just as another mortar shell launched into the air. Hitting the open space between his protective shadows and the checkpoint, both guards spun his direction. Firing a shot in stride, he hit one of the gunmen in the chest as he continued to pull the trigger. Launching into a roll, he sprung up to fire on the last visible guard only to see him knocked backward, a bullet shattering his skull.

Penance swung his aim from a half-kneeling position targeted and locked on a *piratas* delivering a shell to a man behind the mortar. With a well-aimed shot, the man fell, the shell bouncing off the pavement. As the second man bent to retrieve it, Penance fired a quick burst, dropping him as well.

Rushing to the barrier, Penance peered out beyond the checkpoint. He could see three men scrambling by the line of cars a football field away. Penance wheeled the mortar around, ratcheted the telemetry, and fired a shot in the direction of the men.

His shot was not on target, but its effect was. The men dove to either side of the road for safety, providing Penance the opportunity to remove the firing pin, rendering the mortar useless.

"Now, Bubba, now! Get all checkpoints to retreat!" Penance called into his radio.

Penance darted to the building used as one of the checkpoint sniper nests. Halfway up the stairs to the post, Penance found a man lying in the stairwell. A glance showed several injuries. The weary man looked up at the FBI agent with frightened, hopeful eyes.

"It's alright buddy, let's get you to safety, and we'll get you fixed up," Penance said. Slipping his arm under the man's shoulder, he hoisted him up. Bearing most of the weight, Penance guided the man to the front door.

A pair of headlight beams cut the night. Penance rolled the injured man out of view. The tactical stopped in the middle of the street. Two armed men hopped out and cautiously approached the checkpoint where the mortar fired while the man in the bed of the truck slowly arched the machine gun turret in a 350 degree turn to the limit of the belt ammo feeder.

As the machine gunner moved the barrel away from where Penance stood, the agent rolled to his right, aiming a careful and decisive shot at the gunner. In an instant, the two inspecting the checkpoint turned and fired at Penance.

The driver in the technical got out and darted for the turret. Penance concentrated his shot at the driver, dropping him just as his head breached the bed of the truck. In doing so, Penance was the recipient of a clear shot himself, hitting his tricep with a through and through. Rolling behind cover, wincing in pain, Penance readied himself for the imminent shoot out. Before the man could reach him, he was knocked to the ground by a large caliber round. The second man tried to duck behind a planter, but the shooter had a better vantage and took him out anyway.

Penance could hear the shouts of the *Las Piratas* closing in from beyond the barrier, where they had long recovered from the wild shell attack. Wasting no time, he hoisted the injured man up to his feet, ignored his own growing list of searingly painful injuries, and pushed towards the technical.

"The other men from the checkpoint...," Penance started as they moved towards the vehicle.

The man looked at Penance and shook his head solemnly.

Understanding, Penance slid the man into the passenger seat. Rolling over the hood of the truck, he grabbed the steering wheel and accelerated away from the checkpoint.

Sliding the technical into a hasty stop outside of the final barriers set around the market place square that served as the bank's final layer of protection and the town's final fallback position, Penance hopped out of the driver's seat. Seeing the relief on the faces of those manning this new set of checkpoints, he motioned for one to come over and help him.

One of the men quickly left his post and met Penance at the passenger door of the truck. "This man is pretty banged up in need of immediate medical attention," Penance declared. "Can you help see him inside?"

The man nodded and helped the inured checkpoint guard to his feet and inside the barrier.

To the other men at the marketplace square position, he shared, "The mortar is disabled, and clearly, they are down to one technical, but they are closing in. The full force of the cartel is focusing on this spot. They have breached the barriers. Dig in, make sure you have protective cover."

"I hear the other technical! Let's fight fire with fire!" a man from the square yelled, running to the tuck. Two more men joined.

"That'll work. Good luck, I am going to try and make sure everyone else makes it here safely from the drawback," Penance declared, once more disappearing into the shadows.

Slithering through the dogwood and magnolia shrouded streets, Alex Penance made his way around the checkpoints. Most had cleared out with Bubba's call to fall back. Hanging his head on two too many occasions, he identified casualties of Sawyer townspeople that bravely fought but were taken out by the *Las Piratas* cartel gang members.

His stealthy movements paid off when he arrived just short of the water tower. Two *Las Piratas* gunmen were splitting up to divide Bubba's attention in the water tower allowing the other to snipe him while distracted.

Moving carefully and quickly, Penance rushed the sniper setting up for his shot. By the time the man heard the ruffle of the FBI agent's clothing, Penance was on him. One hand over his mouth, the opposite forearm wrenched on the man's throat.

The man's initial protests of flailed arms and muffled screams ultimately fell to silence as he collapsed in Penance's arms. Flipping and zip-tying the man, the agent quickly ducked under the shadows after the other gang member.

As the *Las Piratas* member did his job of distraction, taking potshots wildly towards the water tower a quarter-turn from the sniper, Penance did not have to reach him before a well-placed shot from the water tower ended the antics.

"Alright, Bubba!" Penance whispered to himself. "Now, to get you to safety, big man."

Ascending the tower quickly, he was surprised to see a gun barrel aimed at his forehead. He was even more surprised to see who was holding the long barrel rifle.

"Hello, Agent Penance," the unmistakable southern drawl of Shannon Whatcom cooed.

"Shannon! What the…," Penance began as stared in bewilderment as he climbed completely onto the water tower scaffolding.

Shannon pulled the gun away from his head and scanned the terrain before looking at the agent. A grin swept across the girl's face. "What? Surprised to see me? I saved your ass on more than one occasion out there, didn't I?"

Penance nodded in acknowledgment, a half-smile crossing his own lips, "That was *you*. Nice shooting."

"Don't be so surprised. I can outshoot most of the fellas in this town. And ol' Bubba here is a better spotter than a shooter," Shannon said.

"I thought you were a goner at the mortar," Bubba said, the concern evident in his voice. "But Shannon, she didn't hesitate. Pop! Pop!"

"Well, not to break this party short, I came here to pull you…and now Shannon, to the fallback position," Penance said.

"I hate to argue with a lawman, but I think I am better use and frankly, safer here," Shannon protested.

"You had two *Las Piratas* flanking you," Penance said.

"The guy at nine o'clock I popped and the guy at six I assume you took care of? I know. Bubba saw them. I mean, the mortar shell explosives had me plenty worried and those crazy trucks a bit, but I gather you took them offline. There ain't no way, outside of a lucky shot, one of them is gettin' me up here. In town, I'm scared for all y'all," Shannon argued.

"Bubba?" Penance pressed.

"If it's alright with you, I'd just as soon stand here with her. Stay her spotter," Bubba said in earnest.

Penance gazed at the trio of long rifles and the pair of ARs next to the open backpack overflowing with ammunition. Shannon arrived with a full arsenal at the top of the tower.

The FBI agent nodded reluctantly, "Alright."

"What are you gonna do?" Bubba asked.

"I'm going to defend the bank and the town's people in the market square with everything I've got," Penance said.

With an extended hand, he looked Bubba in the eye. The officer's large hand grasped Penance's. With a jerk, he pulled the agent into a hug.

"You be careful," Bubba said. "I ain't got that many friends."

"You have one more than you had a few weeks ago," Penance said, giving in to the hug.

Pulling away, he faced Shannon. "You continue to impress, in your own, very outside of the box ways, Ms. Whatcom," he said.

Shannon flashed a coy smile and lunged towards the agent. With a hand clasped around his neck, she pushed her lips onto his. "I'll see you when this is all over, Agent Penance," she whispered.

Penance, far from his usual unflappable stance, "Yeah," was all that he could mutter. "Stay sharp, stay alive," he said and made his way down the steel tower ladder. In the distance, the sound of two fully automatic machine guns trading fire echoed through the town.

THIRTY-SEVEN

J onas Frye took the turret controls in his hand.
He steadied his feet on the bed of the pickup
truck and began to scan the streets through the iron sights
of the machine gun. He felt the truck suspension give a
little as the substantial body of Dwight James joined him.

"Oh good, can you maintain the feed? When this
stuff starts, if we don't keep the flow, we're both toast,"
Jonas declared.

"Yeah, I got you, man," Dwight said.

Jonas paused and looked slightly over his shoulder at
the man who was helping him. He was a little surprised.
"Dwight?"

"Jonas," the man nodded.

"I uhh, it's good to have you here," Jonas
stammered.

"Yep."

"Uh, in high school...I was...an ass," Jonas
admitted.

"Yep."

"I'm, I'm sorry."

"It's all good. We *all* family tonight," Dwight said, the tone of his voice sincere, but never changing.

"Thanks, man. I won't forget this. You're a good man," Jonas said.

"Yep, don't forget."

"Right," Dwight returned his focus to the streetscape in front of him. His eyes widened, "Oh, sh….!"

The entire truck shook as he squeezed the trigger of the machine, the bullet spray painting an indiscernible pattern, yet the incoming technical stopped at the end of the intersection. Its turret slow and controlled, rolled its muzzle towards their truck.

Watching the erratic spray of asphalt and concrete shrapnel in their own gun's path, Jonas looked at Dwight, "Uh, maybe you'd better do this, and I help you instead?"

"Probably," Dwight nodded and stepped into position, replacing Jonas as the gunner.

As the muzzle flash from the opposite technical came to life, Dwight moved his own turret with strong hands and stared down the sight, letting loose on his.

From the side alley, Sheriff Day took careful aim at the *Las Piratas* technical gunner and levied a kill shot. Before he could move back undercover, a swarm of cartel gunmen opened fire, dropping the sheriff.

Dwight pulled the trigger and held on, moving the gun in incremental, smooth movements until he painted the technical and any spot sidewalk to sidewalk with 7.62 mm rounds. Jonas carefully fed the belt rounds through the turret so that Dwight could operate the machine until the case ran dry.

For a moment, the night air fell silent. Smoke spewed from the other technical. Concrete dust hung in the humidity. Any *Las Piratas* remotely in range of the muzzle of Dwight's machine gun laid to waste.

The next layer of *Las Piratas* gang members began to filter into place as the gun slowed to a stop, and shots began to lobby towards Dwight and Jonas.

Jonas tugged at the large framed man, "Let's go!"

As Jonas put his hand on Dwight's back and guided him off the end of the technical, he felt the sting of hot steel rip through his back and carry through his chest. Instantly, he fell forward, tumbling off of the truck.

Dwight caught him by his shirt with one hand. Adjusting so that he had a solid grip around Jonas' waste, he carried him through the market square checkpoint. "I got you, brother!"

With one hand, and with bullets impounding into his own back, Dwight rushed like a football running back, weaving through the obstacles until he and Jonas reached the front door of the bank, both collapsing unconscious at its entrance.

Penance moved quickly but cautiously through the town, making his way to the market square. The barrage of 7.62 mm machine gun fire reached a crescendo before temporarily descending into silence. Small arms fire soon replaced the heavy gunners.

A mass of Las Piratas began to circle the square, at least one hundred men strong, well dwarfing the town's fighters, which had dropped to the teens since the inception for the evening. Most held vigil in the bank, as Penance had instructed, ensure it remained secure. Some fled, worse, others lost their lives in the battle.

The water tower lost visibility to all but a quarter of the square. Penance could see Shannon doing what she could to thin the crowd. The *Las Piratas* had the inner circle border crew pinned down. Most ducking in whatever protective concrete crawlspace they could wedge themselves. Taking an offensive stance was primarily removed from the equation.

Penance had a decision to make. He could rush in and make what would likely be his, and the town's last stand, or he could stick to the shadows and keep on the move, taking potshots as the situation presented itself. Either way, he knew his impact would not be enough.

Ultimately, the *Las Piratas* numbers were too high, and help was too far away to turn the tide effectively.

Minimizing his gear to fast and light arms, he began to circulate the outer ring of the square. He timed his shots with those of the *Las Piratas*, covering the sound of his gunshots. Still, with every squeeze of the trigger and strike on a *Piratas*, the scrutiny of a gun barrel or two began to isolate him.

Dancing amongst the shadows, sliding in and out of the building alleyways, ducking behind planters, mailboxes, and vehicles, he levied what damage he could. The cartel began picking off the final checkpoint guards one by one.

Penance steadied himself using two trees several feet apart. He angled so that his position between the two squeezed down to mere inches. He held his breath as one cartel member slowly lined their orbit with another. Squeezing the trigger in rapid succession, Penance took the opportunity to double up on his chances and impact.

After completing a full circle with *Las Piratas* gun muzzles closing further and further in on his position, he knew he had run out of time. He was hunted from all sides, and they were closing in. Breathing deep, he was ready to spring from the shadows and take out as many *Las Piratas* as he could in his final stand as an FBI agent, as a member of Earth.

He consciously never closed his eyes in a skirmish, never knowing what iota of a moment might be the difference-maker. In this instance, he bowed his head and closed his eyes. Despite the battle still taking place, his world went oddly silent. He wondered in his mind if he had already been killed.

A voice inside his head whispered, "I've got you. It's okay. It's going to be okay."

Real or not, Penance took a deep breath, opened his eyes, and sprang from his spot. He fired a shot immediately, spun, whirling one-hundred and eighty degrees while changing his height stance, firing another shot. He continued this erratic dance, until his clip was nearly empty, each bullet in his magazine finding a host. Several rounds fired his direction sliced through his muscles, and many skimmed his flesh. When the magazine emptied, he reached for a replacement as the near full force of *Las Piratas* was honed on him precisely.

Suddenly, cartel members started dropping. In slow motion, Penance dropped to a knee. The *Las Piratas* members that had converged on him stumbled and fell while those closing in scattered.

He survived with a fresh magazine and a handful of painful, but not immediately life-threatening new scars. Through the haze of onslaught, walked Delvin Whatcom, his sons, and his men.

"Agent Penance, looked like you could use a hand," the Whatcom patriarch said.

"Yeah, I guess I could. Thank you," Penance gasped.

"Well, let's see if we can't clean up this stinking town," Whatcom said and began providing strategic orders to his men.

"You alright?" Delvin said, extending his hand to help Penance to his feet.

"I'll live," Penance said, subconsciously patting himself down, looking for holes more substantial than he realized.

"You're a tough son of a bitch," Delvin observed. "Not as smart as you look, though. Gotta know when to fish and when to cut bait. I'd say you were way past cuttin' bait."

Penance looked at the man; his mind still not reconciling that he was alive. "Captain of the ship goes down with it, I suppose. I started this with the cartel, figured I had better finish one or the other."

"Your ship? This ain't your ship, agent. You're just a stowaway along for the ride," Delvin laughed. "Now, let's put a proper end to this!"

Penance grinned, collected himself and joined the Whatcoms and their men in trying to repel the *Las Piratas* assault on Sawyer.

Slicing through a portion of the cartel ranks, Penance and Devlin's men fortified the marketplace square. The guards cautiously peered out from their protective nooks, and the fight renewed.

The ranks of the *Las Piratas* dwindled by death and by withdrawal.

By the time a handful of lieutenants were left, seething but surrounded, they dropped their guns and raised their hands. Delvin's men moved in, knocking the weapons out of reach and kicking them to their knees.

"Keep your hands up, gang-bangers!" Delvin snarled as he strode forward. His eyes twitched as he glared at the cartel members. His finger shook on the trigger of the sawed-off shotgun he levied at the group of men.

"Agent…I guess this is where I call you in to arrest them…or….," the Whatcom patriarch called.

"Arresting them at this point will do fine, thank you, Devlin," Penance said, moving towards the group pulling a wad of zip-tie handcuffs from his pocket.

Devlin nodded, his men took the plastic ties from the agent and began securing the cartel lieutenants.

Penance turned to Devlin. The agent was exasperated and exhausted. Confused, grateful, and completely at a loss for words. "I didn't expect you here."

"This is my town. My people. Like family, we have our squabbles. I'll kick my own son's asses, but if anyone else touches them...," Devlin shook his head.

"Got it. I'm thankful you came when you did," Penance admitted.

"I don't know what to think about you, Agent Penance. You're a problem and a promise," Devlin said, eyeing the agent.

Penance scoffed, "I feel the same, sir. Regardless, today, we're friends." Reaching out his hand, he shook the Whatcom family patriarch's hand firmly. It was seemingly the last gasp of energy he had.

"If it's alright, I'm going to check on the people in the bank. Think your boys can be proper hosts to these guys and ensure no straggling gang members get any crazy ideas?" the agent asked.

Devlin nodded.

Suddenly, each wound Penance had suffered seemed to declare itself at full volume. As he started to hobble towards the bank, Devlin called, "Hey, agent. Have you seen my daughter?"

Penance turned and laughed. "You weren't the first Whatcom to save the day in this mess. She's up in the water tower, sniping with Officer Jeffries. Quite the girl you have their, sir."

Devlin looked betwixt, started to speak, and then just nodded.

The lobby of the bank transitioned into a makeshift trauma center. Dwight and Jonas lie next to each other, their outstretched hands clasped, despite each man asleep with sizable morphine drips keeping their pain at bay.

Finding Pastor Roberts dutifully managing the exchange from the lobby to the teller area and ultimately the executive section of the bank, he nodded his appreciation.

"We should talk when this is over," Penance suggested as he stumbled by.

Penance staggered through, waving off the medic as he made his way towards the executive suites. Working his way through the gratefully secure stages of the bank, he found himself at the door of the bank president.

Leaning against the door jamb, he knocked with what force he could muster. "It's Alex!"

"Is it over?" he heard Annie call from the other side while she manipulated a series of locks ringing in satisfying metallic clicks.

"We hope so," Penance admitted, his brain questioning whether it was true. He suddenly wondered whether he should approach them, unsure whether their defenses with the Whatcoms would hold.

He stammered as the door opened, about to suggest they lock up and leave. Annie Hunt stood in the doorway. Her face pale with exhaustion and worry, yet exquisitely welcoming and beautiful. Without a word, she stepped forward, wrapping her arms around the weary, dirty, and bloody FBI agent.

For a moment, her embrace seemed like it took all of his pain away. Her warmth, her heartbeat radiated from her chest to his. It fueled him. It woke him from his battle-weary, zombie-like, well-earned malaise.

"You guys are okay?" he asked, his voice a hoarse whisper.

"Us?" Annie spat, taking a step back, she studied him, "We are fine. You look like a hot mess that needs a hospital bed."

Placing her hand to her mouth, she gasped, "Have you been shot?"

Penance grimaced, "A few times, I think."

"Agent Penance, sit down! That is a direct order that if you disobey, I will kick you out of the bureau myself," Deputy Director Dixon warned.

Wincing Penance nodded, "Yeah, I could sit."

THIRTY-EIGHT

Penance wasn't sure how long he had been out, but he woke abruptly to find a medic and the town family physician combing him over.

"Ah, Agent Penance, you're still with us. Your pulse was weak but viable. Welcome back," the doctor said. "I'm Doctor Walker. The EMT, Stephen, and I have assessed most of your injuries. You were bleeding in multiple locations and have countless abrasions, bruising, and swelling. You have at least two bullets or bullet fragments lodged in your upper torso. Fortunately, neither is necessarily close to an organ or your spine. You should consider yourself lucky."

"Yeah, I feel lucky," Penance gasped and winced.

"Why don't we fix a spot for you to lie down? I was just about to inject an infusion line into you," Dr. Walker suggested.

Penance shook his head, "No. No, thank you."

"At least something for your pain, I can only imagine what you are feeling," Dr. Walker pressed.

"You know what, doc? I'll take a few ibuprofen," Penance shifted in his seat and winced again, "Okay, *several* ibuprofen."

Doctor Walker raised an eyebrow, "I have…"

"No!" Penance cut him off. "I need to keep my wits about me. Who knows if this is over…I need to get back out there."

Doctor Walker looked back at Deputy Director Dixon, who just shrugged.

"Alright," he conceded. Turning to the EMT, he instructed, "Give him 800 milligrams."

The EMT nodded and produced the dose suggested.

"That's not going to…," he began.

"It's going to have to do. Thank you," Penance acknowledged accepting the medicine.

Releasing a deep breath, he stood, shaking the weariness from his head. "Time to check the lines."

"Let me go with you," Dixon offered.

Penance looked at him and then Annie somewhat feebly and nodded, "Alright, boss. Let's see how much of Sawyer still exists. Annie…"

"I know, man the comms until you give the official 'all clear'," the assistant district attorney rolled her eyes.

"Thank you," Penance pressed.

Motioning the doctor and the EMT out with Dixon and himself, he ensured the executive office door was once more secure. Moving through the hallways, they managed the layered security of the bank building.

"Alex," Pastor Roberts called. "Good to see you up and about. I was worried when I saw the doc rush in."

"I'm good," Penance nodded. "Would you…"

"Keep vigil at my post? Yes," Pastor Roberts assured.

"Thank you, Pastor," Penance waved and headed out into the lobby.

Most of the injured were stabilized and waiting for the call to medivac. Through the lobby windows, a faint pink glow mixed with the dark shades of blue filling the early morning sky. There were voices, but no gunfire in the streets. The FBI agent was grateful for that.

Delvin Whatcom remained the central commanding figure in the town center. He ordered men at each post. Seeing the FBI agents, he offered a wave.

"Delvin…," Dixon cocked his head at the presence of the head of the Whatcom household.

"Oh yeah, we'd probably all be dead by now if Delvin and his men didn't show up," Penance shrugged.

Delvin offered an outstretched hand to the Deputy Director, "Your man held his own, damn near pulled the whole thing off, right up to the end."

"Right up to the end is the proverbial part of all that," Penance admitted humbly.

"Glad you're here," Dixon said, shaking Whatcom's hand.

Penance looked grave, "You heard from Shannon and Bubba?"

Delvin nodded, "I sent a small team to go fetch them and escort them back safely. She's a strong-willed one. Slipped out on her own accord long before we decided to act."

"How did you know to step in?" Penance asked.

"We were observin'," Delvin said. "Didn't want to step in if we didn't have to. As the troops pulled into town center, I knew it was time."

"Lucky for me, for all of us, you did," Penance offered. "How's it looking?"

"Been quiet since you went inside," Delvin reported.

"Glad to hear that," Penance admitted. "Turning to Dixon, let's put a team together, two-man lead, four-man back up in a med wagon."

"You and I are the lead team if you're sure you're up for it," Dixon said, pointing back and forth at the two of them.

"I'm up for it," Penance declared defiant.

"That technical still work? Make a fine lead vehicle," Dixon said.

"Ammo's wasted, though there may be some in the defunct one down the block," Penance suggested.

"If it runs…," Dixon suggested. "I'll get the EMT, a driver, and two gunners."

As the FBI deputy director ran off to find his assignments, Penance and Delvin eyed one another. "Didn't think you liked this town," Delvin asked. "You sure put your backside on the line for it."

"Didn't think you liked it much, either. You could've waited this thing out safely from your compound," Penance prodded.

Delvin flashed a wicked grin and winked, "I won't tell anyone if you won't."

Penance returned a smile, "Agreed."

Penance searched the second technical for spare ammunition while he waited for Dixon to assemble a recon and rescue team. While the pickup was irreparably damaged, he was pleased to find an available cache of ammo in the truck bed.

Seeing the agent's successful discovery, but challenge lifting the case with his injuries, Delvin Whatcom sent two of his men to fetch the case and install in the other truck. He waved back over to wait for Dixon.

Penance willingly accepted and began making his way back to the marketplace square. A dozen feet from the checkpoint, he caught a shadow in his peripheral vision. His reaction and his draw speed retarded by pain, inflamed muscle constriction and sheer weariness. By the time he had his handgun to belt level, the shadow had already steadied a bead on him. For the countless time that day, his brain told him his time was up.

Carrying through with his draw, he was surprised when he heard the resolute crack of a nine millimeter, not in front of him, but from behind him. As he rounded into full position versus the gunman, he saw him fall and relaxed the finger on his trigger.

Spinning to where the shot had come from, he saw Bubba with his pistol drawn, smoke streaming out of the muzzle. Behind him was Shannon Whatcom, her weapons riding on her shoulders. The sight of his friend backdropped by the crimson glow of morning sun as light fought through the trees and streaming down the streets of Sawyer.

"Bubba!" Penance gasped. Amazed that his presence was lifesaving and that his friend confidently took the life of the would-be shooter.

"Penance!" Bubba returned. He looked down at his pistol for a long moment, surveyed the fallen gunman who was writhing and gasping.

Before either of the men could react, one of Whatcom's men put the struggling man out of his misery.

Penance whirled, started to speak in an official context, but then shook it off with a glance over to Devlin, who shrugged.

"Daddy!" Shannon squealed and ran over to her father. "You aren't mad at me, are you?"

Devlin looked proud, "How could I be? I hear you're the town angel."

"Well, the earthbound one maybe," Shannon grinned and did the slightest curtsy.

"How many is that?" Devlin asked.

"How many times has my butt been saved today? Too many to count," Penance said. Turning to Bubba and Shannon, he shared, "Saving my life aside. It's good to see you. I was worried about you two."

"I told you we had it covered," Shannon said.

Dixon joined them, motioning several men at the door to hold. "Are we still good out here?"

"For the most part," Penance said. "We need to be cautious and realize there may be stragglers that can still very much do us harm."

Nodding, Dixon waved the men over. "We'll take the lead in the technical, did you find ammo?"

"Yes. Delvin's men just fit the new belt supply into the feeder," Penance pointed towards the pick-up truck.

"Good. You four take the truck we used for supplies earlier. Trail us by half a block. If we stop, you stop. If we back up, you back up. We'll look for threats and survivors from either team," Dixon commanded.

Whispering to Penance, he asked, "You sure you're up for this?"

"I'm fine. Not going to say I haven't lost a step, but I'll pull through. We're good," the agent nodded.

"Fine, but let's pull another man to run the gun on our ride," Dixon said, accepting Whatcom's offer to supply one of his better shots.

Special Agent Penance and Bureau Deputy Director Dixon led the way through the streets of Sawyer. Dixon drove while Penance rode shotgun. They started off slow, careful not to miss a sign of *Las Piratas* activity or town's survivors.

The streets looked as though they had survived a war—asphalt damaged to the point that not all roads were passable. The mortar shells destroyed storefronts and houses. Two structures were burning, threatening to leap to a third building.

Only a few blocks from the marketplace square, they got out and surveyed the area. Deeming it clear, they pushed further out, calling into the bank that if any firefighters were among the crew that stayed behind, they might tend to the fire.

At each stop, Penance and Dixon explored for survivors and threats. Survivors were helped or carried to the pick up where the EMT could attend to them. Most threats came by way of injured cartel members that were left behind by the handful that retreated. Once disarmed, medical care was afforded for in the same manner the townspeople were. If they still presented a risk, they were restrained.

Combing through the town, they made a thorough sweep, returning twice with a full pick up truck of injured passengers. On their third tour, the sound of helicopters cracked overhead. Four Blackhawks and three medical transports streamed past the town and circled in a field just outside of the northern checkpoint.

Dixon and Penance looked at each other, "*Now* the cavalry is here!"

Motioning for the trailing truck to return to the marketplace square, Dixon drove the technical towards the field. Getting out, the field director flanked by four agents with assault rifles made a beeline for the Deputy Director. One of the Blackhawks remained over the town, sweeping the area. A pair of drones lifted into the air and began making lower level sweeps, each making a thorough grid-shaped pattern over their respective half of the town.

"Deputy Director Dixon, this looks like a war zone. What the hell happened here?" the Field director asked.

"Exactly what I warned D.C. was going to happen. The cartel sent nearly every man in their ranks here. Well over one hundred men dispatched. They were armed to the teeth, even had a pair of machine gun mounted technicals and a mortar," Dixon replied.

"This your man," the field director nodded towards Penance.

"He is," Dixon nodded. "Special Agent Penance, this is Field Director Peter Davison."

Davison eyed Penance.

"He's the reason there is any town left at all," Dixon announced.

"Pleasure to meet you. I can't begin to imagine what you all have been through. Have you…been shot?" Davison asked.

"A few times," Penance shrugged.

"Jones, take Agent Penance to the Medivac and have him looked after," Davison called over his shoulder to an agent who nodded and quickly moved to guide Penance to the chopper.

The Field Director looked Dixon, "What's the current sitrep?"

"We were looping for survivors and remaining threats when you buzzed overhead. Can't promise it's all puppies and kittens out there, but we eliminated most of the threat. Mostly quiet for the past hour with a few spot fires," Dixon reported.

"Alright, Dixon. Nice work holding things together. I wish we could have been here sooner. The moment they gave me green, we were airborne," Davison admitted. "We've got ground crews from nearly every direction coming in."

"They'll want to be on the lookout for fleeing cartel members," Dixon warned.

"Roger that, we'll get it called in. Comms up?"

"Cell towers still working, we have an internet feed to HQ. Powers down, no reason to have left the streets lined with gold for the cartel," Dixon replied.

Davison made a note, "We'll get that taken care of as well. Got a trauma unit?"

"Ragtag at the town bank. Patch jobs like Penance, a few on bags," Dixon reported.

"Roger that, we'll get better set up ricky-tick," the Field Director asserted. "Johnson, four-by-four teams, sweep, rescue, and spot fire. Start with a three-block path for med transport."

The agent named Johnson quickly assigned his teams, and they moved out less than forty seconds after ordered.

"Let's go check on your man, see if we can't get this town secure and healthy," Davison suggested.

As the two made their way to the Medivac helicopter, the found Penance embroiled in an argument with the medic.

"What's going on, boys?" Davison asked.

"Agent Penance needs transport for care at a hospital. He has multiple severe wounds. Most are through and through. Two are frags. They need surgical removal to avoid sepsis and further damage," the medic explained.

Davison frowned, "What's the problem?"

"He refuses to go, sir," the medic said.

"I see," Davison turned his attention to Penance. "You did a helluva job here today, agent. Aren't you good to get patched up and put back together whole?"

"Not until the day is done. This town...the cartel's fight was with me. I want to see the town with the storm clouds cleared," Penance declared. "Give me antibiotics to fight infection. If I start oozing or pass out from a fever, I'll crawl back to the helo myself."

Davison looked at Dixon, "He's your agent. It's your call."

Dixon laughed, "He's no one's agent but the FBI's. I don't see how anything less than an order from D.C. is going to get him on a helo until the town's people are safe to come out of their holes."

"So be it. Give the agent your best dose and strap a vitals watch on him. Track him from the Medi-vac. If his system goes haywire, I'll march him back by gunpoint if I have to," Davison told the medic.

The medic complied and injected Penance with a high dose antibiotic.

"Alright, let's get this town on its feet, so your man here feels good about flying out of here," Davison suggested.

THIRTY-NINE

The FBI team, armed with additional manpower, made a building by building search of Sawyer. Every door of every house, of every business, was marked to denote it had been searched and what or who they found.

The medical team marched through the town, following the safe path the search teams carved for them. In short order, they had a triage and a trauma tent set up to provide better interim field care for the injured while they waited for proper transport.

Another tent was set up to receive the bodies of the less fortunate, those that did not survive the night.

At long last, the "all clear" broadcasted from loudspeakers and emergency radios. While families who left town were encouraged to remain away, those cooped up in the local shelters, were allowed under escort to go to the marketplace square.

Penance made his way to the executive offices in the bank. Stopping to thank Pastor Roberts for his sentry duties, he agreed to catch up with him later in the day.

Knocking on the president's door, Penance waited. A minute clicked by, and he could not detect any movement from inside. Knocking again, a bit louder, he called out, "Annie!"

This time, his inquiry was met with the mechanical sounds of locks turning, and latches clicked into place. A sleepy Annie Hunt swung the door open. "I'm sorry, I guess I dozed off."

Penance laughed, "It was a *very* long night."

"That it was. I'm glad to see you," Annie took a hard study of him from head to toe. "No more holes?"

Penance shook his head, "No more than the last time you saw me."

"That's a relief. How's the world outside?" Annie asked, brushing her hair out of her face.

"Come with me, take a look for yourself," Penance said. Taking her hand, he strode through the bank halls one more time. Entering the town square, which was just trickling in with town's people from the recently opened shelters, Annie took in the busy scene.

"I see help from the outside finally came," the ADA noticed.

"They did. Med tents, a search and sweep team, and a security team are all on hand. More help is coming for ground med transport and infrastructure assistance," Penance said.

"What about the town?"

"Red Cross will come in when the bureau clears the next security level. They'll bring water and comfort care until the town is truly back to power," Penance said.

"What about you?"

"What about me?"

"Aren't you still a walking pinata with surprises inside?" Annie asked, touching him gently.

"I'll be alright," Penance said curtly.

Annie frowned, "You saved the town, time to take care of yourself."

"The town saved the town," Penance defended.

"They...*we* wouldn't have made it without you," Annie looked at him directly in the eyes.

As they talked and stood in the center of the marketplace square, townspeople began streaming in. Their moment was broken up by hugs and thank yous as the people of Sawyer showed their appreciation for the agent and his efforts.

As the sun arched its way overhead, authorities accounted for the casualties. The critically injured were flown to area hospitals and Penance and the responding agents rounded up the remaining *Las Piratas* members

Davison laughed as he and Dixon found the agent to bring him up to speed on the cartel members that had been rounded up on area highways fleeing Sawyer. "Quite the bizarre Easter egg hunt you made for us. We found cartel members zip tied all over the place- at the jail, in the woods, in ditches…did we miss any?"

Penance shrugged, "I'll have to think through it. Might be like when I was kid, we didn't find some of the eggs until the Fourth of July playing in the yard."

"We used real eggs. Usually find them by smell in a couple of weeks," Dixon recalled.

"Probably the same case here, I'd suppose," Penance quipped.

Davison wrinkled his nose at the prospect, "Better work on that list."

"Right," Penance grinned. Turning to Annie, he said, "Catch up with you in a bit?"

Leaving the square had become more cumbersome than entering it. Before Penance and Dixon reached the edge, Mayor Kittridge flagged them down as he stood on the steps of the bank. "Hang on a minute fellas. I want you here for this."

Raising his voice, the mayor called above the crowd, "People of Sawyer, under the light of day, our nightmare is finally over. An evil had inflicted our town like none other. They frightened us, chased us, damaged our roads and our buildings, hurt us and heartbreakingly, took a few of our loved ones from us.

Today, I stand before you, as humble as I have ever been. This isn't just the town of Sawyer. After this day, it is the Sawyer family. Our town has been great. It has seen its failures and a few ugly times. The past few days have been as horrific as it gets. The whole time, I was amazed by how the town came together. Those that needed to leave, left. Quickly and safely and God bless them, I look forward to their safe return as I am sure you all do. Those that stayed, bunkered down together, taking care of each other. Some of the bravest men and women this town has ever seen stayed to defend the town and her people.

Some of the brave lost their lives. Others were hurt, some medivaced to area hospitals, we'll work to keep you updated on how they are doing.

There are heroes at almost every turn in this square. Look left, look right. Thank someone, shake their hand, hug them. I love and appreciate every single one of you," the mayor wiped a tear from his cheek. "Pastor Roberts, could you, would you..."

Pastor Roberts stepped up to join the mayor. "Would you all mind, let's take a quick knee for our fallen."

The pastor dropped to a knee. The mayor followed suit. One by, from the Whatcoms, to the police officers, to Penance and Dixon, the entire town took a knee and held a long moment of silence.

"Dear Lord, we are so grateful for all of us to see daylight, each other, another amazing day. We are grateful for those you kept safe at a distance or in our shelters. We are grateful for those who strapped on your armor and stayed to protect the innocent. We are mournful for those we lost and pray those who are receiving medical care come back to us in the safety of your protective hands. We pray days like this don't afflict Sawyer or any other town ever again. That the children the cartel preyed on are under your protective care, and no one has to fall into their fate with the monsters after today.

Lord, we pray you to help us put our community and our lives back together. Not like before, but even better. We came together because we had to. I pray we stay together because we want to. Amen."

Prior to resuming their duties or whatever task they had been about to embark on, the people of Sawyer spent time appreciating one another and one time pausing to give a round of applause to the FBI and medic teams that came to help bring solace to the town.

Additional crews arrived to put power back on and ensure any buildings damaged in the fight were still safe for occupancy.

Penance and Dixon squirreled away from the crowd to ensure that they had indeed covered their bases. Penance, in particular, concentrated on retracing his steps to ensure he didn't forget anyone.

Borrowing a golf cart, the two sped around town, moving through the evening as best as Penance could recall. The exercise helped them create the critical points for a draft report and allowed Penance to find any missing Easter eggs, as Davison suggested.

Slowing by the Sawyer High School football stadium, Penance nudged Dixon and pointed towards the far end of the field.

With power restored, the football stadium scoreboard lit up, reading Home 136, Visitors 7.

"Is that…?" Penance gaped.

Sheepishly, Dixon nodded, "Yes."

Penance shakes his head. "Seven's too many," he whispers.

"I know." Dixon.

The numbers seared in Penance's brain.

"There are twenty-three more cartel members in secure medical and another forty-six detained, including those who fled," Dixon noted.

"Unbelievable. All for what? Some idiot drug lieutenant who wanted to make a few extra bucks by adding trafficking little girls to his drug trade?" Penance pressed.

"You see how they were willing to come here, to fight, to murder, and to die. They aren't like us. They're twisted and desperate. Brainwashed," Dixon said.

"Doesn't make sense. Such a lack of humanity."

"We don't have to make sense of them. We just have to stop them. And you did," Dixon declared.

Penance and Dixon returned to the marketplace square. Penance reported to Davison that he was "reasonably satisfied" that there weren't additional cartel members he left bound and gagged anywhere strewn about the community, including a very defeated "Dirty" Sanchez.

Snapping his fingers, Penance spun back, "The freezer at the meat locker!"

Davison shook his head and instructed a team to fetch the stowed gang members. As they laughed, Penance caught Bubba in the corner of his eye. The officer sat on a ledge just on the fringe of the busy town center. Excusing himself, Penance walked over to check on Bubba.

"How're you doing, Bubba?" Penance asked. Pointing to a spot on the ledge opposite of the big man, he received a nod to join.

"I'm…I don't know," Bubba admitted. "My thoughts bounce around. They seem like they should be celebratory or others should sting. Mostly, just kind of numb."

Penance looked thoughtful for a moment. "You know how when you cut yourself on a piece of glass…you expect it to hurt, but it doesn't, at least not right away. Or when you make that game-winning play, you're so excited, but your mind kind of puts you into a weird third-person mode. The noise, the action, the crowd, your teammates all become just a little bit surreal. I think it is your mind's way of letting you process to either great and wonderful things or tough and painful things. That glass cut…you'll feel it later, but you've been able to stop the bleeding in the meantime."

Bubba nodded slowly, "I guess that makes sense."

"Check in with your Mom?"

"She'll come back tomorrow," Bubba nodded again.

"That'll be good. You two are kind of each other's anchors," Penance observed. "We did some good things. Tough things…but good."

"Yeah," Bubba agreed solemnly. "So many bad people. So many dead. Sheriff Day…so many."

"Fighting is kind of stupid when you put actual lives on the scorecard, isn't it?"

"The guy I shot. I don't feel it. I don't feel good. I don't feel bad," Bubba said.

"You didn't decide to shoot someone. You merely did what you had to do. The bad guys decided for you," Penance replied.

"You're right. That is kind of how I feel. Even watching him fall. I watched so many fall, but that one was at *my* hands. I expected to feel bad, I don't," Bubba recalled.

"My mom would never let us kill spiders. We would have to scoop them up with a thin piece of cardboard and cover them with a glass and take them outside and set them free. One day, near the headboard of my bed she spied a black widow. She didn't hesitate. She didn't think twice. She grabbed a tissue, swooped in, squeezed it, and flushed it down the toilet. Not a moment's thought, not a slight bit of remorse," Penance shared.

Bubba cocked his head slightly as he was absorbing the story.

"She cared for all creatures, but if any of them posed a threat to those she loved, they didn't stand a chance. We aren't evil or bad for defending those we love from those imposing imminent, real harm. We just aren't," Penance said.

"What about you?" Bubba asked. "You've done that a lot."

"I don't take a single one lightly. If I shot to kill a suspect, it was because they put me in a position where I had no other choice," Penance said. Grinning sheepishly, "Now, those I just kinda winged, maybe I had other options."

Bubba laughed and shook his head. "You're just a little on the crazy side, but I like you, Penance."

Penance got up and, in an uncharacteristic move, clasped Bubba's hand in his and pulled him in for a muscular hug, adding a few slaps on the back for measure.

"I like you too, Bubba. You have single-handedly made me appreciate coming to this town," Penance said. Giving the chaotic scene a scan, smoke still rising from the extinguished fires, bullet holes riddling near every vehicle and piece of architecture, roadways in brutal disarray, "I gotta say, your town's kind of a mess. Not nearly as boring as I originally thought, however."

FORTY

The FBI expanded the marketplace square barrier to encompass several additional blocks to accommodate the growing mass of people in Sawyer. While maintaining patrols, sentries, and drone flyovers, they were cataloging their massive investigation. The Army Criminal Investigation Command arrived to assist with the scale of the incident.

Penance noticed the expansion of the border encompassed the church. Instinctively drawn to the edges of the new borders, he ended up on the church's steps. Pausing, he looked up at the building—one of the few in town that did not seem to be distinctively damaged.

"You gonna come in or are you just going to stand there?" Pastor Roberts asked as he walked through the open door.

"I, uh, I can come in," Penance nodded nonchalantly.

The agent strode up the steps, joining the pastor. Inside the sanctuary, the pews scattered with individuals, families, and friends. Some were praying independently, some praying as a group. A few people ambled with bowed heads, praying as they paced through the sanctuary.

"Welcome to head in and pray," Pastor Roberts suggested.

"Well, I...," Penance shrugged and began.

"Come on, join me in my office," the pastor led the FBI agent to his office. Setting two chairs opposite each other, the pastor offered Penance a seat. While the agent obliged, the pastor went to the cabinet behind his desk, he pulled a bottle and two glasses out and placed them on his desk.

"No Pappy on a pastor's income, but Buffalo Trace ain't a bad swill," Roberts said, pouring two heavy glasses and handed one to Penance.

Raising his glass, letting the amber liquid crawl up the edges but not eclipsing the lip of it, he shared, "I'm not sure how I feel about the scoreboard, not sure who's idea that was, though I could guess...I am pleased by the outcome."

"A sad and crazy, unnecessary business," Penance noted.

"No doubt," Pastor Roberts nodded. "You saved this town. It's innocent sons and daughters."

Penance wrinkled his nose at the comment. Taking a sip of bourbon, he replied, "I caused this mess, Pastor. My arrogant, bold actions brought all this misery to this little town in the middle of nowhere."

"You had your hand in it, to be sure. But not in the way that you think. Young girls throughout Louisiana and Mississippi…and who knows where else…were being abducted by the cartel. A drug bust here or there were nuisances, but they were never going to stop. Maybe your actions were a little over the top, but that plug was never going to get pulled without something…bold, as you put it," the pastor suggested.

"I go back and look at everything I did, how could I have prevented any one of those seven deaths on the Home Team scoreboard? What did I set in motion that put those seven in harm's way?" Penance asked.

"The Las Piratas put them in harm's way. They were already there before you arrived in Sawyer. You just pulled back the curtain and revealed the ugliness behind it," Pastor Roberts took a sip from his glass. "I pray for every one of those lives, home team, or otherwise."

The two sat in silence, taking small sips savoring their bourbon.

"There were so many points where I thought, this is it. I can't stop that bullet from coming at me. Towards the end, in the town square, the cartel was converging on me. I had to stop and change mags. I dropped to a knee, and I could feel the gun barrels condensing, zeroing in," Penance shared. "I've been in those scenarios before. My training taught me just to keep focusing, keep on my task, and not worry about the others that I cannot control. Take advantage if the advantage is there, and accept what the result is. Keep moving."

Penance looked up and swallowed hard. "For just a moment, I stopped moving. I think I...prayed. I swear, in all the chaos, in all the gunfire, I heard a whisper. Not from my ears, but inside my head, 'I've got you'. I closed my eyes...I *never* close my eyes in combat...looked up and saw Delvin Whatcom standing over me, the cartel members dropped."

Pastor Roberts nearly spit his whiskey, "Delvin Whatcom was your savior? I mean, God can appoint whomever he chooses, but Delvin? The Whatcoms come to church. They're good about that. But there is hearing the Word and living it out. Delvin Whatcom..."

"Delvin wasn't the only Whatcom to save me that night either," Penance relayed the scene at the checkpoint with the mortar and the well-timed sniper shots. "Shannon, I don't know how she came to be there, but if she wasn't..."

"The Whatcom family as answers to your prayers. There are plenty of stories where God had chosen even less likely participants," Pastor Roberts was thoughtful for a moment. "You know, I like it. The Whatcoms have been on the fringe. Walking the line between listeners and followers, between neighbors and enemies. There is good in all, and all can be redeemed!"

Pastor Roberts took a sip of bourbon and smiled, "Yes, even you, Agent Penance."

"There are a lot of mistakes. A lot of bodies…," Penance protested.

The pastor pointed a finger with his drink hand, "Without you, which way would the body count have fallen?"

Both men were silent at the sobering thought.

"You were here for a reason. The Whatcoms were timely to your defense, not by accident. Bubba's courage at just the right moment. And then, how many times were you the right guy in the right place at the right time to save someone else?" Roberts pressed.

Penance studied the pastor for a moment before the events of the prior evening flashed through his head. One by one, images of the cartel members with a bead on Bubba, a security guard at the jail, or a Sawyer civilian who stayed to take a stand or even himself flashed through his mind.

The FBI agent leaned back into his chair, absorbed in the air that had been like a thick wool blanket, heavy and dense, suddenly lifted.

Leaving the church, rounding the corner towards the main throng of the town square, Penance ran nearly full force into Shannon Whatcom. Her eyes lit up as she put her arms out on either side of him to halt their collision.

"Agent Penance, I've been looking for you," the Whatcom girl cooed.

Penance eyed her, cautiously, "You...." Shaking his head at her, not in a disdainful, but rather thoughtful way.

"You kinda like me, don't you? Admit it," Shannon pressed.

Penance sighed, "I kind of like you, Shannon. You were, without a doubt, amazing out there."

"I was," Shannon wrinkled her nose. "You weren't so bad yourself. Watching you scurry around, taking out bad guys, rescuing so many of Sawyer's people."

"This town of yours, it's not so bad," Penance admitted. "Your family...I haven't figured them out. I haven't figured *you* out."

"What's to figure out? We are who we are. Simple people, simple goals, just want to live our lives," Shannon said.

"Simple...no. You are anything but simple," Penance smiled.

Shannon furrowed a brow, "Is that a bad thing?"

"No," Penance shook his head. "Not necessarily. Just a thing. A very complicated thing."

Shannon placed a hand gently on his chest, not knowing what minefield of wounds she might hit, "Don't have to be complicated. Just needs to be."

For a brief moment of hesitation, some profound, complicated crossroads in the map of Penance's mind, the insistence of the defiantly charming southern girl could have sent him down a different path, he leaned in, planting a firm but tender kiss on Shannon's cheekbone.

"I am very glad to know you, Shannon," the FBI agent said softly.

"But…"

"But," Penance nodded.

Shannon's brief look of defeat displaced by bubbly optimism, "I ain't done trying to break you. Kinda like that whiskey, takes a little time to warm you, get into your soul, and then mmm, it's got you, and you like it."

Penance chuckled at the girl's illustration.

Pulling her in for a warm embrace, "I like you, girl. You have definitely burned an impression in my life. I think that place is just better served as friends."

Pulling away from the hug that she felt to be more fraternal than romantic, she looked up at the agent. "I ain't giving up. I can be *real* friendly." With a wicked grin, that somehow melted into a kind innocence, the Whatcom girl disappeared into the crowd of the marketplace square.

FORTY-ONE

As darkness fell, the FBI's security stepped up. The town made makeshift sleeping quarters throughout the expanded safe zone. Penance had checked in with Dixon and was immediately put on immediate orders to stand down until his flight the next day to take him to Jackson for proper treatment of his wounds.

He found himself wandering the town, smiling, shaking hands, and receiving the occasional hug from the people of Sawyer. He surprised himself with how much he enjoyed the interaction and felt a genuine, mutual warmth amongst the crowd.

Underneath a street lamp, he found Annie Hunt. She leaned back with a leg propped up against the light post. With an outstretched finger, she beckoned him over. Not hesitating to oblige, he walked over, wondering why he felt so sheepish in doing so.

Maybe it was the vision of her bathed in the light. Or her confident posture that matched the knowing, confident smile that stretched across her lips. Or maybe it was Penance's own stirred up hornet's nest of emotions buzzing around inside of his chest.

"The town hero, I was wondering when you might notice me," Annie said, her smile sly.

"I, uh, the people...," he stammered.

Annie laughed, "I know. I was watching you. A very different vision than your first few days in our little backwoods hamlet."

Penance wrinkled his nose, "Its...there are parts of it that might have, maybe grown on me a little bit. It's not *completely* devoid of charm."

Annie admired his charisma, which was only more apparent when his stoicism had boiled away. "I have something for you," she lifted a box for him to see.

Penance reached for it with curiosity, but she pulled it quickly away.

"Not so fast. Let's go somewhere a little more...a little more just you and me," Annie suggested.

The agent's interest peaked, "Where to?"

"How about my place?" Annie asked.

Penance frowned, "That's out of the safe zone."

"I believe anywhere with you is a safe zone, well, *almost* anywhere," Annie said coyly.

"Okay," Penance approved. "Let's go."

Arm in arm, they walked the handful of blocks to Annie's bungalow. The deserted streets were eerie and yet somehow charming with just the two of them. It felt as though they were alone in the world, and at that moment, they were both very much okay with that.

Once at her house, the FBI search team marker sketched on her front door momentarily broke the aura.

"Just to be safe, let me clear the house," Penance said, instinctively drawing his pistol and shining his tactical flashlight ahead of him as maneuvered through the house. Annie stuck to his side as he did so.

Satisfied, they were alone and safe, he turned to her in the kitchen, his curiosity getting the better of him, "So…"

Annie grinned, "Oh, the box." Holding it in front of her, she offered.

Penance cracked an edge, trying to reveal a peek before he fully committed to opening it. He was a little surprised by what he found—a meal of grilled chicken. "What's this for?" he asked, his head cocked to one side.

Annie's grin perpetuated, "You told me you liked Bubba and your neighbor Frank because they brought you chicken. Maybe I want to be one of those people that you like. So, I brought you chicken." Annie rose to her toes as she completed her sentence.

Penance looked directly and deeply into her bright brown eyes, "I like you."

Moving into a kiss only took a fraction of a movement, but the distance felt like it took forever to close. Once their lips met, the pressure between them felt like gravity, joining the two ever closer together. Penance's head spun. He closed his eyes, feeling as desperately lost as he had when he reloaded on the battlefield, only this time within reach of a brilliant curtain of light and warmth.

"I like you too," Annie whispered as she pulled her lips away, just for a moment.

The two remained intertwined in Annie's kitchen, next to an open box of grilled chicken for several long, soul-searching minutes.

When the finally parted, though their hands remained together, Annie confessed, "I was so worried about you."

"I was worried about you too," Penance said.

Annie frowned and lightly stomped her foot on the floor, "I was locked in highly secured office in a bank…"

"I know. That was the only thing that kept you from being a heavier distraction on my mind. But when things hit the fan in the town center, I…I didn't think there was anything I could do to protect you. Protect everyone."

"But you did. You did," Annie said.

Penance shrugged, "The town did."

"The town would have continued the siphoning of girls into the black market and drugs seeping into our schools. The town would not have risen up and fought back, fought *together*. You did that," Annie defended.

"Well, *if* I had a hand in it, I had a heck of a supporting crew," Penance admitted.

Annie let out a grin and wrapped her hands around his neck and looked directly into his eyes, "Does that crew include me?"

"You're the ring leader," Penance looked incredulous.

With the slightest pull on the back of his neck, Annie led the FBI agent to match his lips with hers.

"So, what happens now?" Annie whispered.

"What do you mean? I figured we would eat chicken and then...," Penance teased.

Annie looked more serious than she had the entire evening. "I mean with us. With you in Sawyer..."

Penance pulled away just slightly, "I don't know. My ticket was punched for a minimum docket of two years, potentially lost to the shuttered agent file for...eternity."

"And now?" Annie pressed.

"Now, I don't know. D.C. can see this as a huge win, I get repositioned for promotion and maybe get recommissioned, and...," Penance shrugged.

"And?"

"And I would have to move," he admitted, his voice going quiet.

Annie looked dejected, "I see."

Penance gently lifted her chin, "I'd have a healthy travel budget and probably land somewhere you'd love to visit."

The message didn't seem to help.

"Or…or they see this whole event as one giant cluster and throw my personnel file in the trash and leave me forever or fire me," Penance said and then grew dramatic like he had an epiphany, "In which case, I'd have to get a job here at the hardware store or maybe become a fry cook for Bubba's mama…"

Annie laughed, "Oh, stop."

Penance squared up with her, "Look, I don't know if my stop here is close to an end, or I'm destined to stay here forever. What I do know is how incredibly grateful that I am to have come here. To meet the infectiously kind Bubba, who taught me a whole lot at being a good human being. Or Pastor Roberts and connecting me to something *way* bigger than me, a chapter that I have only begun to explore and understand.

And then there's you. The moment you came into the Bureau office, carting me off to my now infamous first Sawyer crime scene, which I think I handled deftly- I might add. You have crushed and ground up and demolished every image of grace, beauty and loving soul that I ever pictured in a woman.

When I came here, I didn't want to stay for a minute. You make me doubt ever wanting to leave."

Annie licked her lips and dropped her eyes for a moment, her voice cracking when she spoke, "But if the call comes, you'll still leave."

Penance's face answered her question. He nodded, "It's my job. It's my life. There may be another Sawyer that needs, well needs to be turned upside down, I guess, but needs my help anyways. This time it could be a million people in Boston, or Miami, or Los Angeles...or the country."

Annie swatted him in the chest and giggled, "That's such an unfair argument. I guess that's what I get for wanting to date a superhero."

"Oh, you want to date me, that's what this is all about," Penance teased.

Annie scowled, her voice rose, "Of course, that's what I'm talking about. But if you're going to leave, I...I can't do it. I can put my heart in that box just for you to pack it in your luggage the next day and fly off."

"Let's take it a step at a time. For now, we have tonight. And chicken. We have tonight and chicken!" Penance declared triumphantly.

Annie laughed, "You are not the stuffy grey man that flew in here from your ivory tower. You're pretty darn great."

"I think you're pretty special, too," Penance said. "Now, let's eat some chicken, seriously, I'm starving."

The evening grew from late to exceptionally late. Annie and Penance maintained their conversation over dinner and then migrated to the couch amidst the glow of candles, and red wine warmed cheeks.

Penance glanced at his watch, "It is really late. We are well past curfew."

Annie studies his face in the flickering light of the candles. "I don't want to sleep at the bank or the shelter."

"It's not safe, not yet to leave you out here by yourself," Penance protested.

"I'm not suggesting I stay here alone," Annie said.

Penance froze with the thought, his mind whirling.

"I'm not suggesting *that*, either," Annie frowned. "I feel safe with you. I'm safer here with you than anywhere else with anyone else."

"Fine, I should at least text Dixon, so he doesn't worry," Penance suggested.

Annie shook her head, "I already told him I was stealing you. He agreed if there was one person in this town that could make you sit still and not injure yourself further, it was, well... me."

"Fair enough, I can tuck you into your bed and settle on the couch," Penance said.

"If it's alright with you," Annie cooed, and then snapped, "*And* you can be a gentleman, I think I'd just as soon stay just like we are right now. I'm in no hurry for this night to end or for you to fly away."

Penance kissed her gently, "Me either."

FORTY-TWO

The day Penance was out of surgery, removing the shrapnel and bullet fragments dotting his body, he was in front of a closed-door Congressional panel explaining what happened with the *Las Piratas* cartel and how it exploded into a mini-war in the Mississippi backcountry.

Neither he nor Deputy Director Dixon knew how the panel, how the bureau, or the Army's CID investigation would define the agent's actions or the results of the operation. Grilled for three days in either deposition or in front of the joint panel, regurgitating every detail that Dixon had already laid out in the hefty report that he filed, they finally closed the testimony.

After a brief adjournment, the panel reconvened.

"Special Agent Alex Penance," the top-ranking Justice Committee member, Jeffrey Owens from Texas, led the closing comments. "The joint panel finds your actions, while at times reckless, consistent with the pursuit of justice and the ultimate safety of the lives of residents throughout the Mississippi delta. You, nearly, single-handedly dismantled one of the most extensive and most insidious drug and human trafficking cartels to breach our southern border, I know we have felt their sting in my home state of Texas.

We hereby find your actions in good standing and deserving of Congressional Accommodation. In short, we are grateful for your service, Agent Penance. In fact, it is our panel's recommendation that you finish what you started."

"Started, sir?" Penance asked.

"While the Las Piratas crime cartel is largely dismantled, there are remnants that continue to exist. We have intel on some of the missing girls from the Mississippi delta. *Las Piratas* fragments have them holed up in at least one possible location. We would like you to take this intel and see if you can't clean up the remaining members of the cartel, and by the grace of God, see if you can bring some lost kids home," Owens declared.

"Of course I will, sir," Penance replied.

"Good. Then we are adjourned."

Dixon turned to Penance, "Looks like your flight plans take you back to Sawyer after all."

Made in the USA
Monee, IL
24 October 2020